MURDER IN MALAYA

MURDER IN MALAYA

FATAL SHADOWS

DEATH OVER HER SHOULDER

DOROTHY COLE MEADE

COACHWHIP PUBLICATIONS
Greenville, Ohio

Murder in Malaya, by Dorothy Cole Meade
© 2019 Coachwhip Publications

Fatal Shadows published 1933
Death Over Her Shoulder published 1939
No claims made on public domain material.
Cover image: Leaves © Marhero

CoachwhipBooks.com

ISBN 1-61646-475-5
ISBN-13 978-1-61646-475-2

CALL HIM ISMAEL
THE MALAYSIAN DETECTIVE FICTION
OF DOROTHY COLE MEADE

CURTIS EVANS

Part One

"I have it on the very best authority that no really great writer fails to write at least one pretty snappy detective story before he or she dies."
—G.C.N., "Malayan Detective Fiction," *Singapore Free Press and Mercantile Advertiser*, 12 March 1930

Dorothy Cole Meade (1893-1979), the author of three detective novels, published between 1933 and 1939, that are set in British Malaya, came from a prominent American family composed partly of old New England Puritan stock. In contrast with modern anti-globalist attitudes (so redolent of pre-World War Two anti-globalist attitudes), however, the Coles wholeheartedly embraced the outside world.

The eldest of three children of Harold Wyatt Cole (1873-1922), a leading figure in the American ice and refrigeration industry, and his wife Susan Marilla Callender (1871-1950), daughter of an Albany, New York, newspaper editor, Dorothy Cole (1893-1979) grew up first on Madison Avenue, New York and then in Montclair, New Jersey, with her younger siblings, sister Marilla Rathbun (1901-1939) and brother John Orton (1906-1961). In the 1920s Dorothy married world adventurer Captain Patrick Alexander Meade (1894-1972), a larger-than-life Scots-Irishman originally from the United Kingdom who for many years led a colorful martial life abroad, serving in Cairo

Dorothy Cole Meade
She manufactures mystery in the jungle in "Death Over Her Shoulder."

Captain Patrick A. Meade.

and the Sudan with the Egyptian Camel Corps when
barely out of his teens, in Archangel with the British Army during the ill-fated Allied anti-Bolshevik
North Russia intervention of 1918-19, and in Singapore with the Singapore Police Force between 1920
and 1928. Through her marriage to Captain Meade,
Dorothy gained experiences in Southeast Asia in the
Twenties that would lend distinction to her Thirties
detective fiction, which chronicles the investigations
of an unprepossessing but canny Malayan Muslim
police investigator named Ismael. The phlegmatic
yet wily Ismael stands inevitably apart from the European and American colonials whose seamy and secret
affairs he politely yet remorselessly examines during
his murder inquiries, yet he proves again and again

that it is he, not the incidental occidental interlopers
in his native land, who is the Great Detective.

Commitment to their expansive conceptions of
liberty and justice for all characterized the family of
Dorothy Cole. The author's father, Howard Wyatt
Cole, was a grandson of John Orton Cole, a prominent state judge and War of 1812 veteran who had
been part of the official delegation accompanying
iconic American Revolutionary War hero the Marquis
de Lafayette on his stop, during his triumphal 1824-
25 return to America, in the state of New York. Howard's parents were Charles Wadsworth Cole, Superin-
tendent of the Schools in Albany, New York, among
whose accomplishments was, as his 1912 obituary in
American Education proudly stated, seeing "corpo-
ral punishment overthrown never to rise again," and
Joan McKown Cole, the descendant of a Scottish tav-
ern keeper at McKownsville, New York, who became
the first president and "leading spirit" of the Albany
Mothers' Club, which organized and maintained five
playgrounds for children in the city, while his sister,
Elsie LaGrange Cole Phillips, distinguished herself as
a Vassar graduate, social worker, trade unionist, suf-
fragist, and socialist. Harold himself, though less obviously iconoclastic than his crusading sibling Elsie,
was obliquely though still suggestively described, in
his 1922 obituary in the trade journal *Ice and Refrigeration*, as a consummate American idealist: "Hating

injustice and unnecessary suffering, believing deeply that a new and better social order was essential and possible, he stood courageously for ideas little understood and hence often unpopular."

In 1893 Harold married Susan Marilla Callender, a daughter of Albany newspaper publisher and editor William Nelson Callender and a granddaughter of Scots-Irish immigrant and lumber manufacturer David Callender. Through his connection to his father-in-law, Harold became the editor of *The Ice World*, which he soon consolidated with another magazine as *Cold Storage and Ice Trade Journal*; he would later become the moving force behind the establishment of the Natural Ice Association of America. For her part, Marilla, it was said, "always displayed an active interest in Mr. Cole's activities in behalf of the ice industry." During the early years of their marriage, Howard and Marilla lived at Madison Avenue, New York, with young Dorothy and Marilla's younger brother William Nelson Callender, Jr., advertising manager of the *New York Journal*. After the turn of the century, William married stage actress Sadie Lauer and the Coles moved to a large 1900 Tudor arts and crafts style house at Nine Mountain Terrace in Montclair, New Jersey, a rapidly growing city of some 15,000 souls located not far from New York. There Howard and Marilla would raise Dorothy and their two younger children, enjoying the services of gardener Richard McCluskey, who came, like Patrick

Meade, from Northern Ireland, and James and Fanny
Carroll, a black couple from Virginia employed
respectively as chauffeur and cook. There too the
Coles became pillars of Montclair's progressive Unity
(Unitarian) Church, led by Reverend Edgar Swan
Wiers, President of the Unitarian Fellowship for
Social Justice, who was lauded by the late African-
American author Carrie Allen McCray as "a white
fighter for justice for negroes in our town."

It was at Unity Church on September 22, 1928, in
a ceremony over which Reverend Wiers, three years
before his death, officiated, that Howard and Marilla
Cole's second daughter, Marilla Rathbun (Marilla 2),
wed a second cousin, Harvard graduate and diplo-
mat Felix Cole (1887-1969), a grandson of the first
governor of Wisconsin, Nelson Dewey. Dorothy, now
Dorothy Cole Meade, served as Marilla 2's matron of
honor; and Felix's best man was Donald D. Shepard,
tax attorney for none other than millionaire Republi-
can U. S. Secretary of the Treasury Andrew Mellon, a
man of rather a different political and economic outlook from the President of the Unitarian Fellowship
for Social Justice. Some years prior to his marriage to
Marilla 2, Felix had served in 1916-17 and 1918-19
as U. S. Vice Consul at, respectively, Petrograd and
Archangel (probably meeting Patrick Meade in the
latter location); and during this time of troubles he
had wed a Russian woman, Tatiana (Tanya) Sergeia
Imshenetzki, with whom he had a daughter, Marion

(1916-1998). After returning to the United States in 1919, Felix become the State Department's Chief of the Division of Russian Affairs, from which position he resigned in December 1920 in order to become Consul General at Bucharest, Rumania, an office he held for a year before resigning to take a position investigating economic conditions in Russia on behalf of the Department of Commerce. After his marriage to Marilla 2, he and his new bride departed from the United States for Warsaw, Poland, where he had been appointed Consul General. Felix later became Consul General at Frankfurt, Germany, and Charge d'Affaires at Riga, in the Baltic state of Latvia.[1]

During this period Felix and Marilla Cole had two daughters: Marilla Callender (1931-1999) and Catherine Dewey (1933-1974). In 1938 Felix became Consul General at Algiers, the largest city in the French African colony of Algeria, where he would serve until 1943. Not long after her arrival in Algeria with her husband and daughters, Marilla 2 died from the grave nerve disease known as Guillain-Barre syndrome (most commonly triggered by a bacterial infection derived from consuming undercooked poultry) and her now motherless daughters, Marilla 3 and Catherine, returned to the United States to live with their widowed grandmother, Marilla 1, their Uncle John, an insurance broker, and his wife and their two children, Susan and Karolyn. In the spring and summer of 1940, however, sixty-eight-year-old Marilla 1 returned to Algeria with Marilla 3 and Catherine (eight and six years old respectively) to visit their father Felix. On May 10, the Germans launched the Battle of France, which culminated in the Fall of Paris on June 14 and the signing of the Armistice between Germany and France on June 22. The next day, June 23, Marilla 1 and her two young granddaughters departed from Casablanca, in the French protectorate of Morocco, for Lisbon, Portugal, where Marilla 1 had booked passage for a return journey to the United States aboard the luxury liner SS *Manhattan*. Once arrived in Lisbon, the three Coles fatefully encountered another family of three seeking passage to America: Abraham and Eugenia Rozenfeld and their six-year-old son Stefan, Polish Jews fleeing the decimating Nazi advance across Europe. Marilla 1 and her granddaughters naturally were quite familiar with Poles, with Felix Cole having served as Consul General in Warsaw. When Felix became Consul General at Algiers, he and the late Marilla 2 had even brought with them to his opulent Algiers residence two Polish servants, Marianna the cook and Lutzina the maid, both of whom were deemed "treasures."[2]

In January 1940 Eugenia Rozenfeld had dauntlessly managed with her young son Stefan to make a harrowing trek by train from conquered Poland across Germany to Belgium to join her husband Abraham, a ribbon manufacturer who had been in Belgium on business when the German army invaded

Poland. However, the family soon found themselves compelled to flee Belgium for new shelter after the Germans stormed the Low Countries on May 10. Two weeks later Abraham Rozenfeld obtained for the family visas to Portugal from the kindly Portuguese Consul General in Bordeaux, Aristide de Sousa Mendes; yet after their arrival in Lisbon, Abraham finally ran out of funds. Most happily for the Rozenfelds, however, Marilla Cole, upon her encounter with the little family in Lisbon, used her pull with the Foreign Service to book the family passage on a ship, the *Nea Hellas*, which was bound for America, and lent them the money to pay for their passage (incidentally refusing to accept as collateral jewelry which Eugenia had smuggled out of Poland). The Rozenfelds arrived at Hoboken, New Jersey on July 12, six days before the *Manhattan* docked in New York with the Coles. (Fortunately, Abraham was from Ukraine, rather than Poland, a country for which restrictionist American immigration legislation had set a low immigrant quota.)

Later that year the Rozenfelds were guests of Marilla 1 at her house in Montclair. Abraham corresponded with Marilla 1 during the war, writing her in February 1941, for example, that "Stephen [as he was now called] is going to school and is doing very well. He speaks already English and you and the children [Marilla 3 and Catherine] would be surprised hearing him." Unfortunately, Abraham noted that, aside from his brother-in-law and his wife, who had escaped from Poland to Lithuania and thence to Japan, the position of his and Eugenia's relatives, who had remained behind in Poland under Nazi occupation, "is very bad." He added grimly: "One thing is clear: it is impossible to get them out from there." Stephen Rozenfeld, today eighty-five years old and a citizen of the United States for nearly eighty of those years, had grandparents and an uncle who never did make it out of Europe, becoming casualties of the Nazis' many crimes against humanity. Of Marilla 1's benevolent intervention in his and his parents' lives, Stephen has stated that he deems it to have been a "miracle."[3]

By this time Dorothy Cole Meade had published her final detective novels and she and Patrick had moved to Woodstock, Connecticut, after having resided for over a decade, since their return to the United States from Singapore, at the Cole house in Montclair. Apparently in Woodstock they initially occupied themselves by raising Seeing Eye dogs for the blind. With the advent of World War Two, however, Patrick commenced working for the Atlantic Arms Company, located in Jersey City, New Jersey, and the Office of Strategic Services in Washington, D. C. In those capacities, recalls historian Richard Rabinowitz, the "exotic" Patrick was "mysteriously involved in providing more war materiel to the British forces than was publicly acknowledged in the Lend-Lease agreement."[4]

After the war, Dorothy's brother-in-law Felix reached the formal pinnacle of his career (though in fact his early service in Russia during and after the First World War, later praised by George F. Kennan, remained his most important contribution to history), serving as Minister to Ethiopia and Ambassador to Ceylon. Felix retired from the Foreign Service in 1949 and returned to the house in Montclair, where he passed away two decades later. Marilla 1 died in 1950, at the age of seventy-eight, a year after Felix returned, and the teenaged Marilla 2 and Catherine went to live with their Aunt Dorothy and her husband in Woodstock, where they both married a few years afterward. Thereafter Dorothy and particularly the outsized Patrick became well-known personages in the area, the latter serving as a longtime host and lecturer at Old Sturbridge Village, a living museum located across the border from Woodstock in Massachusetts. Richard Rabinowitz recalled Patrick, whom he met a year before Patrick's death in 1972, as "the embodiment of Anglo-American order and tradition, my own personal Churchill. He cherished rural New England as the perfect tempering of British courtesy and American democracy." Dorothy followed her charming husband Patrick to a grave in the flinty and uncompromising New England earth in 1979, passing away at the age of eighty-six. She had survived not just her husband but her father, mother, sister, brother, and brother-in-law.

Part Two

"This is certainly one devil of a case, Ismael," Campbell admitted, knitting his sandy eyebrows. . . . Give me a nice straightforward Malay or Chinese killing every time, what?"

"They are simpler certainly. When a Malay kills it is plain sailing. . . . Nevertheless . . . I have found that the same passions rule the hearts of all races."

—*Fatal Shadows* (1933)

"I've tried to play cricket with you, but it's impossible. A man is coming up from Johore to take over the investigation, and he wants everyone kept here until he arrives."

"Who's coming? Anyone we know?" Mike Sullivan asked, with an undertone of anxiety in the voice he tried to keep casual.

McCleary, who had started to turn away, stared at him with hard eyes. "Sergeant Ismael will take charge. He is leaving at once."

"Ismael!" Betty Harvy sniffed. "Sounds like a native."

Sullivan, with a worried expression in his cat-green eyes, said slowly, "He is a native—and one of the smartest detectives in the East."

—*Death over Her Shoulder* (1939)

Chauvinistic white interlopers' perceptions of the native peoples of the foreign lands over which they have presumptuously attempted to exert lasting dominion figure throughout Dorothy Cole Meade's corpus of detective fiction, consisting of three novels, *Fatal Shadows* (1933), *The Shadow of a Hair* (1939), and *Death over Her Shoulder* (1939), the first and last of which are included in this volume. (From 1938 there is also a fourth, mainstream or "straight" novel, *Hostages*, set in Batavia in the Dutch East Indies, aka modern-day Jakarta, Indonesia.) All three of the author's detective novels are set in colonial British Malaya, not long before the deluge of the devastating Japanese invasion that would help precipitate the sweeping away of European colonial regimes in the Eastern hemisphere after the Second World War. *Fatal Shadows* introduces the Malayan Muslim series sleuth Ismael, a police sub-inspector in the Sultanate of Johor (spelled Johore in the novels), one of Britain's so-called protected states in the Malay Peninsula throughout the 1930s, the decade in which Dorothy Cole Meade published her mysteries. On first encounters with Detective Sergeant Ismael, native European sojourners in British Malaya tend to underestimate the diminutive and self-effacing Malayan, who resembles "an ordinary Malay servant dressed up in a khaki uniform." Yet later they find to their dismay what Ismael's white police colleagues already know: that those who discount Ismael do so very much

at their own peril, for the shrewd and misleadingly
mild Muslim is no white man's (or woman's) patsy. As
Ismael's superior, the Scotsman Campbell, reflects to
his assistant in *Fatal Shadows*: "It has been you who
has solved most of the crimes in Johore. I just do the
hack work that gives you the inspiration."

Campbell goes on with unintended irony to ob-
serve to Ismael, "It's a damn shame that you aren't
white so that you could have proper recognition,"
never perceiving that the larger "damn shame" might
be the entire colonial system which prevents non-
white men (or women) from receiving "proper recognition" for their abilities and accomplishments.
However, Ismael responds politely to his superior (in
title) with reflections that are both practical ("My
place is in the background beside you. With you before me, no one notices a fat old native, and I can
work better.") and philosophical ("What could the
government give me that could bring me happiness?
The Malays have the art of living. I wouldn't change
with a white man.") To which Campbell concedes:
"I guess you're right at that, Ismael. Look at these
people we've been talking to tonight. All of them are
miserable about something or other."

In *Fatal Shadows* (dedicated to Dorothy Cole
Meade's mother Marilla), Ismael's criminal investigation concerns the stabbing slaying, on the grounds
of the old stone Rest House in Johor Bahru, capital
of Johor, during the evening of the natives' raucous

celebration of the Sultan's birthday, of beautiful and compulsively alluring Ailsa Brownley, whom many a miserable white man (and woman) in Johor had more than enough reason to want to murder. In *Death over Her Shoulder* (dedicated to William Milton Rockwell, office manager of the school and college textbook department at publisher Charles Scribner's Sons and former president of the Montclair Heights Community Club), Ismael's criminal investigation concerns the stabbing slaying, at her bungalow on the isolated Semang Rubber Estate (fifteen miles outside of the city of Kluang), of another, this time seemingly inoffensive, woman, Lydia Bosworth, of whom it emerges that many may have had ample reason to want to see her dead too. These two novels were the only Dorothy Cole Meade mysteries published in the United States, the first by short-lived but interesting publishing firm Ray Long & Richard R. Smith, the second by Charles Scribner's Sons (which likely explains the dedication of the novel to William Rockwell, a Scribner's employee and Cole family friend from Montclair). Dorothy's other two novels, *Hostages* and *The Shadow of a Hair*, were published in England by John Hamilton.

Both *Fatal Shadows* and *Death over Her Shoulder* (and for that matter *The Shadow of a Hair*) are interestingly plotted and peopled, with real characters of flesh and blood and sometimes surprisingly "modern" passions and a sleuth who is unique, as far as I

am aware, in Golden Age Anglo-American mystery;
yet the quality in them which most stood out for
contemporary reviewers was the atmospheric tropical
setting. A review of *Fatal Shadows* in the Catholic
journal *America* stresses this point:

> Dorothy Cole Meade has given us a mys-
> tery that is decidedly out of the ordinary,
> not so much in the skeleton of the plot,
> but in the unique setting and the mode
> of development. It is always refreshing to
> read a story in a land we little wot of,
> provided we feel sure the events narrated
> really occurred in the alleged place. There
> is no better word to describe what is meant
> than the trite one—atmosphere. Fatal
> Shadows darken the picture in Johore,
> and the Malayan atmosphere forms a fit-
> ting background for Ismael, "an inscru-
> table native, whose soul technique is the
> application of his intuitive knowledge of
> human nature." Over all the characters,
> American, English, Dutch, there blazes
> down the merciless Asiatic sun, render-
> ing away the folds of pretense with which
> caution is wont to cloak the human emo-
> tions. Thus Ismael is able to read aright
> the riddle of several deaths and the Fatal
> Shadows are lifted.

Similarly "Judge Lynch" of the *Saturday Review* delivered a very favorable summation of *Death over Her Shoulder*: "Good background, tense atmosphere, ready-made hero, sophisticated friends and cross-currents of emotion help make a pretty tangle." The novel marks a step up, in my view, from *Fatal Shadows*, both in concealment and characterization and in the fact that Ismael pleasingly plays a greater role in the narrative, taking over the investigation from the floundering local man, McCleary, who admits to being "out of my element" in this, his "first white murder case." The investigation which follows is, indeed, Ismael's final recorded triumph, though Ismael, calculatedly self-effacing to the end, on parting from the dazed surviving white people at the Semang Rubber Estate once again dons the humble yet deceiving mask of the polite and proper Malay servant, leading one of his former suspects to reflect, now with some measure of disappointment, "Why . . . he's nothing but a native after all. I'd forgotten."

The artful Ismael has fooled them yet again.

Notes

1 On Felix Cole's appointments in the early 1920s see the Consular Bulletins for the period. This matter is significant in light of Daniel Okrent's contention, in his recent book *The Guarded Gate: Bigotry, Eugenics and the Law That*

Kept Two Generations of Jews, Italians, and Other European Immigrants out of America (Scribner, 2019), that Felix Cole, in his supposed capacity as Consul General in Warsaw, was to blame for the Warsaw section of a State Department report which condemned prospective immigrants (largely Jewish) as "filthy and ignorant and the majority . . . verminous" (p. 282). This report was influential in the passage and signing into law of the severely restrictionist 1921 Emergency Immigration Act. Were Felix to have been responsible for this section of the report, it would not have been merely reprehensible on his part but deeply ironic, given his future mother-in-law Marilla's gallant action on behalf of the Rozenfeld family two decades leader (see main text).

2 Hal Vaughan, *FDR's Twelve Apostles: The Spies Who Paved the Way for the Invasion of North Africa* (Lyons Press, 2006), 106.

3 See the page on the Rozenfeld family at the Sousa Mendes Foundation website at http://sousamendesfoundation.org/family/rozenfeld. Quotation from Abaraham Rozenfeld's letter with permission from Leah Rozenfeld Sills.

4 Richard Rabinowitz's *Curating America: Journeys through Storyscapes of the American Past* (The University of North Carolina Press, 2016), 61.

FATAL SHADOWS

Our acts our angels are, for good or ill,
Our fatal shadows that walk by us still.
                    JOHN FLETCHER

To Mother
Without whose encouragement this story would never have been written.

Author's Note
The characters in this story are all fictitious, and although the old stone Rest House still exists in Johore, to meet the exigencies of my plot, I have taken some liberties in my description of the house and grounds.

CHAPTER I

A girl's scream, sharp and agonized, shattered the brooding stillness of the tropic night. Lights sprang up suddenly like restless fireflies in the dark stone Rest House in Johore, and the sound of pattering feet and excited voices reached the straining ears of Bruce MacAlistair as he stood rooted to the lawn in the squat shadow of the building.

The scream had seemed to come from the other side of the grounds where hibiscus and mimosa and frangipani grew in scented profusion along the western boundary of the property. The tropic moon flooded the lawn and garden with a ghostly light which served to emphasize the black shadows where waving palm trees towered and bushes sprawled.

Still shaken by the terror of that scream, Bruce sped around the back of the Rest House, cutting across the lawn in a direct line to the shrubbery. Trailing vines caught at his feet as he groped his way through the tangled wall of leaves and flowers to the narrow path that twisted snakelike through the length of the miniature jungle. Cautiously he felt his way toward the front of the grounds, where in a small clearing the moonlight flickered down in patches on an empty marble seat gleaming faintly white amid the shadows.

"Ailsa!" he called anxiously peering into the darkness. There was no reply, but somehow he knew that she was there as she had said she would be. Controlling his rising fears, he brushed his way into the clearing, his eager eyes searching the shadows. On the ground, half under the marble seat lay a silvery figure.

"Ailsa!" Bruce exclaimed again, dropping to his knees beside the still form. The girl's body was limp as he lifted her in his arms and stumbled through the bushes onto the moonlit brightness of the lawn.

"Here you fellows, get a light!" he called to the white men and Chinese boys who had rushed out of the Rest House and were trying to locate the source of the scream. "No, I don't know what's the matter!" Bruce said impatiently in reply to the excited inquiries. "I think it's Ailsa. Guess she's fainted. I found her lying in the bushes. Hold the door open for me, somebody, and get some water," he panted mounting the shallow veranda steps.

Carefully Bruce laid his burden, a crumpled heap of green and silver, on one of the tables in the long combination dining hall and bar into which the veranda door opened. The competent Chinese head boy, Oom Ling, touched a button, and the room which had been only dimly illuminated by the remote chandeliers in the roof, above the gallery, was suddenly flooded with light.

"Good God!" Bruce exclaimed staring stupidly at the body lying before him, "she's been hurt. The front of her dress is covered with blood!" His own hands too were sticky, and the whiteness of the monkey jacket he had donned for dinner six hours before, was stained with crimson.

Leaning forward, he put his hand on the scarlet patch over the girl's heart. "Why, she's dead!" he cried to the horrified men who had crowded around the table. For the first time he recognized them: Harry Gordon's red, good natured face, now strangely white; Dick Durham's pale eyes blinking nervously through his gold-rimmed spectacles; the officious little Wetherby shrinking away from the ugly reality of the figure on the table; Oom Ling placidly regarding the scene like an inscrutable Buddha, while the other Chinese boys chattered in an excited group behind him. Leaning over the balcony, which, half way to the roof surrounded the room, he saw the plump, scared face of the Dutch woman. It must have been she who was on the upper veranda a few minutes ago when he had tiptoed down the outside stairway. Even as he watched her, she disappeared into the shadows and he heard one of the bedroom doors, which opened on the gallery, slammed shut.

A minute later another door on the opposite side of the balcony was thrown open and an angry American voice called out, "What the devil do you mean by making such a racket at this hour of the morning? How do you expect respectable folks to get any sleep?" The blurred face of the middle-aged American tourist glared down at them from the railing, while over his shoulder peered the inquisitive faces of his wife and young daughter.

The group around the table moved aside automatically disclosing the figure of the murdered woman. "Good Lord!" the American stepped back hastily colliding with his wife. "Go back, mama! Gertrude! Get back in your room!"

"What is it? What's the matter?" the women's voices were shrill with excitement.

"Go back to your room, both of you. There's been an accident. We don't want to get mixed up in it!" Forcefully he marshalled his family away from the railing, and a door closed on the duet of female protests.

Swift light footsteps sounded on the wooden stairway leading from the upper veranda to the porch below, and the front door burst open. "What has happened?" demanded Berenice Gordon, clasping a filmy negligée tightly around her slight figure as she ran into the room.

"Keep back, Berenice!" ordered her husband starting around the table to intercept her. She moved too quickly for him, however, and in a second was staring with wide frightened eyes at the body of her friend.

"Ailsa!" she screamed, "O Harry, how could you!" Berenice swayed as she looked up at her husband,

and then with a little moan pitched forward into his arms.

"She doesn't know what she is saying, Bruce," Harry muttered with a pleading look at his friend, "I didn't do it."

"No, old man, of course you didn't," Bruce assured him, but there was a troubled gleam in his keen, grey eyes as he watched the big man lift his wife and carry her gently across the hall to the rear stairway near the deserted bar.

"Is there anything I can do?" called a fresh young voice, and Bruce realized that the figure in red lounging pajamas, hesitating at the foot of the stairs was Susan Ames, the young American girl he had met at dinner.

"Yes, Susan," he answered, unaware that he was using her first name, "Berenice has fainted. Go up with Harry and see whether you can't bring her around. We'll want Harry back here as soon as he can come."

"All right, I'll take care of her." Susan stepped aside to let Harry pass with his burden, and then followed him swiftly up the stairs. "Don't go down, Janet," the men below heard her say in response to Janet Durham's murmured inquiry, "come in and help me with Berenice." Once more a bedroom door opened and closed.

In the hall there was a stunned silence, but the monotonous sound of Malay music from the native kampong beyond the hill drifted in through the open veranda door. All evening, with only short intervals of silence, the natives had been celebrating the Sultan's birthday with wayangs, dances and singing. On and on it went maddeningly, its humdrum chords nagging at the nerves of the white men like the droning of a million mosquitoes.

"We ought to call the police, don't you think?" Wetherby asked in a voice which he vainly tried to make authoritative. "And nothing should be touched until they get here. It's too bad you didn't leave Mrs. Brownley outside where you found her, MacAlistair."

"Don't be an ass," Bruce snapped, "how could I know she was dead? You could hardly see your hand before your face in those damn' bushes. I just thought she had been frightened and had fainted."

"I'm not accusing you," Wetherby said hastily, "but I'm afraid the police won't like it." With an effort he shifted his gaze from the ugly blood stains on Bruce's jacket. He was a lonely, fussy little man, and all evening he had jealously watched the gay and carefree houseparty which had invaded his domain. He was glad now that he hadn't been mixed up with them. "I'll telephone the police," he announced in a self satisfied voice, and hurried toward the telephone on the wall near the bar, as though fearful that he might be circumvented.

"This is one hell of a note," Dick Durham grumbled. "I wish I'd never come on this damn' party. It was a crazy idea of Ailsa's having us up here this weekend when they were putting on a show for the Sultan's birthday."

"You were glad enough to come, Durham," Harry Gordon said sharply as he rejoined the group. His level gaze reminded the other man of his infatuation for the beautiful woman lying dead beside them. Hastily Dick changed the subject, "Someone ought to tell Bob. It's funny he hasn't come down. Shall I go up and break the news?"

"Bob's asleep. I looked in at him on my way downstairs. He's been having insomnia, and at bridge tonight he said he thought he'd have to take some of the dope his doctor in Singapore gave him. He's sleeping the sleep of the dead, poor chap. I think we might leave him alone until the police get here, what do you think, Bruce?"

"Let him sleep while he can, poor devil. It's going to be pretty ghastly for him when he hears about Ailsa," Bruce agreed, "but I do think we'd better have someone stand guard over the seat where she was killed. There may be something out there to help the police."

As he spoke, Oom Ling glided into the room, although up to the moment of his reappearance no one had noticed his absence. In his hand he was holding something, something which gleamed dully.

"Here is the pesoh, Tuan," he said in Malay to Bruce. "It was lying on the ground beneath the seat."

Mechanically Bruce reached for the dagger and examined it curiously. The handle was an intricately carved parrot's head outlined in gold, and on the wavy, six inch blade, there was a dark stain. "This must be the weapon that killed her. Any of you ever see it before?"

"Let's have a look!" Harry said, leaning across Bruce's shoulder, "I think I've seen it before."

"Why, that's the kris I bought yesterday in one of the native bazaars!" Dick Durham exclaimed. "I wanted a souvenir, and Ailsa and I hunted up a shop. The rest of you waited outside while she went in with me to bargain. Her Malay was better than mine—I don't know much of the damned lingo. I bought the kris for myself, and I got her those jade earrings—the ones she has on now," Dick rambled along nervously.

"Yes, I remember," Harry stated. The scene flashed back to him—Ailsa stepping out of the dark doorway, her laughing face upturned to the complacent Durham's; her gay little gesture as she held out the earrings for Berenice and Janet to admire; Berenice's exclamation of approval; the malevolent look that Janet Durham had given Ailsa as she shrugged her thin shoulders in silence.

"Where did you leave the kris, Durham?" Bruce asked, placing the weapon carefully on the table.

"I don't remember," Dick's voice was troubled. "I put it down somewhere in my room, on the dresser, or maybe the table."

"The police officer, Campbell, will be over as soon as he can dress," interrupted Wetherby coming back to the group by the table. "He will bring Ismael along with him—he's a Malay detective, as smart as you make 'em." He stopped short and his eyes widened as he noticed the kris. "That weapon,—if it was in the hotel, it rather eliminates the possibility of an outside native, doesn't it?"

Bruce frowned at hearing his own thoughts put into words. "Oom Ling, you'd better go back and stand guard in the shrubbery. Don't let anyone go in there. There may be other clues that the police will need."

"Baik-lah, Tuan," the slim figure in white coat and flapping black trousers once more slipped from the room.

Quick steps sounded on the wooden veranda which stretched across the front of the Rest House, and Jack Ames strode into the room.

"Hello, you fellows," he hailed. "What are you doing down here at this hour? Looks as if you were holding a wake!" His voice lost its buoyancy as Bruce and Harry turned to greet him, and he became conscious first of the gravity of their faces, and then of the figure on the table.

"Good Lord, it's Ailsa! What's happened to her?" He stepped forward and stared down into the still face of the woman he had left in such a rage only a short time before.

"She isn't dead!" he cried wildly. "She can't be dead!" His voice broke, and he stumbled into a chair that Harry pushed toward him.

"Get him a drink, Durham," Bruce suggested, "I was afraid he'd take it hard. He's just a kid."

"That's a good idea, MacAlistair. I guess we could all do with a bracer. Hey, boy," he called to one of the Chinamen, "get us some whisky sodas." As though welcoming an excuse to get away, Durham followed the Chinese boy to the bar at the end of the room to superintend the mixing of the drinks.

The American boy raised his bloodshot eyes, his face still twisted with emotion. "Who did it, Gordon? Who could have killed her? My God! I'll strangle him with my own hands when I find out." He started to his feet, but half way from his chair collapsed heavily, burying his face in the crook of his arm.

The only sounds in the room were the clink of glasses and the choked sobs of Jack Ames, but in the distance, the monotony of the native instruments beat on and on with rhythmic fury. Harry had slumped into a chair and was gazing straight before him, his usually ruddy face white and haggard. Wetherby was pacing noiselessly up and down the long room, mechanically avoiding the tables and chairs that stood about in scattered confusion. At the bar, under pretense of directing the Chinese boy, Dick Durham was gulping down glasses of neat whisky in an effort to steady the trembling of his thick, pale hands.

Bruce stood at the open door where the slight, sea breeze from across the Straits of Johore struck coolly against his damp forehead. It wouldn't be long now before the police arrived. Soon they would be cross-questioning him, tripping him up, dragging the dark, bitter past from him little by little, munching over it, distorting it. Would he be able to avoid telling them everything, and if he did, how could he explain convincingly the accident of his presence? Impulsively he crossed the room and laid his hand on Harry's shoulder. "Come on outside with me, old man, I want to talk to you."

Harry gazed at him blankly as though unable to bridge the distance between his own unhappy thoughts and the voice of his friend and then with an effort heaved his huge body from the chair and followed Bruce on to the deserted veranda.

For a moment the two friends stood together in silence, contrasting their tragic surroundings with the sound of native music and revelry in the kampong behind the hill. "Look here, Harry," Bruce said in a husky voice, "I'm in a devil of a fix. The police will be here in just a little while, and I don't know what to tell them. I can't seem to think." He rubbed a restless brown hand impatiently through his dark hair. "I wish to heavens I'd never stopped at this infernal place tonight."

Harry stared in amazement at this outburst, trying vainly to reconcile it with the reserved, self-contained man he knew so well. Funny how people reacted to a crisis of this sort. "There's nothing for you to worry about, old man," he said soothingly. "All you did was to discover Ailsa's body, and they can't hang you for that!"

"O, that's the least of it," Bruce's voice was bitter. "It's a long story, one I've been trying to bury for the last ten years, and now I'm afraid it will all come out. Nice pickings for all the dinner tables in Singapore and Johore!"

"What are you driving at?" demanded Harry. "Your personal affairs have nothing to do with this. All you'll have to tell anyone is that you dropped in here to spend the night, that Ailsa asked you to join her party and that you refused until I begged you at least to have dinner with the crowd. There's nothing to get your wind up about."

Bruce tried to smile. "Sorry, old man. You don't understand. The truth of the matter is that I used to know Bob and Ailsa years ago, and they were the last people in the world I wanted to meet again." He broke off abruptly and took two or three nervous paces. He couldn't go on—not even to Harry. Perhaps the police wouldn't delve into the past—perhaps no one need ever know. Once more he cursed the circumstances that had brought him to Johore. If only he hadn't been so keen for a hot bath, a good supper and a night in a real bed after his three weeks in the jungle, he and Ahmat might be in Singapore this minute. Of course he hadn't remembered the Sultan's birthday until he had stepped into the hall of the Rest House and found it crowded with people

in evening clothes, the air blue with smoke, a gramophone blaring out ancient American jazz, and the
Chinese boys flapping from table to table balancing
tin trays laden with glasses. Even as he had threaded
his way toward the overcrowded bar to make arrangements for the night with Oom Ling, he had no idea
that his old friend of India days, Harry Gordon, was
in the center of the group, and that after all these
years he was once more to be involved with Ailsa
and Bob Brownley. Glad as he had been when Harry
hailed him, he'd have gone six hundred miles to avoid
the meeting had he realized that Harry was the guest
of the Brownleys, and that in five minutes Ailsa herself, with her tawny eyes and camellia-like face under her gleaming cap of red brown hair, would be
holding out a slim hand as she urged him to join her
house-party. Nobody but Ailsa would ever have organized a party at the quiet Rest House in Johore and
include the gorgeous pageantry of the Sultan's birthday as part of her entertainment. He'd felt frozen,
and he'd probably acted that way, for even now he
couldn't remember the words he had used to combat
her cordial insistence. Finally she had given him up
as a bad job and gone back to dance with the blond
giant who was dry nursing the gramophone.

Harry seemed to have been following his thoughts,
for he said quietly, "I was wrong to make you stay,
Bruce, when you so obviously wanted to get away. I
didn't know you had more than a casual acquaintance

with the Brownleys, and I was so beside myself with worry just then that you seemed like a gift from the gods. I know you only stayed on to oblige me, and I'll do anything I can to help you now."

"How about you, Harry?" Bruce's voice was apologetic. "I'm afraid I let you down last night. I tried to stay awake, but I drifted off in spite of myself."

"O that's all right. I stopped in your room but you were asleep so I didn't wake you. I was only going to tell you that I wouldn't bother you with my troubles after all. I'd had time to think things out, and I wanted to kick myself for having said anything to you at all."

Bruce nodded sympathetically. "The trouble with both of us is that we are too damn British. We can't talk about ourselves. Even when we need advice or help, the words stick in our throats, and we'd go through hell fire rather than give ourselves away. Probably we'd all be a lot better off if we weren't so close-mouthed. Look at Bob! If ever a man seemed to be devil ridden, he does, but no one could ever break down that English reticence of his!" He smiled across at Harry. "Anyway, old man, I know damn' well that you never killed Ailsa, and no matter how black things may look for me later on, I want to give you my word that I had nothing to do with her death either."

"I never thought you did, Bruce," Harry's voice sounded shocked at the suggestion, "but I'm glad you are giving me a clean bill of health—Lord knows I had motive enough." His fingers shook slightly as he reached for a cigarette and passed his case to Bruce. Having secured a light, he leaned back once more and added, "The important thing is to find out who did kill Ailsa."

Bruce puffed thoughtfully on his cigarette. "You know this crowd better than I do—but it struck me that there were some very queer undercurrents at that dinner party last night, and once or twice I thought there was going to be an ugly scene. Do you remember?" Harry nodded, and Bruce continued, "Since I've been sitting out here, I've had a hunch that the clue to the murder lay in the things that were said, or the things that happened earlier in the evening."

"Perhaps," Harry agreed doubtfully. "I hadn't thought of it before, but now you mention it, I remember a lot of funny things cropped up at dinner." He relapsed into silence. Somberly Bruce stared out across the lawn. If he could only track down that elusive feeling he had, trace it to something definite so that he might have a clue to offer the police in exchange for the sanctity of the past!

CHAPTER II

It had been exactly eight o'clock that evening, Bruce recalled, when he had come out of his bedroom and paused beside the balcony railing to glance down at the room below. In the interval that it had taken him to bathe and change into dinner clothes, the hall had achieved an air of orderliness, save for the Chinese waiters scurrying to and fro, from table to kitchen, and from table to bar. The guests, who only a short time before had been milling around the bar, dancing between the tables, or gossiping in scattered groups, were now settled decorously into patterns at their allotted tables.

The big round table in the center was occupied by Ailsa and her friends. On her right was the important-looking Mr. Durham to whom Harry had already introduced him; next was the flower-like Berenice Gordon, in a black lace frock that emphasized the fairness of her skin and the gold of her hair. The vacant place beside Berenice was obviously meant for Bruce; then came the curly brown head of the

American girl, Susan Ames, above a wisp of orange
evening dress. On her right sat Bob, a worn, battered edition of the charming lad who had once been
Bruce's closest friend. Next to Bob, Harry Gordon
was making a strained effort to be his usual, jolly
self. On Ailsa's left sat the broad-shouldered, colle-
giate American youth, obviously the brother of the
girl beside Bob. From a place between the boy and
Harry, an older woman in an unbecoming, chartreuse
green dress, was watching, with smoldering brown
eyes, the clumsy efforts of Dick Durham to distract
Ailsa's attention from the American lad. She must
be Mrs. Durham, Bruce had decided with a cynical
smile. With the exception of Harry Gordon and Mrs.
Durham, they all seemed to be having a hilarious
time, due doubtless to the cocktails which Bruce had
missed, for their laughter drowned out the milder
babble from the small tables surrounding them. Many
of these were occupied by local people who had taken
the occasion of the Sultan's birthday to celebrate with
a change from the monotony of their home menus.
There were also two tables of out-of-town guests,—
the inevitable American tourists, middle-aged business man with plump eager wife and flapper daughter who was showering embarrassing attentions
upon a young ship's officer whom she had annexed
somewhere; and at a table by herself, a quiet Dutch
woman in a baggy white silk dress, probably the wife
of a planter from up country, a kindly, timid-looking

woman who seemed to be fascinated by the group at the big table. In the far corner, from another solitary table, a Mr. Wetherby, who, Bruce remembered was the secretary to the Resident and lived at the Rest House, was also greedily watching Ailsa's party.

There was no use putting off the evil moment any longer. Mentally bracing himself for the ordeal, Bruce hurried down the outside stairs and a minute later was standing at his hostess' side. Ailsa glanced up at him smiling, as he apologized for his delay, and introduced him in turn to Janet Durham, and Susan and Jack Ames. He shook hands with the American boy, murmured a friendly greeting to Berenice, bowed to the women, then turned to meet his host. Bob had risen with the other men and was holding out his hand uncertainly. "Hello, Bob," Bruce tried to make his voice sound natural as he took Bob's feverish hand in a brief grip. That was something he had never expected to do again, he thought as he settled into his place.

"We didn't wait for you, Bruce, but you are only a couple of courses behind, and I'm sure your army training will enable you to catch up," Ailsa said, directing one of the hovering Chinese boys to attend to his wants.

"I'll be right with you," Bruce assured her. "My army training is well supplemented just now by a ravenous appetite. I've been on a diet of rice, tea and wild pig for the last three weeks." He turned with appreciation to the shrimp cocktail that had been placed in front of him.

"I hear you've just come back from a hunting trip, Mr. Mac-Alistair," the American boy said. "Did you have any luck?"

"Nothing to boast about,—just a few pig and one tiger."

"You can bet I'd boast about it," the youngster's voice was admiring. "I've never shot anything bigger than a squirrel or a jack-rabbit."

"It's too bad your style has been so cramped, Jack," his sister mocked. "Daddy should have brought us up in Chicago where you could have had some real, big-game hunting."

"You're looking very fit, Bruce," Bob said diffidently. "You haven't changed much in the last ten years. The East is a small place when it comes to gossip, you know, so even in Shanghai I heard of you from time to time. I was sorry when you crocked up in the Soudan and had to give up the Camel Corps. You were always so active that I can't imagine you tied down to a desk in Calcutta."

"O, it's not so bad," Bruce's tone was casual. "I get in a hunting trip now and then, and I guess there's some of my Governor's mercantile blood in my veins after all, for I get quite a kick out of the export game."

"What did you think of the Sultan's birthday party, Miss Ames," Bruce said, turning to the little American girl who seemed to be at loose ends, since her brother and Durham had resumed their contest for Ailsa's interest.

"It was simply gorgeous." She lifted starry grey eyes to Bruce's tanned face. "The gold and crimson, and the fierce looking Indian soldiers! I haven't been so thrilled since my first circus. It was a shock though, when I saw the Sultan himself, somehow I expected him to be white. Doesn't he look exactly like the Lord High Executioner or someone in Gilbert and Sullivan—" her eagerness died away as she saw that Bruce's attention had wandered.

It was the troubled look on Harry Gordon's face which had distracted Bruce and recalled to his mind the reason for his presence at that alien table. Something was wrong. Berenice looked more than ever like an expensive French doll, but there were purple shadows under her blue eyes, and her delicate rouge stared out from the pallor of her cheeks. Ailsa had been rallying her on her silence, and with a frightened glance at Harry's grim face, Berenice was making an effort to join in the conversation.

"How do you and Bob happen to be in Johore, Ailsa?" Bruce diverted his hostess' attention. "I thought you were still in Shanghai."

"Thought, or hoped, Bruce?" Ailsa's tone was malicious, but she went on swiftly, "We left Shanghai when the Japanese started their fireworks. Bob's business expired on our hands, and we decided that the world owed us a living. We've practically been

beachcombers for the last year. Eventually we drifted down to Singapore with some other flotsam, and
the kindhearted inhabitants there supplied us with
a bamboo roof and our daily rations of coconuts."

"Ha ha!" cackled Dick Durham. "I guess the
management of the Raffles Hotel wouldn't be flattered at your description." He shook his large, bul-
let-shaped head. "I don't know how the Straits newspapers got along, before you two arrived to supply
them with copy. After that last party of yours, they
ran three editorials about the postwar decade, and
their circulation went up five hundred."

"It's all a deep-laid plot of Bob's and mine, Dick,"
Ailsa leaned forward with a pretty, confidential gesture to the table. "We are gradually leading up to a
grand denouement when we will both be clapped in
jail and be sure of three meals a day, to say nothing
of freedom from our creditors. The jail is really the
coolest place in town, and I've planned just how I
am going to decorate our cell. I'm going to paint
it in squares of red and black, like a checkerboard,
and we'll spend our time practicing the moves of the
game. I prophesy that the checker era will arrive as
soon as backgammon is done to death, and when the
time comes we are going to be ready to clean up."

"Thanks for the warning, Ailsa. If your checker
game is as deadly as your bridge, Berenice and I will
take passage for parts unknown, the day you get out
of jail,—that is, if we have the price of our passage

left, after we've paid off Berenice's bridge debts." There was a disquieting note of bitterness in Harry's booming voice.

"O Berenice would never desert me, would you, darling?" Ailsa's red lips suggested a pout as she looked at her friend.

"I'd be between the devil and the deep sea as usual." Berenice glanced helplessly from Ailsa's gay face to Harry's frowning one.

"There are lots of good husbands lying around loose out here, dear. I'll get you another one any time Harry turns temperamental." Ailsa's voice was caressing, but her tigerish eyes held a menace as they met Harry's.

"Damn it all, I've left my cigarette case upstairs," Harry muttered, feeling in the pockets of his evening clothes. "Hey, boy, find Mahat and tell him to bring my cigarette case down to me," he said in Malay to their waiter.

"No mere husband is going to separate us, is he, Berenice?" Ailsa persisted.

"I don't know about that," Dick Durham cut in. "Bob and I have a little surprise to spring on you. We fixed it up after tea this afternoon. I've offered to take Bob on as one of my managers. If he cuts out his drinking and gambling, and tones down a bit, it'll be a good thing for all of us." Bob flinched at the crudeness of the words, but there was an eager appeal in the look he bent on his wife.

"O Dick, how marvelous!" Ailsa's face lost its hardness in the lovely ardor that Bruce remembered. "Now our troubles will all be over. We can leave the Raffles and move into that adorable house I've been coveting on Thompson Road."

For a moment Dick Durham looked puzzled, and then he interrupted, "Not so fast, Ailsa. The position I've offered Bob isn't out here. I have a man already for Singapore. I'm going to take you and Bob back to Manchester with Janet and me. He'll be right in the main office where I can keep my eye on him. Don't think I'd leave you two in charge out here, do you? Ha! ha! Old Dick Durham isn't quite in his dotage yet, is he Janet?" He glanced at his wife's frozen face. As he started to speak to Ailsa she had clenched her hands tightly to conceal their trembling, and there was a quiver of emotion in her voice as she said, "I think Ailsa and Bob would be happier out here, Dick. I don't believe either of them would like to live in Manchester."

"Nonsense," he frowned. "Bob wants to get back to England. He's just rotting out here, and he knows it. Manchester is a great place, and Ailsa will give it a new lease on life, once she gets there. She's got a social gift, and she'll make the people there forget that you were just a stenographer working in my office, once they see what friends we all are. It will be a good move for everybody concerned."

"Lord what a cad!" Bruce muttered under his breath as he saw Janet wince.

"I'm sorry to upset your plan, Dick," Ailsa's voice was cool, "but I'm afraid it will be impossible. Bob could never stand the climate of England."

"What do you mean?" Dick stared at her as if unable to believe the evidence of his ears. "Here you've been trying to wangle a job for Bob ever since I met you, and now when I offer him one and we have things all fixed up, you go and renege."

Bob's eyes pleaded with his wife as he leaned forward to hear her reply.

"There's no use discussing the matter," Ailsa's lips were set in a stubborn line, "I won't go. If Bob wants to go without me, he can, but I've lived out here too long to face Manchester." Slowly the hope drained out of Bob's face and he sank back in his chair.

"Ah, here's Mahat with my cigarettes," exclaimed Harry, blessing the interruption. "He's a fine boy, only one thing wrong with him," he addressed the table full of people. "He's latah!"

"What's that?" asked Susan, her grey eyes wide with interest.

"Why, it's a kind of disease some of the natives have. You can make them imitate anything you do. It's a sort of nervous affliction. Watch now!" As the boy approached the table, Harry caught his eye and with an exclamation threw his napkin on the floor.

Quick as a flash the boy dashed the cigarette case likewise to the stone pavement. "Hey!" exclaimed Harry as a laugh went up, "I forgot he was carrying that. Wait, try again." Leaning over he spoke sharply to the boy, at the same time giving Bob a gentle push. Immediately the native responded by pushing Bob too. "Jangang (*Don't*), Tuan," the boy entreated abashed, handing Harry the cigarette case which he had retrieved from the floor.

"How queer!" the American girl breathed leaning forward. "It must be a kind of St. Vitus dance."

"No, it's not like that," Bruce answered. "Mahat is perfectly all right, unless someone speaks to him sharply, and then he only imitates what he sees enacted."

"Let me try him out," Dick Durham said, calling to the boy and dashing a glass on the floor. Instantly a second glass crashed as the native mechanically repeated the white man's gesture.

"Don't!" exclaimed Bob. "It's not sporting to take advantage of the poor chap. He doesn't know what he is doing, and it's not fair to make a show of him. Send him away, Harry."

"I guess you're right, Bob. The poor devil has a bad enough time as soon as the other natives find out about his weakness. They used to have him performing by the hour, back on the estate, until I put a stop to it. Whenever I take him off on a trip with me like this, he refuses to have anything to do with the other servants. Spends most of his time in my room, or crouched outside my door. He even sleeps there, rather than go to the servants' quarters." He motioned the boy to go away, and like a brown shadow Mahat glided out of sight.

"I think we'll have coffee outside," Ailsa said. "It will be cooler. All the other guests seem to have left the dining room, and as soon as we go, I've told Oom Ling to put up some bridge tables." She rose as she spoke and the rest of the party followed her out onto the shadowy veranda.

"Ailsa," said Susan going to her hostess' side, "if you'll excuse me, I don't believe I'll play bridge to-night."

"Nonsense, child, of course you will play, won't she, Jack?" She appealed to the tall American who was holding a chair for her.

"Really, I'd rather not," Susan insisted.

"Don't be a kill-joy, Sis," Jack exclaimed impatiently.

"It isn't that, Jack, but I honestly can't afford to lose any more money," blurted Susan.

"O, so that's it, is it? Well, I'll stake you. Your bad luck won't last forever. She should never quit when she's losing, should she, Ailsa?"

"No, that's always fatal. Of course Susan is going to play,—it will spoil a table if she doesn't," Ailsa said absently, as she watched her husband and Bruce framed together in the lighted doorway.

"Bruce," Bob put out an impetuous hand, "let me say just one thing, won't you? I've wanted to tell you for years that I didn't know about your father's failure and death when Ailsa and I ran off that night. I didn't hear about it for weeks."

"You didn't know?" Bruce echoed. "But you must have known."

"No, on my honor! Neither Ailsa nor I knew a thing about it. She told me, of course, that your engagement was broken, that she had found she didn't care enough for you to marry you, and that you'd released her. I wasn't rotter enough to cut in otherwise, surely you knew that?"

"You mean," Bruce picked his words slowly, "that neither you nor Ailsa knew about that cable?" He was remembering the scene in the quiet corner of Shepheard's Hotel in Cairo, when dazed and broken at the news of his father's suicide, he had shown the cable to Ailsa. His mind still recoiled from the shock of her reaction. What he had done, or where he had gone the rest of that night, he never remembered. When he came back to the hotel the next afternoon and inquired for Bob, he had received the short note that had killed his friendship—"Ailsa and I were married this morning. We're off on our honeymoon. Will write you from the next port of call!" He had been left stranded, with just enough money to pay his hotel bill. The world tour, on which he and his chum had set forth so blithely, had ended for Bruce in Egypt. It was then he had joined the Camel Corps. He had had two or three letters from Bob later, and had torn them unread into bits, stamping them into the burning sand somewhere in the Soudan.

"On my word," Bob's voice continued eagerly, "I never knew you were broke. I'd have shared my last farthing with you if I'd dreamed it. I had plenty in those days for all three of us, but you never answered my letters, and I thought maybe you wanted to forget both Ailsa and me."

So that was it! He should have known Bob better, known that Ailsa had never told him. If Bob had had any inkling of the real facts, he'd never have married her. She'd played her cards swiftly and well. He cast a look of burning hatred at the beautiful woman who was sitting a few feet away, gracefully pouring hot milk and syrupy coffee into fragile cups. Bob's anxious eyes followed Bruce's glance, and a spasm crossed his face.

Well, that was that, Bruce was thinking. Bob had married her and as long as she lived her shadow would fall between them. With an effort he turned to Bob, "I was off my head for awhile back there. Let's forget it." For a second his hand rested on the other man's shoulder, then he went swiftly down the steps into the welcome darkness of the night.

The sea wall across the road was deserted, save for a solitary figure leaning across the parapet some distance away, and for many minutes overwhelmed with bitterness, Bruce stood staring with unseeing eyes at the limpid sea, while a soft, salt breeze cooled his burning forehead.

"Don't you love the little golden threads the minnows, or whatever you call them out here, weave through the water when the nights are dark like this?" a low voice broke in upon his memories. With a start he came back to the present and realized that the vague figure he had noticed was the little American girl, and that she had moved to a place beside him.

"I'm sorry, I didn't know you were out here," he apologized. "I was hundreds of miles away for the moment."

"Yes, I saw you were, and it wasn't a very pleasant ride you took yourself on, judging by your tenseness. You looked so grim even in the starlight, that I thought you were going to do a Steve Brodie right before my eyes."

"A Steve Brodie? I'm afraid I don't know what you mean," Bruce said blankly.

The girl's laughter rang out, "He was an American who jumped off Brooklyn Bridge, back in the mauve decade."

Bruce chuckled, "You flatter me. I'm not contemplating anything as altruistic as suicide. I'm far more apt to commit a murder."

"I think that's a splendid idea," Susan approved. "Is your aim good, or do you think you ought to practice a little before you stage the really perfect crime?

There are one or two targets I might suggest—people I'd be glad to spare from my immediate social circle."

"I'd do a great deal to oblige a damsel in distress, although I'm still in the amateur class when it comes to crime. Whom would you like to have removed?"

"You make me feel just like the Queen in Alice in Wonderland,—all I have to say is 'Off with her head!' Well, by way of being the perfect guest, it will be all right with me if you begin with my hostess."

Bruce checked his start of surprise. "Why pick on the fair Ailsa?" he asked. "She seems very fond of you and your brother."

"Of my brother, yes, but not of me. I spend all my waking hours making a respectable third to their little triangle. Jack, poor darling, doesn't know yet what it's all about. But I'm going to save him from that man-eating-she-shark if it's the last thing I ever do." The girl's voice had lost its playfulness, and uncomfortably Bruce realized that she was serious.

"You know, Miss Ames," he said abruptly, "you and your brother don't belong out here. You should both be back in America."

"O, but I love the East—the blue-black nights, the perfumed air, the natives in their bright sarongs, all the strange flowers and fruits, the bamboo huts—I could spend hours just watching a palm tree against the burning blue of the sky." Her voice was wistful. "Yet I'm afraid of it too, it twists and distorts people so. You all seem to take things so seriously out here."

"What do you mean?" Bruce asked, interested in so novel a point of view. "I thought the chief criticism was that we didn't take things seriously enough."

"O, you do, but it's the wrong things that you are serious about. You make a business of your pleasures,—a business of bridge, and of drinking, and of lovemaking. All the other things you take too lightly, friendship, loyalty, business!"

"Whew!" Bruce whistled. "What an indictment! And how long did you have to be out here to discover all our weaknesses and vices?" he asked in amusement.

"You score," the girl admitted after a minute's thought. "I've not been here long enough to judge. But, in a way that proves my first point, that the East distorts everybody. It has already warped my perspective."

"It is just because you are worried, I think, Miss Ames," Bruce's voice was gentle. "You have only been out here a short time and haven't your bearings yet. You got in with the wrong crowd. When you've been here longer and have met people more congenial, you'll feel different. Don't judge too hastily."

"I suppose you are right," Susan sighed, "but I can't help being afraid of what the East is doing to Jack and me. It is bringing out all the weakness in him, and it is bringing out all the vindictiveness in me. Jack is too fine to be spoiled. If that woman ruins him as she has her husband, and other men, I'll kill her!"

"Hey, Bruce!" Harry Gordon's voice hailed them from the road. "Is that you? I've been looking for you."

"Sorry, old man, I went off for a stroll, and then Miss Ames and I stopped to watch the phosphorus. It's unusually fine tonight because the moon isn't up yet. Come and join us."

"It's too late now," Harry sounded reproachful. "Ailsa sent me out to round up a couple of tables of bridge. You're playing, aren't you, Miss Ames?"

"I'm afraid I must," Susan said reluctantly as she turned away from the sea, "but what's that noise, music, I guess it is meant to be?" She stopped to listen to the weird sounds in the distance.

"That's the natives celebrating the Sultan's birthday. It's a big night for them. They'll keep on with their music and dancing for hours, just stopping long enough to get their breath and refreshments," Bruce explained.

"It's terrible," Susan shuddered. "It gives me the jitters. Well, thank you for your fatherly advice, Mr. MacAlistair. I'll try to remember it."

"Not at all," Bruce said, embarrassed. "I'm going to have some friends of mine in Singapore look you up and try to change your unfavorable impressions of us."

"All right, if it's not too late," the girl called back cryptically over her shoulder as she crossed the lawn toward the yellow lights of the Rest House, leaving Bruce and Harry to follow at their leisure.

"Are you going to cut in with us, Bruce?" Harry asked.

"No, I'm off to bed. At best I never have much time for bridge, you know, and tonight I'm too tired to face it. I'm sorry I didn't have a chance to talk to you, old man, but I heard something that upset me, and it knocked everything else clean out of my mind."

"That's all right. I've practically decided what I'll have to do. That byplay at dinner settled things as far as I'm concerned. I may stop in your room on my way up to bed, if you are still awake, but perhaps I'd better not drag you into the mess. She's a devil incarnate, that woman!" he added under his breath as they reached the veranda steps and Ailsa came toward them.

"You'll play, won't you Bruce? We can cut in," Ailsa greeted him.

"Thanks just the same, but I'm turning in now. I have to be on my way early tomorrow and I want a decent night's sleep."

"O, but Bruce, you mustn't," Ailsa came so close to him that the fragrance of the sandalwood perfume she used choked him with the involuntary memories it evoked. "I've been waiting to talk to you all evening. There is something I must say, and you haven't given me an opportunity."

With a muttered apology, Harry Gordon pushed past her and through the open door Bruce saw him make his way toward the bar.

"I'm sorry, Ailsa," Bruce said evenly, "but it's too late."

"No it isn't, Bruce. It's never too late. I must see you, if it's only for five minutes," her voice held an unusual note, one almost of fear, it seemed.

"It's no use, Ailsa, there's nothing to be gained by it, and I've nothing to say to you except goodnight, and thank you for the dinner," his voice rose as Dick Durham approached.

"Ah, little lady, here you are," Durham exclaimed. "You've been avoiding me all evening, but you can't put me off any longer. I want to know just what you mean—"

"Ssh!" warned Ailsa, "I'll see you later. I promise you I'll make an opportunity, but you mustn't drink any more. I'm afraid of you when you've been drinking." With a shrug of disgust, Bruce mounted the outside stairs but not before he had heard Ailsa add, "Here comes Janet, be careful! She looks as though she'd like to murder me."

His room seemed oppressively hot as Bruce sat in the darkness by the shuttered window, staring with blank eyes at the stretch of lawn and its border of shrubbery below. The plaintive whine of the native instruments seemed a fitting accompaniment to his gloomy, chaotic thoughts—Harry and Berenice! Bob and Ailsa! The little American girl and her ass of a brother. The unpleasant menace of Durham's voice! The cat-like watchfulness of his wife! A disagreeable evening, and one that he was glad to have behind him. Tomorrow he would be free from them all. He shivered in spite of the heat.

There was a soft knock at his door, and thinking that it must be Harry, Bruce sprang to his feet as he called out, "Come in!" It was only one of the Chinese boys with a chit. Of course it was too early yet to expect Harry. He'd be stuck at the bridge table until the wee sma' hours probably, Bruce realized as he took the note and dismissed the boy. As he switched on his light he saw that the envelope was addressed in Ailsa's distinctive handwriting—"Bruce, you must meet me. For the sake of what we once were to each other, you must come to me. I will be on the stone seat in the shrubbery at 1:30 and will wait until you come. Ailsa."

"Damn the woman!" he exclaimed in disgust ripping the note in two and dropping it into the waste basket. "She can wait until hell freezes over for all I care." Viciously he switched off the light and threw himself on the bed. For a long time he lay there too angry and upset to sleep, but eventually weariness overcame him and he dozed off.

The tropic moon was slanting through the shutters, touching the mattinged floor and rattan furniture with familiar beams when, with a start, Bruce woke. For a moment or two he lay still trying to remember where he was, then stiffly he rose to his feet, automatically smoothing down the wrinkles in his crumpled evening clothes. Ailsa was waiting for him in the garden. Damn the woman! What time was it? The illuminated dial on his watch showed 1:50. The native music had stopped for the time being, and the house itself seemed wrapped in silence. Peering through the shutters he saw the garden ghostly in the moonlight, but the shadows cast by the shrubbery at the edge of the lawn were so deep that he couldn't see the marble seat. Was Ailsa really down there at that hour? It was no place for a woman, especially on a night when the natives were excited. Not that she deserved any consideration, but just the same, much as he hated her, no woman should be allowed out alone at that hour. He supposed he'd have to go down and make sure she wasn't there, or if she were by any chance, then he'd have to make her come in. If he didn't, he'd never get to sleep again, and sleep was the only thing that really mattered to him just then.

Reluctantly he opened his door. The Rest House was still. The lights downstairs were out, and only the faint illumination from the ceiling lamps showed him the way across the dark balcony to the door that led onto the veranda. Someone was standing by the railing there in the corner of the porch, he noticed as he stepped outside, and for a second he hoped it was Ailsa. If it were she, he'd creep back to his room without a word. A second glance, however, showed him that the figure, although that of a woman, was too dumpy to be Ailsa, or indeed any of her party.

She gave no sign that she saw him, but she couldn't have helped hearing the wooden steps creak under his weight. He decided that he would circle the Rest House, approaching the shrubbery from the rear and following the little path that twisted through the bushes to the marble seat. In that way he would be out of sight of the watcher on the veranda. He had just reached the lawn on the east side of the Rest House, when Ailsa's scream had rung out. Could he have gone to her more quickly,—in time, perhaps to see the murderer slinking away? He didn't know. He would never know.

Wearily Bruce shifted his position and turned to Harry who was still sunk in thought. "I've gone over everything I can remember about last night, and all I know is that Ailsa seemed to be pretty unpopular with everybody except Bob, Ames and Durham. Toward the end of dinner, even Durham's behavior was threatening, and who knows, Ailsa may have quarreled later with poor, old Bob, and disillusioned the American chap, just by way of making the hatred unanimous!"

Harry roused himself with an effort. "I've been trying to get hold of something significant too, but it's beyond me. Brains never were my strong point. Thank God it's not up to us. It's a job for the police, and, by George! here they are." He and Bruce rose hastily to their feet as a car raced up the driveway.

CHAPTER III

A large, loose-jointed man in police uniform untangled himself from behind the steering wheel, and strode across the veranda, followed by a short, thick-set Malay.

"My name is Campbell," the officer said to Bruce, "and this is my assistant, Ismael. I hear there's been a murder in the Rest House."

Bruce introduced himself. "Yes, Mrs. Brownley has been killed, stabbed. I found her body out in the shrubbery and brought it inside." Campbell nodded, and with long strides covered the distance between the door and the table where Ailsa's body lay. The Chinese boys stiffened to attention as Ismael passed them, and their beady little eyes gleamed with interest as they watched his deliberate examination of the murdered woman.

"The doctor will be along in a few minutes," the white officer was explaining. "He was out on a baby case. There doesn't seem to be much he can do here though. Mrs. Brownley was obviously stabbed to death, and from what Wetherby told me over the telephone, it happened about two A.M."

"Yes, Mr. Campbell," Wetherby put in, "it was exactly 2:03 when she screamed. It woke me out of a sound sleep—a perfectly ghastly shriek, but I remembered to look at my watch after I switched on the light. Then I pulled on some trousers and ran downstairs to see what the trouble was."

Ismael turned from his contemplation of the body. "Was this kris found in the wound?"

"No, the kris was found later by Oom Ling. It was lying under the marble seat," Bruce volunteered.

"Does it belong to any of you?" Campbell asked, looking around the little group.

"Yes, it is one I bought this afternoon as a souvenir. I left it in my room and didn't miss it until Oom Ling brought it in. I don't know who could have taken it," Dick Durham said in a worried tone.

"Where's Oom Ling now?" asked Ismael, his dark eyes resting in turn on Bruce, Harry, Dick, Jack and the silent, huddled Chinamen.

"I told him to stand guard out in the shrubbery, so that nothing more should be disturbed until the police got here," Bruce said.

"Good," a pleased expression lighted the stolidity of the Malay's face. He turned to his chief, "I think we should go out and look around, Tuan. By that time, Tuan McCloud should have come to take notes on the testimony."

"That's a good idea, Ismael, and will save us a lot of time," Campbell approved the suggestion. He glanced at the group of white men and added to them, "We have to have a magistrate present to take notes, so I arranged for young McCloud to get here as soon as he could. In the meantime, just make yourselves as comfortable as you can while Ismael and I take a look."

The scant fifteen minutes that elapsed before their strained ears caught the explosive clatter of a motorcycle on the driveway seemed an eternity to Bruce. An eager figure, surprisingly young, came into the room, peeling off goggles and gauntlets as he nodded to the men assembled in the hall. "My name is McCloud," he said. "Where's Mr. Campbell?"

"Right here, McCloud, you made good time," the officer answered from the doorway. Behind him came the squat figure of the Malay detective, followed by Oom Ling. Over Campbell's arm trailed a scarf of silver net embroidered with green dragons. "This is the total result of our search, gentlemen. The scarf lay at the back of the marble seat. I presume it belonged to Mrs. Brownley,—it seems to match her costume. Do any of you recognize it?"

The men shook their heads. A flicker of surprise crossed the officer's face, "Which of you is Mr. Brownley?"

"None of us," Harry Gordon said. "Mr. Brownley is still asleep upstairs. He doesn't know what has happened."

"Asleep!" exclaimed McCloud. "And his wife murdered!"

Harry looked uncomfortable as he explained, "Mr. Brownley is troubled with insomnia and when I looked into his room a few minutes ago, he was breathing heavily, so I thought he had taken some of the pills his doctor prescribed for bad nights. Bob is very highly strung and he has a touch of malaria, so we thought it would be better not to break the news to him until you got here, and there was a doctor in attendance."

"I see, you were probably right." Campbell looked thoughtfully at the five men. "Now suppose you all sit down, and tell me what you know about this murder. Ready, McCloud?"

The young magistrate pulled a small table in front of a chair, took out a notebook and pen. "All set!" he affirmed.

"As I visualize the crime," the officer stated, "Mrs. Brownley was seated on that marble bench in the shrubbery, perhaps resting, perhaps waiting for someone to join her. Somebody came along that path. Ismael's flashlight showed that several people had passed that way, but unfortunately the ground was too dry to hold any footprints. I think that if Mrs. Brownley hadn't been expecting someone, she would have been alarmed at the sound of his approach—the rustle of twigs and branches and dried leaves. At any rate, she rose as her murderer came into view, for the position of the wound shows us that the kris must have been plunged into her breast as she stood facing her assailant. And from the way her scarf lay on the bench, we know she must have been sitting there previously. Apparently it slipped from her shoulders as she stood up. She probably wasn't alarmed until she saw the murderer with the knife in his hand, otherwise she would have tried to run away, or she would have screamed for help. She only screamed once—and that must have been when the knife was plunging toward her."

"By Jove!" exclaimed McCloud, "that means she must have recognized the murderer. That it was someone she knew. If it had been a stranger she'd have yelled for help, or struggled."

"Exactly!" Campbell was watching the faces of the men around him. His words had purposely made the picture very real, very terrible and his listeners were reacting characteristically.

Bruce's lean, tanned face stiffened into a mask for his emotions. Dick Durham's eyes blinked behind his glasses. Harry Gordon grew white. Wetherby took two or three nervous steps back and forth. Jack Ames turned aside his miserable, boyish face. There was a complete silence in the room while the officer and the little Malay stared at each of the men in turn.

Finally Campbell said in his pleasant voice, "Suppose each of you tell me what you know of the crime. Sit down, Wetherby," he motioned impatiently to the one man who had remained standing. Then settling himself astride one of the chairs, with his back to the table he faced the semi-circle of witnesses. "Suppose each of you tell me what you know of the crime. Since you discovered the body, MacAlistair, you had better start. Where were you when you heard the scream?" McCloud's pen was poised expectantly, and Ismael's almond-shaped eyes were fixed on Bruce with the open frankness of a child as he noted each word, each fleeting expression of hand, mouth and eyes.

"I was outside on the east lawn," Bruce began slowly, "when Mrs. Brownley screamed. For a moment I was so startled that I couldn't move. Then I ran across the back lawn and cut into the shrubbery, because the cry had seemed to come from there. It was dark, but as I came into the little clearing around the marble seat, I saw something lying on the ground there. It was Mrs. Brownley. I picked her up and carried her into the Rest House. Put her on the table there in the center—it was the only one that seemed large enough. I thought she had fainted, but when I laid her down, I saw the blood. I felt her heart, and knew she was dead."

"You said you heard Mrs. Brownley scream. Did you know then that it was she, or didn't you know who it was until you got inside?" Campbell asked.

"I knew it was Ailsa," Bruce said as though surprised at the realization.

"How could you know that?" Campbell looked interested.

"I don't know how I was so sure, but I didn't have any doubt. I just knew it was Ailsa."

"Did you know Mrs. Brownley well?"

"I used to know her years ago, but I hadn't seen her for ten years until tonight."

"You must have a pretty good memory then, Mr. MacAlistair, to be able to recognize her voice under those conditions." Campbell's tone was dry. "Suppose you tell us now how you happened to be outside the Rest House at that hour."

Bruce's feeling of discomfort increased. "It was hot in my room. I went out for some air."

"O, and did you see anyone else around?"

"No, not until I crossed the lawn carrying Mrs. Brownley. I had seen lights go on in the house right after the scream, and I could hear people moving, but I didn't see anyone. Wait a minute, yes, I did see one person! As I crossed the upper veranda to come down the outside staircase, I saw a woman. I didn't recognize her then, but after I'd put the body down, I saw her again, leaning over the balcony up there. It was the Dutch woman I'd noticed at dinner."

"That would be Mrs. DeKok," interrupted Wetherby.

"That's interesting. Where is she now?" Campbell asked glancing up at the empty balcony.

"I don't know. She disappeared after a minute or two. I suppose she went back into her room."

Campbell changed the line of his inquiry. "I understood from Mr. Wetherby that Mrs. Brownley was having a house-party here over the weekend. Were you one of the guests?"

Bruce shook his head. "No, I had been on a hunting trip up in the Endau. I just stopped here for the night. I ran into Mr. Gordon whom I had known in India, and later met Mrs. Brownley. She asked me to join her party at dinner. My participation was quite inadvertent."

"Did you know Mrs. Brownley was here in Johore?"

"No, I thought she and her husband were still in Shanghai."

"How well did you know Mr. and Mrs. Brownley?"

"I used to know them very well, but as I said, I haven't seen either of them for ten years."

"Your relations with them were friendly when you last saw them, before tonight, I mean?"

Bruce bit his lip. He could feel himself becoming more and more involved, and again he silently cursed the mischance that had brought him to the Rest House. That confounded Malay's eyes seemed to be boring into his very mind.

"I used to go to school in England with Bob Brownley. We were taking a trip around the world together when Mr. Brownley met the girl he later married. In fact he married her in Cairo, and they went on to Shanghai where they settled."

Harry Gordon started at Bruce's words. There was a disagreeable glitter in Durham's eyes, and both Campbell and McCloud straightened with interest. Only Ismael's face was inscrutable.

"Wasn't it rather strange that you should have lost track of your friend when you had been so intimate with him, when you were both out here in the East?"

"I don't think so. Marriage makes a difference. Bob was in Shanghai, and I got a berth in Calcutta. We were hardly next door neighbors."

"I suppose you heard from them often, wrote back and forth even if you didn't exchange visits?"

"No, I heard nothing from them direct, until to-night," Bruce snapped.

"If your friendship with Mr. Brownley suffered such a lapse, there must have been a reason, Mr. Mac-Alistair." The officer leaned forward, "Was it because you disliked Mrs. Brownley, or was it because perhaps you liked her—too well?"

"It's none of your damned business!" shouted Bruce. "That is my affair. I didn't kill her, if that's what you are driving at." There was a murmur of surprise, and Bruce sank back in his chair ashamed of his outburst.

"Suppose we let that go now," Campbell sounded pleased with himself as he turned suavely to Harry.

"Mr. Gordon, will you please tell us where you were when Mrs. Brownley screamed?" Ismael's speculative stare shifted from Bruce's face to Harry's. McCloud began a new page in his note book.

Harry Gordon looked embarrassed as he said, "I was in the Recreation Room—that little room back there in the rear." He nodded toward a door opening on the left of the bar.

The officer raised his eyebrows. "What were you doing there? Playing billiards?"

"No, I had come down to look for a magazine I'd left there in the afternoon. It was beastly hot in my room and that confounded native music kept me awake. I had nothing to read, and after tossing about for a long time, I decided to come down and get the magazine I'd picked up before tea."

"Did you find the magazine?"

"Unfortunately I didn't. It was dark in there, and I couldn't locate the light switch. I groped around the room feeling on the tables and chairs, but I didn't have any luck. Then I stepped on a billiard cue that some idiot had left on the floor, and wrenched my ankle. I couldn't step on my foot for a few minutes. Had to sit down and rub it. It's still swollen a bit," he pointed down to his enlarged ankle. "I was just going to rout out one of the Chinese boys to turn on the lights, when I heard the scream."

"What did you do then?"

"I hobbled as fast as I could out on the lawn trying to find what was wrong. Dick Durham joined me, and I saw some of the Chinese boys rushing around. Then Bruce appeared carrying Mrs. Brownley."

"You knew it was Mrs. Brownley?"

"Not until Bruce mentioned that he thought Ailsa had fainted. In fact I'd been greatly worried because I was afraid it was my wife who had screamed."

"Wasn't your wife in your room when you came downstairs?"

"No, she had gone in to speak to Mrs. Durham. They went up from bridge together."

"What happened after Mr. MacAlistair put the body down?"

"Well, we realized immediately that she was dead. My wife came bursting into the room and fainted when she saw the body. I carried her upstairs. Miss Ames and Mrs. Durham are looking after her."

"I see. You were a member of the Brownley party, Mr. Gordon?"

"Yes, they invited my wife and me, together with Mr. and Mrs. Durham, and Mr. and Miss Ames to be their guests. We arrived in Johore Thursday. We were planning to spend the weekend."

"Have you known Mrs. Brownley long?"

"I've only known her and her husband about two years, but my wife has been a friend of Mrs. Brownley's since she was a child. In fact she was living with the Brownleys in Shanghai when I met her."

"Have you seen much of them since you were married?"

"Yes, they have visited us several times on my rubber estate in Sumatra, and my wife spent three or four months with them in Shanghai."

"Were you with her at that time?"

"Not all of it. I took her up there and stayed about a week. I went up again to bring her home."

"O!" The officer looked at him quizzically. "How long have you been married, Mr. Gordon?"

"About eighteen months."

"Isn't it a bit unusual for a bride to be away from her husband so much?"

Harry stiffened. "My wife is delicate and she needed a change. Surely it was natural for her to visit her closest friend."

"You didn't resent the friendship then? I want to get these relationships straightened out, if you don't mind. I'm trying to find out whether you approved of the friendship between your wife and Mrs. Brownley."

"I approve of anything which adds to my wife's happiness," was Harry's evasive reply.

"Quite so. What did your wife say, Mr. Gordon, when she saw her friend's body lying here?" Campbell leaned forward and stared earnestly into Harry's face.

Harry whitened, but he looked directly into the officer's eyes as he said in a low voice, "She said, 'O Harry, how could you!'—then she fainted."

"What did she mean by that? Had she reason to believe you killed her friend?"

Harry brushed a hand across his damp brow. "I don't know what she meant. She wasn't herself. She is still half crazy from the shock. I hope, Mr. Campbell, you won't question her tonight."

"I'm afraid I'll have to see her later, but I'll put it off as long as I can. That will do for now."

"Oom Ling, Oom Ling!" a voice shouted from the balcony. "Have all the boys gone off on a strike? I've been ringing my bell for the last ten minutes!" The American tourist was leaning over the railing. With a murmured apology Oom Ling stepped forward, "I'm sorry, Tuan. The boys are all out here. What is it you want?"

"My wife is very much upset by this affair," he waved a large hand that included the body on the table, the police officers, and the group of white men. "She wants a club sandwich and a pot of coffee."

Oom Ling looked questioningly at Campbell. Annoyed at the interruption, the officer hesitated before saying, "All right, Oom Ling, tell one of the boys to fix it, but tell him to make it nippy." Then he raised his head and addressed the American. "While you are out here, Mr.—er?"

"Thompson!" snapped the bath-robed figure above him, "Gerald B. Thompson of Columbus, Ohio. If you are planning to ask me any questions, you can save your breath. I don't know anything about these people or their quarrels or their crimes. Never saw any of 'em until today, and I hope I never see any of 'em again."

"You were in your room all evening?" Campbell controlled his temper with an effort.

"Yes. And so was my wife and daughter. We don't know anything. That's all I have to say. Just tell that chink to make things snappy. I'd like to have some service around here." With a final gesture of disgust he stalked back to his room and slammed the door.

Campbell glanced uncertainly at Ismael, as one of the Chinese boys, under the direction of Oom Ling, sidled toward the kitchen. "It doesn't matter, Tuan," Ismael said, "I do not think that American family is involved. It is waste of time and temper to talk to Tuan Thompson. Let us rather hear the words of Tuan Durham."

Once more the group settled themselves in their chairs, while McCloud bent his amused face over a fresh sheet of paper.

"Mr. Durham, where do you fit into this picture?" Campbell turned his attention to the prosperous manufacturer.

"My wife and I were also guests of Mr. and Mrs. Brownley. We have been traveling through the East,— part business and part pleasure. I am planning to expand my cotton market, open offices in some of the strategic centers out here. I ran into the Brownleys in

Shanghai first, and then a couple of months ago, met them again in Singapore. They were very cordial, and I liked them both. I thought perhaps I could offer Brownley a job, he seemed to be a bit on his uppers— in fact only yesterday I put a proposition to him to take over the management of my Manchester office." Durham's voice was complacent.

"Did he accept your offer, Mr. Durham?"

"He seemed very pleased with it. However, Mrs. Brownley put a damper on the idea. She didn't want to go back to England."

"And where were you when you heard the scream?"

For the first time during his questioning, Dick Durham seemed to lose some of his assurance. "To tell you the truth, Inspector, I was asleep out on the veranda."

"Asleep on the veranda!" echoed the officer.

"Yes, I'd had a lot to drink, and after the bridge game, I went outside to cool down a bit. I dropped into one of those long wicker chairs on the porch, the one at the far end, and I must have dozed off. The first thing I knew, I was aroused by that scream. I didn't know what time it was. I was still dazed. I nipped across the veranda and out on the lawn just as MacAlistair came out of the shrubbery with something in his arms. Of course, you understand, I didn't know then that it was MacAlistair, or whom he was carrying,—not until I had followed him into the room and the lights were put on."

"I understand that the weapon is yours, Mr. Durham. Can you explain how it got here?"

"No, I left it in my room when we came back to the Rest House. I don't remember seeing it again until Oom Ling brought it in a little while ago."

"Who would have access to your room, Mr. Durham?"

"Practically everybody in the Rest House, I should say; the native servants, or anyone who wanted to slip in when my wife and I weren't there."

"It rather makes this murder an inside job, then, doesn't it?"

"I'm afraid so. Until I saw my kris, I supposed she had been killed by some strange native. Now I suppose it was one of the house boys."

The Chinese boys began babbling excitedly among themselves as they saw Ismael step forward.

"What makes you think that, Tuan Durham? Did Mrs. Brownley have any difficulties with any of the servants," the Malay's soft voice was unusually stern.

"O no! She seemed to have a way with servants, they always liked her. She spoke Malay and Chinese very well, and she was always generous with them. I just said that one of these boys must have killed her because it is unbelievable that one of us should have done it."

At his words a shudder passed through the room, as each person present realized the implication. Ismael turned and stared thoughtfully at the frightened faces of the Chinese boys, then once more his gaze returned to the group of white men.

"What were your relations and your wife's with the Brownleys?" the officer resumed.

"Very friendly. Didn't I just tell you I had offered him a berth in my outfit? That is hardly the gesture of an enemy, you know," Dick said with heavy sarcasm.

"The East is a small place, Mr. Durham," Campbell continued unperturbed by Dick's belligerence, "and Mr. Brownley's reputation is well known to me. He is scarcely the type of man that I would expect you to choose for an important position, particularly in view of the fact that his only business venture was an unsuccessful automobile agency in Shanghai. He can't have much knowledge of cotton manufacture."

Durham's face purpled with annoyance. "I should think those facts were sufficient proof then of my friendship. I wanted to give him a lift. He was down and out. He comes from a good county family in England, and I believe he has the right stuff in him, if he once has a chance to pull himself together. That's why I insisted on his taking the Manchester job or nothing."

Ismael stooped down and whispered in his chief's ear.

Campbell nodded, "I see, Mr. Durham,—very commendable of you. Yet it seems a little strange. You look like a very hardheaded business man." His voice changed and a harsh note sounded in it as he stared at the plump, well-fed figure in front of him. "Just why did you offer Mr. Brownley that job? Was it because you were concerned about his welfare, or because you were interested in his wife?"

Dick Durham jumped to his feet, "I won't put up with your insinuations. I refuse to answer any more of your questions. Further than that, I shall report you to your superiors for insolence."

"Just as you please, Mr. Durham. My job is to get to the bottom of this murder, not to spare the feelings of the people who are involved in it. If you have anything to hide, it is my business to find it out." With a wave of his long, bony hand, Campbell dismissed Dick from the center of the stage, and hitched his chair about until he faced the American lad. Jack still seemed to be dazed, indifferent to the questions that had been asked and answered.

"I presume you are Mr. Ames," the officer said pleasantly, "and that you are the other gentleman in the house-party."

Jack nodded.

"Have you been here in the East long?"

"No, only three months. I came out for a large American oil company."

"I see. Then your acquaintance with Mrs. Brownley is a recent one?"

"Yes," the boy answered. "She was very kind to my sister and me. She was the only real friend we had here." Again he seemed to be overcome with the knowledge of his loss.

"About tonight," Campbell continued. "Where were you when Mrs. Brownley screamed?"

"I don't know. I didn't know anything about it until I came in half an hour or so ago. I wish to God I had been here. If I'd only stayed with her it would never have happened!"

"So you had been with Mrs. Brownley shortly before her death?"

"Yes, we took a little walk after the bridge game broke up."

"Where did you go?"

"O, just around the grounds and then over to the sea wall."

"Did she seem to be in good spirits then?"

"No, she was upset. She had been having a stormy interview with someone—she didn't tell me who, but she took hold of my arm and asked me to come along with her until she could calm down."

"Do you know who the person was who had upset her?"

"I have my own ideas about that, but I'm not going to tell you who it was. I'll settle with him myself."

Campbell stared thoughtfully at the excited, boyish face. "If you have any information, Mr. Ames, you should give it to me. Don't you want to see Mrs. Brownley's murderer punished?"

"I'll see that he's punished all right. He's not going to get away with it," Jack shut his mouth stubbornly.

The officer dropped the subject. "Did you succeed in quieting Mrs. Brownley?"

For the first time the boy hesitated. "I told her to leave the fellow to me, that I'd see he didn't bother her again, but she only laughed. It seemed to make her feel better though. She began kidding me, but I wasn't feeling in any mood for it just then. I was in dead earnest, and she wouldn't see it."

"What happened then?"

"Well, I got pretty sore because she wouldn't take me seriously and let me do the things I wanted to do for her. We had a sort of quarrel—" his voice trailed off.

"What sort of things did you want to do?" Campbell asked gently.

"I wanted to take care of her, protect her!" the boy said wildly, "I wanted to beat up the man who had been annoying her. I wanted to get her away from the things and the people who worried her. It drove me crazy to see her wasting herself on that ineffectual husband of hers, and all the people that hung around her."

The officer's eyebrows twitched at the picture the lad's words evoked. "What did she say to your offer?"

"O, she wouldn't listen to me. She said I was just a baby and that it was past my bedtime." His voice choked over the bitterness of the recollection.

"And then what did you say?"

"I saw red. I accused her of all sorts of things,—of leading me on, of being in love with Durham," he stopped and then continued with an effort. "Finally I told her I was all through, and I brought her back to the Rest House. I must have been off my head. All I wanted then was to get away by myself."

"What did she say?"

"She just laughed, a funny little gurgle, and she patted my cheek. She was standing two steps above me,—and she told me I'd feel better in the morning."

"What did you do?"

"I left her standing there. That was the last I saw of her, with the light from the doorway streaming out on her dress and hair," Jack brushed his hands across his eyes as though to erase the picture. "I walked then, I don't know where. I had heard that devilish native music all night and after a time I wandered in that direction. I came to a native village, and stood watching their dances for awhile. I got interested in their costumes and their funny, jerky movements. It wasn't my idea of dancing at all, but the natives were tremendously excited—like children at a party. They were so happy that after a time I began to feel better myself. I guess I'd known all the time that Ailsa was right, that I hadn't any business to lose my head and expect more than she could give me. I made up my mind then that I'd content myself with her friendship and make her realize that she could always count on me when she needed anyone. I planned to apologize and tell her how I felt. I came back happier than I had been for weeks, and I found this had happened." His shoulders sagged, and his head drooped at the realization.

"What time did you leave Mrs. Brownley?"

"I don't know exactly. It must have been about one o'clock when we finished playing. I stopped at the bar and had a whisky soda. Then I went out on the veranda for a minute before turning in. It was while I was standing there that I saw Ailsa cut across the lawn. It must have been about twenty minutes past one. I don't know how long we talked together, probably twenty minutes, or maybe twenty five. I was so keyed up I didn't pay any attention to the time."

"Did you see anyone else while you were talking to her?"

"No, most of the crowd went off to bed as soon as the bridge was over. I thought Ailsa had gone upstairs too. You see, there are two stairs, the one back by the bar where I was standing, and the one on the veranda. I thought she had used the outside stairway. I saw Susan go up the inside one, and then Bob, and Berenice and Janet. MacAlistair had gone up before we settled down at the tables."

"You didn't see Mr. Gordon, or Mr. Durham go upstairs?"

"No, I wasn't paying any particular attention. I was just hanging around in the hope of having a word alone with Ailsa, but everyone seemed to clear off at once. I supposed anyone who didn't pass me had used the outside stairs."

"I see. Now about the bridge game. Who were the losers there, and what were the stakes?"

"The stakes were low last night. We played for a penny a point, Straits, of course. I wasn't at the table with Ailsa. I played with Mrs. Durham, against Harry and Susan. The score was fairly even. Mrs. Durham and I only lost about a dollar. Susan was terribly pleased. Poor kid, it was the first time she'd won a penny since we left America. She said at last her luck had changed and she was riding high."

"Did you hear how they made out at the other table?"

"I heard them say that Berenice had lost a lot. She was playing with Durham, and Bob and Ailsa were playing together. We'd cut for partners and tables, and Ailsa was quite put out when she drew her own husband. She said that bridge had broken up more families than blondes. They cleaned up nicely though. Berenice can't seem to resist putting in psychic bids that are absolutely ruinous, and she always has rotten luck with her finesses."

A car rattled up the driveway, and Campbell rose. "I expect that's Dr. Bailey. Will you gentlemen go out on the veranda for a little while? I'd like to see you later when the doctor has made his examination."

As the guests hurried out of the room, Ismael walked over to the group of servants and spoke to them reassuringly. At his words their fearful faces brightened, and like a flock of obedient children they shuffled behind him toward the little Recreation Room.

"You, Fu Wang," Ismael said in his musical Malay, stopping to address the Chinese boy who padded out of the kitchen carrying a covered tray, "when you have taken the nourishment to the American Mem, return to the little room. I want to talk to you." With a grunt of assent the boy plodded up the stairs, and Ismael marshalling the other servants into the room, closed the door behind him.

The, young magistrate finished his notations, and then, notebook in hand, his blue eyes brimming with repressed excitement, he joined Campbell and Dr. Bailey who were gravely bent over the body of the murdered woman.

CHAPTER IV

Outside on the moonlit veranda, Bruce drew a long breath of the fresh night air.

"Whew, Bruce, I'll wager I lost ten pounds in there," Harry said nodding toward the hall they had just left.

"It was pretty bad," Bruce agreed pacing the length of the piazza beside his friend. "That man certainly put us all over the hurdles. Wonder what he has in his mind."

"I don't know," Harry rejoined. "When he was examining you, I was sure he thought you were the murderer. Then he tackled me, and by the time he'd finished, he had me wondering whether I hadn't killed Ailsa myself. When he got to Durham, I heaved a sigh of relief, for he seemed to think Dick was the murderer, and just between you and me, I think Durham is a bit of a bounder, eh what? But, then he started on young Ames, and I didn't know what the deuce to think. He can't suspect all of us, and yet, he was pretty clever in dragging out motives from each of us.

I had no idea that you and Bob had been such pals once."

"No reason why you should," Bruce showed all too plainly that he had no intention of pursuing that subject.

Harry looked troubled. "You know, old chap, this is a rotten mess any way you look at it."

"It's worse than that," Bruce's laugh was harsh, "I don't envy the police their job. Everyone they've talked to so far has had a motive of one sort or another, and no one has had an alibi. Did you notice that? Any one of us could have killed Ailsa so far as cause and opportunity is concerned."

"Well, the women are clear anyway," Harry said with a sigh of satisfaction.

"I hope so. But don't forget that Campbell hasn't had a go at them yet. There's no knowing what that chap may dig up. After all, a woman could have stabbed Ailsa as easily as a man." They relapsed into a gloomy silence as they patrolled the veranda. Dick Durham was listening to the excited theories which Wetherby was pouring into his ear, while the American boy glowered at them all from the doorpost against which he was leaning.

At the end of twenty minutes, Campbell beckoned them to come inside. "Dr. Bailey simply confirmed what we already knew. Mrs. Brownley was stabbed, obviously by the kris. Now which one of you will go up and break the news to Mr. Brownley? I'll have to talk to him."

With one accord the men all turned to Harry.

"I suppose it is up to me," Harry said reluctantly, "but I'd rather be shot." Slowly he turned and walked out of the front door. His heavy, unwilling footsteps could be heard mounting the steps. As he crossed the balcony, Campbell called, "While you are up there, Mr. Gordon, you might ask your wife, and Mrs. Durham, and Miss Ames to come down in a few minutes. I'll have to hear what they have to say, but I'll make it as easy for them as I can." At Gordon's nod of understanding the officer resumed his low-voiced conversation with the doctor. Above the chatter of broken Malay in the Recreation Room, could be heard the staccato of Ismael's questions as he patiently interviewed the excited servants. The young magistrate had resumed his seat at the little side table, but his eager gaze followed each movement made by the men who had testified.

A door opened upstairs and two figures moved along the shadowy balcony. For a second they were lost to sight, but their footsteps could be heard clumping down the wooden steps. All eyes were fixed on the front door. Bob came in first, walking directly across the hall to that table in the center of the room, slowly followed by Harry. Bob's face was grey, his eyes sunken, and he looked neither to right nor left as he approached the body of his wife. Quietly the doctor moved forward to his elbow. The very room seemed to be holding its breath.

"Ailsa," Bob muttered wonderingly, "Ailsa Dead!" He shook his head impatiently as though to rid himself of a delusion. "So, it's true. I can't believe it even now!" He appealed to the doctor, "She's really dead? There's nothing you can do?" The doctor shook his head.

Bob began to laugh hysterically. "Ailsa dead! and I don't feel anything. I'm just numb. I can't believe it. I always thought I'd crock up first. I never dreamed that she would be the one to go, and that I'd be left."

Dr. Bailey took hold of his arm shaking him, "Stop that at once. You mustn't go to pieces. Stop it, I say!"

Bruce put his hands over his ears to shut out the sound of Bob's wild, uncontrolled laughter.

"Campbell," the doctor said in a low tone, "you won't be able to talk to him tonight. I'm going to put him to bed and give him a bromide."

The officer nodded. "All right. I'll talk to him in the morning."

With a visible effort Bob stopped his crazy laughter, and pulled himself together. "Sorry to make such a fool of myself. I'll be all right. It was the shock of seeing her like this." He shuddered. "If I could just have a drink?"

"Hey boy!" Campbell yelled, and a badly scared Chinaman, released by Ismael ran out of the Recreation Room. "Kaseh brandy sâma Tuan (*Bring some brandy for Tuan*)." The boy scurried back toward the bar and in a couple of minutes was handing a glass half filled with spirits to Bob, who gulped the contents at a draught.

"Thank you, Sir," he addressed the officer, "I'll be all right now. I'll tell you anything you want to know, and then perhaps you will be good enough to tell me how this terrible thing happened. Harry told me upstairs, but I was so confused, so stunned that I'm afraid I didn't take it all in."

Campbell's look was solicitous. "Just tell me, in your own way what you did after you finished playing bridge tonight."

"I felt rotten, so I went right up to bed. I'm about due for another bout of malaria and I hadn't been up to much all day. That was just after one o'clock. I undressed, but I couldn't sleep. The natives were making a row in their kampong, and their music always gets on my nerves. After I'd tossed around for half an hour or so, I got up and took a couple of codeine tablets. I don't like to take dope, and I only use those pills as a last resort, when I know I have to get some rest. I had slept very little all week."

"Are you often troubled with insomnia, Mr. Brownley?"

"I've only been bothered with it the last few months. The doctor in Singapore said it was because I was a bit run down, and gave me the codeine to take when I'd had two or three bad nights in succession." Bob's gesture was apologetic. "He said I needed sleep in order to build up resistance against my malaria, which has been recurring more and more frequently."

"How long before the codeine takes effect, Mr. Brownley?"

"It sends me off in about fifteen or twenty minutes."

"So you were asleep at the time your wife cried out?"

"I must have been. I heard nothing."

"The last time you saw Mrs. Brownley was in this room after the bridge game?"

"O no, I saw her again later. It was just after I got up to take the pills. She came into the room to get a scarf."

"Did you speak to her?"

"Of course. I asked her where she was going. She said it was too warm to go to bed yet and that she was going outside to cool off. I told her I didn't like her to be out there alone at that hour, but she said I was being silly, that I was to get back in bed and go to sleep, she'd be up presently. She gave me a glass of water and tucked in the klambu (*Mosquito netting over the bed*).* Then she opened the door and went out. I didn't see her again." There was a dignified pathos in the scene his words created that made them all avert their eyes.

"That will be all, Mr. Brownley. I'm sorry to have troubled you," the officer said after a moment's silence.

Bob straightened himself in his chair and leaned forward. "Mr. Campbell, will you tell me what you have discovered? Have you any clue to the person who did this dreadful thing?"

"We have no idea who did it, Mr. Brownley. The murder was committed with a kris belonging to Mr. Durham. Apparently it was taken from his room. Mr. MacAlistair discovered the body in the shrubbery outside and brought it in here. That's all we know definitely."

A dozen Chinamen hurried from the Recreation Room and darted across the hall, only to vanish through the door beside the rear stairs which led to the servants' quarters. A second later two other Chinese boys silently slipped up the stairs. Ismael stood by the door until they had disappeared into the upper regions, then he moved across the floor to Campbell's side.

"Get a line on anything, Ismael?" the officer asked, glancing up at the inscrutable brown face of his assistant.

"One or two slight happenings that may be important. I will investigate them further. Just now I would like to be here while you continue your questioning. Could Tuan Brownley tell you anything?"

"No, he had taken some medicine as Mr. Gordon said, and was asleep at the time of the crime. He saw Mrs. Brownley when she went up to get her scarf, just before she went out to the seat."

Ismael nodded.

"And now we will talk to the ladies. They come down the stairs."

Harry Gordon sprang to his feet and hurried to the foot of the narrow staircase to meet his wife who was clinging to Susan's arm. Janet Durham followed, a step or two behind the younger women. With a movement of repulsion, Berenice shrank away from her husband's outstretched hand.

"She's still upset, Harry," Susan said quickly as she saw the hurt expression in Harry's eyes. "You'd better let me look after her."

Together the two girls crossed the room, followed by the dark, aloof figure of Mrs. Durham. As they sank into the chairs which had been placed for them at a distance from the center table with its tragic shrouded burden, Campbell shifted his position so that he faced them.

"I'll try to make things as easy as I can. Mrs. Durham, will you tell me what you did after the bridge game tonight, up to the time when you heard of the crime?"

Janet's bitter, brown eyes were fixed suspiciously on the officer, and her voice was brusque. "I can't help you. I know nothing about it."

"Just tell me where you went and what you did and saw after one o'clock. It may seem unimportant to you, but it will help us if we can know where everybody was from one o'clock until two."

She shrugged her thin shoulders under the black satin kimono. "I left the hall as soon as we had finished the last rubber. Mrs. Gordon came with me to my room and we stayed there talking for some time. As soon as she left, I undressed and went to bed. Shortly afterwards I heard a scream. I supposed it was one of the natives, but it made me nervous and I lay awake listening. Then people began stirring around and I could hear excited voices downstairs. I got up, threw on a kimono and went out on the balcony to see what was the matter. Berenice screamed, and looking over the railing I could see Ailsa lying on the table."

"How did you know it was Mrs. Brownley?" interrupted Campbell.

"I'm not blind, and I'm not an imbecile," her voice was scornful, "I recognized her dress. I ought to know it—she told me herself that she had bought it with the money she won from me at bridge."

"And then?" prompted the officer ignoring her hostility.

"Nothing. I saw Harry carrying Berenice upstairs, and as Susan came abreast of me I asked what had happened. She told me to come and help her with Berenice. When we got in the room Susan told me that Ailsa had been killed."

"I see. Where was your husband after bridge was over? Did you see him again?"

"Only from the balcony. But there's nothing unusual in that. I have seen very little of him since he met the Brownleys." She cast a malevolent look at her husband who jerked uneasily in his chair.

"What time did Mrs. Gordon leave you, Mrs. Durham?"

"I don't know. About quarter of two or a few minutes earlier. Time means nothing in this heathen country. I don't even bother to wind my watch out here. There is always some slinky yellow or brown boy to wake you up in the morning, and to call you to meals."

"So you were alone in your room then from about quarter of two until after the murder?"

"Yes," her hard eyes stared defiance. "Just try to prove that I wasn't in my room all that time if you can. I'd be glad to see some of you men out here do a little work for a change."

Campbell's long face flushed darkly, but his tone was even as he went on. "I understand that Mr. Durham offered Mr. Brownley a position in Manchester."

"So I heard at dinner. But the Lord who looks after fools and drunkards helped him. Ailsa refused to let Bob accept. She knew she couldn't get away with the things in Manchester that she did out here. O I know it isn't polite to speak evil of the dead, but whatever else you can say about me, I'm no hypocrite."

"What were you and Mrs. Gordon discussing in your room?"

"That's our business," she snapped.

"Well, that will be all for the present, Mrs. Durham." With a sigh of relief he turned to Susan.

One of the Chinese boys leaned across the balustrade and motioned to Ismael who quickly sped up the stairs to join him.

"You are Miss Ames?" Campbell asked, and at her nod, went on. "Where were you from one o'clock until two, Miss Ames?"

"I was in my room. I went upstairs as soon as we had finished playing bridge and went to bed. Some time later I was wakened by that terrible scream." Her slight, scarlet clad body shivered at the memory. "I got up and turned on my light. I peeked out on the balcony, but it was dark and I couldn't see anyone. The lights were all out downstairs. I came back into my room to look out of the window. I could hear voices and people moving around on the lawn below, but my light was on and I couldn't distinguish anything definite for that reason. I kept getting more and more uneasy, and finally I changed into my lounging pajamas so that I could come down and see what the trouble was. By that time the lights were on down here, and when I leaned over the banister, I could see Ailsa lying on the table, her dress all stained with blood. Just then Berenice ran in the front door and then fell down in a faint. I hurried downstairs and Mr. MacAlistair asked me to take care of her. Harry carried Berenice up to her room, and Janet and I went in there to look after her."

Unnoticed by anyone except Bruce, the thickset figure of the Malay detective had returned to the hall and once more taken his position behind his chief.

"Thank you, that is very clear. Miss Ames, how well did you know Mrs. Brownley?"

"Not very well," the girl's answer was guarded, "I don't believe anyone could really know Ailsa."

"Perhaps I should have asked, how long did you know her?"

"We have been in Singapore just three months. We met Mr. and Mrs. Brownley the day after we arrived. We were all staying at the Raffles. Later my brother and I found a house, but we continued to see a lot of the Brownleys."

"How did you like Mrs. Brownley, Miss Ames, how did she impress you?"

Susan raised candid, grey eyes to the officer. "That is a very difficult question, Mr. Campbell. I admired Mrs. Brownley's smoothness, her finish. She always looked like a million dollars, and she had a positive genius for managing people. She was very plucky, very gay, very amusing, and very beautiful. That is a combination that is hard for any woman to forgive, you know." A faint smile relaxed the earnestness of her vivid, heart-shaped little face.

"Your brother seemed very fond of Mrs. Brownley, Miss Ames. Just what was your reaction to that?"

"O, I regarded it as part of his education, like his first long trousers, and his college diploma. I knew

Mrs. Brownley would never consider him seriously."
Susan's words seemed spontaneous, but Ismael's shrewd
gaze was fixed on her tightly clenched brown fists.

"You weren't worried about his playing bridge for
such high stakes?"

Her brown short curls shook an emphatic nega-
tive. "No, he played a good game, and he is invari-
ably lucky at cards."

"And you yourself? How did you make out?"

"Not so well," she admitted.

"Had you lost very much?"

"More than I liked. There's a bit of Scotch in me,
too." Under the shade of black lashes, her eyes twinkled at the officer, but her small hands were so closely
clasped that the knuckles were white.

"To whom did you lose?"

"To Mrs. Brownley. In cataloguing her charms for
you, I forgot to mention that she was a marvelous
bridge player. I was way out of my element with her."

Quietly Ismael handed Campbell a slip of paper.
"This was found in Mem Ames' room, Tuan." The
officer's eyes narrowed as he examined it.

"How much money had you lost to Mrs. Brownley,
Miss Ames?"

Susan's eyes were fixed on the slip of paper in
Campbell's hand, and she didn't seem to hear the
question.

"Is this a memorandum of your bridge debts, Miss
Ames?" the officer held the note out for Susan to

identify. She made a slight, despairing gesture of assent.

"Then you owed Mrs. Brownley a thousand dollars?"

"Yes," Susan whispered, "but that's Straits. It's only five hundred dollars in gold."

"Good Lord, Sue!" her brother broke in. "Why didn't you tell me? I'd no idea you'd lost so much. I'd have paid it for you."

"With what?" Susan's smile was bitter. "You didn't have five hundred dollars any more than I did." With returned composure she addressed the officer, "My check from Dad's estate is due next week, and I expected to pay Ailsa with that." Jack hastily averted his eyes.

"Did Mrs. Brownley know that?" Campbell asked.

"Yes, I told her a couple of weeks ago that I'd be broke until after the first of the month. I get my allowance quarterly. She said it was quite all right, that she would just keep a memorandum of my scores."

"Then why did she give you this note? It is dated yesterday and she says she has to have the money immediately."

"Perhaps she had forgotten. I was awfully surprised when I read it."

"When did she give it to you?"

"Last night, just before I went upstairs. I didn't read it until I got to my room."

"And then you were upset?"

"I think I was more annoyed than anything else. I knew I could get the money, but I couldn't understand why she had asked me for it in that way."

Campbell stared at her in perplexity. There seemed to be a reservation in her statements that baffled him in spite of the frankness of her smile. Reluctantly he turned to Berenice.

"Now, Mrs. Gordon, will you tell me briefly what you did between one and two o'clock this morning?"

With a frightened look at her husband, Berenice sat forward on the edge of her chair. "After we had finished playing bridge, I went upstairs with Mrs. Durham," she began in a low voice. "We talked in her room as she said, for a long while. Then I left her and went to bed. The scream came a few minutes later. I was terribly frightened. I got up and looked out of my window, but I could see nothing. I could hear voices on the other side of the house, and they seemed to come nearer. I expected my husband to come up and tell me what had happened. He didn't come, and I kept getting more terrified. Finally I put on a negligée and ran downstairs. When I saw Ailsa lying there dead, I fainted." Her words were almost inaudible, and young McCloud had to lean far across his table in order to capture them for his notes.

"What did you say to your husband when you saw that Mrs. Brownley had been killed?"

"I don't remember," she raised a piteous small hand to her forehead, "I was upset. I—" her body sagged, and Susan caught her as she was about to slip to the floor.

"That's enough, Mr. Campbell. You mustn't torture the poor child any more," Susan flared. "Harry, carry her upstairs! Come, Janet!" Without another glance at the astonished officer, Susan and Janet waited for Harry to lift his wife in his arms, and silently the little procession filed out of the door.

CHAPTER V

As the women left the room, Ismael leaned down and spoke a few words to his disconcerted officer. At Campbell's nod of approval, the Malay detective turned and once more went up the stairs. The interested group below could hear him rap on one of the bedroom doors, and could catch the murmur of a brief conversation. A moment later they saw Mrs. DeKok, still dressed in the shapeless white gown that she had worn at dinner, cross the balcony closely attended by Ismael, and slowly descend the stairway.

Campbell rose to meet her and pushed forward a chair into which she lowered herself. She had lost her high color, and only with an effort controlled the tremor of hands that were surprisingly beautiful. "You wish to speak to me, mynheer?"

A smile lighted the grimness of the officer's face. "Yes, if you please, madam. I am glad you speak English. My Dutch is very limited, and I was afraid we would have difficulty understanding one another."

"I learned English when I was a girl in Holland. One must learn it in the schools there." She picked her words with care.

"What is your name?"

"Mefrouw Heinrich DeKok, mynheer. My husband is a rubber planter in Rengam."

"You came here for the Sultan's birthday?"

"Ja! My husband also was to come for the holiday, but some machinery broke before we could start, and he must stay to mend it. He sent me on alone so that I should not miss the spectacle. He will come later. Tomorrow, I think."

"I see. Did you know these people?" Campbell nodded toward the group behind her.

She turned in her chair and surveyed them with the deliberation that marked all her movements. "No, mynheer. I do not know them, but I have seen them and heard them since I came here. I was very interested to watch them. They act so different from my people."

"You know Mrs. Brownley was killed tonight?"

"Ja, *cachon!* (*Poor little thing.*) Terrible was it. She so beautiful—so gay, and now gone!" Sadly she shook her head.

"Did you see anything that would help us discover the murderer, madam?"

The woman shuddered, but did not reply.

The officer shifted his tactics. "What did you do tonight after dinner?"

"After dinner, I walked. I went down to see the native dances in the kampong. Their music and dances were different, a little, from those I have seen in Jawa, and I watched them a long time. When I came back, these people were playing a card game in the hall, so I went up the outside stairs to my room. I read my newspaper a little, but it was very warm. I missed Heinrich, and I felt nervous. I didn't like it, to go to bed. I slept a long time by the window where there was air. When I woke, I was all a—perspiration is it? I turned out my light, and went out to the foregallery to cool myself."

"While you were on the veranda did you see anybody, anything?" With an effort Campbell controlled his eagerness and spoke casually.

She hesitated, "Ja, I saw this mynheer come out of the door," she pointed a slim finger at Bruce. "He went downstairs. Then I heard a scream from the shrubbery. Awful was it! I heard people speaking inside, and men came running out onto the lawn. Then I saw one of them come out of the bushes carrying something in his arms. Everyone came into the house, and the lights went on. I came in too, to see what was it, the trouble. I looked down from the balcony. The lovely English lady lay on the table, and she was no longer lovely. I saw her face, like wax, and her beautiful dress all over blood. I was very sad, and very frightened. I went quickly to my room. I am still very

afraid, mynheer." Her pale, troubled eyes sought his
as if asking protection.

"Why are you frightened, Mrs. DeKok?" Campbell's voice was gentle. "It was a terrible thing, but it
is over now. There is nothing for you to fear."

"I do not think it is all over, mynheer." She shook
her head and several locks of her drab hair straggled
down her back from the untidy knot at the nape of
her short neck. "I feel that death will come again,
and yet again to this house, and I am afraid. I wish
my husband were here."

At the solemnity of her words a wave of uneasiness swept over the little group. Ismael's dark head
nodded in agreement, but he said nothing, and the
officer continued his questioning.

"Did you see anything else, Mrs. DeKok? You were
on the veranda a long time."

The woman sighed and shifted uncomfortably in
her chair. "Nay, mynheer, not so long a time—but
even so I saw much, too much I think for my peace."

Campbell bit back an exclamation of satisfaction,
and with forced calmness asked, "What did you see,
madam?"

Mrs. DeKok hesitated as though seeking some way
of avoiding the question, then said reluctantly, "I saw
mefrouw cross the lawn and go into the shrubbery."

A murmur of excitement rose from the onlookers,
but was immediately suppressed as Campbell's glance
swooped over them. "When was this, what time?"

"I do not know. It was soon after I went on the veranda, a few minutes before that mynheer went downstairs." Again she pointed at Bruce.

"Was Mrs. Brownley alone?"

"Ja, alone. But soon I saw another follow her into the bushes." She spoke as though hypnotized.

Ismael leaned down and spoke urgently to his chief. An expression of annoyance clouded the eagerness of Campbell's face as he shook his head. "No, Ismael. I can't wait. I must know now."

In sudden panic the Dutch woman cast a frightened glance over her shoulder and half rose from the creaking rattan chair.

"Who was the person you saw follow Mrs. Brownley?" Campbell asked.

"No, that I will not tell you. I am frightened. To-morrow my husband comes. If he says I must tell you, I will do so, but tonight I say no more. I am very unfortunate. I saw too much." Obstinately she shut her lips, and in spite of all that the officer could say, heaved herself to her feet. "Already I have said too much, mynheer. Now I go to my room." With surprising speed she moved her cumbersome body across the hall and mounted the stairs.

"An eyewitness, Ismael!" Campbell exulted. "What a stroke of luck!" The little Malay was watching the Dutch woman as she plodded up the stairs, and not until he heard her door firmly closed, did he answer his chief. "We were too hasty, Tuan," he murmured in Malay.

The officer frowned. "We should have had the name of the murderer if she hadn't been as stubborn as a water buffalo. Now we'll have to wait till tomorrow." He unfolded his long legs, and rose stiffly to his feet. "I guess that will be all for tonight."

"You are leaving now?" Bob asked turning his ravaged face to Campbell.

"No, Ismael and I are going to stay on, but the rest of you may as well go to bed and get some sleep. Dr. Bailey is going to have Mrs. Brownley's body moved into one of the empty rooms upstairs for the present. Tomorrow you can make whatever arrangements you wish for the burial."

"Thank you! I can't think clearly now." Bob passed a weary hand across his eyes. "Tomorrow I'll be able to plan." He paused, then added nervously, "There will be someone on guard, won't there Mr. Campbell? I don't want the murderer to escape."

"Of course, you aren't any more anxious to catch him than we are, Mr. Brownley. Ismael will be stationed outside, and I am going to bunk in here. It will hardly be necessary though. Any attempt to leave would be an admission of guilt, and no one could get out of the country anyway."

Half an hour later the Rest House was once more quiet. Ailsa's body had been moved, and the doctor, finding that none of the guests required his services, had gone home to a well deserved bed. The competent Oom Ling had straightened the chairs and tables into their usual places and left the orderly room to the possession of Campbell, Ismael and McCloud. The young magistrate glanced up from his work.

"This informal questioning of yours makes a devil of a lot of trouble, Campbell. I have to go back and fill in all the red tape afterwards." The officer grinned. "It's good practice for you. I find it puts the witnesses off, if you start in asking their names and residences and all the rest of it. Gives them time too, to figure out what they will say when the crucial questions are asked. We can always get the other dope later."

"They're a rummy lot, if you ask me," McCloud said gathering up his papers. "Not one of them with an alibi, and every last soul of them with a motive. Who do you think did it, Ismael?"

Ismael showed a row of white teeth. "It is too soon to venture an opinion. Middle age teaches one to be patient."

The young magistrate laughed. "You can't put me off, Ismael. I've seen you in action before. You stand around, looking like a brown sphinx until, Bingo! the criminal wakes up in jail. I'll never forget those terrible days in the old palace on Jalan Ayer Mulut when I kept thinking I'd be the next to go west." Even yet he could feel the hair prickle on the back of his neck, as he recalled the deaths of his friends, and the terror that stalked through the once happy-go-lucky mess.

Ismael shrugged his plump shoulders deprecatingly, "I was fortunate then to discover the murderer. I hope Allah will continue to smile upon me in this case."

"Well, unless the Dutch lady crashes through, you are going to need more than Allah's smile, old thing. 'Night, Campbell. I'll be over the first thing in the morning. I wouldn't miss a scene in this show for money!" With a motion of salute, the youngster ran across the veranda and a moment later his motorcycle chugged off.

"I sent a policeman to Singapore with the kris, and your chit to the detective station. We will hear about fingerprints by midday, but I think they will not tell us much. The handle is too heavily carved, and we know already that Tuan Durham, Oom Ling and Tuan MacAlistair have held it," Ismael announced.

Campbell nodded. "I don't hope for much from that. It is lucky we have Mrs. DeKok. She knows who committed the murder as sure as I'm a Scotsman, and once her husband gets here, she'll tell us."

"Perhaps—perhaps not, Tuan. If she doesn't speak, what have we? Nine people. All with motives. All without alibis."

"Yes, it would be tough. We'd have to weed out the innocent, one by one. We can't even eliminate the women in the party. That Mrs. Durham is a wild cat, if ever I saw one. And the American girl was holding out something too. Even Mrs. Gordon could have done it, if she were desperate enough."

"I have more information about some of them, Tuan, if you will give ear."

"O yes, what did you learn from the servants, Ismael? Do you think any of them were mixed up in it?"

Ismael shook his sleek head. "I never thought it was a native crime, Tuan. The servants were all ready to talk. Mem Brownley was liked by all of them. Her jewels were not touched, and beside, what is jade to a native?"

"I didn't think it was a servant," Campbell agreed. "Did you pick up anything from them about the house guests?"

Ismael seated himself on the edge of a chair beside his chief, and pulled out two pieces of paper from his pocket. "This was found in the waste basket in Tuan MacAlistair's room." He fitted the edges together on the table and waited for Campbell to read the note that Ailsa had written to Bruce.

"I knew there was something fishy about his story," Campbell exclaimed. "I'll get him on the mat in the morning. Meet her at 1:30 eh! and at 2:03 he was still outside getting a little air on the lawn! Was he late going to the appointment, or was he coming away from it?"

"That we have still to learn." The Malay dismissed speculation about Bruce. "The roomboy who takes care of Mrs. Durham's room told me he overheard angry words between her and another lady before dinner last night. Her voice was loud and she threatened her visitor, but he didn't know whether the other lady was Mem Brownley or not. The visitor said little and her voice was soft."

"Hm, we'll have to look into that too. What else?"

"I think perhaps things were not so well between Tuan and Mem Brownley as they might have been. Their roomboy told me they had many arguments. He couldn't understand their words, but he said she was cold and bitter to her husband when they were alone, that he would plead with her, and when she turned on him angrily, he would shrink away like a pariah dog."

"That's interestin'. Funny the things that go on behind the scenes between apparently happy couples, isn't it Ismael?"

"The white race could learn much in that respect from the brown, I think, Tuan. It is not good yet for women to think they are the equals of men. Power rests unbecomingly on a female head."

Campbell chuckled. "Well, Solomon, being only a bachelor myself, I'm in no position to argue with you. What more did you discover? I know from that pleased expression of yours that you've got another headache waiting for me."

"Just one more, Tuan," Ismael said benignantly. "You remember Tuan Ames said Mem Brownley was upset when he met her because she had been having trouble with someone? That someone was Tuan Durham. One of the kitchen boys had been at the kampong and on his way back he passed Mem Brownley and Tuan Durham on the road near the Rest House. He did not understand their English, of course, but their voices were raised in passion."

"What time was that?"

"The boy thought it was about quarter past one, maybe a few minutes earlier."

"This is certainly one devil of a case, Ismael," Campbell admitted knitting his sandy eyebrows. "What do you think about it?"

"I think that for all her beauty, Mem Brownley was a very unfortunate lady. Those who did not hate her, loved her overmuch."

"And either emotion would provide motive for her murder," the officer finished. "Well, thank God for Mrs. DeKok. Give me a nice straightforward Malay or Chinese killing every time, what?"

"They are simpler, certainly. When a Malay kills it is plain sailing. He does merely what any other Malay would do under the circumstances. Put yourself in his place, and you know who the murderer is. But white men are more complicated, and their motives are more difficult to fathom. Nevertheless, Tuan, in

spite of their color, I have found that the same passions rule the hearts of all races. It will take a little
longer to discover this murderer, for we will have to
understand first the hearts of each of the guests, but
it can be done."

Campbell looked affectionately at his assistant.
"You always have the gift of understanding, Ismael.
It has been you who has solved most of the crimes
in Johore. I just do the hack work that gives you the
inspiration. It's a damn shame you aren't white so
that you could have proper recognition."

The Malay shook his head. "That I don't want.
My place is in the background beside you. With you
before me, no one notices a fat old native, and I can
work better. What could the government give me that
could bring me happiness? The Malays have the art of
living. I wouldn't change with a white man."

"I guess you're right at that, Ismael. Look at these
people we've been talking to tonight. All of them are
miserable about something or other. Well, I'm going
to get some sleep." Campbell stood up wearily. "If
our luck holds, Mrs. DeKok's story will put us on
the right trail tomorrow. You'd better keep an eye on
things outside. Just make yourself comfortable on the
veranda near the outside stairs, and I'll bunk here on
that long chair by the rear staircase."

"All right, Tuan." Ismael glanced around the deserted room with an air of uneasiness. "Somehow, my
mind is not at peace." His dark gaze was raised to

the silent balcony for an instant before he moved reluctantly toward the door. "It is only an hour or so
before dawn. I can smell its fragrance even now."

As soon as Ismael had gone to his post, Campbell
walked across the room and switched off the lights.
The dim glow from the ceiling left the center of the
hall in a grey twilight, but the balcony itself and the
space beneath it was wrapped in mystery and shadow. Stretching himself gratefully on the long wicker
chair, the officer immediately fell into a dreamless
sleep. On the veranda outside Ismael crouched on
the steps leading to the upper veranda. His usually
impassive face was troubled and there was a strained
expectancy about his homely, thickset figure. "If I
were the murderer, what would I do next?" he stared
into the darkness beyond the Straits of Johore quest-
ing for an answer.

Upstairs, very quietly a door opened on the balcony. A shadowy figure stood in the gloom listening
with satisfaction to the heavy silence that muffled the
Rest House, then, with snakelike rapidity it moved
along the wall and vanished.

CHAPTER VI

Two hours later the fragrant smell of wood smoke drifted out into the cool, grey dawn. In the huge, stone kitchen at the back of the Rest House, the sleepy Chinese boys were starting their daily routine with a cheerful clatter of pans and dishes. The stimulating aroma of fresh coffee began to permeate the building. Ismael entered the hall from the kitchen where he had again been questioning the servants, and bent over the sleeping form of his chief.

"Tuan," his voice was gentle.

Instantly Campbell was awake and on his feet. "What's wrong, Ismael?"

"Nothing, so far as I know. I still have an uneasy feeling that all is not well. I didn't sleep. I walked about, but I heard nothing, saw nothing. Yet my heart will not be at peace. I have tried to put myself in the place of the murderer,—and my fear has grown."

Campbell glanced at his watch. "Seven o'clock! I'll just have time for a bathe and a shave." He rubbed his rough, sandy bristled chin. "We'll let the guests have their breakfast in peace. McCloud will be here by that time, and then each one of our suspects is going to have some tall explaining to do. Mr. DeKok ought to get here before noon. If he doesn't, I'll send a car for him."

Two barefooted Chinese boys came into the hall and busied themselves with coconut fiber brushes, casting curious, sidelong glances at the policemen as they swept up the scattered cigarette ashes, and dusted the rattan furniture. At the rear of the room, still other boys were going swiftly up the stairs carrying small trays with pots of tea or coffee.

Before Campbell could move to carry out his wishes, he was startled by the crash of breaking dishes upstairs, and in another instant a terrified young Chinaman leaned over the balcony calling in Malay, "Tuan, Tuan, come quick!"

With a swift glance at the sickly yellow face of the shaking boy, the officer started up the steps, closely followed by Ismael. "What's the matter?" he demanded of the boy who pattered to meet him.

"Mem Blandah (*Dutch Woman*)! She didn't answer when I knocked, so I pushed open the door. I thought she must be in the bath since her door was unlocked, so I entered to leave her coffee. Then I saw her, lying in the bed, and there was blood all around, much blood. The cup spilled itself from my hands and I ran," the boy gasped in swift Malay.

Without another word, Campbell pushed past him and entered the room toward which the boy silently pointed.

Shafts of early morning light spread across the bed revealing brutally the bloodstained sheet that partially covered the quiet body of the Dutch woman. The mosquito netting had been loosened on the side of the bed nearer the door, and the body, clad in a cambric nightgown lay on its right side facing the window.

"There's our witness, Ismael," Campbell said, in a choked voice. "Stabbed in the back while she slept. The poor soul probably never knew what happened."

"Yes, Tuan, it was a mistake for the lady to tell us that she knew the murderer. I blame myself. I should have heeded better my instincts." Ismael's voice was strangely subdued as he moved quietly around the bed to stare at the waxen face of the Dutch woman. "She had no time to cry out, or to struggle. See, the bed is not disarranged, only the sheet twisted as though she had pulled it when she turned toward the window to sleep." The Malay's restless eyes darted around the immaculate order of the small room—the pile of clothes neatly folded on one of the wicker chairs, the Dutch newspaper on the table beside the bed, the few toilet articles on the wooden dresser.

Campbell stood as if stunned. "Why didn't she lock her door, Ismael?" he muttered. "That's what I can't understand. The poor thing was fairly shaking with fear when she left us. You'd think her first impulse would have been to bolt her door."

The Malay's smooth brown face was wrinkled in perplexity. "That is what puzzles me too, Tuan. I watched her go safely up the stairs, and I heard her door close. I thought the door would be locked and all would be well with her for the night." He moved away from the bed to examine the door. "See, Tuan, come here!" he called in excitement a moment later. "The bolt is out of order. It will not close properly. It goes just so far, but not far enough to secure the door!"

In two strides Campbell was beside him, and together the two men stared at the bolt. "It looks all right," the officer said experimentally sliding the bar along the metal groove on the door. Ismael's slender brown fingers were busy with the socket of the bolt attached to the door jamb. An instant later he pulled forth some white substance. "Cotton wool, Tuan! Stuffed in here so that the bolt could not enter. When Mem DeKok pushed the iron bar across, thinking the door was fastened, it did not reach far enough to secure the door because this wad of cotton prevented. In her agitation, the poor lady could not have noticed."

"Yes, you're right, Ismael. The murderer made sure of his entrance," Campbell said closing the door and trying the bolt, "but when could he have done it?

Mrs. DeKok went directly to her room when she left the hall. All the men were downstairs at the time."

"But not the women, Tuan. They had retired before Mem DeKok came down. A woman could have committed both murders as easily as a man."

"If it was a man, he must have been very forehanded. He knew the Dutch woman was dangerous, and fixed the lock even before I talked to her."

"Yes, it seems to me there is no doubt but that the Dutch lady was silenced so that she couldn't betray the murderer to us today. If the murderer is a man, then he must have seen this poor lady on the veranda, and decided then that she was to die. But when did he have the opportunity to fix the lock, I ask myself. If the murderer is one of the women, then it is simpler, for they were all upstairs much of the time. The murderess could have listened to the Dutch lady's statements in the shadow of the balcony and had time to stuff the cotton wool in the bolt."

Campbell turned again to the bed. "There's no weapon that I can see, Ismael, unless it is around the room somewhere."

"I don't think the knife was left behind this time, but I will make sure." With dexterous fingers that didn't disturb either bed clothes or the body, Ismael searched the bed,—the mosquito netting. With amazing agility he wriggled his bulky frame under the bed to examine the floor, the wooden bed slats and the mattress, while Campbell stood by watching with troubled eyes. Emerging from his fruitless task, the rotund little Malay scanned the expanse of matting, feeling along its edges, testing the floor boards, all without result. The bureau drawers and wooden clothes press likewise received minute attention, but there was no sign of the knife, nor any clue to reward his efforts.

"There is nothing, Tuan. The murderer must have taken the knife away."

"Well, if we can find it in one of the other rooms, that ought to be a help," Campbell said thoughtfully, "and if we can pin some of these people down to exact time and place, we may discover who could have fixed the lock between the time of the murder, and approximately 3:40 when Mrs. DeKok returned to her room."

"I think we can narrow the time down even closer, Tuan, for Mrs. DeKok was in her room, you will remember, from 2:15 until about 3:25 when I brought her downstairs. The only time she was away from it was the twenty minutes or so she was on the veranda, and the fifteen minutes she was downstairs talking to us. The door could hardly have been tampered with early in the evening, for the murderer could not possibly foresee that the Dutch woman would be an incriminating witness, even granting that the murder of Mem Brownley was planned so far in advance. As I construct the crimes, Mem Brownley was killed on the spur of the moment. The murderer, coming from the shrubbery, saw Mem DeKok on the veranda, and realized that she too must be killed to preserve his safety. The lock must have been fixed either during the next fifteen minutes, before the Dutch lady returned to her room, or, if the murderer was a woman, it could have been done in the fifteen minutes while we were questioning Mem DeKok."

"That's probably what happened, Ismael, but how we are going to pin it on anyone is more than I can see just now." Campbell shook his head despondently as he moved toward the door. "There's nothing more we can do here. I'll go down and tackle some of the guests, I can hear signs of life and they'll soon be appearing for breakfast. You'd better telephone for Dr. Bailey, and get McCloud to hurry over. While I'm talking to the suspects, you can search their rooms for the weapon or anything that looks suspicious."

"Here boy," Campbell addressed the Chinese roomboy who was still hovering on the balcony outside. "Watch this door and don't let anyone go into the room until the doctor gets here."

"Ja, Tuan," the boy murmured taking his place stolidly beside the door while his small almond eyes watched the two officers make their way along the balcony and down the stairs.

CHAPTER VII

It was nearly eight o'clock when Bruce MacAlistair opened his eyes and saw Ahmat standing beside his bed with a cup of coffee. The harrowing events of the previous night, and the realization of his own equivocal position had kept him awake for a long time, and it wasn't until the final darkness before dawn that he had fallen into an uneasy slumber.

As he sat up and reached for his coffee, Bruce sensed the suppressed excitement in his boy's manner. "What's the matter Ahmat? Have the police been questioning you?"

"Yes, Tuan. I told the police that I was at the kampong with my friends last night when Mem Brownley was killed. I knew nothing about it until I returned to the Rest House. It was late, but the other boys were still awake and talking. But, there is yet more trouble this morning, Tuan, have you heard?" Ahmat ceased his cascade of Malay and looked hopefully at his master.

"I suppose the police are buzzing all over the place. Did they find anything new?"

"Ada, Tuan, Mem Blandah, in the next room was killed last night,—with a knife!" the boy announced, beaming at the sensation his words were causing.

"What's that?" exclaimed Bruce, and his coffee cup tipped perilously on its tilted saucer.

"Yes, Tuan,—with a knife, she was killed. Tuan Gordon's boy told me. The Chinese roomboy discovered it when he took her kahua (*coffee*) in, and he called over the balcony to the mata mata (*police*). Mahat had just wakened and was going down to get tea for his Tuan and Mem, so he was fortunate to hear it all." Ahmat's tone was envious. "He slept outside their door last night, as always. He will not mix with other servants."

"Funny," Bruce said absently, "I don't remember seeing him there last night."

"O, he was late to sleep. He also went to see the wayangs at the kampong."

"So, that was it." Bruce dismissed Mahat from the conversation. "Do they know who killed Mem De-Kok? How did the murderer get into the room?"

"I don't know. Mahat heard only what I have told you. The policeman is very angry."

"Hmph, I don't wonder, with his chief witness killed right under his nose," Bruce grinned at the thought of Campbell's discomfiture, then his face grew serious. "It is bad obat (*medicine*), Ahmat. I expect we will all be put on the gridiron this morning."

"Yes, I think so," Mahat said complacently. "The mata mata questioned Mahat and me for a long time this morning. We are the only outside boys in the house, but of course, we could tell him nothing. Tuan Campbell is talking to the guests as they appear downstairs. The old American tuan is very loud and angry. He says he and his family know nothing and he wants to leave, but the police say they must stay, that no one can go until the killer is discovered."

"Well, in that case, I guess you needn't start packing my things either. Just lay out a fresh suit for me and I'll get my bath so I'll be ready when Campbell wants to see me."

"There is plenty time," Ahmat soothed him, "Tuan Campbell is talking to Mem Thompson, and the young daughter. Tuan Ames has just gone downstairs so that he will be next. Inche Ismael called the doctor and now he is searching the room of Tuan Ames. I think he will look in every room, while the tuan or mem is being questioned. Inche Ismael is very wise and clever, the Chinese boys tell me. Always he discovers the evil doer. He is more seeing than a white man!"

With a muttered oath, Bruce cut short Ahmat's eulogy, and leaping from his bed, dashed toward his waste basket. Holding it to the light he stared at its empty bottom. "Did you empty this, Ahmat?" he asked the startled boy.

"Tidak (*No*), Tuan. The roomboy does that each morning, but he has not yet been here today."

"What a fool I was," muttered Bruce to himself, "I know I dropped that note of Ailsa's in the basket. I suppose that damned policeman has it by this time, and thinks he has the goods on me." His lips tightened under Ahmat's worried look. For several minutes he stood there absently holding the empty basket while he wondered what attitude to take in the interview that was looming before him. Finally with a wry smile he put the basket back in its place and turned to his boy. "Just keep your eyes and ears open, Ahmat. I'll be all right, don't worry about me. I'm going to dress now."

Fifteen minutes later, Bruce, immaculate in a starched white suit, went down to breakfast. The hall seemed deserted, only two of the many tables being occupied. At one, Mrs. Durham sat toying with a cup of coffee and a piece of toast, while in a low sharp tone she conversed with her husband, who, slumped in the opposite chair, was eating nothing. A dozen yards away, Susan Ames sat alone, her grey eyes fixed on the door of the Recreation Room as she mechanically peeled a mangosteen. Outside on the veranda Mr. Gerald Thompson was holding an indignation meeting with his wife and daughter, and his rasping voice drifted into the hall, "It's outrageous, keeping us here where we may all be murdered in our beds.

I'm going to telephone the Consul General in Singapore and find out whether they can treat an American citizen like this—take our money and then act like we're all criminals!"

"Good morning, Miss Ames," Bruce stopped beside her table. "Do you mind if I sit here with you, or are you expecting your brother?"

She glanced up at him with a start. "O, good morning, Mr. MacAlistair. Do sit down. I'm as nervous as a witch this morning, and I need diversion. Jack gulped down a cup of coffee. Probably by the time Mr. Campbell gets through with him in there," she nodded toward the Recreation Room, "he won't want anything to eat."

Bruce looked sympathetically at her small white face and dark circled eyes. "You mustn't take things too hard. The British police are very efficient and they'll soon have the murderer."

"It is so terrible though—that poor Dutch woman! I can't get her out of my mind. How could anyone have been brutal enough to kill her?"

"It was a case of the survival of the cleverest, I fancy," Bruce said. "She knew too much. Either she should have spoken last night and told us who the murderer was, or she should have kept absolutely quiet."

"But who could have done it?" Susan leaned across the table and spoke in a low, tense voice. "That is

what is driving me mad,—the knowledge that someone I know, someone in our party should be a murderer. I scarcely slept a wink last night trying to figure out which of us it was."

Bruce's smile was grim. "Well, I imagine you are
with the majority in that, if it's any comfort to you.
Apparently Mrs. DeKok and the murderer were the
only ones informed on the point, and now the murderer has the secret to himself."

"I guess this is a case where ignorance really is
bliss," Susan said thoughtfully. "Apparently it isn't
healthy to know too much." Her troubled eyes again
sought the closed door of the Recreation Room. "Anyway, I know that Jack didn't do it. They can't pin the
murder on him. The poor dear is almost beside himself with grief. It hasn't penetrated yet that his idol's
feet were not only clay, but mud."

"He'll get over it," Bruce assured her, "and the
genuineness of his sorrow must clear him with the
police. In fact he and Bob are the only ones Campbell
appeared to eliminate, though, of course, he may have
just been holding off his fire on them last night."

"That's what I'm afraid of. They may think Jack
killed her because he found out she was making a
donkey out of him."

"I wouldn't worry about that, Miss Ames. Your
brother left Ailsa about half past one or so, if I remember rightly, and Bob and Mrs. DeKok both saw
her after that. If he was down at the kampong, as

he says, you may rest assured that there will be dozens of natives who saw him there. Most Europeans and Americans regard the natives as just part of the landscape out here, not as human beings at all, so while Jack probably couldn't identify a single Malay or Chinaman that he saw last night, every one of them who saw him will remember it."

Susan's face brightened. "You are right, of course. All natives look alike to me except my own babu and cookie. I don't believe I could even recognize the Chinese roomboy here, though I must have seen him a dozen times. The only one who really stands out in my mind is Oom Ling."

For a few minutes they sat without speaking while Bruce busied himself with the kippers he had ordered, and Susan sipped her coffee.

"Mr. MacAlistair," she said suddenly, "I'd like to have your advice about something. Somehow I am sure you didn't kill Ailsa, and with Jack in the state of mind he is, there's no one else I can talk to."

Bruce looked up from his plate with interest. "You mean that you aren't sure that any of the others didn't commit the murders?"

"Well, I'm afraid that is the situation. Last night after I went to bed, I thought over everything I knew about the rest of the party, and there isn't one, I'm sure, who didn't have some reason for wishing Ailsa was out of the way, unless it is Bob. He has always been an unknown quantity to me. He seems to have just one dimension, like a picture of an English gentleman."

"Bob is a thoroughbred," Bruce said abruptly. "Of course I haven't seen him for years, but it is simply impossible for me to imagine him as a murderer."

"The East works strange miracles, as I said last night," Susan reminded him. "But to go on—Harry Gordon hated Ailsa because of her influence over Berenice. I've seen the look in his eyes when Ailsa baited him as she did at dinner last night, and I wouldn't have been in her shoes for a good deal. Certainly Berenice believes he killed Ailsa."

"Well then, that eliminates one suspect for you!" Bruce said with forced cheerfulness. "If Berenice thinks Harry is the murderer, it means that she herself can't be. Though personally I don't believe for a minute that Harry did it."

"In my opinion that is about the only thing in Berenice's favor. If it weren't for that I'd be inclined to think she is guilty. She's very fragile and doll-like to look at, but she's really as strong as a horse, and she just plays up that helpless attitude of hers. Underneath she is as shrewd and cold blooded as a New England Yankee, and Ailsa had to hold the reins very firmly in order to keep the upper hand. I don't know what hold Ailsa had over her, but it must have been a terrible one. Berenice didn't really faint last night," Susan blurted. "She was just stalling so that she wouldn't be questioned."

Bruce regarded the girl with interest. "It seemed to me that Berenice was devoted to Harry, that she was torn between her love for him, and her feeling for Ailsa," he protested.

Susan grimaced. "You would think that! It's just what she wanted everyone to think, but you flatter her. That girl hasn't a thought beyond Berenice Gordon."

"Well, what do you think about the Durhams?" he asked.

"I think either of them is quite capable of murder. Mrs. Durham is as hard as nails, and she is frantically jealous of her husband and her position. I don't know which comes first with her, but I imagine she worked like a slave to get both, and she would go to any lengths to keep them. She hated Ailsa because Ailsa not only had the beauty, the charm and the background that she envied, but because it was obvious that if Ailsa wanted them, she could also have Dick and his money."

"What do you mean by Ailsa's background?" Bruce asked, "I thought the Brownley's position was pretty precarious."

"I don't mean their present social status. Both Bob and Ailsa have been scrambling along on their wits for some time. What I meant is that Ailsa obviously came from a good family, she had the assurance, the poise and the breeding that would simply be gall and wormwood to a woman like Mrs. Durham. And as for Dick Durham," Susan's voice was scornful, "he is just a miserable little toad who thinks his money can buy him anything he happens to want. He tried to 'make' Ailsa, and when that didn't work, he was so infatuated that he was ready even to divorce his wife. Ailsa saw through him like a plate glass window. She didn't want to marry him, she was only playing him along to get a job for Bob. She thought she had managed it when he said last night at dinner that he had offered Bob a position. And then, when she found that it was in Manchester, she looked as though Dick had slapped her face. She knew then she had lost out. I was sorry for Bob. He wanted that position dreadfully, and when Ailsa turned it down, every bit of light and hope went out of his poor face as though someone had turned off a switch." She paused as if recalling the scene.

"So you think that Durham might have been so enraged at Ailsa for eluding him that he killed her?" asked Bruce.

"He could forgive anything but an affront to his vanity," Susan said simply. "Anyone who penetrated that would arouse his undying hatred. I think he might very easily have killed Ailsa when he realized that she was simply trying to use him to further her husband's interests."

"All this discourse is merely a preamble to my own position," Susan went on with a faint smile. "Women always argue from the general to the particular, you know. I didn't kill Ailsa, of course you must believe that, but I've been awfully foolish, and I'd like your opinion,—your help, if you can give it to me."

"It never occurred to me that you might have killed Ailsa," Bruce said in a shocked voice. "You aren't capable of such a thing."

"O, yes I am, don't overestimate me," Susan announced bluntly. "I'd commit murder rather than have Jack's life ruined, but fortunately it didn't come to that. The worst he was headed for was disillusion. Ailsa would never have married him, and Jack is such a dumb Dora that anything less than marriage would never have occurred to him. Even granted that Ailsa cared for him in her own way, and was willing to take him on as a lover, her very willingness would have jolted him back to his senses. He was really in love with her in his idealistic way. Yesterday afternoon he told me that he was going to persuade her to divorce Bob and marry him—the poor lamb! I tried to reason with him. I hated to have Ailsa dangling his scalp from her belt, along with the rest of her victims. He turned on me like a whirlwind." Susan crumpled a piece of toast between nervous fingers. "And I lost my temper. I told him I'd kill her before I'd let her marry him. I was so furious at him for being such an idiot, that my voice was raised, and I'm sure the native gardener heard me. We were out on the lawn and the kabun (*gardener*) was pottering around the flower beds."

"And now you are afraid he will tell the police,"

Bruce finished for her. "Well, you needn't worry on that score—there isn't one chance in a hundred that he understood English. Practically none of the boys here do, except Oom Ling. All he could say if he were questioned would be that you and Tuan Ames had angry voices, and unless you are unlike most brothers and sisters, there could be a dozen reasons for an argument between you."

Susan drew a little breath of relief. "I forgot all about the language, wasn't that stupid of me? You see, while I was building up a case against each of the others in our party, I tried to look at my own position from the point of view of the police, and then I remembered the scene I'd had with Jack about Ailsa." She hesitated. "You've relieved my mind tremendously about that, but there is something else that I'm afraid you won't be able to reassure me about."

A smile lighted Bruce's keen, grey eyes as he watched her. "Have you a dark past too, or is there a family skeleton rattling his bones in your closet?"

"It isn't a dark past," Susan said slowly. "Just a sort of murky present that worries me. I don't see how I could have been such a fool!"

"Do you want to tell me about it?" Bruce's voice was kind. "Or will you let me help you without going into the matter at all? I'll do anything I can."

"That's awfully good of you," Susan said gratefully, "but I think I'd better put all my cards on the table, if you don't mind. I couldn't accept your help unless you know the worst about me. It wouldn't be fair."

"Just as you like. How about a cigarette before we go into a confessional?" Bruce passed his case to her and then bent across the table with a lighted match.

"It is my bridge debts," Susan announced abruptly. "I really had no business to play with Ailsa at all. She is, was, I mean, a superb player, and I am barely average. In addition to that, the cards ran against me consistently. Even if I'd been good, my cards would have sunk me. And the stakes were high, at least for me."

"Why did you keep on playing then? Ailsa couldn't make you play if you didn't want to."

"That's just what she could do, and did. She made me feel like a spoilsport, a crybaby, and it seemed to me that I had no alternative but to complete the table when she made such a point of it. I had a motive too, beside the hope that my luck would turn. I was convinced that Ailsa was a card sharp, and I kept hoping that I'd catch her at it." She shrugged her slim shoulders: "Needless to say, I never succeeded, but I still believe she wasn't on the level."

"Well, there's nothing to incriminate you in what you've said. You were just a bit foolish, that's all."

"No, that isn't all," Susan bent her curly head over a pattern that her nervous fingers were marking on the white cloth, "I lost a lot of money. You heard,—a thousand dollars. I told Ailsa that I couldn't pay it

until I got my check, and at first that satisfied her.
Then last night she must have become suspicious because she gave me that note saying that she must have
the money right away. Mr. MacAlistair, I didn't have
the money, and I'm not going to get a check next
week. The stocks in which my Dad invested his money all passed their dividends this quarter. The exec-
utor wrote me last week. It put Jack in a hole too,
for we had both been counting on that money to pay
our bills. Our trip out here was very expensive, and
then we had to furnish the house, and everything. I'm
afraid we are both dreadfully extravagant. Jack has a
good salary for a youngster, and we thought, with our
little income, we could manage. And now there isn't
any income. Jack knew last night that I was lying. He
looked as though I'd hit him below the belt, when he
heard what I had told Ailsa."

Bruce's lean, tan face was grave. "You think Ailsa
knew you couldn't pay your debts next week?"

"Yes, I'm sure she did. I think Jack told her our
financial position sometime yesterday. He is so quix-
otic that he'd want her to know exactly what he had
to offer her. You see how black things were for me. I
couldn't possibly have paid her last night as she demanded, and if the fact were known that I reneged
on my bridge debts, it would finish both Jack and me
socially."

Bruce was silent, appalled by what the girl was
telling him. He knew his East. That story would echo

from Shanghai to Calcutta, if it once got out, and it would be remembered long after Susan's connection with the murder was forgotten. Beside that angle, there was the immediate menace from the police. In their opinion social ruin of that sort was ample motive for murder, even without the complication of her brother's infatuation for Ailsa.

"You'll have to have the money to pay your bridge debt next week, as you said you would," Bruce announced. "Do you think you can sell your stocks?"

The girl shook her head without looking up. "No, I can't touch the principal until I'm twenty-five, and that is three years off. Jack has only a year to go. There's just one thing I can do." She hesitated. "I have a string of pearls that belonged to my grandmother. They are small, but they are supposed to be very good. I must sell them, but I don't know how to do it. I was afraid to try the big jewelers in Singapore in case people should hear about it. I thought perhaps you'd help me." Her grey eyes were raised appealingly. "You see, if I can get the money by the time the next American mail gets in, I'll be all right."

The cloud disappeared from Bruce's face. He was glad now that he hadn't cynically offered to pay her bridge debts himself. She would never have forgiven such misunderstanding of her confession. "I can arrange it for you quite easily, if you'd like me to. I know an old Chinaman in Singapore who will give me all the pearls are worth, but I'm sure now that Bob will never take the money from you."

"O he must! No one must ever know. Why I couldn't even face myself in the mirror, if I didn't pay those beastly debts. Promise me you won't say anything to Bob!"

"I won't say a word to anyone," Bruce assured her. "Just stick to your story when the police question you again, and you'll be all right. You might tip your brother off too, in case Campbell goes into the question of finances with him."

"Yes, I've been afraid of that. I didn't have a chance to speak to Jack this morning, but he heard my story last night, and I'm sure he won't give me away. The pearls are in my safe deposit box in Singapore. I'm so dark that they aren't particularly becoming, and I don't wear them very often. I'll get them for you as soon as the police let us leave here. I can't tell you how grateful I am, or how relieved." Impulsively she stretched her hand across the table and her slim brown fingers pressed his. "Please don't think too badly of me!"

"That's all right," Bruce said awkwardly, "just don't worry any more. Here comes your brother now, and Campbell seems to be looking my way. I guess I'm for it next." Bruce rose to his feet with a murmured apology as the police official crossed the room. Campbell's face was grim, and there was none of the geniality of the night before. He greeted Bruce curtly, "Good morning, Mr. MacAlistair, Will you come into the other room? There are some questions I want to ask you." With a strange feeling of dread, Bruce followed the officer into the Recreation Room.

CHAPTER VIII

"Sit down, Mr. MacAlistair," Campbell pointed to a chair opposite the one into which he flung himself, and near the table over which McCloud's bright head was bent. "I presume you know of Mrs. DeKok's murder?"

"Yes," Bruce said, "I was sorry to hear it. She seemed like a harmless soul."

Campbell watched him with narrowed eyes. "Your room is next to Mrs. DeKok's, MacAlistair. Did you hear any sound in there during the night?"

Bruce shook his head. "No, as soon as I learned of her murder I tried to recall anything that might be helpful, but there was nothing. I was awake for some time, but these walls are thick, so unless there had been a scream or loud sounds of a struggle, it wasn't likely that I'd hear anything."

"About how long were you awake, do you suppose?"

"An hour, perhaps longer. It is hard to judge. I was going over Mrs. Brownley's murder in my mind, trying to figure out who could have killed her, and I was cursing myself for my own stupidity." Bruce looked steadily at the officer who was eyeing him so warily. "I wasn't completely frank with you last night, Mr. Campbell," he continued, "and although the things I omitted to tell you have no direct bearing on the murder, I decided I had been very foolish to try to suppress any information."

The officer's only reply was a grunt but his regard was questioning.

"My reason for not talking freely was understandable, I think. I am naturally reticent. I hate to discuss my personal affairs with anyone. I've lived alone too long, I guess. Anyway, the idea of speaking before a group of strangers was simply unthinkable. However, last night after I left you, I realized that although my story throws no light on the murder, except to put me in a very unfavorable position, at least it was my duty to save you the time and trouble necessary in ferreting out the facts." Bruce smiled, "I knew, of course, that I was your prime suspect, and that you would check up on me immediately. All I'm really doing is to save you some time."

Campbell nodded. "That's true. Go on!"

"What I told you was the truth, but it wasn't the whole truth," Bruce explained, "I knew both the Brownleys years ago. Bob was my best friend in those days. We went through public school together, spent our holidays at either his family's

or mine, and when we graduated, we started out
by ourselves to see the world. Bob's mother and
father had been killed in an automobile accident
the year previous, so he had come into quite a bit
of money. My father was terribly decent about
our plan. There were just the two of us, for my
mother had died when I was a little shaver, and
the governor was anxious, naturally, for me to go
into business with him—he was a manufacturer
of machinery. When he saw that my heart was set
on travelling, he told me to take a year and that then
I'd be glad enough to come home and settle down.
So Bob and I set out. We were just twenty-two,
and the world was our oyster. We spent several
months on the Continent doing the usual fool things
that youngsters that age will do, and then we crossed
the Mediterranean, and eventually wound up in
Cairo. We stayed at Shepheard's, of course, and
while we were there, we met Ailsa Courtney. She
had come out to spend the winter with a wealthy
old aunt who wanted a companion and offered to
pay her niece's way. Ailsa's father was a younger son,
and his family never had much in the way of worldly
possessions, so Ailsa had jumped at the chance. The
aunt was pretty difficult, and Ailsa's position was
almost unbearable. Instead of being the beautiful
and popular niece of a wealthy visitor, she was nothing more or less than a lady's maid, minus the salary
and the time to herself. I'm sorry to dig into all this,

but I think you ought to have a bit of the background," Bruce apologized.

Campbell waved his remark aside with a sweep of his big hand. "It's all right, MacAlistair, take your time. The threads of this murder may go back a long way, and anything you tell me may be useful."

"I fell in love with Ailsa the moment I saw her. She was very lovely, and the Cinderella aspect of her position appealed to us, naturally. I was so absorbed in my courtship that I don't believe I even thought about Bob's reaction to it. I'm sure it never occurred to me that he might be smitten too. We three were together whenever Ailsa could escape her aunt's eagle eye, and Bob seemed wholeheartedly happy to be an onlooker to our romance. That idyllic state lasted about a month, as I remember. I had had one or two letters from my father, which under ordinary circumstances would have been most disquieting, but I was so rapt up in Ailsa that they made no impression on me. I thought the old man was simply trying to interest me in the business, flatter me into thinking I was essential there. By that time I'd made up my mind to go in with him anyway, so that I might give Ailsa the things she wanted. Then, like the proverbial bolt from the blue, I received a cable one evening. Bob was out trying a new gambling place he'd heard about, and I was hanging about the hotel hoping for a word or two with Ailsa. The cable told me of my father's suicide and of his financial ruin. Ill-advised investments, betrayal by his friends—the usual story. I was almost beside myself with grief and self-reproach. Not unnaturally I counted on Ailsa to buck me up, to assure me that I wasn't to blame for deserting the old man—and Ailsa's only comment was to hand back my ring and tell me it was all off, that she couldn't marry a poor man." Bruce grimaced. "I was a spoiled cub in those days. My father's death was the first bit of trouble I had ever known, and when on top of that Ailsa defected, I simply went haywire. To this day I don't know what I did the rest of that night or the following morning. When I turned up at the hotel in the afternoon, my first thought was to find Bob, and to clear out with him. Bob wasn't in our suite, and at the desk the clerk gave me a note when I inquired for Mr. Brownley. The note simply informed me that Bob and Ailsa had been married that morning and gone off on their honeymoon. There wasn't a word about my father in it. That finished me. The loss of Bob's friendship cut deeper than Ailsa's cold-bloodedness. I had barely enough money to pay my hotel bill—nothing for passage to England, and nothing really to go back there for. I spent the few remaining dollars on one grand binge that must have lasted a week. When I snapped out of it and realized that I'd have to earn my own living somehow, I joined the Camel Corps. I spent about a year in the Soudan, then I was crocked up by a Mandi spear in a surprise attack. That year in the desert was the making of me, and it was a bitter disappointment when I realized that I couldn't go on with it. The spear had gone through my thigh and I was quite lame for years. Even now it bothers me a bit in damp weather." Bruce smiled, "I'm almost through with my autobiography, Mr. Campbell."

"While I was still in the hospital wondering what on earth I was to do with myself, I had a letter from an old friend of my father's, a Mr. Cartright. He'd been trying to get track of me ever since my father's death, and he was decent enough to offer me a job with his branch office in Calcutta. As soon as I was well enough, I went to India, and there I have been more or less ever since."

"You heard nothing from the Brownleys?" Campbell asked.

"I had a couple of letters from Bob when I was in the Soudan, but I tore them up unread. Since then I've had no communication from them. You know what the East is. You hear gossip about everybody. I heard that they had gone to Shanghai and were making a big splurge. Then after a few years, someone told me that Bob's money was all gone and that he was running an automobile agency. When I saw Harry and Berenice in India,—they came there on their honeymoon,—they said that Bob's agency was going to pot. I knew nothing about them beyond that, until I breezed in here last night and met them."

Bruce lighted the cigarette which Campbell passed him, and then resumed his story. "I'd been hunting up in Endau for three weeks, and I stopped in here for the night, expecting to go on to Singapore this morning and catch Monday's boat back to Calcutta. The last people I expected, or wanted to see, were the Brownleys. I'd lost much of my bitterness in the Soudan, the desert has a tendency to make everything else seem small and unimportant, and then, I'd been working hard in India for nine years, which is a pretty effective antidote for most troubles. Just the same, I wasn't keen to have old memories revived. I hadn't forgiven Ailsa and Bob, but I'd pretty well forgotten them." He was thinking fast now, he mustn't involve Harry, and yet he had to make his story plausible to the hawkeyed man opposite him.

"While I was arranging with Oom Ling about a room for the night, I met Harry Gordon, and he told me he was here as the guest of the Brownleys. Ailsa came up just then, and greeted me like a long lost brother as she urged me to join her party. I didn't want to have anything to do with Ailsa, and I didn't want to see Bob, but I couldn't figure out how I could suddenly shift my plans without making Harry wonder. I had never told him, or anyone else, about my blighted romance. The upshot of it was that I agreed to have dinner with the crowd but I begged off bridge and the other festivities Ailsa had planned for the weekend, by saying that I had to leave

Johore this morning." His eyes twinkled at the policeman. "Another case of the best laid plans of mice and men—eh, Campbell?"

Campbell's stern face relaxed into an unwilling smile. "Is that the end of your story, MacAlistair?"

"No, unfortunately," Bruce's voice was serious, "I'm really just reaching the part that should interest you. After I had agreed to have dinner with them, I went up to dress. It must have been nearly seven-thirty then, and I didn't see any of the party until I joined them at eight o'clock. They had already started to eat when I came down."

"You hadn't seen Mr. Brownley up to that time?"

"No, but he was pathetically cordial when I met him at dinner. I think it is only fair to tell you about Bob, although it won't do my own case any good. After dinner, when we went out on the veranda to have our coffee, Bob told me that he didn't know anything about my father's death until months after he had left Cairo. Apparently Ailsa hadn't seen fit to enlighten him."

Campbell straightened up in his chair. "Are you sure of that, MacAlistair?" he asked sharply.

"Yes. Ailsa had simply told him that she didn't care for me after all, and that she had broken the engagement, so he naturally supposed the field was clear. I am sure Bob was telling the truth. It fits in with everything I knew about him, and if I hadn't gone off my chump, I'd have realized at the time that

Bob simply didn't have it in him to pull a stunt of that sort. Even though Ailsa swept him off his feet, he would never have left me in such a financial jam. He was always the soul of generosity."

"Did you tell him what had really happened between Mrs. Brownley and yourself?"

"No, poor devil. Ailsa was his wife, the only thing he had left in the world, what was the use of going into past history? I was glad for my own sake though, to be able to exonerate Bob from any blame. Nevertheless, I was upset to have the affair revived, and sorry for the things I'd been thinking about Bob all those years, so I went off by myself for a stroll." Again Bruce trod lightly, he didn't want to bring Susan into the picture. "When I came back, the guests were all going into the hall for some bridge. I begged off when Ailsa asked me to cut in, and then, when I still held out, she told me that she wanted very much to see me. I thought it was part of her come-on game, that she simply wanted to rehash old times and alibi herself, though now, as I think back, I don't believe that was it at all. I think she was frightened."

Campbell started. "What makes you think that?"

"I don't know," Bruce admitted with a puzzled frown, "it is the memory of her face in the light from the doorway—something about her eyes. At the time it didn't register, I was only anxious to get away, but it has haunted me since. I shall always feel that if I had talked to her, I might have prevented the tragedy.

Durham came up just then, and his wife, and I went on upstairs."

He lit another cigarette. "This part is going to be a strain on your credulity, I'm afraid. I had only been in my room for a few minutes when one of the house-boys brought me a note from Ailsa asking me to meet her in the garden at half past one."

The officer checked an exclamation of surprise, and with an effort asked formally, "Have you the note?"

"No," Bruce admitted with a quizzical look, "I tore it up and threw it in my basket. She didn't say much, just appealed to me to meet her for old time's sake. It made me angry. I thought immediately that she was up to her old tricks again. She never could bear to have a man resist her. I had no intention of going out to meet her, but I was pretty tired. I'd had a strenuous day, and I fell asleep."

"Still dressed?" Campbell's voice was skeptical.

"Yes," Bruce said evenly, "as you saw later. Harry had told me that he might stop in my room for a chin if I was still awake, and since I hadn't had a chance to talk to him all evening, I didn't want to miss him. When I awoke it was about ten minutes of two. I remembered then about Ailsa. I didn't want to meet her, but I knew the natives had been celebrating all evening—their infernal racket had nearly driven me crazy—and I hated to think of any woman being down in the garden alone. I looked out of my window, but I couldn't see into the shrubbery where she had said she would be. Finally I decided that I'd better go down and see whether she was really there. If she wasn't, fine. If she was, I'd simply make her come back into the house and be quit of her. On my way downstairs, as I told you last night, I saw the woman whom I later learned was Mrs. DeKok. I thought it would be just as well if she didn't see me meeting Mrs. Brownley at that hour, so instead of going the shortest way toward the shrubbery, which would have kept me within Mrs. DeKok's sight, I went around the other side of the house, planning to cut across the back lawn. I had just reached the lawn at the east side of the Rest House, when I heard the scream. You see now why I was so sure it was Ailsa."

Campbell nodded. "You saw nothing, I suppose?"

"No," Bruce said slowly, reliving the moments when he had been searching for Ailsa. "It was dark in the shrubbery, and of course I had no idea then that she had been murdered. I didn't know until I had carried her into the hall that she was dead. Of course the murderer could easily have been lurking in the bushes until it was safe for him to come out and join the rest of us. There was a lot of confusion and people running around. I've tried to remember, but at the time I was too intent upon getting Ailsa indoors to notice anything. I didn't even know who was present until after I'd discovered that Ailsa was dead."

"Just who was there at that time, do you mind telling me, Mr. MacAlistair?" McCloud asked, pausing in the middle of his notes. "I didn't get here until later, you know."

"Harry Gordon, Durham, Wetherby, Oom Ling, and a bunch of the Chinese boys," Bruce said promptly. "Mrs. DeKok was leaning over the balcony railing, and the American came out of his room in a huff over the noise. Berenice ran downstairs, and Susan Ames. Mrs. Durham didn't leave the balcony. Jack Ames came in some time later, and, as you know, Bob was in his room the whole time. I've gone over the whole scene until my brain was in a whirl, but there was nothing that I can remember that sheds any light on the murder,—on either murder."

"MacAlistair," Campbell's voice was impressive, "from the time you brought the body in here, did you, or any of the people who had been on the lawn go upstairs?"

Bruce reflected for a minute. "I can't say positively, for I don't know who was out on the lawn. They were just dark figures, shadows to me. Any one of them could have slipped up the outside stairway without attracting attention from below, although of course, Mrs. DeKok was on the upper veranda at that time. By Jove! perhaps that was where she recognized the murderer!"

"Perhaps," Campbell said noncommittally. "I want you to think carefully, MacAlistair. Do you think that any of those figures you saw on the lawn could have been a woman?"

Bruce started at the question, and its significance. "My God, Campbell, I don't know. I only remember seeing men, but I wouldn't swear that a woman couldn't have been there."

The officer sighed as he rose from his chair. "Well, thank you for your frankness, Mr. MacAlistair. You have cleared up a number of points for us. If anything else occurs to you, I hope you will tell me. Two women have been killed here, and for the safety of everyone in the Rest House, we've got to get the murderer. Don't forget that justice should come before loyalty, or chivalry," he added cryptically as he followed Bruce to the door.

"Now what the deuce is in his mind," Bruce wondered making his way toward the veranda. "He's a deep one. Never a word about finding that note of Ailsa's, though I'll wager it was in his pocket the whole time. And that remark about loyalty and chivalry. Did he mean Harry, and Susan?" Absorbed in his own unpleasant thoughts, Bruce crossed the piazza without noticing the people who were gossiping there in groups, and wandered down the driveway.

Campbell stood for a moment at the door of the Recreation Room waiting to catch the eye of Dick

Durham, without success. The man seemed to be deliberately avoiding his gaze. "Mr. Durham," he exclaimed in an annoyed tone, "I'd like to talk to you.
Will you kindly come in here." Reluctantly Durham
rose, and with lagging feet crossed the hall. Left alone
at the table, his wife watched his exit with tightened
lips and an anxious glow in her usually hard eyes.

CHAPTER IX

"Sit down, Mr. Durham," Campbell directed as he carefully closed the door of the Recreation Room. "As you probably know, there has been a second murder."

"Yes, I heard that Mrs. DeKok had been killed," Durham said quickly, as, with a suspicious stare at the officer and McCloud, he gingerly seated himself on the edge of a chair. "But I know nothing about it. My wife and I retired as soon as you had finished with us last night, and neither of us stirred out of our room until we came down to breakfast."

Campbell's gaze was reflective. Both Durham and his wife would stick to that story, he was sure, and unless he could prove that they had worked together, there was no use pursuing the question further.

"It seems obvious that Mrs. DeKok's murder was a direct result of Mrs. Brownley's," he said, shifting his line of attack. "She was undoubtedly killed so that she couldn't identify Mrs. Brownley's slayer."

"I don't know about that," Durham protested. "How can you be sure that the murderer didn't have some grudge against the Dutch woman too, some of these natives? I wouldn't trust any of 'em as far as I could see 'em."

Campbell smiled. "It isn't a native crime, Durham. My assistant has gone into the matter very thoroughly. A native might kill through hatred, or for the sake of robbery, but both Mrs. Brownley and Mrs. De-Kok were very popular with all the boys, and neither woman had jewels to tempt them with. Furthermore, as you know, Mrs. Brownley was still wearing the jade earrings you gave her, and the carved jade necklace and bracelets." He raised his hand as the Englishman started to speak. "You are going to say that the murderer may not have had time to remove them, but jade doesn't appeal particularly to the average native—it is too common out here, and Mrs. Brownley's wasn't especially valuable."

Durham winced, and McCloud hastily bent his face to conceal his amusement at Campbell's thrust.

"Furthermore," the officer went on smoothly, "in the case of Mrs. DeKok, while she had no jewelry except a plain gold wedding ring and watch, her purse with several hundred dollars in it was beneath her pillow. The murderer certainly had time to make off with that if robbery had been his motive."

Durham was still unconvinced, "Well then, how do you know that the murderer isn't just a crazy native who kills for the sake of killing?"

"A native doesn't go about it in that way. When a native runs amok, he does it openly, kills everybody who crosses his path. He doesn't plan things as carefully as these murders were planned. No, Mr. Durham, your theories don't fit these cases at all."

"How do you know that one of the white people isn't crazy, hasn't a hereditary taint of some kind?" Durham's pale little eyes gleamed triumphantly behind his thick glasses.

"That is possible, of course," Campbell admitted, "but I hardly think it likely. If it is true, of course, the murderer will probably go on killing until his identity is discovered."

Durham blinked nervously as he digested this bit of logic. "Why don't you do something, then. Are you waiting until we are all murdered in our beds?" His voice was shrill with fear.

"We are doing all we can, Mr. Durham," Campbell said patiently. "Personally I don't believe we are dealing with a madman, but with a very clever individual whose primary desire was to remove Mrs. Brownley, and who killed Mrs. DeKok merely in order to safeguard himself."

Dick grunted. "What's to prevent him from killing the rest of us for the same reason?"

The conversation was shaping as the officer wanted it to, but his voice showed nothing of his satisfaction as he said smoothly, "The murderer isn't apt to kill

anyone who isn't a menace to his safety. Unless you
know something vital to the investigation, you are in
no danger. If you do know anything, Mr. Durham,
then for your own sake and your wife's, you should
tell me, so that we can arrest the criminal."

"I know nothing, nothing at all," Durham disclaimed, "I'd be only too glad to tell you if I did."

"Well, since you can tell me nothing about Mrs.
DeKok's murder, suppose we go back to Mrs. Brownley's. That is the crux of the whole matter. Let's see
now." He made a pretense of consulting the memoranda which he drew from his pocket. "You said that
you had drunk too much last evening, and fell asleep
on the veranda."

Durham eyed the memoranda anxiously. "I wasn't
drunk, if that is what you are implying," he protested, "I'd had quite a few drinks, and I was feeling
drowsy."

Campbell shrugged, "That's too bad. I thought
you had passed out altogether."

"Why is it too bad?" Dick demanded.

"Because if you were really drunk, you couldn't
possibly have committed the two murders—you'd
have stumbled or bungled. If you were in full possession of your faculties, then I'll have to include
you among the suspects." Campbell was thoroughly
enjoying the dilemma in which he had placed the
self-satisfied manufacturer. There was a moment's

silence while Durham weighed distastefully the two alternatives, then Campbell went on. "Did you see Mrs. Brownley after the bridge game broke up?"

Durham hesitated for the fraction of a second.

"No. I went over to the bar and had a couple more drinks, and then I went out on the veranda and fell asleep."

"I wonder why Mr. Ames didn't see you then, or the bar boy?" Campbell said quickly, "Mr. Ames had a nightcap at the bar just before he went out and joined Mrs. Brownley. He said distinctly this morning that he was the only one at the bar at that time, and the bar boy's records show that no one else had a drink until after the murder. No, Mr. Durham, that's not good enough." His eyes were flinty as he stared at the discomfited little man, and his voice harsh. "You sought Mrs. Brownley out after the bridge game, and you walked with her down the road. You were seen there quarreling with her."

Durham wriggled uncomfortably.

"What if I did?" he blustered. "That doesn't mean I killed her does it? Ames and Brownley and Mrs. DeKok all saw her after that."

"It means that you have lied about your actions. It means that to all intents and purposes you were sober. It means that after she went into the shrubbery, you could very easily have slipped across the lawn and killed her. Your own statement places you nearer her than any one else."

"O my God!" Durham exclaimed. "You don't really think that I killed her do you? I didn't, I'll swear I didn't." He mopped his face with a dapper handkerchief. "I did go for a walk with her, and we did have a few words,—but all the rest I told you was true. I was asleep on the veranda, and I didn't hear a thing until she screamed."

Campbell looked noncommittal. "What did you quarrel about?"

Durham drew a long breath, "Look here, Campbell, I'll tell you everything, only don't let it go any further. I don't want my wife to hear about it. I'm a successful man. I'm forty-five years old, and I've always been law-abiding and respectable. I can't afford a scandal. It would ruin me. That woman bewitched me, she made me forget everything. I wish to God I'd never seen her." He moistened his too-red lips with the tip of a pointed tongue.

"I can't make any promises, Mr. Durham. If your testimony is relevant to the crime, it has to go on record," Campbell warned him.

"Well," Durham said reluctantly, "I'd better chance it, I suppose. Rather that, than have you think I'm the murderer.—I met Ailsa and Bob Brownley in Shanghai first, and right from the start she fascinated me. She was different from any other woman I'd ever known, more alive. But, even then, I'd have stayed in the traces, if I hadn't run into them again in Singapore. That was four months ago. When I met her here in Malay she was much more,—well, I can't say nicer, because she had always been that, but more accessible. I began to hope—" he smirked irritatingly, "well, that she'd be kind to me, if you understand what I mean."

With an effort Campbell controlled his distaste, but the less disciplined McCloud glowered across his table at the back of the complacent Lothario.

"After a little while though, I realized that she was keeping me at arm's length," the manufacturer went on, "I didn't seem to be making any progress with her at all, and that made me more crazy about her than ever. She was encouraging, but somehow, I never saw her alone. She always had a crowd around her, and then that Ames cub came on the scene and she paid him a lot of attention. I knew that Ailsa and Bob were hard up. It was only her bridge that kept them going. He'd told me that he would give anything in the world to go back to England; that he was homesick for the old country and fed up to the teeth with the East. He had malaria too, and was altogether in bad shape physically. That gave me an idea. If I could once get Ailsa to Manchester, I'd have the field to myself. If she still held out when she saw all that I could give her, all that I could do for her, why I even thought I might divorce my wife and marry Ailsa. She was in my blood. I had to have her at any cost.

So, I fixed things up with Bob; offered him the management of my Manchester office." He paused once more to wipe his perspiring forehead.

"Wasn't that pretty risky, Mr. Durham? Mr. Brownley didn't know anything about cotton manufacture did he?" Campbell asked.

"It wouldn't have been as risky as it seemed," Durham grinned cunningly. "I'd have kept my eye on him, and if he didn't make good, and I really didn't expect he would, why I'd have soon got him out of the way. I mean," he added hastily, "I'd have given him a pension."

"You mean that as soon as you'd made Mrs. Brownley your mistress, or your wife, you'd have given him money to get out?" Campbell inquired.

Durham stuck out his chin. "What of it? He'd have been well paid. He wasn't any sort of provider for Ailsa. She needed a strong man, not a milksop that she could twist around her finger the way she did Brownley. You can bet your bottom crown, that if she'd been my wife in the first place, she wouldn't have made ducks and drakes of my fortune the way she did his. No sir! Neither one of them had any idea of the value of money, but if anything, he was worse than she. She had learned what it was to do without things these last few years, how to get hold of it, and how to make a show with it. Just between you and me she pulled some pretty raw stuff when she got the chance, but he was too dumb to see it."

"What did she say to your scheme?" the officer asked.

"She didn't know about it until I sprang it on her at dinner last night. She saw through it then, and turned it down cold." There was admiration in his voice. "But if she saw through me, I saw through her too. She was out to get something for nothing. A job for her husband here in the East. She didn't stand an earthly!" Durham jumped to his feet and began to pace back and forth in his excitement.

"What did her husband say when she refused the position? You remarked that he was very keen on it."

"He started to say something, but he shut up when she looked at him. I guess he realized it was no use. I'd never have taken him on without her. I was mad clean through when I realized how she had been playing me along, but at the same time, it made me want her more than ever."

Campbell nodded. "What did you do then?"

"I couldn't do much, except some heavy thinking, for we all had to play bridge. I was so stirred up that I kept ordering drinks during the games, and I couldn't get my mind on the hands. I decided that I would put things squarely up to Ailsa. She had promised me a few minutes' talk later on. I hadn't yet offered to divorce Janet for her, you see,—I'd been keeping that up my sleeve in case everything else failed. As soon as we finished the last rubber, I went out on the veranda and waited for her. When she came out, we walked across the lawn and up the road a ways. I told her that I'd divorce Janet and marry her."

"How did she like that proposition?" Campbell asked.

"She didn't seem to like it." Durham's voice still echoed the surprise of that discovery. "She acted furious because I even thought she would consider it. She said she could get further with the husband she already had, than she could with me and all my money. She said I was only a shopkeeper on a big scale, and that I had nothing but money, while Bob had family and distinction even if he was broke. She said a gentleman could always make his way, but that with all my fortune I'd never be anything but lower middle class." He still flinched at the memory of her words. "She laughed at me," he admitted, flushing.

"What happened then?"

"Nothing more, she went back to the Rest House. I walked down the road a bit for I was still pretty angry. Then I came back and sat on the veranda. I didn't want Janet to see me until I'd calmed down. Janet is as sharp as you make 'em, and I knew I couldn't fool her. She raised merry hell with me every time I looked at Ailsa and I knew she had seen me go off after bridge. Well, what with the drinks I'd had, and the night air, and the emotional strain, I was all in. As I told you, I fell asleep and didn't hear a thing until Ailsa's scream woke me. Lord, I can still hear it!" His face held a look of sustained horror.

"Did you regard Mrs. Brownley's refusal as final then?"

Durham shook his head. "Not after the first shock of it wore off. She was pretty cagey, and it wouldn't have done for her to snap up my offer. I think she was holding out for a big settlement. I've never seen anything yet that money couldn't buy, if you just offer enough for it. No, I believe I'd have got her all right if she hadn't been killed. She couldn't really prefer a weak sister like Brownley to a man like me—and besides, there were all the things I could have given her."

Campbell looked at him incredulously, but the manufacturer seemed to be quite sincere. His vanity simply refused to let him accept Ailsa's refusal. Perhaps he was right. Perhaps she was holding out for more, you never could tell with a woman like that. If she was, then that let Durham out, but at the same time it provided a strong motive for either Mr. Brownley or Mrs. Durham. If, on the other hand, she had convinced Durham of her scorn, he might easily have been furious enough to have killed her.

"Mr. Durham," the officer said suddenly, "do you think your wife knew of your plan to divorce her?"

The manufacturer looked startled. "Lord, I hope not! I certainly never said anything to her. It would have been bad enough when Ailsa and I had everything arranged."

"Do you think she may have guessed what was in your mind?"

Durham took two or three nervous steps, "I don't know," he admitted, "she's been giving me hell every time I've seen her for the last two days,—I couldn't please her, and I couldn't shut her up, though she never mentioned the idea of divorce."

"If she had suspected your intentions, how far would she have gone in an effort to prevent them?"

The realization of the trend of Campbell's intentions seemed suddenly to dawn on the self-centered little man. "Look here, Campbell, Janet never killed her. She might bawl her out, might raise hell with me, but she'd never commit murder." He was thinking fast. "Besides, she couldn't have done it! You said yourself that both Ailsa's murder and Mrs. DeKok's were done by the same person, and Janet never left our room last night!"

"All right, Mr. Durham, I think, unless you have something else to add, you can go now," the officer announced.

At the door, Dick hesitated. "You won't say anything about all this to my wife, will you,—the divorce, and all that,—you know how wives are—"

"I don't know anything about them, Mr. Durham," Campbell said coldly, "and I'll have to use the information you gave us as I see fit." With an unhappy look at the stony face of the officer, Durham hurried out of the room.

CHAPTER X

Campbell had just finished an unenlightening interview with Susan Ames, when Bob Brownley, looking
white and harrowed, burst into the Recreation Room.
"What's all this about Mrs. DeKok being murdered?"
he demanded.

"She was stabbed some time early this morning,"
the officer answered.

"Do you know who did it? Have you any clues?"
Bob asked eagerly. "Why should anyone want to kill
that harmless old soul?"

"One question at a time, please, Mr. Brownley.
You'd better sit down." The officer motioned toward
a chair into which Bob threw himself. "Now, I'll tell
you that we don't know who killed Mrs. DeKok, nor
have we any clues yet. As for why she was killed, well
it seems obvious that it was done to prevent her from
identifying the murderer of your wife."

Bob ran distracted fingers through his mop of
light hair. "And I don't suppose you have any more
idea who killed Ailsa?" he asked.

Campbell shook his head. "I'm sorry, but I have no news for you there either. We are working on it, but so far there is nothing tangible. The murderer is very clever, but somewhere he must have made a slip, and when we find that, we'll know who committed the crimes."

Bob's blue eyes sparkled. "What kind of a slip?"

The officer shrugged. "That's what we have to discover. It is common sense though, that nobody can commit two crimes like this without leaving some trace of his or her personality, either in the things he did, or the things he left undone."

"I suppose all he has to do is to keep on killing people long enough, and you'll be bound to catch him. That is, if he doesn't kill us all first." His voice was bitter, but a second later he leaned forward with an impulsive gesture. "I'm sorry, Mr. Campbell, that was uncalled for. My nerves are simply shot to hell and half the time I don't know what I am saying. I know you are doing all you can."

"That's all right, Mr. Brownley," Campbell smiled, "I don't blame you in the least. It is perfectly natural that you should be impatient to see your wife's murderer brought to justice. But you will have to give us a little time. Did you get some sleep last night?" he inquired with a solicitous glance at Bob's ravaged face.

"Yes, thanks. I took a couple of codeines after I went upstairs and they sent me off immediately. I never heard a sound until I woke up a few minutes ago. The roomboy had orders not to disturb me until I rang for him. He told me with great gusto of Mrs. DeKok's murder, and I came down as quickly as I could to get the details from you. I thought perhaps she had left some word, a note or something, telling you what she had seen last night."

"I only wish she had," Campbell said ruefully, "But we found nothing, though Ismael went over her room with a fine-tooth comb. No, Mr. Brownley, I'm sorry to state that we are just where we were last night, except that we have one more crime to solve."

"If there is anything I can do to help you, you can count on me, Mr. Campbell. This inaction is going to be terrible. I feel as though I ought to be doing something to avenge my wife."

"There isn't very much that anyone can do at present, except sit tight and wait for developments," the officer said slowly. "At present I'm trying to get a clear picture of all the people involved. The solution of the problem must lie in the relationships in your group of friends, unless we are to believe that these murders are simply wanton affairs, without rhyme or reason. I can't bring myself to accept that thesis yet. Suppose you tell me what you know about the people in your party, and your wife's attitude toward them."

Bob leaned back in his chair and thoughtfully lit a cigarette. "That seems a bit thick, you know, Campbell. These people are all my friends,—my guests."

Campbell's eyes flashed, "And one of them is your wife's murderer, don't forget that, Brownley. This is no time for misguided loyalty, as I told Mr. MacAlistair."

Bob's face softened. "Poor old Bruce. It's a damned shame to let him in for all this. I've caused him enough worry in my time. Funny isn't it, how you hurt the people you care for most! Bruce MacAlistair is the only man in the world who means a thing to me, the only one whose good opinion I've ever wanted. These public school friendships have a powerful hold on a man." His eyes grew dreamy. "Bruce will always seem darn near perfect to me, because I think of him, not as he is now, but as he was in those old days—strong, handsome, popular,—all the things that I wasn't. I still can't get over the pride I felt when he singled me out of the whole class to be his friend. O well, that's neither here nor there, unless it helps you to rule Bruce out of your list of suspects." He smiled an apology for his eulogy.

"It hardly does that, Mr. Brownley, but nevertheless I am interested in your attitude toward him. Mr. MacAlistair had more opportunity than anyone I've talked to, to commit the murder, and apparently he had a motive."

"He had motive for killing us both, if it comes to that." Bob's voice was bitter. "But Bruce simply isn't that sort. Years ago—I assume you know the facts of our stay in Cairo—he might have killed me, but even then he'd never have touched Ailsa."

"And yet," Campbell leaned forward, "last night he had a note from your wife asking him to meet her in the garden."

Bob's face was impassive. "I'm not surprised. Ailsa doubtless wanted to square us if she could. She knew how much his friendship meant to me, and she had always regretted the fact that she had come between us. This was the first opportunity she had had, but it wouldn't have got her anywhere with Bruce, I'd told her she couldn't change his attitude. Without knowing anything about it, I'm willing to wager that Bruce never answered her note, and never met her."

"No, he claims he didn't. He says he fell asleep and that when he awoke it made him uneasy to think of her down there alone. He was on his way to make sure she was all right when he heard her cry out."

"What did I tell you?" Bob said triumphantly. "You are just wasting your time trying to connect Bruce with the murder."

In spite of himself, the officer was impressed by Bob's faith. "How about the rest of the people?"

Bob reflected for a moment, and then said slowly. "Let's rule out those that I think are above suspicion, though you must understand that I have nothing important to tell you, either one way or the other, about any of them. I haven't a notion who could have killed Ailsa or I'd tell you like a shot. As a starter, I don't believe that the little American girl did it. She's too direct. If she had a good reason for doing so, she might have shot Ailsa, but she would never have stabbed her, and she would never in the world have killed Mrs. DeKok. For quite a different reason, I am sure her brother didn't commit either crime. It was quite obvious that he adored my wife."

"And you didn't mind that, Mr. Brownley?"

Bob shrugged, "I was used to it, and so was my wife. She was very beautiful, very alluring. Men always have admired her, and their admiration was essential to her, but that was all. I have always understood that, and I trusted her," Bob said simply. "I can't visualize her without her coterie of admirers. It didn't affect our relationship at all. You see there was never just one, but always a group, and I have never been jealous, perhaps for that reason. Ailsa needed me, just as I needed her, and although she could undoubtedly have divorced me and married any number of better and wealthier men than I, I don't believe she ever thought of doing it. We suited each other."

"Do you think that young Ames might have killed her in a fit of pique?"

"No! He didn't feel intensely enough for that. He hasn't grown up yet. If Ailsa rebuffed him, his blighted young affections would simply have made him more interesting to himself. When he got tired of contemplating them alone, he would pick out some young girl and pose to her as a disillusioned man of the world. Then he'd fall in love and marry her."

With a wave of his long, slim hand, Bob dismissed Jack from their consideration.

Campbell smiled, "Go on, Mr. Brownley, this is very interesting."

"Well, there's Berenice Gordon. There might have been times when she wished Ailsa out of the way, but she would never have done anything about it, for such flashes of anger were promptly succeeded by waves of admiration and affection. She fairly basked in Ailsa's popularity, and she shivered with delight at Ailsa's unconventionality. She got a vicarious enjoyment out of everything Ailsa did. Even though Ailsa did tease her on occasion, after all she was awfully good to Berenice, had her out from England to live with us, and kept her there until she married Berenice off to Harry. A darn good job it was too. Berenice will never have to worry about money again, lucky girl, and she won't have to go back to that stuffy family of hers either. No, Berenice would never have touched Ailsa. Every bit of enjoyment or luxury she has ever known is due to Ailsa's friendship."

"You don't think that very fact may have driven her to desperation?" Campbell leaned forward earnestly.

"Lord no!" Bob scoffed, "All Ailsa ever had to do was to look at her and she subsided like a pricked balloon. If Berenice had ever been crazy enough to pull a knife on her, Ailsa would have laughed in her face, and Berenice would have broken down and wept for forgiveness. No, Berenice is not the person you are looking for."

"Well, what about the other three, the Durhams and Harry Gordon?"

Bob frowned. "They are more difficult. I think any one of them could conceivably have done it. Harry is a good egg, but he might have had some twisted resentment of Ailsa's influence over Berenice. Dick might have done it because Ailsa made a public monkey out of him, and Janet might have killed her out of jealousy. But it is impossible for me to really feel that any of them did kill her."

"Someone did, Mr. Brownley," Campbell reminded him.

"Yes, and that is the only possible excuse for this conversation about my guests," Bob snapped. "Personally I don't believe that any of them did it."

"Then who did?"

"Some native perhaps, some madman! I don't know. That is up to the police."

"What was your wife's feeling toward these people? Let's tackle it from that angle."

"O Ailsa seemed to like them all. She loved to have parties and have a crowd around, but it didn't matter much to her who was in the crowd. She never liked women very much, except Berenice, so she probably didn't care particularly for Susan or Janet. Durham and Ames simply happened to be her present admirers, she didn't take them seriously. She sincerely liked Bruce, I think, in spite of the way she once treated him. I don't know what she thought about Harry. I can't remember that she ever discussed him with me. He was always a genial host, and a pleasant guest, and I personally thought him a darn good scout."

"What were her feelings toward you, Mr. Brownley?"

Bob stiffened, and his eyes flashed dangerously at the inscrutable face of the officer. "I suppose that question too, is relevant to your investigation, Mr. Campbell, or you wouldn't have asked it. All I can say is that my wife stuck by me through thick and thin, when it was decidedly against her own interest to do so, even after I'd become a physical and financial liability."

"And your feeling for her?" pursued the officer doggedly.

"Well, what would you feel for a woman that had given you everything, and who in spite of your failure continued to stand by?"

"I'm sorry it was necessary to ask those questions, Mr. Brownley, but I had heard rumors that you and your wife were not as happy as you seemed."

"Happy!" Bob's lips twisted at the word, "Well, happiness is something else again. I never said we were happy. How could we be happy when every day was a struggle to keep up pretenses, when we never knew when we might be dumped out in the street by some hotel management! How could anyone be happy under those conditions! There were times when both our nerves were rubbed raw, what married couples' aren't? But that isn't grounds for murder. If it were, there'd be mighty few inhabitants left in this weary old world."

Campbell smiled. "I wasn't accusing you of your wife's murder, Mr. Brownley. As I told you, I'm simply trying to get a picture of the lives and relationships of all the people concerned. You have helped me considerably."

Bob looked startled. "I don't see how. I hope I haven't cast suspicion on any of my guests. I want to see my wife's murderer punished, but I don't want an innocent person to suffer, and I can't honestly believe that any of our friends are guilty."

"Time will tell," Campbell murmured tritely. "And now, Mr. Brownley, don't you think you had better have some breakfast. You look as though you needed some solid food."

Bob shuddered at the suggestion. "Ugh, food! no! But perhaps I could do with a cup of coffee." He struggled to his feet. "You'll let me know how the investigation comes along, won't you?" he asked as he opened the door.

"Yes, I'll keep you informed, Mr. Brownley," Campbell replied following him across the room and nodding to Ismael who was standing just outside in the dining hall. "Come in, Ismael."

The door closed on the two policemen.

CHAPTER XI

"Another reprieve!" Susan exclaimed to herself as she slipped out of the Recreation Room leaving the baffled police officer behind. So absorbed was she in the interview just past, that until a small voice hailed her, she had thought the hall was deserted.

"Susan!" Berenice called from a small table near the front windows, "Please come and talk to me."

Reluctantly the American girl regarded the slight figure in the blue linen dress, and then unable to resist the appeal in the childlike face turned toward her, went quickly to the table.

"What's the matter, Berenice? You look worried. Is there anything I can do?"

"I shouldn't bother you with my troubles, Susan, but I'm almost crazy, and there's no one left for me to talk to, now that Ailsa is gone." The blue eyes filled with tears. "You looked so calm and cool and capable as you came into the hall, even after you'd been talking to that terrible officer, that I thought perhaps you could help me."

Susan's smile was cynical as she thought how little any of those adjectives described her feelings. "Well, you certainly flatter my ability as an actress when you say that. I'm as hot and jumpy as a frog on a gridiron. Would you like me to sit here with you until you finish your breakfast?"

Berenice glanced down at the untouched plate before her. "No, I don't want any breakfast. The very thought of it makes me ill." With a petulant movement she pushed her coffee cup away from her.

"What do you want then?" Susan's voice was soothing as though she were dealing with a sick child.

"I'm so worried I'm almost crazy. I hardly know what I am doing or saying. I couldn't sleep all last night thinking about Ailsa and wondering what that terrible policeman would make me say today." She pushed back the loose curls from her white forehead with shaking fingers. "I'm so afraid!" Her voice dropped to a husky whisper.

"There's nothing to be afraid of, Berenice. No one is going to hurt you. If you are frightened, let me get Harry!"

"No, no!" Stark terror flashed into Berenice's face. "Not Harry, I never want to see him again! He is the one I'm afraid of,—he and that awful Campbell. You must help me, Susan, tell me what I should do!"

"Why, of course, I'll help you if I can," Susan said as Berenice rose shakily to her feet.

"Come up to my room with me then," the English girl whispered, "Harry is apt to come in here any minute, and I want to get away from him."

With a puzzled frown Susan followed her upstairs to the Gordon room, where with utter disregard for her freshly ironed dress, Berenice in an abandonment of grief, flung herself on the unmade bed.

"Berenice, stop that at once. You are simply making yourself sick!" Susan said in a sharp voice. Berenice continued to sob. "If you don't control yourself, I won't stay here. I'll go out and leave you alone."

At that threat, the crying stopped and Berenice lifted a tear crumpled face. "Don't leave me, Susan. I'll be good. Sit down in that chair beside me."

"Well," Susan said perching on the edge of the wicker chair, "if I can help you, I will, but I'm not going to stay here and watch you work yourself into hysterics. What's the matter with you anyway?"

Berenice's lips trembled, and she threw a frightened look at the closed door. "It's Harry. I'm afraid of him. I'm afraid he will kill me the way he did Ailsa!"

"Nonsense! Harry never hurt Ailsa. Why he's one of the kindest men I know! I don't see how you can believe such an awful thing!" Susan said indignantly.

"He hated Ailsa," Berenice declared. "He told me he was going to settle with her once and for all, and he was downstairs at the time she was killed. O, I just know he did it. But I don't want to betray him to the police, because he was justified in doing it. He has a terrible temper, and I always knew that if he found how Ailsa and I fooled him, he'd kill us. I don't really blame him, but O Susan, I don't want to die!"

"You are wrong, Berenice," Susan said earnestly, "I'm sure Harry didn't kill Ailsa, and he wouldn't touch a hair of your head. Why he simply worships you!"

"Yes, he did love me," Berenice admitted, "but that was before he discovered what we did."

"What was it?" Susan's native curiosity quite overcame her reluctance to be involved in Berenice's affairs.

"It's a long story," Berenice said. "I'll have to go back to my childhood in order to make you understand. You'll have to see the sort of life I lived in England, the straggly, uninteresting little town in Surrey where my father was the vicar. I have three sisters, all much older than I, and we lived in a big, cold, rambling house on the main street. The house was always draughty and it always smelled of cabbage and boiled beef, though I don't know how it could, for all I remember eating there was mutton, hot mutton, warmed-over mutton, cold mutton. We only kept one servant, and we were always changing her. My father was a scholar and a dreamer. My mother was the real worker of the family. She organized all the Church societies and was always out visiting the parishioners and attending meetings. My sisters were interested in that sort of thing too. They were all big, husky, capable girls that dashed all over the county on their bicycles and thought a tennis party was the height of social functions." Berenice's lips curled. "They couldn't understand why I hated that life, why I wanted pretty clothes and beaux, and nice things to eat. There was just one person in the town who interested me, and that was Ailsa. She was always beautiful and gay, and she lived in a lovely, old, red brick house that seemed like a palace to me, though I know now that it was terribly run down and that she was as discontented as I was. We weren't exactly friends, but I used to see her quite a lot, and sometimes, when she noticed the way I hung around after Church watching for her, she'd go with me for a walk across the downs." Berenice paused as though trying to realize her old life and make it seem more than the dream it had become. Fascinated by the picture of a life so different than her own, Susan sat forward listening with eager interest as Berenice went on with her narrative.

"The last time Ailsa went for a walk with me there, she was terribly excited over a letter her father had received from his sister. She told me that her Aunt Madge had invited her to go to Egypt for the winter, and she felt it was the opportunity she had been waiting for all those years. She said that she'd meet lots of men, and that she'd marry someone out there so that she'd never have to come back home again. I was awfully envious of her luck, and at the thought of what that town would be without her to watch and talk to occasionally, I broke down. I don't think she realized until then how dreadfully I hated it all too, and how much she meant to me. Anyway, she promised me then that if she could carry out her plan, she'd help me escape too.

"Ailsa went away the next week, and I didn't see her again, or hear from her, except occasional postcards, when she happened to remember me. At home things were more ghastly than ever, for my mother and sisters thought I ought to take a more active part in the Church work—take a Sunday school class, sing in the choir, sew for the heathen. They were always nagging at me about something. I wanted to take a position and earn my own living, but my family wouldn't hear of it, and I had no training, no money. There wasn't even a chance to get married there, for all the eligible men who had managed to survive the war, had gone off to London or some place. Heavens! those tennis parties!—women everywhere dressed in their frumpy best and giggling and gabbling over each stray man that could be persuaded to come. And such men— Gangling boys of sixteen, or fat married ones of forty-five! The grass courts all bumpy, the nets grey and sagging in the middle—the lukewarm tea and biscuits and the sour strawberries. Ugh! how I loathed it!"

Susan nodded her sympathy. What an incongruous setting for a girl like Berenice.

"I stuck it out for four years, feeling all the while that life was slipping past me. Then, for some unknown reason, Ailsa wrote me. I don't know yet whether it was just kindness, or because she wanted to show the contrast between her old life and the one she was living in Shanghai. I'd heard of her marriage, of course, and for months I'd watched for a letter, praying that she'd remember her promise, but for four years there had been nothing. As soon as I read her note, I sat down and answered it. It was a wild sort of letter, I guess, but I was desperate. It was my only hope, and I was determined to make the most of it. It worked though." Berenice's eyes were wide with the miracle wrought by her frantic appeal. "Ailsa not only answered my letter right away and invited me to come out for a visit, but she sent me the passage money. I think that was the most wonderful moment I have ever known," she said simply.

"It was marvelous," Susan agreed warmly, "I didn't think Ailsa could be so kind."

Berenice's eyes grew vague. "She was always impulsive. My letter must have reached her at the psychological moment. A day sooner, a day later—and I'd probably still be eating mutton and going to Church three times on Sunday. But Ailsa," her voice dropped, "Ailsa might still be alive."

Susan shivered. Could it be true that the threads of Ailsa's murder ran back through the years to her kindness to the forlorn, young English girl in the little Surrey town?

"Ailsa was very good to me though, particularly at first. I was like a new toy," Berenice resumed her story. "She took me in hand and made me over. She said my clothes were all wrong, and the way I walked and talked and did my hair. We went shopping together, and Ailsa bought me a complete new outfit. Then she told me that I looked fragile and appealing, and that that must be the cue to my personality. She wouldn't let me use slang, or move hurriedly. She made me let my hair grow and taught me how to wear it back smoothly from my forehead in a knot at the back of my neck. She wouldn't let me wear bright colors, nothing but black or white, or shades of blue. It was months before I got used to myself and could act the way I looked. At first it was awfully hard to remember. I would get so tired of eternally posing that I'd have to get away from the house and then I'd whoop and run and let off steam but I was careful not to let anyone know. Finally Ailsa was satisfied with me, and began to introduce me to people and take me about with her. It was very gay in Shanghai, and I was glad she had made me wait. If those people had seen what a fright I was when I came from England, they would never have forgotten their first impression of my rawness. Ailsa understood people, you see, and both of us knew that my one chance was to marry well. Even with the changes though, I'm not the sort of girl that attracts men immediately, as Ailsa did. Young boys liked me, and old men, but no one that was particularly eligible. Ailsa chaperoned me very carefully. I had less freedom than almost any girl in the foreign colony. She wouldn't let me take a drink, or smoke—said she'd made me look like a Fra Angelico angel, and she wasn't going to have her work of art ruined."

"Didn't you have any life of your own at all?" Susan asked indignantly. "Didn't you have any good times?"

"O, I enjoyed it," Berenice declared, "Ailsa was much cleverer than I, and she always got her own way. I knew she would make more of a success of my life than I ever could alone. Besides, I had no money. I was absolutely dependent on her. Any time she became tired of the game she was playing, she could just ship me back to England—and I'd have done anything rather than have that happen."

"I see," Susan's curly head nodded.

"After I'd been in Shanghai two years, Bob's money was all used up. He put the last of it in an automobile agency, but that wasn't very successful. We had to give up the house and go to one of the hotels to live. Ailsa made some arrangements about bringing them business,—she was one of the most popular hostesses in Shanghai,—so we got a cheap rate. She did the same thing with some of the exclusive shops there,—brought them new customers so that our clothes cost us practically nothing. We played bridge every day, and most evenings, and Ailsa and I got our pocket money from that."

Susan's eyes opened wide and she started to speak.

Berenice smiled wisely. "You thought I couldn't play, didn't you, just because I've lost so much since you've known me? Didn't you ever notice that the only person I ever lost to was Ailsa? Didn't you notice that when I stuck in my famous psychic bids, it was always when the cards were running with me, and against Ailsa? Nothing but a wild bid, or a silly finesse would have brought up Ailsa's score, and I never used them unless I was playing against her!"

"You mean you deliberately lost?" asked Susan unable to grasp the significance of Berenice's words.

"Of course I did it deliberately! I'm not as good a player as Ailsa, of course, but my bridge is way above the average. Ailsa and I almost always won when we played together, and when I played against her, I made it a point to lose."

"But that was dishonest!" Susan said sharply. "What about your partners?"

"If they couldn't afford to lose, they didn't have to play with us," Berenice shrugged, "it was very nearly life and death with us, you know. We had to have money to get along on."

"Didn't anyone suspect you?"

"No, at least I don't think so. We were very careful. People simply thought that Ailsa was a remarkably good player, and that I lost my head. We both did all we could to create that impression. Don't look so disgusted," Berenice snapped, "your own ethics aren't above reproach, and you didn't have the provocation we did. At least when we lost we always paid our debts."

Susan flushed. "So, Ailsa told you that I couldn't pay my debts? Well, she was wrong, they will be paid in full next week."

Again Berenice shrugged, "I don't care anything about that—that was between you and Ailsa, but at least I should think it would help you to understand the position we were in. If we'd had enough money to live decently, we wouldn't have done any of the things we had to do,—it wasn't very much fun."

"No, it couldn't have been much fun," Susan echoed, trying to put herself in their place. "But why try to keep up a position you couldn't afford?"

"The only way either of us could earn a penny was by doing just what we did. The hotel wouldn't have given us rooms, the shops wouldn't have clothed us, we'd have been ruined, if our friends had guessed how hard up we were. By that time we didn't even have the passage money to take us back to England. All we could do was to stay where we were and try to keep our heads above water."

"What did Bob say to all that maneuvering?"

"Bob didn't know about any of it except the hotel arrangements. He made such a fuss about that before Ailsa convinced him that there was no alternative, that she didn't tell him about our other sources of income. Bob isn't a good business man, you know. He'd been brought up to have everything he wanted, and he'd simply no idea of the value of money. When things began to go wrong with him, he was as bewildered and helpless as a little child. He made a small amount from his automobile business, and he turned it all over to Ailsa. He supposed that kept us all clothed and in funds."

"How did you happen to marry Harry?" Susan asked, trying to bring the long story to a focus, "Did he know the straits you were in?"

"O no, he never guessed. Even now he has no idea how bad things were. He couldn't understand the way we lived, he'd think we had been dishonest, and he'd never forgive any of us," Berenice explained. "If he had been different,—well, none of this would have happened. You see, in spite of all Ailsa could do, things went from bad to worse. Lots of our crowd gave parties at the hotel, but the manager kept expecting more and more, and of course, Ailsa couldn't force her friends to entertain there all the time, or they'd have suspected the truth. The shops were impatient too, and finally began to threaten us. It was just at that time that Harry came to Shanghai. Ailsa met him first at a reception given by one of the consuls. When she got home that evening she told me that she'd found a solution to all our troubles, that all I had to do was to marry Harry—he had every one of the qualifications we'd been looking for in a prospective husband for me. He was a bachelor and his father had just died and left him oodles of money. Ailsa had arranged for me to meet him a couple of days later, and she coached me carefully on the line to take with him. So, I met him," she paused for a second, then added naïvely, "I was awfully disappointed. He was so big and red, and quite old, almost forty. He was very shy too, and if it hadn't been for Ailsa, his first call would have been his last. I was scared to death, but Ailsa carried things off in that breezy way she had, and after that, he came often. Harry gave quite a lot of parties at the hotel, and spent so much money that the manager stopped nagging us. Gradually he began to be attentive to me, but he never made love to me, or even hinted at marriage. Ailsa would make me tell her everything he said, recall every look and gesture after he'd left, and try to figure out what my chances were, and with all the optimism in the world, she couldn't be sure that he would propose. She used to get awfully angry at my stupidity in handling him, but no matter how hard I tried, I just couldn't make any headway. I hated his big hands, and his booming voice and his red face and his little, funny eyes. After he'd been coming to see me for a couple of months, Ailsa told me that unless I married him, I'd have to go back home,—that we couldn't stick things any longer. She didn't actually say so, but I knew she was thinking of

all the money she'd spent on me. I began to cry and
I told her I'd do anything she suggested, but that I
didn't know how to make Harry marry me if he didn't
want to, and apparently he didn't. She was disgusted
with me and said I was a fool not to be able to bring
it off myself, but since I was so dumb, she'd tell me
exactly what I was to do. I promised her, and then
she explained—" Berenice shivered at the humiliat-
ing memory.

"Harry never drank much. He was afraid to, because he always forgot what happened when he'd been
drinking. The next night was my birthday, and Ailsa
spent every cent she and Bob and I had between us
on a birthday party for me. She purposely gave the
little dinner—there were four other guests beside
Harry,—at a very expensive restaurant out in the
French settlement. You've never been to Shanghai
have you?"

Susan shook her head.

"Well, you wouldn't know it then, but that doesn't
matter. The dinner was a grand success. Ailsa and I
both had new dresses,—mine was of cream colored
lace, with little bowknots of blue velvet. It was the
prettiest dress I'd ever had, and everyone made a lot
of me, so I was excited, and forgot to be shy. There
was loads of champagne, and after a couple of glasses
—Ailsa let me have some because it was my birthday—I even flirted a little with Harry, though I don't

think I did it very well. Harry had quite a lot to drink, and Ailsa kept motioning the waiter to fill his glass. When the party broke up, Ailsa arranged for Harry to drive me home in his car. My only part, she had told me, was to make sure that we got back to the hotel very late, long after the others. It worried me a lot, because it was really not a long drive from the restaurant to the hotel, and Harry's car was faster than the others.

"I suggested that it would be fun to take a little drive instead of going right back. Harry agreed, and he headed for the race track, but his idea of a moonlight ride was to tear like seventeen devils along any good road he could find, and when he hit the race track I thought my last day had come. I yelled myself hoarse trying to make him stop, and then I tugged at his sleeve until he slowed down to listen to me. Then I told him I wanted to stop so that I could light a cigarette. He thought that was a great joke, because he knew Ailsa disapproved of my smoking, and after he had given me a light, I pulled out Bob's silver flask of brandy that Ailsa had given me, and made him drink my health. The brandy, on top of all the champagne began to affect him, and he got sentimental, put his arm around me and kissed me a few times. I peeked at my watch, and it said 3:30, so I thought I could go back to the hotel then. Harry was perfectly willing. He'd begun to get sleepy anyway. So, he brought me back and left me in the lobby. That was all I had to do. Ailsa did the rest." She paused, and a cloud passed over her face.

"What rest, what do you mean?" Susan's eyes were wide with interest.

"The next morning she sent for Harry to come to the hotel, and then she told him that he had seduced me. You see, Harry never remembers a thing that happens when he has been drinking!"

"O!" exclaimed Susan, shrinking back in her chair.

"Harry was terribly upset. He walked up and down the sitting room trying to remember what had really happened," Berenice went on, unconscious of her listener's gesture of repulsion, "but apparently the evening was all a blank. Then Ailsa showed him my poor little lace dress with the front all torn, and the skirt ripped,—she'd done that before he got there. That broke him up, he said he didn't see how he could ever have been such a beast, and that he could never make amends for the terrible wrong he had done, but that if I would consent to marry him, he would try to make me happy. Ailsa sent for me then, and I came creeping into the room. I was scared to death, and sick about the whole affair. He spoke to me very gently, and I liked him better then than I ever had before. A couple of weeks later we were married."

With an effort the American girl controlled her disgust. "But what did Ailsa get out of it? She didn't do it just for you, did she?"

"We had arranged all that. Harry settled all our bills, and of course that included Ailsa's, and he paid all the wedding expenses. Then he settled a very generous allowance on me, and I promised Ailsa that I would give her half of it. She managed to get along on that until Bob's business went smash, then it wasn't enough for them both to live on. After that, whenever she got short of money, she'd send for me, or else come to us for a visit, and I'd lose a lot of money to her at bridge. Harry didn't like me to gamble so heavily, but he would always settle my debts. He thought Ailsa was a bad influence, and lately he has been trying to break off our friendship."

"After you had married Harry and gone to Sumatra, why didn't you cut loose from Ailsa? You were giving her half the money you got."

"I couldn't. I've always been afraid of Ailsa, and I was terrified that she would tell Harry. I knew he would never forgive me,—he is so straightforward and scrupulous, and I was terrified lest he send me back to my people."

"Why do you think he found out that you and Ailsa had fooled him?" Susan asked.

"Things had been very strained between us lately. He knew that Ailsa had some sort of hold over me, and he used to question me by the hour trying to find out what it was. Of course I never told him,—I didn't dare. He'd been doing everything he could to make me happy, to make up for the wrong he thought he had done me—I couldn't tell him the truth. Then one day, he asked me for my checkbooks, and of course when he went through them, he discovered that I was giving Ailsa half of all he gave me. He was simply furious. His mind works slowly, but it is like the 'mills of the gods', I knew that it was only a question of time before he would piece together the whole story. The only reason he consented to come up to Johore this weekend was to have a showdown with Ailsa. Instead of helping me, she taunted him at every opportunity, with her power over me. Every time he looked at Ailsa there was hatred in his eyes, and his behavior to me was strained. When we were alone, he hardly spoke, just sat watching me with a brooding expression in his little eyes until I thought I'd go mad."

"You think then, that he had figured things out pretty well for himself, that he had a talk with Ailsa and she flung the truth at him, and he killed her in a sudden rage?"

Berenice's eyes filled with tears as she nodded her ruffled head. "Even if he did, I don't want him to be arrested. It is really all my fault. I should never have married him in the first place."

"I can't believe Harry did it," Susan murmured to herself, but her positiveness was gone. All she was conscious of was a deep sympathy for the big, generous man who had been a victim of his chivalry. "If I were you, Berenice," she said with sudden decision, "I'd have a frank talk with Harry. I'd tell him everything. I'm sure he loves you enough to for-give you,—I saw the tenderness in his eyes last night when you fainted, and the gentleness with which he carried you upstairs. Talk to him now, at once, before Mr. Campbell sees either of you! I'll find Harry for you!" She sprang to her feet.

With a cry of fear, Berenice shrank back against her pillows, "No, Susan! Don't! I won't see Harry. I'm afraid of him, I tell you. O, I wish he were dead instead of Ailsa. I hate that plantation in Sumatra, nothing but Dutch people within fifty miles of us. It's nearly as bad as Surrey. And I'll have to stay there the rest of my life,—I won't even have my visits to Ailsa. I hate Harry! I've always hated him!"

Susan looked down contemptuously at the piti-ful little creature on the bed. "Why did you tell me your story? You said you wanted advice, and now you won't take it!"

"I don't know why I told you," Berenice sobbed, "I thought you could help me the way Ailsa always did. She'd have found a way out for me. Ailsa would never have suggested my going to Harry. She knew it would be impossible!"

"I'm not Ailsa, thank heavens!" Susan exclaimed. "If you hadn't followed her advice so long you'd never have been in the jam you are now, or Harry either."

Berenice pulled a pillow over her head to shut out the sound of Susan's words.

With an angry glance at the stubborn blue-clad figure on the rumpled bed, the American girl opened the door and went out. As she went slowly down the stairs in a sudden craving for sunshine and fresh air, there was a troubled frown on her young face. What if Berenice was right, what if Harry really was the murderer? The story she had listened to made her feel unclean. Swiftly she ran down the veranda steps, across the lawn fleeing from the grey shadows of the Rest House.

CHAPTER XII

"What luck, Ismael?" Campbell asked eagerly as he closed the door upon Brownley's receding back, and turned to his assistant.

Ismael shook his head. "I didn't find the weapon, Tuan, though I searched every room. The doctor has come and gone. He states that the knife that caused the wound must have had a four-inch blade. Tuan Durham has a gold pen knife, and Tuan Gordon has one with a bone handle, but both blades are too short to have been used, and they show no trace of blood. Tuan MacAlistair has a hunting knife, but its blade is too wide to fit the wound. Tuan Brownley had no knife at all."

Campbell's face fell, and he flung himself dispiritedly into the chair beside McCloud. "What about blood stains, Ismael? Did you find any on their clothes or in their rooms?"

The Malay reached into his pocket and drew forth a handkerchief. "I found this in Tuan Brownley's room. It was stuck beneath the mattress of his bed." Carefully he spread the square of linen on the card table that the young magistrate was using for a desk, exposing the ugly brown smears that stained its whiteness.

"By Jove!" exclaimed McCloud, "that looks bad for Brownley. Unless I miss my guess, this handkerchief was used to wipe the blood off a knife."

"Yes," Campbell said leaning forward to examine the handkerchief more closely, "it's Brownley's handkerchief all right. Here are his initials in the corner—R. L. B."

Ismael nodded. "There are five more like it in his suit-case."

The police officer frowned, "It's a bit too good to be true, it seems to me. Why would Brownley leave incriminating evidence like this in his own room?"

Ismael's face brightened. "That is what I ask myself, Tuan. And why should he use an initialed handkerchief such as this, when in his bureau there was a pile of plain uninitialed handkerchiefs?"

"A murderer always makes a slip of some kind, you know Ismael, otherwise you'd never catch any of them," McCloud protested.

"Ah yes, but not so bald a slip as this. The handkerchief was left there for us to find. If I had not searched the room, then the roomboy would have found it when he made the bed, and would have brought it to us."

"That's just about the sort of break we would get," Campbell said in a glum voice. "We have two clues, and both of them were left behind to mislead us. First Durham's knife, and now this handkerchief. It doesn't stand to reason that if Durham committed the murder he would have used his own knife and left it for us to pick up, but that is more conceivable than that Brownley should have wiped the blood from the second knife on his own handkerchief and calmly stuffed it under his mattress for us. It won't wash."

"That is how I read it, Tuan," Ismael said somberly. "The murderer is very clever, and the two clues he left were not oversights, but deliberate efforts to confuse us."

"Let's try to figure a bit," Campbell said rising restlessly and pacing up and down the room. "Who would have had the opportunity to put the handkerchief in Brownley's room? It must have been done this morning while Brownley was down here talking to me. Who was upstairs at the time?"

Ismael looked thoughtful, "I am afraid that won't help us much. Mem Gordon was the last person to descend, but we cannot suspect her alone, because the boys in the dining room told me Tuan Durham went directly upstairs after he left this room, and that Tuan Gordon also returned upstairs for a brief interval after breakfast. Either of them might have slipped the handkerchief into Tuan Brownley's room. Likewise, Mem Durham went up to her room."

"Where were the roomboys, perhaps they saw something?" suggested McCloud.

"No, I told them I did not wish them to clean the rooms until I had searched them, so they were all below stairs. They just went up now when I told Oom Ling it was all right."

"I don't suppose you saw anything yourself, Ismael?" Campbell asked.

"Unfortunately not, Tuan. I was busy with each room in turn, and not knowing of this development then, I paid no attention to the guests. Besides, Tuan, we can't be sure that the handkerchief was placed there after Tuan Brownley came downstairs. It might have been done earlier, when he was in his bath. His bed is near the door—three steps inside the room was all that was required. If the murderer was a man, he risked little, even should Tuan Brownley have seen him—just a friendly inquiry as to his health, or any little excuse."

"Yes, that is true, I suppose," Campbell sighed. "Everywhere we turn we are up against a stone wall. How about that cotton wool? Did you find who had a supply of that on hand?"

Ismael threw out his hands expressively. "Mem Gordon, Mem Brownley, Mem Durham and Mem Ames, all had a small quantity in their manicure boxes. Tuan MacAlistair had some in a medicine kit, as did also Tuan Brownley. All the cotton was the same quality, first class, absorbent, like that stuffed in the lock,—and all the rolls had been opened."

"I guessed as much. It would have been a miracle if just one of our suspects had had a supply on hand. Where was the cotton kept? Did it look as though it had been recently used in each case, or was it stowed away in their baggage?"

Ismael's white teeth flashed. "The ladies' manicure boxes were all in plain sight on their dressers. Tuan MacAlistair's medicine kit was in his duffle bag. His boy had not unpacked anything except what was needed by his Tuan last night and this morning. Tuan Brownley's suitcase was partly unpacked and his clothes arranged in the wardrobe and in the chest drawers. His medicine kit was in one of the little top drawers. Tuan Ames alone had none."

Reluctantly Campbell dismissed the question of the cotton. "None of our clues lead anywhere it seems. You'd better send this handkerchief along to the hospital to have the stains analyzed. We'll need it for evidence, if we are ever lucky enough to get this case in the courts. Haven't heard about the kris yet, I suppose?"

Ismael carefully gathered up the handkerchief. "It is not yet time to hear about the fingerprints. In the chit, I told them I would call the detective bureau about two o'clock. I thought it better that they should not telephone us here, lest the conversation be overheard. And you, Tuan, did you learn anything from those you have interviewed this morning?"

"Nothing tangible, Ismael. MacAlistair volunteered the fact that he had had a note from Mrs. Brownley last night, though just between you and me, I don't believe he would have opened his mouth if he hadn't suspected that we had the note. It was clever of him to spike our guns about it."

"What did he say?" Ismael asked eagerly.

"Why he admitted that he was once engaged to Mrs. Brownley and that she jilted him to marry Brownley. He says he hadn't seen or heard from either of them directly until he ran into them here on Friday night."

"Did he meet Mem Brownley?"

"Well, he says he didn't. He claims that he fell asleep and didn't wake up until ten minutes of two. Then he started out to see whether she was still waiting for him, and he was on the way to the marble seat when he heard her scream."

"How did he act, Tuan, when he told you all this? Was he nervous?"

"He was a bit worried, but he didn't show much other emotion. I don't believe he was still in love with Mrs. Brownley, if that is what you mean. He seemed far more concerned about his friendship for Mr. Brownley and the fact that he had misjudged him all these years."

"Friendship, pah!" Ismael exclaimed, "that is not a strong enough feeling for murder. Somewhere we must find someone who loved the unfortunate lady overmuch, or who hated her. And those others you saw, how did they feel?"

"I didn't get anything from the American tourists, nor from young Ames or his sister. I discovered that Durham is just as big a cad as I'd thought him. He admitted he was angry at his interview with Mrs. Brownley. Apparently she told him exactly what she thought of him, and it didn't go down any too well, but his conceit rallied even from that, and he is now convinced that she didn't mean what she said and that she would have divorced her husband eventually and married him, if he paid her enough. I don't know whether he was lying or not. Apparently his chief fear now is that his wife may learn of the episode. I wouldn't wish him any worse punishment than to have her hear about it either."

"Perhaps she already knows, Tuan. She is a woman of passion. Perhaps she committed the murder?"

"That occurred to me right away. If Durham was telling the truth and felt that Mrs. Brownley would marry him if he divorced his wife, then both Brownley and Mrs. Durham had a powerful motive for the murder. But Brownley was upstairs doped at the time, which would seem to let him out, and while Mrs. Durham has no alibi for the time of the first murder, she couldn't very well have slipped out of her room and killed Mrs. DeKok without Durham's knowing something about it," Campbell said frowning.

"Perhaps Durham was in on it," McCloud ventured. "Or maybe he was a sound sleeper and didn't know when she left the room."

"It would be pretty difficult to prove either of those guesses, at this stage in the game," the officer's voice was discouraged. "No, I'm afraid we'll have to wait for something more definite to turn up."

Ismael nodded an agreement. "Did Tuan Brownley contribute nothing?"

"I persuaded him to tell me what he knew about his guests. I thought perhaps I'd unearth something there, but I didn't get very much. It came hard to him to talk about his friends at all, but eventually he divided them into the sheep and the goats,—those he thought had the character and motive to kill his wife, and those who didn't. He ruled out MacAlistair, Miss Ames, Jack Ames and Mrs. Gordon. He said he couldn't believe that the others killed her, but he felt that Mr. Gordon and the Durhams might conceivably have done it."

"That is how I myself have sized them up. Those three are all capable of great feeling—Tuan Gordon of love; Mem Durham of jealousy and Tuan Durham of greed. And yet, I think the little American girl could also feel deeply were she aroused. Tuan MacAlistair and Tuan Brownley are too English for me yet to fathom. They seem cold, but even ice can harm."

"So, you don't really rule them out then, Ismael?" Campbell asked.

"They are still unknown to me, Tuan. The others I can understand more easily. I do not think the American boy committed the murder. His feeling for Mem Brownley was only a wind that blew across his emotions, it did not stir them deeply. Besides, I found several of the house boys who saw him at the kampong last night at two o'clock," Ismael added naïvely.

Campbell's grim face relaxed into a grin. "Well, thank God he's out of it anyway. He is the only one with an alibi, and he doesn't know yet that he has one."

"Did you telephone for Tuan DeKok?" Ismael asked.

"Yes, it was bad business. The poor fellow was terribly broken up. Said he would start at once. He ought to be along any time now, I should imagine."

"Have you had breakfast, Tuan?" The Malay's glance rested affectionately on the harassed face of his chief.

"No, I forgot all about it," Campbell admitted.

"I shall tell the boy to bring you something at once. One cannot do without food. The body must be nourished before the brain can do its work," Ismael reproved him.

"Have it sent in here then, and ask Tuan Gordon to come in too. I'll talk to him at the same time."

With a nod of understanding the little Malay went swiftly out of the room.

Ten minutes later Campbell was aroused from the brown study into which he had sunk, by the arrival of a Chinese waiter bearing a tray, closely followed by the tall figure of Harry Gordon.

"Have a seat, Mr. Gordon," the officer said genially. "You don't mind if I have a spot of breakfast while we chat, do you?"

"Go right ahead," Harry said, pulling a chair to the opposite side of the card table on which the Chinese boy had arranged the officer's meal. "I'm always willing to talk when I can buttonhole anyone into listening, as my friends know to their sorrow. Just what topic will form the best digestive accompaniment?"

"Shop!" said Campbell with a smile, pouring out a cup of steaming coffee, "I'm so used to thinking of it, eating with it, sleeping with it, that any other subject would probably give me indigestion. You know about Mrs. DeKok's murder, of course?"

"Yes,—a ghastly thing. Somehow it hit me even harder than Ailsa's. I mean—" he said hastily as Campbell looked up from his plate in surprise, "one could imagine Ailsa creating trouble and havoc enough to motivate a murder, but Mrs. DeKok was so obviously a good, placid creature who would never hurt anyone, that such a horrible fate seems utterly incredible."

"Yes, I understand what you mean. Some people are born to drama and tragedy, as apparently Mrs. Brownley was, and others seemed assigned to play unimportant roles. It is always a surprise to find such a person holding the center of the stage. Even now, though,—it is Mrs. Brownley's murder which is the more important. Mrs. DeKok's seems to be merely a result of that."

Harry's face was sober. "That is what I think. If it weren't for Ailsa, Mrs. DeKok would be meeting her husband this morning, taking a slow walk about the town with him, doing a bit of shopping in the native kedais, buying presents for her children, if she has any. Instead, she is lying dead in her room upstairs. It is horrible to think of." His eyes rested broodingly on the green lawn and waving palm trees outside the open window.

The officer glanced at him sharply, surprised at the imagination displayed by his words. "Can you tell me anything that will help us clear up these crimes, Mr. Gordon?"

Harry shook his head. "Not a thing, I'm afraid. I told you last night all I knew about Mrs. Brownley's murder. If I only hadn't twisted that confounded ankle of mine, I might have seen more, got out on the lawn faster."

"How is it this morning, Gordon? Does it bother you?"

"O no! It was merely a wrench, not even a strain, and it stopped aching after a few minutes."

"You heard nothing after you retired last night?"

"Not a thing. Our room is a long way from Mrs. DeKok's. Even if I had stayed awake listening, I doubt if I'd have heard anything."

"Is Mrs. Gordon feeling better today?"

"She's still upset. She came down to breakfast, but I was just upstairs, and I found her crying on the bed. I can't seem to do anything to comfort her. Mrs. Brownley was her closest friend, you know, practically her only one, so her grief is natural."

"Mr. Gordon," Campbell's voice hardened, "why does Mrs. Gordon think you killed Mrs. Brownley?"

Harry flinched. "That is what is worrying me. She is convinced that I committed the murder, and nothing I can say will shake her. I've talked myself hoarse, but she hardly seems to listen. She acts as though she were afraid of me!"

The officer pushed his empty plate aside. "She must have some reason for thinking it,—she must know that you had a motive for wanting Mrs. Brownley out of the way. Come now, don't you think you had better be frank with me? Everybody here apparently had some motive for killing the lady, but you can't all be guilty. If you know you are innocent, why not tell me all about it, and let me eliminate you from the investigation, if your explanation is satisfactory." Campbell's voice was persuasive.

The other man hesitated, obviously tempted to unburden himself of the weight he was carrying, then his lips tightened. "I can't tell you anything that would be any help to you, Campbell. If you suspect me of the murder, then you'll just have to go ahead and prove it."

"If you don't talk, Gordon, it means that I will have to question your wife again, force her to tell me what she knows," Campbell announced in a matter-of-fact tone.

Harry's ruddy face paled. "You wouldn't do that, Campbell, not in the state she is in!"

"You leave me no alternative, Mr. Gordon. I'll have to talk to Mrs. Gordon again anyway, but I thought you were better able to stand the strain of a long, difficult interview than she. If you can't or won't tell me the things I want to know, then I will have to find them out from Mrs. Gordon."

Harry's small blue eyes stared at him miserably while Campbell waited in silence for him to speak.

"You've placed me in a deuce of a hole, Campbell," he said at last. "I don't want Berenice to be worried, and yet, dash it, I can't discuss my wife with another man, you know. It just isn't done."

"I'm not asking you to discuss your wife, Mr. Gordon. All I am interested in, is why she thinks you murdered Mrs. Brownley."

"I'd have to talk about my wife, and her relation to Mrs. Brownley in order to explain her attitude," Harry said dismally.

"You would really be sparing Mrs. Gordon an ordeal which she dreads. I am bound to discover the facts sooner or later," Campbell said craftily.

"That's true." Harry's face brightened. "Would you have to put it down in the records, anything I told you in confidence?" He nodded toward McCloud.

"Yes, Mr. McCloud would have to take down your testimony, but unless it is relevant to the murder, it wouldn't have to be made public."

Again Harry hesitated, and then his face changed as he came to a decision. "Campbell, I'm going to ask a favor of you. My mind is a slow one. I can't do things on impulse. Give me a few hours to think this over. Nothing I can tell you now would be of any use in finding the murderer, but there is something that I might be able to tell you later, that would solve the crime."

"What do you mean?" Campbell asked sharply.

"I don't know exactly," Harry's words were slow. "But I have a feeling that I have the clue to the murder buried in my mind, my memory. It just eludes me. I have been so upset about Berenice that I haven't really had time to think it out yet. But it's there. I'll swear that it is!" His deep voice rose in excitement. "Twice it has almost come to me, and then it escaped. Let me be by myself awhile so that I can think quietly. If I can't dig it up by teatime, say, then I will answer any questions you ask."

Campbell's eyes were inscrutable as he stared at the open, ingenuous face opposite him. Harry smiled boyishly. "I know it sounds fanatical, but I'm really not trying to hedge. I'd almost made up my mind to tell you the unimportant things you want to know, when I had again that sensation of being on the verge of a discovery. If I were to talk to you now, that little isolated fact is going to be buried under such an avalanche of emotion that I'll never be able to unearth it. Didn't you ever feel that way when you tried to remember a name or a word,—that it was on the tip of your tongue? That's the way I feel. Somewhere, sometime, something happened that seemed quite unimportant at the moment, but is now of tremendous significance. Just let me remember what it was, and I'll know the murderer!"

Against his will Campbell was impressed. "Haven't you any idea when this happened, what it was?"

Harry shook his head. "No, except that it was recent. Somehow I associate it with dinner last night. But I can't go beyond that."

The officer gazed at him thoughtfully. The interview with Gordon could easily wait until teatime. There were plenty of other odds and ends to follow up in the interim, and there was a chance that Gordon might be able to give him the clue he so desperately needed. He could afford to chance the slight risk that the man was stalling for time, but he couldn't afford to lose the information which Gordon sincerely seemed to feel he could supply.

"All right, Mr. Gordon, your request is unusual but I am going to grant it. I won't trouble either you or Mrs. Gordon until teatime. Furthermore, in case your clue is associated with last night's meal, I'll arrange to have you sit at the same places at lunch today. Perhaps that may help a bit. There's one thing I'm going to ask of you, though,—that you say nothing to anyone except me if you do find the clue. You must take every precaution for your safety. Remember what happened to Mrs. DeKok."

Harry rose eagerly. "Thanks Campbell. It's awfully decent of you, and I'm sure you won't be the loser. I won't discuss the matter with anyone, not even Berenice."

"O, by the way, Mr. Gordon," the officer suddenly remembered the handkerchief as Harry started to open the door, "did you go to Mr. Brownley's room for anything this morning?"

Harry stopped in surprise. "Why no! His door was shut when I came downstairs and I supposed he was asleep."

"You didn't go back upstairs after breakfast?"

"Yes, I ran up to get my topee. I wanted to take a turn around the grounds, and I was up there again a few minutes ago looking for Berenice, but I didn't see Bob. Nothing wrong with him is there? I thought I saw him having breakfast as I came in."

"No, there's nothing wrong with him. I'm just trying to check up on a couple of things. That will be
all, thank you, Mr. Gordon."

In spite of his feeling that he was doing the right
thing in giving Gordon the respite he had requested,
Campbell's eyes were troubled as he watched the big
man disappear through the doorway.

CHAPTER XIII

The hot, tropic sun had mounted half way up the
deep blue dome of the sky, burning away all the early
freshness of the morning, thirstily drinking up the
last drop of dew from the close-cropped lawn and the
green tangle of shrubbery. Roses drooped wearily on
their trellises, and the passion flowers, mimosa and
hibiscus blossoms hoarded their fragrance until sun-
down should again release it. Only the royal coconut
palms were impervious to the heat, defiantly lifting
their feather duster heads to the battery of sunshine.

Not a breath of air ruffled leaf or flower as Bruce
strolled slowly down the shallow veranda steps and
across the lawn, past the white glare of the road, to
the seawall. The water beyond was as blue and motionless as the sky above, a dazzling mirror that tortured the eyes. Malay fishermen with bright sarongs
tucked about their smooth, brown thighs were wad-
ing in the lukewarm water near the shore, joyously
scooping up shrimps with home-made nets. Occasionally a heavy twakow crawled slowly past, or a

native fishing boat, with brown sails drooping, passed before Bruce's unseeing eyes. He was as oblivious to the traffic on the Straits before him, as he was to the lumbering oxcarts, the padding feet of rickshaw runners, and the rattling cars streaming along the thoroughfare behind him.

"It couldn't have been Harry," Bruce was insisting to himself, "and I know it wasn't Susan or Jack. I don't believe it was Berenice either, in spite of what Susan said about her faked faint. Lord! I'd have knocked myself out too, about that time, if I'd thought I could put it over on that hawkeyed officer. That brings it down to one of the Durhams. It's a toss-up which of them did it. Dick was closer at hand. His story about being asleep on the veranda sounded pretty thin, and yet somehow that wife of his seems more capable of murder than he does—a regular Lady Macbeth. I can imagine her carrying through a crime, but he'd always have an eye to his own safety, if you ask me. I wonder how long it would have taken Mrs. Durham to go downstairs, out to the shrubbery, kill Ailsa and get back! Of course she could have hidden in the shrubbery until we'd taken Ailsa into the Rest House, then slipped up the front stairs, but Mrs. DeKok would have seen her, or the American, or Susan or Berenice. Could she have waited on the veranda until Berenice and Susan had come downstairs! Mrs. DeKok was there for a time, and it was bright moonlight. She couldn't have stayed in the shrubbery very well, for

Oom Ling was poking around there. Besides, there is the later murder. Not much chance of her going out and committing that without her husband knowing all about it. I wonder whether they could have acted together? If they did, I'll wager he'll crack first and give the show away."

"Well, Mr. MacAlistair," exclaimed a voice behind him, "here you are in exactly the same position I left you in last night." Startled he turned to face Susan's mischievous grin, which faded as she said wistfully, "Wouldn't it be nice if it were true?"

"If what were true?" asked Bruce bewildered.

"Why that we were both still here—that neither of us had moved—that last night hadn't happened at all. It seems like a nightmare, wouldn't it be wonderful just to open our eyes and find that it was one!"

"I fancy we'd be feeling pretty stiff and uncomfortable by this time if we'd been standing here for twelve hours or more," Bruce said practically.

"Just the same it would be an improvement," Susan insisted. "I'd rather have an uncomfortable body any time than an uncomfortable mind, and I guess there isn't one of us who isn't worried to distraction—even the murderer." She shivered in spite of the blasting heat.

"I don't know about the murderer," Bruce put in. "He or she is probably enjoying the situation, watching us stumbling around in the dark, chasing shadows, and suspecting each other."

Susan nodded thoughtfully as she rested her bare
arms on the hot sea wall and glanced up into his
bronzed face. "Mr. MacAlistair, who do you think
did it? You came in from the outside and you can't be
so confused with its closeness as I am. Tell me what
you think."

"I'm not quite so remote from it all as you seem to
think," he said slowly. "You know Harry is a friend
of mine, and Berenice too, in a lesser degree, and I
knew Bob and Ailsa very well in the old days."

The girl's grey eyes were suddenly veiled by long
black lashes and her voice sounded small. "I knew
you were a friend of Harry's,—but I thought Bob and
Ailsa were just casual acquaintances. I didn't know—
I'm sorry." Her slender figure in the starched white
linen dress stiffened.

"There's nothing to be sorry for, Susan," Bruce assured her. "Perhaps I should have told you last night,
or this morning, that I knew the Brownleys well."

"There's no reason why you should have told me
anything, Mr. MacAlistair, but I don't think it was
fair of you to let me talk so frankly and critically
about your friends." Her small pointed chin quivered
as she turned away.

"Don't be silly, Susan," Bruce seized her hand and
pulled her back to the wall. "You know perfectly well
that none of these people mean much to me except
Harry and you. Bob was once very close, and Ailsa—
but that was ten years ago."

"Just the same you deceived me," Susan stamped her small white shoe angrily. "You shouldn't have let me say the things I did. What can you have thought of me?"

"I thought you were very frank, and that it was very good of you to treat me like a friend." Bruce smiled down at her as she struggled to free her hands. "No, you are going to stand still and listen to me for a change."

Susan looked up into his friendly eyes, and was reassured. Her lips crept into the boyish grin that transformed her into a bewitching street gamin. "Well, I'm not going to stand here in this sun a minute longer, but if you want to walk beside me while I go to explore the old palace over yonder, I don't suppose I can help myself."

"Fine," Bruce said, releasing her hands. "Let's go. It's an interesting old place and it's just a short walk up the road."

"And now," Susan announced as they turned and strolled along the parched grass beside the road, "what's on your mind?"

Bruce hesitated. "It's hard for me to talk about myself."

"Don't tell me you are one of those strong, silent men!" she mocked. "And a woman hater too, I'll bet. I never expected to find one outside the movies, and even they aren't silent anymore."

His smile was reluctant. "I'm no hero, in fact I'm the comic relief if there is any."

"No, you don't qualify for that. Your eyes aren't crossed, and your shoes aren't the right size. You'd better get on with your little bedtime story and I'll be thinking what role to cast you for."

"Well, there isn't much to tell, and none of it reflects any credit on me," Bruce said grimly. "Bob Brownley was my best friend. We went through school together, then both of us having more money than brains, we started out to see the world. In Cairo we met Ailsa. I fell in love with her and we became engaged. Then my father lost his money and killed himself, and Ailsa decided that she preferred Bob. They settled in Shanghai, and eventually I got a berth in India. That's all." Susan was very quiet while he was speaking and it was some minutes before she said softly, "Thank you for telling me. I didn't know things were like that or I would never have said anything."

He stopped short and looked down at her severely. "Now don't get any romantic ideas about me in that curly head of yours. I'm no blighted lover. Ailsa's decision was the best thing that ever happened to me. Until then, I had been nothing but a spoiled young cub, and I needed a severe jolt to shake some sense into me. I've had to make my own way, work for everything I've managed to get, and now I am beholden to no one. I'm free to do what I please, within reason, and I'm perfectly happy."

"Don't worry. I'm not sympathizing with you, Bruce MacAlistair. I think you had a narrow escape. Just think, but by the grace of God you might be in Bob's shoes this minute, instead of being 'perfectly happy'."

Both their faces clouded at the mention of Bob, and Susan desperately pushed away the memory of the tragedy as she said, "I'll bet I know just what your happiness consists of!" Her voice held a challenge.

"What do you mean? How can you know anything about me?"

The girl shrugged her slim shoulders. "Perhaps I'm the seventh daughter of a seventh daughter, who knows? Let's see if I'm right." She stared at him with wide, speculative eyes. "You have a nice bachelor bungalow just outside the city somewhere, with lots of books around, and guns, and a couple of boars' heads on the walls. You have a speedy little red roadster, a dog, and a native boy who pampers you to death. Now what kind of a dog would you have, I wonder. Don't say anything," she interposed as Bruce started to protest. "It wouldn't be a wirehaired fox terrier, or an Irish terrier,—they are too small for you. I have it! It's a police dog!"

"You are all wrong," Bruce said in a triumphant voice. "He's an English bulldog. And my car isn't red. I wouldn't have a red car. Mine is grey, a nice,

sensible shade that won't show the dust and get me
into trouble with my sais (*driver*). And as for Ahmat's
pampering me—why he is a perfect tyrant and bullies
me until I daren't call my soul my own."

Susan's fresh young laughter rang out joyfully.
"Those are only minor details. I was right in all the
essentials—a dog, a gun, a car and a native boy! You
have a limited idea of happiness, it strikes me."

Bruce frowned; as she enumerated his blessings
they did sound rather trivial. "What's wrong with
that? What more could anyone want?"

Her eyes twinkled. "I could suggest several im-
provements, but I don't know you well enough yet.
That can wait."

"We haven't a pass to get into the palace," Bruce
said, ignoring her levity, "but if you like we can follow this road around past the Mosque and then go
into the botanical gardens at the back of the palace."

"Anywhere, to get out of this sun. There seems to
be some shade farther down the road, under those
olive green trees."

"They are mangosteen trees—you had mango-
steens for breakfast this morning, you know." Bruce's,
words were lifeless, as though his thoughts were on
a far different subject. "You know, Susan," he said
abruptly, "you were an awfully good scout to accept
my story at face value, but I'm not at all sure that
Campbell was so amenable to the truth. In fact, I
rather fancy I head his list of suspects. He found a

note that Ailsa wrote me last night asking me to meet her. Like a damn fool, I just tore it up and threw it in the basket."

Susan looked startled. "What did she write you about?"

"O, she just asked me to meet her in the garden for a talk. I had no intention of going down there at all, but when I woke up—I'd dozed off—I didn't like to think of any woman being out alone at that hour with the natives all stirred up, so I decided I'd have to make sure she wasn't waiting for me. I'd just gone out of the Rest House when I heard her scream." He paused, frowning. "You see it does sound improbable. I can't blame Campbell for being skeptical."

Susan sounded troubled. "It never occurred to me that you could be involved—the stranger in our midst, was the way I pictured you. Of course I know you didn't kill Ailsa, but from Mr. Campbell's point of view, things don't look any too good. The wronged lover turning up just before the lady in the case is killed. What did Mr. Campbell say to you?"

"O, he was noncommittal as usual. I think he was surprised when I told him about the note, but he may have figured that I knew he had it and was just trying to take the wind out of his sails, which is only too true. If I hadn't discovered the note was gone, I'd never have mentioned it."

"Mr. Campbell is nobody's fool. Did you notice for all his apparent frankness, he really tells us very little? I asked him how on earth the murderer got into Mrs. DeKok's room—why she hadn't locked the door as the rest of us all did, and he just smiled and switched the conversation to my bridge debts."

"What did you tell him?" Bruce inquired anxiously.

"Just what I told him last night—that I'd pay Mr. Brownley as soon as the next American mail got in. He looked a bit skeptical, but he didn't say anything more about that. He tried to draw me out about the relationships between the people in our crowd, but that didn't get him anywhere either. Our interview was a stalemate."

"Did you speak to your brother?"

"Yes, he stopped and had another cup of coffee with me after you left. I told him that I was going to sell the pearls and settle my debts. He seemed to be in a sort of fog, but he snapped out of it long enough to act relieved. He admitted that my statement last night had rather knocked him for a loop, but he said he knew I'd have something figured out. If I hadn't, he was planning to ask for an advance on his salary. That would have put him in wrong with his company, but I knew I could count on him to stand by me, however much he might disapprove."

Bruce nodded. "How did your brother feel about things this morning?"

"He's badly cut up, of course, but I'm sure he doesn't feel as badly as he thinks he does. He met the little American girl this morning,—the one with the loud-mouthed papa, and they seemed to be hitting it off very well. Just before Mr. Campbell called me she was looking up at him with that 'How-wonderful-you-are' expression, and he was straightening his necktie with a 'You're-right-but-you-aren't-so-hard-to-look-at-yourself' attitude, so I decided he was in good hands. She is very pretty."

The beautifully kept lawns and gardens lay before them, with a glimpse in the distance of the rambling grey stone palace, as they passed the domed and minaretted Mosque and entered a path leading to the palace grounds.

"Oh, there's a stone seat ahead in the shade. Do let's sit down and get our breath," Susan exclaimed, quickening her steps. Bruce followed her and contentedly relaxed on the seat at her side. "This seems like a different world," he said with a long sigh of satisfaction. "Look at the color in those flowers banked up over there, reds and purples and pinks!"

The girl tossed her little white hat aside, and ran her fingers through the damp curls so suddenly revealed. "It's simply heavenly," she breathed, dreamily watching some gay-colored butterflies float past her in the soft, perfumed air. "I hate the thought of ever going back to that dreadful Rest House again."

"Why here comes Harry!" Bruce exclaimed after an interval of silence. "He looks as if he were walking in his sleep. Doesn't see us at all. Hi, Harry," he called as the rugged figure in wilting white clothes

approached the tree under which they were sitting.
"Come out of it!"

Harry stopped with a jerk, and regarded them haz-
ily. "O, it's Bruce and Susan," he said in surprise, "I
didn't see you until you called."

"What's the matter, old man? A touch of the sun?
Come on and sit down with us." Bruce pointed invitingly to a place on the stone bench.

Susan was regarding Harry with compassionate
interest. Could this be the man who had killed two
people last night?

"Can't, I'm sorry. I'm trying to remember something, and I don't dare risk a diversion." A smile light-
ened his broad, red face. "Never mind,—if I have any
luck, I'll have good news for you this evening."

As his big, bulky figure receded in the distance,
Susan and Bruce exchanged puzzled glances. "Now
what on earth is Harry being so mysterious about?"
Bruce wondered aloud.

"He's probably sleuthing. Running down a clue to
the murderer," Susan answered lightly, fighting down
her doubts about Harry. "It seems to be the favorite indoor and outdoor sport hereabouts. I hope he's
cleverer than the rest of us though, or we are apt to
spend the rest of our days in Johore. Mr. Campbell
won't let us go until he finds the murderer."

"I know," Bruce murmured, "I've gone round and
round the facts I know until my mind feels like a
squirrel in a cage. I just get nowhere."

"Whom do you really suspect?" Susan asked leaning toward him until the soft tendrils of her hair
brushed his cheek.

Fascinated at the purity of the face so close to
his, Bruce answered absently, "I don't know. I think
Mrs. Durham seems more capable of it than anyone
else, but I don't see how she could have covered the
necessary ground in the short time she had. She was
with Berenice until quarter of two, and that means
that she had to get downstairs, out to the shrubbery,
commit the murder, and get back upstairs in eighteen
minutes."

"That's a thought," Susan exclaimed. "I'll make
the trip and time myself when I get back to the Rest
House. If it can't be done, why then that eliminates
everyone who was upstairs at 1:45, which means the
female of the species."

"It would help a lot if we could pin it down definitely to one of the men," Bruce said thoughtfully,
"but even if you find that the crime could have been
committed in that length of time, you will still have
to figure how she got back upstairs without being
seen by you or Berenice, or by Oom Ling, or Mrs.
DeKok."

"Perhaps she was seen by Mrs. DeKok," Susan's
voice was eager. "Perhaps that's why Mrs. DeKok was
killed."

"It's possible," Bruce admitted, "but somehow I
got the impression from Mrs. DeKok last night that

she had seen the murderer on his way to commit the crime, not afterwards."

"Well, we're off again!" Susan said despondently, "and now I can't enjoy this dream of a garden any more. I'm going back to the Rest House and time things out for myself."

"You'll have to wait until after tiffin then," Bruce retorted. "It's quarter of one now."

"All the better," the girl returned, crushing on her hat and jumping to her feet. "I'll need a lot of exercise after all the curry I expect to consume."

As they walked slowly back toward the Rest House through the white heat of the noon hour, an unaccountable dread seemed to shackle Susan's feet. She shivered violently and reached out a hand to clutch Bruce's coat, "O, I don't want to go back there, Bruce, I'm afraid,—I'm afraid!"

CHAPTER XIV

One by one the guests assembled in the cool dimness of the large dining hall, and one by one, each guest hesitated at the sight of the round, waiting table in the center of the room. With averted eyes the American family thankfully sought their own table in a far corner, while little Wetherby, with a curious glance, made a wide detour to reach his place on the other side of the room. Several other tables were occupied by local men who regularly had their tiffin at the Rest House, and to each group, the big round table was the center of interest and speculation.

Susan and Jack Ames stood uncertainly in the doorway while Dick Durham, loud in his indignation, sent for Oom Ling. "What's the meaning of this?" he demanded as soon as the suave Chinaman came within hearing distance. "You don't expect us to eat at that table do you? Just have a small table set for Mrs. Durham and myself."

"Yes, and for my sister and me," Jack said thrusting out his chin.

"I'm sorry, Tuan," Oom Ling replied, "Tuan Campbell say that you will all sit as you did at dinner last
night."

"That's outrageous," declared Janet Durham, her
sallow face flushed with anger. "He can't make us sit
together if we don't want to. Where is Mr. Campbell?
I'll talk to him."

Oom Ling spread out his yellow hands expressively. "Those are my orders. I can do nothing. Tuan
Campbell is not here."

"Where is he?" asked Janet sharply.

"Upstairs with Tuan DeKok. He say to tell you
that no one who did not kill Mem Brownley and
Mem DeKok will mind sitting at the table," Oom
Ling said softly. There was a startled silence, during
which each of the waiting groups eyed the other with
suspicion, as though calculating the result of refusal.

"What kind of game is he putting up on us?" Jack
Ames wondered aloud.

"Well, my conscience is clear anyway, come along
Jack." Resolutely Susan walked across the hall and
took her place at the round table. With varying emotions, the others followed her example, keeping their
heads carefully turned away from the empty seat at
the head of the table.

"What do you suppose his idea is?" Bruce murmured to Susan after he had helped Berenice into the
chair on his left.

"I don't know, unless he thinks that someone may crack if he makes us uncomfortable enough. That empty chair dominates the table, just as Ailsa always did. I keep trying not to look at it, and yet my eyes go slinking back as though it were a magnet," Susan whispered.

"Perhaps it won't be so bad when the others come," said Bruce trying to appear more optimistic than he felt. "I wonder where Harry and Bob are?"

"Here they come now," Jack said looking over Berenice's bent head at the two men entering the door. "It's going to be tough on poor old Bob. I think we all ought to act as cheerful as we can." At his words there was a mumble of approval, and each guest made an effort to greet Bob casually.

"I'm awfully sorry you all have to sit here," Bob said, slipping into his chair. "I tried to persuade Oom Ling to let us off, but apparently law and order must be served, even though it works in a 'mysterious way'."

"That's all right, old man, don't worry about us. If you can stand it, I guess we can stick it," Bruce assured him. "After all, it doesn't make much difference where we sit."

"Thanks Bruce," a shadowy smile softened Bob's lips, "I know you'll make the best of a bad bargain."

"Did you enjoy your walk, Harry?" Susan inquired with a quick glance at the worried face opposite her.

"Not particularly," Harry returned, and then as though fearing further questions, addressed Jack.

"How did the shopping expedition go? I'll wager every native kedai in town is rising up and calling your name blessed."

"O Jack, did you go shopping?" asked Susan in a surprised voice.

Jack flushed. "I didn't buy anything myself, just piloted Gertrude and her mother and father around a bit. They wanted some souvenirs to take home with them, and asked me to go along as interpreter. They were more impressed with my limited Malay than the shopkeepers, but thanks to the good old sign language, I managed to get away with it."

Susan and Bruce did their best to encourage Jack in enlarging upon his difficulties, but in spite of their efforts, Ailsa's empty chair usurped the center of their thoughts. Berenice sat silent, toying with her food, only raising her eyes occasionally in fearful expectancy toward her husband. After his first compassionate glance at the pitiful, tear-stained face of his wife, Harry had relapsed into an absent-minded silence, during which he ate mechanically everything set before him by the soft-footed Chinese waiter. Durham applied himself industriously to his heaping plate of curry, zealously sampling each dish that the attentive boy passed him, and answering in sulky monosyllables Janet's sharp undertones. Janet contributed nothing to the general conversation, but her hard, suspicious eyes dwelt distrustfully in turn on each member of the little group. With an obvious effort, Bob was striving to do his duty as host, though his unhappy eyes kept turning expectantly to Ailsa's empty chair, as if to ask her help in diverting their guests.

As the watchful Chinese waiters deftly began to clear away the dishes to make way for the dessert course, Janet turned to Harry. "Have you a cigarette, Harry? Dick never smokes anything but cigars, and I forgot my case."

"Why yes, of course, Janet," Harry's thoughts jerked painfully back to the people around him as he felt in his pocket. "O, damn! I forgot my cigarette case again. Sorry Janet, but I'll have one for you in a minute." He beckoned to a waiter, "Hey boy, tell Mahat to bring me my case!"

"I should think you'd remember your cigarettes once in a while," Berenice said irritably, as Jack passed his cigarettes around the table. "You never have them when anyone wants one."

Startled her husband stared at her, and slowly his face brightened until it shone like a newly risen tropic sun. Bruce watched him curiously, hoping for a word that might explain Harry's unusual preoccupation, but except for a murmured sentence to Mahat, when the native appeared with the cigarette case, Harry said nothing. His face had darkened again, and he gazed straight ahead of him, with a look almost of horror.

All pretense at conversation had stopped. Each
casual remark or reference that was launched was
promptly wrecked on the unpleasant memories it
evoked. The most innocent words developed a sinister application. All eyes except Harry's kept wandering to the empty chair at the head of the table.
Singly and in groups the other diners left the room,
but those at the round table sat on over their coffee
as though under a spell which they feared to break.

There was the echo of footsteps on the stairs outside, and through the open door, those facing in that
direction caught a glimpse of a short, thickset Dutchman, his face twitching with emotion, and the long
familiar figure of Campbell. The Dutchman stumbled as he crossed the veranda and painfully crawled
into the car which was waiting beside the steps. Hurriedly the police officer strode into the dining hall.
"Where's Ismael?" he demanded of Oom Ling who
had hastened to meet him.

"Ismael has gone down to headquarters. He said
there was something important he must do, Tuan,
but that he would be back soon."

Campbell checked an expression of annoyance.

Suddenly Harry Gordon rose from his place at the
center table and started toward the officer, "O Campbell," he called eagerly, "just a minute. I've thought
of that information you wanted."

As though Harry's movement had at last broken the spell that bound them, the other guests had

hurriedly risen and moved toward the door. For an instant the officer stared blankly at Harry, and then apparently remembered their agreement. "That's fine, Gordon, but I can't stop now. Mr. DeKok is in bad shape and I can't keep him waiting. It's his heart! He should never have made the trip alone. Dr. Bailey is having office hours and can't leave, so I'm taking De-Kok down there. I'll be back as soon as I can, and I'll talk to you then. Just sit tight until I come." With a reassuring nod at Harry's disappointed face, Campbell left the room, and a moment later the wheels of the car crunched down the driveway.

"Gee, after all that curry, I feel like a hoptoad," Jack Ames exclaimed as they all moved out on the veranda. He threw a rapid glance around him at the empty chairs backed invitingly against the wall of the house. "I guess I'll go up and sleep it off. There won't be anything doing until teatime."

"I think I'll lie down and rest too," Berenice said as she saw Harry throw himself into one of the long chairs beside the open door. "It's so hot here on this porch, I don't see how you can stand it."

Harry smiled up at her, "I'm used to heat, and I have to wait to speak to Campbell. You go up and get some rest, dear."

Bruce looked around for Susan, and his face broke into a grin as he saw her come down the outside stairs, speed past him, and dash around the corner of the Rest House. She wasn't losing any time in carrying out her experiment. Before he could finish his cigarette, she was back again. "Well, what are the results?" he asked as she dashed past him. She shook her head. "Don't know yet. I'm timing myself from the far end of the balcony. I'm going to make some notes, but I'll tell you about it all later," she called over her shoulder as she hastened up the stairs.

"Good enough," Bruce raised his voice slightly. "I've got to write out a cable and get it off, but I'll see you at teatime." She waved an acquiescence as she vanished.

On the far end of the veranda, Janet Durham was speaking in low, urgent tones to her husband. Apparently he had given up all hope of conciliating her and his anxious eyes were darting frantically from side to side as though looking for a means of escape. Suddenly, as if unable to bear another word, he stepped down off the veranda and hurried across the side lawn in the direction of the shrubbery. For a moment she watched him baffled, undecided whether to follow him or not, and then with tightened lips, she passed Harry's recumbent figure and went slowly up the steps.

Everybody had disappeared and Harry was alone with his thoughts. Sly-footed Chinese boys finished clearing the tables in the dining hall, and two of them pattered out on the veranda to lower the slim bamboo screens that hung from the edge of the porch, shutting out the glare of the angry sun. The heat was

insufferable, a blanket that clouded the eyes and be-
fogged the mind, but in his elation, Harry was oblivious, as he lay there impatiently awaiting Campbell's
return. Silence as heavy and impenetrable as the heat
fell on the Rest House. With a last lingering look
at the immaculate order of the shadowy, grey dining
hall, the Chinese boys slipped away to their quarters in the rear. The native gardeners stretched their
length luxuriously in the shade of trees or shrubbery
and gave themselves up to their particular shurga
(*heaven*).

Restively Harry wondered when Campbell would
get the Dutchman off his hands and come back to
hear the incredible story that Harry had pieced together. No chance of his forgetting now. His mind had
sought and found the clue to the murders, and he had
fitted them together like a crossword puzzle, only
horrible, more horrible than anyone had guessed.
And clever Lord what diabolic cleverness the murderer had shown, every contingency guarded against,
except the one remote chance that someone might
remember that single damning fact that was the weak
link. Harry paused to marvel at the chance that had
helped him unearth it, that made him the instrument
of justice. He moved uneasily in his chair and then
leaned back wearily against the hands he had crossed
behind his head.

Yes, it all fitted in. There were still one or two details that were obscure about Mrs. DeKok's murder—

how the murderer got into the room—how the knife was disposed of. But Ailsa's murder was as clear to him now as if he had been an eyewitness. Harry's eyes closed as he visualized it. The dark clump of shrubbery, with the marble seat gleaming faintly in the moonlight, and Ailsa in her silvery dress sitting there unconscious of danger. There would be the sound of footsteps approaching, the brushing of leaves, the snapping of a twig, perhaps. She'd raise that coppery head of hers, but there would be nothing to alarm her in the familiar figure she would see emerge into the clearing. That was the devilishness of it—that it should have been the one person in the house from whom she thought she had least to fear. There would be nothing to warn her until her eyes caught the flash of the knife—and then she had only time for that terrible scream. Harry shivered and opened his eyes for a reassuring glance at the friendly daylight, the slitted sunshine pouring through the bamboo screen. His damn imagination was too active for comfort— he could actually see that gleaming knife in front of him descending—the familiar hand clutching it around the hilt. For a split second his fascinated eyes watched the knife. His mind flashed danger. Good God, it was real! His hands jerked from behind his head. His dry lips opened for a scream that died in his paralyzed throat as the knife plunged into his heart.

CHAPTER XV

It was just quarter of three when the short, stocky figure of Ismael hurried up the gravel driveway that led to the Rest House. The blazing sun instead of sapping his energy, acted instead as a stimulant. His smart white drill suit was as stiff and immaculate as when he had donned it thirteen hours before, and he strode along the winding, shadeless road like a brown craft under full sail.

The telephone call to police headquarters in Singapore had proved as fruitless as he had expected—there were no distinguishing fingerprints on the kris, the fine carving on the handle had interfered with any impressions that might have been there. The second call he had put in to Singapore had likewise added nothing new to the information he already possessed. It was the third call which he was turning over in his mind, and it was that which caused the sparkle of excitement in his usually fathomless eyes. To be sure it was merely the first link in the chain he had still to forge, but it was the chain which would hang the murderer.

Ismael bounded up the veranda steps, pushed aside the bamboo shade, and then stopped short in his tracks, his eyes narrowing at the scene before him. Recovering almost instantly from the shock, he darted to the long chair beside the door and stooped over the figure lying there so quietly. Harry Gordon's head had dropped over the side of the chair, his arms hanging uselessly on either side, while a dark red stain spread slowly and steadily across the whiteness of his coat. Blood was still oozing from the wound over his heart, but a single glance at the glassy, staring eyes and pallid face had shown Ismael that life was extinct.

"So, the knife struck again!" With silent feet, the Malay stepped into the hall, his beady eyes searching its cool shadows. There was no one there, and yet, scarcely five minutes before someone had stood like the very shadow of death behind the man outside, and ruthlessly stabbed him to the heart. The murderer had moved swiftly and effectively as was his wont. Ismael returned to the porch and began methodically to seek any clue which the slayer might have left behind. There was nothing,—not a button, not a thread. A silence like that of death itself hung over the Rest House.

The rattle of a car and the welcome sound of Campbell's voice interrupted Ismael's search, and he hurriedly pushed aside the screen to meet his chief. With a single, quick glance at his assistant's clouded face, the officer flung himself out of the driver's seat. "What's wrong, Ismael?"

"Another murder, Tuan,—not ten minutes ago. The body is still warm."

"God! who's killed?" Campbell demanded, clearing the shallow steps in a leap.

"Tuan Gordon!" Ismael's answer was unnecessary for already the officer was bent over the Englishman's body.

"It's my fault, Ismael." Campbell's face was grey and he seemed to have aged ten years in as many seconds, as he turned somberly to his assistant. "I didn't think he really had anything important to tell me, and I put him off. Told him to wait. I'm as guilty as if I'd knifed him myself."

"What do you mean, Tuan? Did he know who the murderer was? I don't understand."

"Yes, he must have figured out the truth somehow," Campbell said slowly. "When I talked to him this morning he told me he was sure he had a clue, if he could just remember it—something that had seemed unimportant at the time, and yet which would explain the murders if he could only recall it. He asked me to give him until teatime. I didn't put much stock in his remarks, it all seemed a bit fantastic, but I did warn him not to say anything to anyone but me, if he did succeed in remembering.

Then, just before I took Mr. DeKok to the doctor's, Mr. Gordon came up to me and told me he had remembered. He wanted to speak to me then, but I told him I couldn't stop. The old Dutchman's heart was bad and I was afraid he was going to die on my hands. I had to get him to Dr. Bailey's. He collapsed in the car before we got there, anyway, and doc had the devil's own time bringing him around. He has him in the hospital now. It all took longer than I thought, but I came back as quickly as I could."

"So that explains this murder too. Tuan Gordon discovered the murderer and was waiting here to tell you. Somehow the murderer must have known that. Did anyone overhear him tell you that he had remembered the vital thing?"

Campbell thought back over the scene in the dining hall: Harry Gordon approaching him, Oom Ling already standing beside him, and the other members of the party crowding close behind Gordon,— MacAlistair, Ames, Brownley, Durham, and the three women. The officer made a gesture of despair. "All of them were there, Ismael,—every last one of them."

"Again there is no sign of the knife, Tuan," Ismael broke in on Campbell's bitter thoughts, "but I think it is the same knife that killed Mem DeKok. The wound seems similar in size and appearance. I will telephone the doctor." He paused in the doorway regarding his chief's grim face with concern. "What will you do now, Tuan?"

"What will I do, Ismael?" Campbell repeated, straightening his sagging shoulders, "I'm going to get every member of this house downstairs, make them account for every minute of their time. And God help any of them that hasn't an alibi. Get McCloud on the wire and tell him to get over here as fast as he can. I told him I wouldn't need him until after tea, but all bets are off now."

Ismael shook his head. "I fear such impetuousness will get you just nowhere, Tuan."

Campbell glared at him. "Well, we'll have a chance to find out. After you get McCloud, call on Oom Ling and have him rout out all the guests—all, that is, except the American family. They aren't mixed up in this, and I don't want that old windbag around. Then, after you've telephoned the doctor, go through the rooms upstairs again and see if you can find the knife." Ismael disappeared swiftly into the hall to carry out his instructions.

It was a surprised and indignant little group of people who assembled in the dining hall a quarter of an hour later, and faced the gimlet gaze of the police officer.

"There's been another murder!" he announced brutally. "One more of your friends has been killed."

A shock of horror ran through the party, and quick-ly they glanced from one to another checking those

who were present. Two anguished women called out
simultaneously, "Harry!" "Dick!" Janet Durham was
on her feet looking wildly about her, her face distorted fear, "Is it Dick? Did anything happen to Dick?"
Berenice half rose, and then sank back overwhelmed
with an intuitive knowledge. "No, not Dick,—it's
Harry. I, I know it's Harry!" she whispered.

The officer regarded her gravely. "Yes, it is Mr.
Gordon. He was stabbed as he lay in his chair on the
veranda." With a little moan Berenice covered her
face. Susan started at the words, and her eyes filled
with abhorrence as she stared at Berenice.

"Not Harry!" Bruce exclaimed jumping to his feet
and starting toward the door as if unable to accept
the officer's statement.

"Come back, MacAlistair," Campbell roared, "nobody is going to move out of this room until I get
through with them." He waited until Bruce had again
seated himself beside Susan, and then turned on Mrs.
Durham. "Where is your husband?"

Janet's face looked old and pinched, but her voice
was calm as she answered, "I don't know. He went for
a walk I imagine. I saw him cross the lawn before I
went up to lie down."

The officer stared at the faces turned toward him,
trying vainly to penetrate their inmost thoughts.
Bruce MacAlistair was sitting on the edge of his
chair, his hands clenched, his face a bronze mask.

Bob Brownley leaned forward, his blue eyes blazing from his white, strained face. Jack Ames, flushed and anxious, was automatically squeezing the hand that Susan had slipped into his. Susan herself was watching Bruce with eyes luminous with pity. Berenice was huddled in her chair, staring straight before her with blank, blue eyes. There was a tenseness in Janet Durham's figure and her eyes were anxiously watching the open door. McCloud, still breathless from his swift ride, was arranging a table near the window, on which to take his notes.

"Oom Ling," Campbell called to the Chinese boy who was standing at a respectful distance, "go and find Tuan Durham. Bring him back here, but don't tell him what has happened. Just say I want to see him right away."

"Ya, Tuan, suka (*Your pleasure, Sir*)," Oom Ling faded from the room.

"Now then," Campbell's voice was hard, "I want to know just where you all were, and what you were doing from the time I left this room until Oom Ling called you. We'll start with you, Mr. MacAlistair." He turned his face toward Bruce who was at the extreme right of the half-ring of guests.

With a visible effort Bruce roused himself from the horror of his friend's murder. "After lunch I went out on the veranda and smoked a cigarette. Then I went up to my room. I had to code a cable to send off to my office in India. After I finished that, I lay down on the bed and dozed off. I was still asleep when Oom Ling knocked on my door."

"Have you any confirmation you can offer?"

"Only the copy of the cable I coded. Ahmat took it down to the telegraph office for me."

Campbell made a note on a slip of paper.

"Mr. Brownley," the officer looked at Bob, "what were you doing?"

Bob returned his gaze steadily. "After lunch I went directly to my room. I was tired, but I couldn't sleep. I lay on my bed reading."

"Have you anyone to vouch for that fact?"

"No, I'm afraid not, unless someone happened to see me go into my room."

Berenice spoke up in a small, remote voice. "I saw Bob go into his room just as I turned into mine. His room is right next door. I went up the stairs behind him."

Campbell's stern eyes shifted from Bob to Berenice. "Did anyone see you go into your room?"

Bob's voice was regretful. "I'm sorry, I didn't know anyone was behind me, and I didn't see Berenice."

Berenice's forehead was puckered in her effort to recall the past hour. "I didn't see anyone else, except Mahat—Harry's boy. He was crouching outside the door as I went in. He will probably remember. He wasn't there later though, for I got thirsty and wanted

him to get me some ire blandah (*soda water*). I opened
the door to tell him, and he was gone."

"Hm, did you ring for one of the houseboys then?"

She shook her head. "I knew they would all be off
taking a nap, and that I probably couldn't make them
hear. I decided I could wait until teatime, or until
Mahat came back, or Harry came upstairs."

The officer made another note before he addressed
Jack Ames.

The American boy answered readily. "I went upstairs right after lunch. The Durhams, Susan, Harry
and Bruce were still on the veranda when I left. I was
awfully sleepy after being out in the heat all morning, and I flopped down on my bed as soon as I got
in my room. I didn't know a thing until Oom Ling
shook me. I didn't even hear his knock."

"Can anyone corroborate that?" Campbell asked.

"I saw Jack go upstairs, and later when I went up,
I peeked into his room. He was dead to the world,
and I didn't disturb him," Susan volunteered.

"Why did you go into his room?" Campbell demanded.

Susan's voice was rueful, "It seems very unimportant now. I had been making an experiment. I
thought the time element counted for a good deal in
Ailsa's murder, and I wondered whether anyone who
was supposedly in their room at the time, could have
had time to go downstairs, out to the shrubbery, kill

Ailsa, and get back, all inside of eighteen minutes. If it couldn't be done, then that automatically cleared all of us women."

The officer repressed a start of surprise. "And what did you find out, Miss Ames?"

"It took me just eight minutes from the time I left the far end of the balcony upstairs to go out to the shrubbery and back to my starting place. The murder could have been done in two or three minutes, I should think," Susan said simply.

Campbell nodded. "So, it could have been done by one of you women. That is what Ismael said. However, you must remember the difficulties that the murderer would encounter when he or she returned. The Rest House had been aroused in the meantime by Mrs. Brownley's scream, Mrs. DeKok was on the balcony when MacAlistair brought the body in, the American appeared almost immediately, and you and Mrs. Gordon were using the front and rear stairs. Mrs. Durham was on the balcony. Did any of you see anyone?"

"No," the answer came almost simultaneously from the three women.

"There, you see!" Campbell pointed out, "Unless one or more of you are lying, the murderer must have been on the lawn with the men. However, that has nothing to do with the point at issue now, which is solely with the movements of you people after lunch. Please continue, Miss Ames."

"Directly after lunch I went upstairs, then came down and went out to the shrubbery and back again, timing myself. When I found it had only taken me eight minutes, I felt awfully set up, though I wasn't sure just what it proved. I wanted someone to talk it over with. I went into Jack's room and found him asleep. By that time, I began to see the objections which you yourself raised just now, so instead of looking further for an audience, I went into my own room, and tried to work out a time schedule of where everybody said they were at the time of Ailsa's murder."

Campbell regarded her with surprised respect. "Where is the schedule, Miss Ames? Will you let me see it later?"

"It is very incomplete and amateurish, I'm afraid, but you are perfectly welcome to it," Susan said flushing. "It took me up to the time Oom Ling knocked, to figure it out. I know nothing about Mr. Gordon's murder."

"Now, Mrs. Durham, how about you?" Campbell directed his dark gaze upon Janet.

"I know nothing," she declared. "After lunch I talked for a few minutes on the porch with my husband. He said something about walking off his heavy meal, and left me. The last I saw of him, he was cutting across the lawn in the direction of the shrubbery. Harry was lying in the long chair just outside this door. He smiled sort of vaguely at me as I passed him on my way to the stairs."

"What did you do for the rest of the time?"

"I don't approve of these afternoon naps that everybody takes—sheer laziness I think. I washed out some handkerchiefs and darned two pairs of stockings," Janet's voice was defiant. "I don't believe in throwing my money away, like most of the people out here. These natives' idea of washing anything is to take it down to a river or a canal and pound it with rocks. Well, they did that just once with my things. After that I did my own."

Campbell stared in perplexity around the semi-circle. They had all spoken with apparent frankness. Their explanations of their occupations were all credible, their reaction to Gordon's murder consistent with shock and horror. As Ismael had predicted, his examination had got him exactly nowhere. His memoranda consisted of just three entries: beside MacAlistair's name, was that of Ahmat, and the word cable; opposite Mrs. Gordon's the name Mahat,—and after Susan Ames'—'Get time schedule'."

The unpalatability of his thoughts was interrupted by the sound of footsteps on the veranda and the exclamation "Good God!" as Dick Durham discovered the gruesome contents of the long chair. A shiver rippled through the forlorn little group inside at the picture his words brought to their minds. Durham's steps had lost their jauntiness, and his face was ghastly as he came into the room, followed by the watchful Oom Ling.

"Who did it? Who killed Harry?" he demanded through dried lips as he came up to the officer in charge.

"That's what I'm trying to find out," Campbell snapped. "Where have you been all this time?"

"I! Good Lord you don't think I killed poor Harry do you? Why I liked him! Everybody liked Harry!" Dick exclaimed, groping blindly for a chair and collapsing into it.

"Somebody didn't," the officer stated bluntly. "One of his 'friends' killed him an hour ago. I'm trying to find out which one of you did it. Where have you been since lunch?"

Dick's eyes blinked nervously as he half turned toward the tense figure of his wife. "Why, let's see. I talked to my wife on the porch for a few minutes. Harry was all right then. I saw him sit down in that very chair. There were several people around. I don't remember just who they were. My wife said she was going upstairs, and I decided to take a little walk. I knew if I lay down on top of all that curry, I'd have an attack of indigestion." He paused to wipe the perspiration from his forehead.

"Yes, and where did you go?" Campbell's voice prodded him.

"Well, I rambled about on the lawn a bit. I was busy thinking and didn't pay much attention to where I was going. The first thing I knew, I found myself in the shrubbery in front of the marble seat, where

Ailsa was killed. That was a bit thick. A frightful shock, coming on it unexpectedly, don't you know? I got away from there as fast as I could, out into the sunshine, for that place had given me the shivers. I walked down the road a ways, and I noticed some native shops. I decided I'd go in and buy a present for my wife. We'd had a bit of a disagreement," he smiled feebly, and again his eyes sought Janet's. Her expression remained changeless, but her eyes seemed to give him strength.

"And did you buy a present for Mrs. Durham?" Again the officer's voice jabbed at him.

Dick shook his head. "No,—most of the native shops were closed, lazy beggars, these natives. Finally I found one that was open. It looked just like the rest from the outside, and inside too, just a sort of hole in the wall. There was a fat Chinaman behind the counter, and he held up a pair of earrings," his voice was suddenly husky with emotion. "They were jade. Just like the ones I bought yesterday for Ailsa. It was too horrible! I turned and ran out of the place, right into the arms of Oom Ling who fetched me back here." His thick hands shook as he mopped his face again.

"How long were you here in the grounds before you went to the kedais?" Campbell asked.

"I don't know, twenty minutes perhaps, or maybe half an hour, I wasn't timing myself."

"When you left the shrubbery, how did you go toward the road? Did you go back to the piazza and down the driveway?"

"No. I came out of the shrubbery and cut right down the lawn to the road. I wasn't within fifty feet of the veranda. I didn't see anybody around,—the whole place looked deserted, but I did notice that the bamboo screens had been lowered."

Campbell made a note—"What time were screens lowered."

"That's interesting. Mrs. Durham, were the screens down when you went upstairs?"

Janet hesitated a moment before replying. "No, they couldn't have been, for I remember watching Dick across the lawn."

"And you were the last person to see Mr. Gordon alive," declared Campbell.

"The last person, except the Chinese boys who lowered the screen,—and the murderer," Janet supplemented his statement.

Ismael came slowly down the rear stairs and approached his chief who turned an eager face toward him. "There was no trace of the weapon upstairs, Tuan."

Campbell's shoulders sagged perceptibly, but his voice showed nothing of his disappointment as he asked, "And the servants?"

"I talked with the two who lowered the screens. It was done at half past two, and Tuan Gordon was alive then. At quarter of three when I came on the veranda, he was dead."

The officer nodded. "He was probably killed about 2:35 then. Is the doctor coming?"

"Dr. Bailey is at the hospital working over Tuan DeKok. He will come along as soon as he can safely leave his patient."

"All right, Ismael. Now get Ahmat and Mahat down here. I want to talk to them. Miss Ames," he looked toward the American girl, "I'd like to see that time schedule. The rest of you can go." With a curt nod, he dismissed them, and with slow steps made his way toward the Recreation Room.

CHAPTER XVI

Long after the tall, forbidding figure of the officer had left the dining hall, and McCloud, with notebooks and pencils had trailed after him, the group sat on, reluctant to move. Outside, the lifeless body of Harry Gordon was waiting for the arrival of the doctor, and even the bravest of them shrank from the thought of passing it. The only alternative refuges were the small, hot bedrooms upstairs, and so they waited aimlessly, hopelessly, while the shadows lengthened on the lawns outside.

Dick and Janet Durham had drawn their chairs apart from the rest, and were conversing in low, anxious tones. Bob Brownley, without noticeable success, was trying to comfort Berenice who sobbed on and on desolately against the arm of her chair. Jack Ames sat in a stunned silence, turning a helpless, stricken look on each guest in turn. Susan crouched back in her chair lost in dark and dreadful thoughts. Bruce MacAlistair alone had moved, but only as far as the western window where his broad shoulders blocked the sunlight that was striving to lighten the gloom of the dismal room.

As Campbell closed the door of the Recreation Room, Ahmat came forward, his brown face pale with excitement. "The mata mata say for me to come here, that you would speak with me!"

Campbell's smile was reassuring. "It's all right Ahmat, nothing for you to worry about," the officer said in fluent Malay. "I just want you to tell me if your Tuan called you after lunch."

"Sahaya (*yes*), Tuan. I went to his room about two thirty to see if he wished anything before I went to sleep. He was writing, and he gave me a telegram to take to the telegraph office."

"And you took it there direct?"

"Yes, Tuan, directly."

"You didn't see your master again?"

"No, he said he wouldn't want me until later. I had already laid out a fresh suit for him. When I came back from the telegraph office, I went to the servants' quarters."

"All right, that is all I wanted to know Ahmat."

The boy hesitated on the threshold, "Please, you are not going to make trouble for my Tuan, are you, Sir? I have been with him many years now, since he first came to Johore Bahru and took me hunting. He is a very good man. For him only, would I have given up my friends and my native kampong to go to far away India."

"So that's how he happened to have a Malay boy, is it?" Campbell said. "I wondered why he didn't have an Indian servant."

"Yes, he likes the Malays better," Ahmat straightened himself proudly. "I am quick and strong. On that first hunting trip, he was charged by a wounded pig. Swiftly I ran up and shot the beast. The Tuan was very grateful and took me then to be his boy."

"That was a good day's work for you, eh, Ahmat?" Campbell spoke absently, and then suddenly added, "Do you know anything about these murders, Ahmat? Did you see anything yourself, or did you hear the other boys talking about anything they knew?"

Ahmat shook his head. "I know nothing except that my Tuan is innocent. I have lived with him a long time, and I know him."

"All right, you can go. If you see Ismael outside, tell him to send Mahat in to me." With a quick nod of understanding, the Malay boy was gone.

The door had scarcely closed on him, when it opened once more to admit Susan Ames. "Jack said you were still in here. I'm sorry to have been so long, but after you left, I was simply rooted to my chair while the horror of these murders submerged me. None of us seemed able to move. It was as if something unbelievably awful was waiting to pounce on the first one of us that stirred." She shivered, and her eyes were wide with dread. "It was ghastly. I knew you wanted these notes, and yet if my life depended upon it, I couldn't have left that chair. Finally Mr. MacAlistair moved over to the window. I expected to see him drop to the floor with a knife in him, but nothing happened, and finally I got together enough strength to make a dash for the stairs." Her voice was shaken, and she kept looking nervously over her shoulder.

"Don't let yourself go like that, Miss Ames," the officer said sharply, "you have too much intelligence not to realize that the only people in danger are those with information about the crimes."

Susan bit her lip, and her next words were steadier. "It is awfully foolish of me to let this thing get me so. I guess we are all about at the end of our tether, and Harry's death was the last straw. He was so good, so kind—" her voice choked, and she turned her face away to hide her tear-brimmed eyes. "Mrs. DeKok was a stranger, and Ailsa—well, lots of people didn't care for her, but I think everyone loved Harry. I can't understand it!"

"What you need is a cup of hot tea. The porch is clear now. Dr. Bailey had Mr. Gordon's body moved, and Oom Ling is going to set up the tea tables out on the veranda in the daylight." Campbell's voice was gentle. "Just leave this schedule here with me. Then go up and have a wash. Tea will be ready when you come down and you'll soon be feeling a lot better. You might tell the others to get ready."

"You really are a nice man, Mr. Campbell," Susan smiled faintly. "I'll pass along the word. I don't think these notes will help you very much, but such as they are, they are yours."

As the door dosed behind her, the officer let out a soft whistle. "We're in for trouble with these people, McCloud. If a girl like Miss Ames could get into such a state, I hate to think what the rest of them are like. I hope the tea will calm them down."

"You can hardly blame them," the young magistrate said. "Whew! when Ismael telephoned me that there had been another murder, I had the jimjams, whatever they are. Three murders in less than fourteen hours is a bit too strong even for me, and I didn't know any of the people involved. One of that group out there may be guilty, as you and Ismael seem to think, but the rest of them are going through unadulterated hell."

"Yes," the officer's face was morose, "and it's going to be worse as night comes on, but I don't know what we're going to do about it."

The despondency of the two men was interrupted by a knock at the door, followed almost immediately by Ismael's round, moon face. "I can't find Mahat anywhere, Tuan. He is not upstairs, or in the servants' quarters, or around the grounds. I have dispatched police to look in the kampongs for him. But see!" His voice rose in triumph, "I have the knife!"

"Stout fellah! Ismael, where did you find it?" Campbell asked, stepping to the Malay's side and peering at the weapon held carefully in Ismael's gaudy handkerchief.

"Outside, in the bushes near the road. I was looking for Mahat, thinking perhaps he had crawled into the shade to rest from the sun, when my eyes saw something shining. As soon as I realized it was a knife, I picked it up with my handkerchief. The handle is smooth, and it should hold the murderer's prints."

"I say, Ismael," McCloud said in an excited tone as he leaned eagerly across his table, "that's just an ordinary steel knife, a dinner knife. It's the kind they use here, I've often noticed how sharp and pointed they were."

"Yes," Campbell added, "they are a kind of steak knife. I remember saying once, myself, that they had the knives unusually sharp here so that the guests wouldn't notice how tough the meat is."

"It means, Tuan, that anyone could have used it," Ismael said. "But the prints will tell us who had it. You see, there are still marks of blood. This time the murderer did not stop to clean it with one of Tuan Brownley's handkerchiefs. I go now to dispatch the knife to Singapore." At the door Ismael paused to add, "I telephoned headquarters this afternoon, and they told me there were no prints on the kris. Also I made two other telephone calls to that city, but of those I will tell you later."

He opened the door and stepped outside, but was back almost instantly, "Tuan MacAlistair wishes to speak to you, Sir."

Bruce advanced slowly into the room.

"What's on your mind, MacAlistair?" the officer asked, shocked at the sight of Bruce's haggard face.

"What was Harry trying to remember for you, Campbell, do you mind telling me?" Bruce asked abruptly.

"I don't know, MacAlistair. I only wish I did. This morning when I was talking to him, he told me he felt sure that something had happened sometime which he had thought unimportant, but which really held the clue to these murders. He asked me to give him until teatime to remember. When I stopped in the dining hall at lunch time, he told me that he had re-membered. You heard him,—you must all have heard him. I couldn't wait then to hear what it was, for Mr. DeKok was in a bad way. I thought he'd go out on my hands before I could get him to the doctor. When I came back, I found that Mr. Gordon had been killed. I'd give ten years of my life if I had waited."

"I wish to God you had," muttered Bruce. "To think of Harry struck down like that—" his face twitched, and he had to pause a moment to control his voice. "I knew he had something on his mind," Bruce went on more calmly. "I met him walking in the old pal-ace gardens when I was up there this morning with Miss Ames. He was very abstracted,—he didn't tell us anything definite, just said that he couldn't stop because he was trying to recall something. At tiffin too, he seemed to be in a fog, and when Miss Ames asked him whether he had had a nice walk, he said he hadn't. Then, suddenly something happened. His face lighted up. I happened to be watching him at the moment, and right after that he jumped up to speak to you. Whatever it was he was trying to remember, came back to him at lunch."

Campbell's face was eager. "Well, that's something anyway. Can you recall anything that happened at tiffin today that bore any relation to another event, say to dinner last night?"

Bruce began to pace restlessly back and forth. "That's what is worrying me. Ever since Ailsa's death, I've been convinced that the clue to it lay in the conversation we had at dinner last night,—I mean the general conversation. There were currents, and cross currents, and one or two really nasty moments. I've gone over and over it in my mind, but I'm damned if I can put my finger on it."

The officer watched him anxiously. "Can't you think, MacAlistair? You must be right, for Gordon had the same impression."

Despondently Bruce shook his head. "It's no go. I know the answer is there, and that's the only thing I do know."

For a minute or two Campbell stared into space while a puzzled frown knotted his forehead. "I tell

you what, MacAlistair," he said with sudden determination, "suppose you tell me everything that you can
remember about the dinner last night, every least little detail, and between the three of us, we may hit it.
I'd feel a lot safer if you were here with me when you
remember the vital fact. Your life wouldn't be worth
the snap of my fingers, if the murderer guessed what
you have hidden away in your mind."

Bruce's smile was grim. "I wish to God the swine
would tackle me. All I ask is to get my fingers around
his neck."

"I doubt whether you'd have the opportunity,
MacAlistair. The bird we are up against strikes in the
dark, and from the rear, and I'm not putting you out
as bait. Sit down here, now, and go over every blessed thing you can recall. Take as long as you like, and
just forget I'm here, or McCloud. All you have to do
is to think out loud."

Slowly and painfully at first, Bruce began to relate
the events of the night before. This time there was
no reason to omit the part that Harry had played
in forcing Bruce to join the dinner party. Bruce's
lips were white as he spoke of his friend, and the
officer's eyes gleamed with interest, but he refrained
from interruption lest he break the flow of reminis-
cence. Bruce seemed to himself to be back once more
at that festive dinner, and details, many of them
irrelevant, poured forth—the smooth sheen of Ailsa's burnished hair—the way Berenice's rouge had

stood out against the pallor of her cheeks, the feverish intensity with which Janet had watched her
husband—Bob's set, unhappy face,—Dick Durham's
elephantine efforts to be playful and to divert Ailsa's attention from his young rival,—Harry's flare of
anger as Ailsa flaunted her subjection of Berenice.
Word by word he recreated the scene; sentence by
sentence he repeated the conversation that had taken
place, and his own impressions of the guests' varying reactions. As he came to Dick's sensational offer
of a position, both Campbell and McCloud leaned
forward eagerly. They could visualize the triumph
in Dick's face as he told of the arrangement he had
made with Bob, the relief in Harry's, the dismay in
Janet's, the light in Bob's—and then the anticlimax
of Ailsa's refusal to leave the East. Bob's silent disappointment, Harry once more grim, Jack relieved,—
Janet skeptical. The ugliness then, of the way Dick
had turned on Ailsa!

Gently the door of the Recreation Room opened
and Ismael entered. Annoyed at the interruption,
Campbell waved him to a seat explaining briefly, "Mr.
MacAlistair is describing what took place at dinner
last night. You'd better listen in."

Bruce's attention however, had been distracted,
and he had lost the trend of his thoughts.

"Go on, MacAlistair," Campbell encouraged him,
"what did Mrs. Brownley say in answer to Durham's
accusations?"

Bruce passed an impatient hand across his eyes.

"It's gone. I can't think.—No, I don't believe Ailsa replied directly to Durham. I think she said something about talking to him later, but it was more to quiet him down than anything else, I imagine. I didn't pay much attention to that, I was watching Harry's performance with his boy."

"What was that, Tuan?" Ismael asked sitting up very straight.

"Why nothing much, Harry had forgotten his cigarette case, and he sent one of the Chinese boys to tell Mahat to bring it down to him. Poor Harry always forgot his case—he did the same thing at lunch today. O, Good Lord!" Bruce jumped to his feet, "That must have been it. Something about his cigarette case. Yes, it was just after Mahat had brought him his case that I saw Harry's face light up. But, what could that have had to do with the murders?"

The room was tense with excitement, as three pairs of eyes watched Bruce's struggle to remember more, just a little more.

"What did Mr. Gordon do last night when Mahat brought his case?" Campbell asked softly.

"Why, Mahat is latah, and Harry showed us all how a latah aped whatever he saw done."

"Latah!" Ismael jumped to his feet, his voice trembling with emotion. "Mahat is latah, and no one told me. Allah, why was your servant such a stupid pig? That is the answer, Tuan, that is the answer!"

Bruce and Campbell and McCloud turned to eye Ismael in amazement.

"Chelaka (*wretch, a very strong Malay oath*)! It was Mahat that committed the crimes. Poor, sick Mahat. But he was not the guilty one, he was just the instrument. Some white devil used his affliction."

"My God, Ismael, you're right. That would explain all the impossible things that happened in this case," Campbell's words tumbled over each other in their excitement. "A sharp word, a gesture—and Mahat would have imitated it. Lord, how diabolical. The murderer was safe. If Mahat carried out his instructions, well and good,—if he failed, if anything went wrong, then Mahat was the guilty one. What chance would the poor devil have stood? Ismael, we'll have to get Mahat."

"Yes, Tuan, already I have given instructions. He will be found, never fear, but it may take time. There were many strange natives here for the Sultan's birthday. It means tracking them all to their homes."

"You think Mahat has run away?" asked McCloud.

"But yes, what else was there for him, when he realized he had killed his master. He would have been terrified, for who could be expected to believe that another was directing him? He ran away as soon as he saw his Tuan was dead, and as he went, he threw the knife into the bushes."

"It does seem plausible," Bruce said, "Mahat could have approached Ailsa without alarming her. She'd

assume he had a message for her from Berenice or
Harry, or one of the guests. And Harry, knowing of
Mahat's infirmity would have been likely to remem-
ber it when the same scene was repeated this noon.
But who was devilish enough to devise such a plot?"

"Which of the guests seemed particularly inter-
ested last night in Mahat's being latah, MacAlistair?
Try to remember what everyone said and did," urged
Campbell.

Bruce thought hard for a moment. "As Mahat came
up to the table, Harry spoke to him sharply and threw
his napkin on the floor. Mahat immediately imitated his gesture by throwing down the cigarette case
he was bringing. Everybody laughed. I think Harry
only did it to create a diversion and relieve the strain
we had all felt during the scene Durham made. Miss
Ames was very much interested, I remember, and
asked several questions about latahs. Harry then
pushed Bob, and Mahat promptly pushed him too.
Dick Durham was greatly intrigued and he tried
Mahat out by throwing a glass on the floor. Mahat immediately did the same thing. Bob interfered
then and told Harry to stop the performance, that it
wasn't sporting. Harry agreed and sent Mahat away.
The poor boy looked awfully sheepish and was glad
enough to go."

"Why did no one tell me this before?" Ismael's
voice was almost a moan of anguish, "Not a word of
it have I heard, not even from the servants!"

"I think that is explicable," Bruce said comfortingly. "Harry said that Mahat was very self-conscious, that the other servants made his life such a burden on the estate that Harry had forbidden them to make Mahat perform. He said when he took Mahat off with him on trips such as this, the boy never mixed with the other servants because he was afraid they would discover he was latah. He always slept outside Harry's door, spent most of his time there."

"I'll find out whether anybody saw Mahat the night of Mrs. Brownley's murder. He told me he was at the kampong until late," Ismael announced.

"Ahmat told me he saw him at the wayangs," Bruce volunteered, "but it will be difficult checking up the time of his return, I'm afraid. I don't remember seeing him at all after dinner, either when I went to my room or when I left it, though that doesn't mean much. If he was sitting or lying quietly in the shadow by Harry's door, any of us might pass a dozen times without noticing him."

"Mrs. Gordon said that he was there this afternoon when she went to her room, but that later, when she wanted a drink, he wasn't around. That was just about the time of the third murder, I imagine, but try to pin her down more closely."

"Why didn't the Chinese boys tell me?" Ismael was pursuing his own line of thoughts, "They must have seen what happened at dinner last night. They must have known that Mahat was latah!"

"Not necessarily, Ismael," Bruce objected. "It was toward the end of the meal. Guests were moving away from the other tables, and we were all making a lot of noise. I don't remember that there were any waiters around our table at all just then."

"You know even yet, I can't quite credit this latah business," put in McCloud. "Did you ever hear of a murder being carried out that way before, Ismael?"

"Yes, once, Tuan. Malays are usually kind to people so afflicted. They will make them show off, yes, but they are careful not to get them into serious trouble. This other murder was caused by a Chinese merchant who made one of the boys in his shop kill a man to whom he owed money. It happened many years ago, and all my people were very angry when the truth became known. To them it is like forcing a child to do wrong."

"I suppose Mahat's fingerprints will be on the knife, Ismael," Campbell interrupted, "but you might as well go ahead and take the prints of everyone in the Rest House. There's always a chance that the real murderer may have handled the knife at some time." Ismael and Campbell exchanged a significant look over Bruce's head.

"Thank you for your help, Mr. MacAlistair," the officer said. "I want to impress upon you the necessity for secrecy, not just for our sakes but for your own. Remember that two people have been killed for knowing what you know. You mustn't mention it to a soul, no matter how innocent you may think them."

Bruce nodded his acceptance of the warning. "It is unbelievably horrible. I can't realize it yet." He sensed the desire of the policemen to be rid of him, and went slowly toward the door.

Campbell's anxious eyes followed him. "For God's sake be careful, MacAlistair. Keep away from the shrubbery. Don't sit with your back to an open door or window, and above all, when you go to your room, make sure that the door is bolted. Remember, we don't know yet whether the murderer is a man or a woman, but whoever it is, the murderer is watching every one of you, ready to kill anyone who betrays a suspicion of his identity. Unless you watch your step, you will be the next to die."

CHAPTER XVII

Ismael moved quickly to Campbell's side as the door closed after Bruce. "The murderer used Mahat to kill Mem Brownley, and Tuan Gordon, of that I am sure,—but I do not think Mahat killed Mem DeKok."

"No, I don't see how he could have," Campbell said. "No native would have used that cotton wool in the first place, and even granting that the principal fixed the bolt, I doubt whether he'd have risked using Mahat for that murder. Remember, I was just downstairs, and everyone knew I was there. I sleep lightly and the murderer would not only have had to arouse Mahat, but he, or she, would have had to force the boy to go to Mrs. DeKok's room and stand inside the door with him before making the fatal gesture. It would be dark in the room too, so that the latah couldn't have seen the gesture,—and if he had spoken to Mahat, Mrs. DeKok would have been likely to wake."

"Yes, Tuan. The impulse of a latah dies quickly. Unless the murderer was close at hand, Mahat would have come to himself and run away. He would not carry out the crime alone. With Mem Brownley, it was different. The murderer could accompany Mahat, could whisper the fatal words,—in the bright moonlight, his gesture could be seen. All the murderer had to do then would be to slip back into the Rest House, and then when Mem Brownley cried out, run out on the lawn again. The same with Tuan Gordon. He lay alone on the veranda. All the murderer had to do was to stand inside the door of the hall, make a gesture of stabbing, and point to Tuan Gordon. But, in the case of Mem DeKok, the real murderer must have done the actual stabbing."

"I wish we had Mahat here," Campbell sighed. "We haven't any real proof of our theory until we get a confession from him. We can't even be sure that his fingerprints will be on the knife."

"I think it is as well that Mahat ran away," Ismael remarked drily. "The murderer would never have let him live after his work was done. If Mahat had not fled, he would by this time have been even further beyond our questions."

"You're probably right. It was only by a fluke we were put on to the plot. Twice the murderer was lucky. Mrs. DeKok must have seen the murderer with Mahat on the lawn. Very likely too, she had seen the demonstration Mr. Gordon made with him at dinner, or she may have known from some other sources that Mahat was latah. She has lived out here for years, and was interested in the natives—remember her comment on the difference in the wayangs here and in Java? The murderer must have noticed her on the veranda, after he had sent Mahat on his fatal errand,—and so she died. Again, with Mr. Gordon—the murderer overheard him tell me he had remembered, and so Gordon's lips were closed with the knife."

"Such luck cannot last indefinitely, Tuan," Ismael hesitated, glancing at the eager face of the young magistrate who was absorbing each word of their conversation. "Tuan McCloud, you will pardon me a moment if I take Tuan Campbell aside? What I have to tell him is something too dangerous to share even with so good a friend as yourself."

McCloud flushed, but he answered readily, "Go right ahead, don't mind me. I'm going to take a turn outside and stretch the cramps out of my legs."

"Thank you, Tuan. Five minutes will suffice. You will understand that it is not because I distrust you, but the secret of the murderer's identity must be revealed to no one yet. A look, a word, and we might have still another murder on our hands."

"Good Lord! Do you know who it is?" McCloud stared with awe at Ismael's inscrutable smile. "Don't tell me. I shouldn't have asked. See you later."

Campbell's rugged face twitched with excitement as he and Ismael were left alone. "How in heaven's name did you get on to it, Ismael? Who is it? Don't keep me in suspense. "

"I told you, Tuan, that I made two other telephone calls to Singapore. It was the last that gave me the information I needed." His voice dropped to a whisper as he gave his chief a résumé of the facts.

"Good work, Ismael!" the officer exclaimed. "It all clicks, but I wouldn't have hit it in a thousand years. If only we had some proof!"

"We mustn't go too fast," Ismael warned him. "Our case must be clear before we make a move. I don't yet see how it can be done. I will, of course, take the fingerprints of all in the Rest House, and send them down to Singapore with the knife, for comparison with any that may be on the knife, but I think we will find only Mahat's. Somehow I feel sure that Mahat wouldn't have wiped off the handle. When he realized that he had killed his master, his impulse would be to throw the weapon from him. He didn't even hide it."

"Yes, and that raises the question of where the knife was concealed between the time of Mrs. De-Kok's murder, and that of Gordon's. It wasn't in any of the rooms you searched."

"There is only one place where it could have been, Tuan. It must have been hidden on the person of the murderer."

"Good Lord! that means it was in this very room then when I was innocently questioning the guilty person. I spoke to each person as they came downstairs, before they went outside at all,—all, that is except Gordon,—so the knife must have been here. By George, you know, Ismael, that took nerve."

"O the murderer is clever, Tuan, far cleverer I think than we realize even now. But slowly the tide is turning. We know at last how the crimes were committed, and more important even than that, the guilty one does not know that we know. We will say, I think, nothing at all about Mahat. Let the murderer think we are still groping among the shadows. I go now to take the fingerprints, and I will tell our young friend McCloud that he may return."

"All right, and you might ask Mrs. Gordon casually whether she noticed what time it was when she found Mahat was among the missing."

Campbell's heart was lighter than it had been for many hours, as he sat quietly in his chair and reviewed the case in the light of the information which Ismael had just given him. McCloud slipped into the room and settled himself at his table. Though his eyes danced with ill-concealed excitement, he bent over his work without disturbing the officer.

"Come in!" Campbell started at the sound of a rap on the door, which immediately opened as Bob Brownley stepped across the threshold.

"May I speak to you just a moment, Campbell. I have something important to tell you." His voice trembled with excitement.

"Of course, Brownley, come in. What's wrong?" The officer looked with concern at Bob's white, worried face and trembling hands.

Carefully Bob closed the door, and cast a hurried glance around the small room before he stepped close

to the officer's side and whispered huskily, "My revolver! It's gone!"

"What's that!" Campbell exclaimed.

"My revolver has disappeared," Bob repeated. "I
always carried it with me. It was in my bureau drawer
the last time I saw it, under my handkerchiefs."

Campbell was visibly agitated. "When was that?"
he asked.

"I think it was there this morning, but I'm so used
to seeing it that it is hard to remember."

"What kind of a revolver was it?"

"It was a Webley-Scott,—a thirty-two. I got a bit
nervous this afternoon after Harry was killed, and
I wanted to be sure my revolver was there so that I
could have it under my pillow tonight." Bob's smile
was apologetic. "I admit all these murders have put
my steam up. You don't know who to trust. The atmosphere is thick with suspicion and fear. I went upstairs about twenty minutes ago, thinking I might
get a little confidence from the feel of my revolver,
and it was gone. I've looked for it high and low. I was
sure I'd put it in my drawer, but you know how it is.
I couldn't swear it wasn't somewhere else in the room
until I'd turned all my belongings inside out. I sent
for the roomboy then, and he declared by all the gods
of his fathers that he hadn't seen it."

"Mrs. Brownley wouldn't have taken it would she?"
McCloud asked.

"No. Ailsa was terrified of guns. She wouldn't touch one with a ten foot pole. She hated the very sight of mine. That's why I hid it under my handkerchiefs."

Campbell's face was serious. "I don't like your news at all, Brownley. The person who committed the murders is absolutely ruthless, and if he or she took your revolver, I hate to think what will happen here tonight."

"But what can you do?" Bob asked in a despairing voice. "Will you make a search?"

"I don't know just what tack to take, to tell you the truth, Brownley," the officer said slowly. "The person who took it will be expecting that move. It wouldn't be hidden in the murderer's room, that's certain, and he's not likely to have it on his person. I'll talk it over with Ismael and see what we'd better do. Just leave things to me."

Bob's face showed his disappointment. "I hope you locate it, Campbell. I hate to think what may happen tonight if you don't. The murderer may be planning to clean us all out."

"I don't expect that, Brownley. All of these murders were committed with a purpose. We aren't dealing with a homicidal maniac. The only person who would have anything to fear, would be one who suspected the identity of the murderer."

Bob leaned forward. "Have you any clues? Have you found out anything yet?"

Campbell's glance was sharp, but his voice was suave as he answered, "No, there's nothing to tell yet. You will have to be patient. By the way, has the undertaker come from Singapore?"

"Yes," Bob said, "he's upstairs now. He is going to look after Harry too. We'll just have a simple service for them tomorrow morning in the chapel. Berenice didn't have any idea what she wanted done, but I suggested that Harry be buried here, and she seemed relieved. Harry hasn't any family, no one except Berenice, and I imagine she will sell the estate as soon as she can, so there was no object in burying him in Sumatra. Harry didn't have any roots in England either. He seems to belong here in the East. It's a funny thing, Campbell, but do you know Harry hasn't been back to England for ten years, though he had all the money he wanted and could easily have gone there to live, bought a fine, old place, raised a family. I'd give anything I own, if I could only go back to England once more—just to see grey skies again, and hedgerows, and apple orchards. My eyes ache from the sight of these eternal blue skies and blazing colors."

Campbell's surprise at Brownley's outburst was modified by pity. "I guess you're homesick, Brownley. This exile's life we lead gets all of us once in a while, and you've had a bad time these last couple of days."

"I've had a bad time ever since I left home," Bob corrected. "At first I didn't mind so much, for we were traveling around, but from the moment we settled down, I realized I was one of those damnfool Englishmen who can never be happy away from his native heath."

"Why didn't you go back, Mr. Brownley, if you felt that way?" asked McCloud with eager sympathy.

"I always expected to sometime. But Ailsa wouldn't hear of it. She hated England. Her experience there had been very different from mine, you see. The happiest days of my life were spent there, while her happiest times have been out here." He stopped abruptly as though just aware that he had an audience for his thoughts. "I'm sorry. I didn't mean to bore you. I just can't help feeling that if Ailsa had been willing to accept Durham's offer, she would still be alive, and probably Mrs. DeKok and Harry too. As for me," his face darkened, "it was like having the gates of heaven slammed shut in front of me. I know now that I will never go back, never see England again."

Campbell looked at him helplessly. He had dealt with homesick men in his time, but Bob's feeling was somehow deeper than that, and the officer felt all the typical Britisher's selfconsciousness at seeing into another man's heart. He was relieved when Bob, with an effort, seemed to shake off his depression. "Well, I'll be getting along. Let me know if you find the revolver, or if there is anything I can do."

"Thanks, Brownley. Oom Ling is going to serve tea on the veranda, you'd better go out and get a cup. It will steady those shaky nerves of yours."

Slowly Bob opened the door and went out into the hall.

"That poor devil is lonesome," McCloud said. "I don't believe he has a friend in the world. Gave up everything for that wife of his,—and now that she's gone, he has nothing. I never felt so sorry for anyone in my life as I did for him just now."

"Yes," Campbell agreed, "he's pathetic. The only person he cares about is MacAlistair—he watches him with a sort of doglike expression in his eyes,—and MacAlistair doesn't see it at all. As far as MacAlistair is concerned, the friendship stopped ten years ago. O well, life's a funny thing, and I think sometimes it's funnier in the East than it is anywhere on earth." With a shrug, the officer dismissed his annoying thoughts, they verged on the sentimental, and his job allowed him no time for sentiment. "I must find Ismael and tell him about that revolver right away. It looks to me as though we were in for more trouble tonight. I wonder whether the murderer guessed that MacAlistair put us on to Mahat, or whether that revolver is going to be used on one of the others?"

CHAPTER XVIII

Tea was being served on the veranda by deft-fingered Chinese waiters, and the guests were assembled in small groups around the scattered rattan tables. At a casual glance, the scene was conventionally cheerful, a sun, grown old and feeble with the day's expenditure of energy, sent slanted, benignant rays across the fluttering, bright-colored chiffon dresses of the women, and the starched white suits of the men, but Campbell who stood quietly in the doorway noted only the strained atmosphere, and the nervous tension that had tightened so perceptibly during the day. Teacups rattled in trembling hands, spoons dropped from nerveless fingers, voices were shrill with an excitement that verged on hysteria.

It was interesting to see how the party had split up. MacAlistair and the American girl were seated side by side, and she seemed to be doing her utmost to arouse him from the somberness of his thoughts which were reflected in the grim lines of his tanned face. Her voice was gay, too gay to be natural. Her brother, Jack, had joined forces with the American family and was absent-mindedly answering the staccato questions put to him by the older woman. The father's voice was subdued, and the pretty, pert face of the daughter had lost its vivacity. Her silver-slippered foot swung restlessly back and forth. Wetherby, just returned from work, hovered solicitously around the fragile figure of Berenice who lay motionless in a long chair, her face white and pinched. At the remaining table, Dick and Janet sat rapt in a pregnant silence, their eyes pointedly avoiding each other as they mechanically drank cup after cup of strong, reviving tea. The bamboo screens had been rolled up to the veranda roof, and the chair in which Harry had been killed had been banished to parts unknown, but the freshly swabbed floor boards where the chair had stood, were still damp, a mute reminder of the tragedy which had taken place so short a time before. Unwilling eyes crept toward it, were hastily averted, only to slink back at the first unguarded moment.

At a sound behind him, Campbell turned to let Bob Brownley pass out onto the porch. There seemed to be no place left for him, though Oom Ling quickly motioned for a waiter to bring another table. Bob stood hesitating, uncertain where to go until Bruce jumped to his feet saying, "Come over and sit with us, Bob." At his words, Bob's sagging shoulders lifted and his face brightened. "Thanks, old man, I will, if Susan doesn't mind?" His voice was questioning as he picked his way past the American group, and Berenice and Wetherby.

"Of course not, Bob, sit down here by me, and I'll do an imitation of a mother robin feeding her young!" Susan said with forced gaiety, motioning to the chair which Bruce had drawn up.

"You mean like a mother cockatoo, don't you, Susan? I can't imagine a respectable robin in this tropical setting," Bob said, seating himself.

"O don't be so technical, Bob. It's the mother bird instinct that counts, not the species. Here's some nice hot tea for you,—and toast that once was hot. There's some mango preserve too, to disguise its leathery texture."

"Not much like those teas my old Scotch nurse used to fix up for us, is it Bruce? Remember those scones, and the shortbread, and raisin cookies?" Bob's thoughts, stirred by his conversation with Campbell, were still on England, a refuge from the tragic horror of the present.

"Other times, other customs," murmured Bruce. "You seem to forget the sloppy, lukewarm stuff they fed us at school, and the thick slices of bread and butter,—lots of bread and very little butter."

Bob's strained face grew almost boyish again. "Still, it tasted pretty good to us after a hard game of rugger."

"Don't boast to me about your English schools," Susan said, pleased at the way the men's tenseness was relaxing, "I may be just an ignorant American, but I was brought up on Charles Dickens, and I don't see how any little English boy who was sent away to school ever lived to reach maturity."

Ismael who had been making his way unostentatiously from table to table, now stood in front of them. "Please, if you don't mind, I wish to have your fingerprints on these cards."

Startled, they all looked up into his bland, brown face.

"Why yes, of course, Ismael," Susan said, recovering from her surprise, "ladies first, I suppose. What do I do?"

"The cards are marked, as you see, 'Right thumb, left thumb, right first digit, left first digit,' and so on. Just place each of your fingers on this ink pad, and then on its proper place on the card. So, and turn it, so! That is right." Ismael picked up the card as Susan finished, and placed one in turn for Bruce and Bob.

"What are you taking these for?" Bob asked as Ismael collected the cards. "Did you find another clue, or are you checking up on the kris?"

"It is merely a formality, Tuan, for our records of the case," Ismael said vaguely, as he moved over to the Durhams' table.

"I wonder whether anything has turned up," Bob's forehead was wrinkled into a worried frown. "I wish he hadn't come along just then. These are the first pleasant moments I have had in weeks, and now they are spoiled." His face once more was haggard.

"Ismael seems to be having a tough time convincing Dick and Janet of their civic duty," Bruce whispered, watching the group at the next table.

"I'll put my money on Ismael," Susan said. "He's about as flexible as the Rock of Gibraltar, don't you think so, Bob?"

"And about as communicative, too," Bob muttered. "I think I'm entitled to know what's going on around here. God, it's awful to be so helpless!" With sudden decision, he laid his napkin on the table. "If you will excuse me, I'm going in to see Campbell."

Susan smiled at him vaguely as he rose. She was still intent on the scene at the next table. "There," she breathed to Bruce, "he's got them. Do I win, or —do I win!"

"I don't remember anyone taking you up. Personally, I don't consider it good ethics to bet on a certainty," Bruce chided.

Instead of rallying to her own defense, Susan lapsed into silence, and Bruce sank back into his melancholy thoughts of Harry. A teaspoon clattered to the wooden floor, with all the effect of an exploded bomb and the alarmed guests all turned reproachfully to stare at Berenice. "I'm sorry," Berenice said in a small voice, "it just slipped. My fingers don't seem to be able to hold things anymore."

Susan jumped to her feet, "I can't stand this place any longer. I've got the jitters. If I don't get away for a little while, I'll be chewing the chair rungs."

Bruce looked up in surprise. "What's the matter? I was just thinking that you showed more courage than any of us."

"That was just bluff,—whistling to keep my spirits up, but I can't do it anymore." There were tears in her voice. Swiftly Bruce rose. "Come on, let's take a stroll."

In the meantime, Ismael, having worn down the resistance of the Durhams and obtained the coveted fingerprints, rejoined Campbell in the Recreation Room.

"I have them all now, Tuan, except Mahat's."

"Did you have any trouble getting them?" Campbell asked, shuffling through the pile of cards that Ismael handed him.

Ismael eyed his chief obliquely. "I had no trouble, Tuan, until I reached Tuan and Mem Durham. At the start they both refused, but in due course I persuaded them to be reasonable."

"How did you do it, Ismael?" The officer's eyes twinkled.

"It was quite simple. I just spoke about how uncomfortable the beds were in our local jail. I apologized politely because it had been built to accommodate natives instead of the superior white race."

"You shouldn't have threatened them, Ismael. You know we couldn't have arrested them," Campbell reproached him.

Ismael's childlike eyes opened wide. "But I said nothing of arrest, Tuan. I merely described one of the places of local interest. Surely visitors to Johore would want to know about our public buildings."

McCloud chuckled. "Good for you, Ismael. I hope you scared the fool out of Durham. My hands fairly itch to take a pass at that smug face of his every time I see it."

Abruptly Campbell changed the subject. "Brownley came in a little while ago, all upset about the fingerprinting. Not that he objected to it, but because he felt we were holding out something on him. He said he had the right to know how the inquiry was shaping, and whether we had any new clues. After all, it's natural that he should be anxious, so I felt I ought to tell him that we had discovered the knife that we thought was used to kill Mrs. DeKok and Mr. Gordon. I didn't say anything about Mahat's disappearance though, and I warned him not to tell any of the others about the knife."

Ismael nodded. "I think he will keep it a secret, Tuan. How is he bearing up?"

"He's nervous, apparently, like the rest of them, and he's still very much concerned about the loss of his revolver. I don't like the look of things at all, Ismael. The whole outfit is keyed up to the breaking point, and with one of them possessed of a revolver,—I hate to think of what may happen before the night is over."

"You need not worry longer about the revolver, Tuan. I know where it is," Ismael announced calmly, and stepping close to Campbell's side, whispered something in an undertone. The officer started back. "Are you sure, Ismael? It seems impossible."

"My lips may lie sometimes, Tuan, but not my eyes. I said that the murderer was cleverer than even we thought. Still, we dare not move."

Campbell moved to the window, throwing back the shutters which had barred the sunlight from the room earlier in the day, and stared into the darkness of the tropic night which, like a curtain, had dropped down suddenly over the familiar lawn and trees. "We can't tell where the murderer will strike next, Ismael, and I can't forget that I'm responsible for the lives of the people in this house. Already two of those in my charge have been killed. I'm worried about Mac-Alistair. What are we going to do?"

"First, Tuan, I would come away from that open window. Your suit is not fresh, but it is still white enough to make a good target for a thirty-two bullet," Ismael remarked casually. "You are too modest for your own good. You think the revolver disappeared in order to end the life of one of the guests. You forget that you now have the doubtful honor of being the most dangerous adversary left to the murderer."

Campbell sprang back hastily. "By Jove, I never thought of that."

"As you so wisely said some time back, Tuan," Ismael went on in even tones as he carefully closed the shutters again, "until Mahat is captured, we have no real evidence against the murderer. We can prove nothing. But it is possible that the murderer too, is nervous and overwrought as are the other people in the Rest House. Furthermore, it is now possible that the slayer will make a false move that will enable us to make an arrest."

"Lord, Ismael, I don't dare hope for so lucky a break!"

"I think, if you are willing, Tuan, it might be arranged." Ismael glanced apologetically at McCloud. "Once more, Tuan McCloud, for your own good health, it will be wise for you to close your ears while Tuan Campbell and I converse in soft tones."

The young magistrate grinned. "I'm apt to die any minute of curiosity, but don't let a little thing like that stop you. Shall I go outside?"

"No, that won't be necessary, McCloud," Campbell assured him. "Just cover up your ears, and try to pretend you aren't here. Your Malay isn't equal to Ismael's flow of conversation, once he gets started."

Obediently McCloud covered his ears and began to sing tunelessly "Nearer My God to Thee," while in his own musical language, the little Malay outlined his plan.

"Fine, Ismael. You're a genius to have thought that out," Campbell exclaimed in enthusiasm as his assistant finished. "We'll work things out just as you suggest. After dinner, I will put the screws on all of them. Several of the guests are still holding out important information—"

"Campbell! Ismael! There at the window! Quick!" McCloud yelled dashing for the door. "Someone was outside listening." As he raced from the room, Ismael sprang to the window. "Keep back in that corner, Tuan," he yelled over his shoulder to Campbell who had started to follow him. Throwing open the shutters, Ismael leaned out, his keen eyes piercing the darkness that covered the deserted lawn. "Who was it? Could you see?" he asked as McCloud rounded the corner of the house and came up to the window.

"No, damn it all. I just happened to notice a white blur outside the shutters, and I let off a yell. It might have been anybody." The magistrate's voice was disgruntled. "Whoever it was got clean away. I didn't see hair nor hide of him."

"Could it have been a woman?" inquired Campbell, coming out of his corner.

"It could have been the devil himself, as far as I could see," snorted McCloud.

"Was there anyone on the veranda, or in the hall, as you went through?" asked Ismael.

"No, the place seemed to be deserted, except for the chinks. They were busy setting the tables for dinner."

"Well, it doesn't matter," Ismael soothed the annoyance from McCloud's face. "Whoever it was could have heard nothing of importance, thanks to your vigilance."

"No, I don't believe he, or she, could have heard anything. I happened to be staring at the window the whole time, and I yelled as soon as I saw someone there." McCloud turned away. "I'll go around the other side of the house and see whether anyone is hanging around."

A few minutes later he once more came into the room. "Not a sign of anyone, Campbell, I'm sorry. The Chinese boys said that no one had come into the hall, so I suppose whoever it was slipped up the outside staircase after I'd run around back."

"Well, don't worry," Campbell said. "You'd better cut along now and get some dinner so that you can be back here around nine. I'll want you here when I haul some of our friends over the coals."

"Why, you couldn't keep me away," McCloud declared, picking up his notes and stowing them carefully in the inside pocket of his coat.

Ismael once more firmly closed the shutters, and then turned to face Campbell who was addressing him. "You'd better hop along too, Ismael, and send those fingerprints down to Singapore. The expert there called me up a while ago and said that there was just one set of prints on the handle of the knife. They looked like a woman's, but they might have been Ma-hat's—all Malays have small hands. I told him then that I'd send the fingerprints of all our suspects down to him, and he agreed to match them up with those on the knife, and call me back. He's waiting for them, and we don't want to spoil any more of the poor devil's Saturday night than we can help."

Ismael hesitated. "I don't like to leave you alone, Tuan."

"Don't be an ass, Ismael," Campbell frowned, "I guess I can look out for myself for an hour or so, when I've been doing it for the last forty years."

"Well then," the Malay gave in, "one thing I respectfully request, Tuan. That you do not leave this room until I return. Remember, the whole success of our plan depends upon you, and outside this room, your life hangs by a silken thread."

CHAPTER XIX

The painful ordeal of dinner was almost over, when Ismael slipped unostentatiously into the hall and made his way directly to the Recreation Room. A moment later, the overwrought nerves of the guests were shattered by the roar of a motorcycle on the driveway outside, followed by the appearance of young McCloud. With a nod and wave of greeting at the anxious faces turned fearfully toward him, the magistrate, too, disappeared into the little room beside the bar. The apprehensive silence which settled over the dining hall was finally broken by the opening of the Recreation Room door. All eyes were turned expectantly to the uniformed figure of Campbell silhouetted against the brightly lighted room, where young McCloud could be glimpsed behind a card table, with Ismael standing motionless beside him.

"If you have finished your dinner, I would like to have Mrs. Gordon, Mrs. Durham, Miss Ames, Mr. Durham, Mr. MacAlistair, Mr. Brownley and Mr. Ames come in here for a little while," the officer stated as his quick eyes rested in turn on the owner of each name. Reluctantly they rose and made their way down the long length of the room, filing one by one through the open door. The American family, Wetherby, and the few outside diners who had come to satisfy their curiosity felt defrauded as Oom Ling closed the door and stationed himself impassively in the hall beside it.

Inside the room, Campbell motioned the guests to be seated. "A number of things have come to light in the last few hours, but there are still many facts that the police must have before we can hope to capture the person who committed these brutal murders. I have asked you to come here in the hope that all of you who have withheld information will realize the importance of frankness." Several of the people in front of the officer moved uneasily in their chairs, but none of them offering any comment, Campbell went on. "I can understand your reluctance to divulge certain facts which would be embarrassing to you, and which you may have decided were irrelevant to the murders, but nevertheless, all of those things are essential to the success of the investigation. Only one among you has a real motive for concealing the truth—and that is the murderer. Don't forget that so long as the murderer is free, everyone in this room is in danger. Both Mrs. DeKok and Mr. Gordon were killed because they had information which the murderer feared they would pass on to me." He paused to let his words sink in, and then added, "I hope no one else will make the same mistake. If you have anything to tell me, tell me now, while we are all in this room where you will be protected."

The officer waited, anxiously scanning the faces before him. He could sense their tenseness. Here and there a hand was tightly clenched, a handkerchief was twisted nervously, a swinging foot jerked spasmodically. They eyed each other distrustfully, or watched him with eyes that dreaded his next words, but no one spoke.

With a half-repressed sigh, Campbell straightened his shoulders. "All right then, I'll have to get the information in my own way." His eyes rested on Susan. "Miss Ames, I'm not satisfied with the story you told me last night about your bridge debts."

Susan smothered a gasp of dismay, and Bruce and Jack glared at the officer. "You admitted that you owed Mrs. Brownley a large sum of money. In fact a memorandum addressed to you to that effect, in her handwriting is in our possession. Your explanation of your failure to pay the debt was that you did not have the money, but expected it to arrive next week. You also stated that Mrs. Brownley knew of your temporary embarrassment, and was willing to wait until then. Since she was aware of the situation, it seems to me that there could have been only two reasons for writing you as she did, demanding money which she knew you did not have. Either she wished deliberately to embarrass you because of some enmity, or she knew that you would not receive the money next week, and would not be able to pay her then. Which was it?"

Susan threw out her hands in a little gesture of protest as Jack sprang angrily to his feet. "What's the big idea, Campbell? Are you trying to pin the murders on my sister? She can take care of those debts herself, but if she couldn't pay them, I'd do it for her."

Campbell's voice was unruffled. "I'm not questioning your sister's honor, Mr. Ames, I am merely trying to discover Mrs. Brownley's opinion of it. Now, Miss Ames?"

"Sit down, Jack," Susan said, yanking her brother's coat, "I can look out for myself. I've nothing to hide." As Jack sank sulkily into his chair once more, she continued, "I don't know, of course, what Ailsa's object was in sending me that note, but I believe she thought I couldn't pay her. If that had been the case, I would have had to go to her and more or less throw myself on her mercy. It would naturally have been disastrous to me to have such a story circulated around the bridge tables in Singapore. She may simply have wanted to feel that I was in her power, or she may have resented my influence with my brother. After all, it is just idle speculation. As it happens, I will be able to pay my debts next week, as I said I would."

"Why then should she suppose you wouldn't?"

Susan flushed. "Because I was very foolish. I had told her that I expected a check from America, and in her talks with my brother she learned that our dividends had all been cut and that there wouldn't be any check from there. She didn't know that I had other resources and that I could procure the money without any difficulty."

"What are those resources?" Campbell demanded.

"That is beside the question, Mr. Campbell," Susan said with flashing eyes. "All that concerns you or anybody else is the fact that Mr. Brownley will have the money as soon as I can get to my bank in Singapore."

"Don't worry about that, Susan," Bob interrupted, "I wouldn't touch a penny of your money. I'm sure you can pay it, but I wish to go on record now that any bridge debts owed to Ailsa are cancelled."

Susan smiled at him. "I knew you'd probably feel that way, Bob, but I refuse to be released from my obligation. You can give it to charity if you like."

"Miss Ames, did you have any motive in continuing to play with Mrs. Brownley after you lost so consistently?" Campbell asked.

Susan's startled glance shifted back to the officer, and for the first time, she lost her composure. Her voice was almost pleading as she said, "Do we have to go into that?"

Campbell nodded.

"I'm sorry," she said simply. "Because I have no right to say anything, and I may have been terribly wrong, terribly unfair. I felt that there was something queer about Ailsa's game. I thought if I kept right on playing, I might discover how she always happened to win, but I found nothing. Either I was entirely wrong, or else she was too clever for me." She looked at Bob apologetically, but his eyes were shaded by his long slim hand. Berenice who had leaned forward breathlessly as Campbell started to question Susan, settled back comfortably in her chair.

"Thank you, Miss Ames," Campbell said, "that is what I wanted to know." He turned to the rest of the group. "Did any of you suspect that there was something wrong with Mrs. Brownley's playing?"

Janet Durham spoke up sharply. "I always thought it was too good to be true, and at the hotel I was warned against playing bridge with her, but I never actually saw anything out of the way."

Berenice cowered back in her chair as though to avoid the speculative look which Campbell bent upon her.

"Mrs. Gordon, you have probably played with Mrs. Brownley more often than anyone here. What is your opinion?"

Berenice looked around her, desperately seeking some means of escape. "I don't think you ought to ask me things like that about my friend," she protested.

Campbell's smile was grim. "So, there was something wrong. What was it?"

Berenice drew a fluttering breath and looked at Campbell with frightened eyes. "Yes," she whispered, "I knew she cheated."

A shock of surprise ran through the group.

"How did she manage it?" Campbell asked.

"I helped her. I had to. I had no choice," Berenice admitted with a despairing gesture. "I was under obligation to her, great obligation, and the only way I could repay her was by helping her win. It was nothing very wrong. We didn't stack the cards, or anything like that. Ailsa was a marvelous player, and ordinarily she won without any difficulty, but when the cards ran against her, if I wasn't her partner, why I would seem to lose my head, fumble my finesses, stick in psychic bids."

Campbell nodded. "And didn't your partners ever suspect?"

Berenice shook her head. "No, everyone knew what a good game Ailsa played, and nobody ever thought I had any card sense anyway. We deliberately created that impression, so that when Ailsa and I happened to play together and win, everyone thought it was her remarkable playing. When I was playing against her, and my partner and I lost, people just assumed it was my bad playing."

"I see," Campbell turned to Bob who was staring before him with stricken eyes. "Did you know of this arrangement, Mr. Brownley?"

"Good Lord no! Ailsa was an expert player. I never doubted the honesty of her game for a minute. In fact I don't believe it now." He glared at Berenice.

"Mrs. Gordon, you say that Mrs. Brownley forced you to help her. How could she do that?"

The officer directed his questions once more to Berenice.

"She threatened to tell my husband something. I would have done almost anything to have prevented Harry from learning it. I hope you won't make me go into that. I'd like to forget it all. I want to have a fresh start. Don't, please, make me tell you about it, Mr. Campbell."

"I'm sorry, Mrs. Gordon, but I'm afraid you will have to."

For a moment Berenice covered her face with her hands, and then to everyone's surprise she said, "Perhaps you're right. It may be better for me to tell the thing that has terrified me so long. I will be free of it then, and I won't have anything more to fear. That will be a new feeling for me—all my life I have been afraid of something." Her voice was firm and her eyes calm as she spoke to Campbell. "Up to the time I was twenty, I was afraid that life would pass me by, that I would remain buried alive in that little town in Surrey where I was born. I hated it there, and I was very unhappy until I escaped. Ailsa was the person who rescued me, and no matter what she did, what she was, I will always love her for that. She invited me to visit her in Shanghai. Everything went along beautifully for awhile, and then Bob lost his money. After that Ailsa and I began to take our bridge seriously and to make every cent we could out of it. Some days we'd do very well, and then again we'd have a streak of bad luck, when the cards ran against us. We couldn't afford that. The money we earned at bridge was all we really had to keep us going. The hotel where we stayed let us have rooms there cheap because Ailsa had so many parties, and her friends entertained there a lot, and we brought customers to certain exclusive shops who repaid us by giving us clothes for practically nothing. Bob did his best, but his automobile business didn't do very well. He didn't know about our bridge, or about the shops— he made such a fuss when he heard about the arrangements Ailsa made with the hotel that we didn't tell him about anything else. Finally Ailsa figured out a way that would assure us of always winning, and after that we worked the way I told you. We only played with people who had a lot of money, and they could afford to lose. All the time we counted upon my marrying well. That was our only hope, but nobody worthwhile came along until Harry came to Shanghai. He had all the requirements, and so," she hastily expurgated the story she had told Susan, "Ailsa managed to bring the marriage off. I could never have done it without her help."

"How did that profit Mrs. Brownley?" Campbell asked.

"Well, Harry made me a very generous allowance, and I sent half of it to Ailsa each month. If her expenses were unusually heavy, then I'd go up to Shanghai and visit her, or she'd come down to Sumatra and I'd lose a lot to her at bridge. Harry always paid my bridge debts, though he disapproved of my gambling as much as I did. After the Japanese began to make trouble in China, and Bob's business failed, she needed a lot more money than I dared give her. I was afraid to ask Harry for it, he had always resented my friendship for Ailsa. He thought she was a bad influence. Then one day he asked to see my checkbook, and he found out that I was dividing everything he gave me with her. He flew into a terrible rage and threatened all sorts of things. I was sick with fear. I knew that if I couldn't send Ailsa any more money, she would turn on me and tell Harry everything. Then she asked us to come over to Singapore and join the party she was planning here for the Sultan's birthday. At first Harry refused to come, but finally he said he wanted a showdown with Ailsa anyway and this was as good an opportunity as any. I lived in terror of what he would do. I knew that if he told Ailsa to leave me alone, Ailsa would turn on him and tell him things she knew about me, and I thought he would be so beside himself with rage that he'd kill her, and me too. When Ailsa was killed, I was sure that she had goaded Harry into doing it. If he had killed her, then I knew I was morally responsible, and I couldn't bear that. Ailsa had been awfully good to me. I owed all I had to her, and if she only hadn't been so hard-pressed for money, we would all have been happy. No one was ever more generous than she, when she had money." Her eyes overflowed with tears and her voice choked as she added, "It sounds terrible, but when I heard that Harry had been killed, I was almost glad, for it meant that he wasn't the murderer,—that I hadn't driven him to kill Ailsa." There was silence in the room as she finished.

Susan's lips twitched with cynical amusement as she listened to the carefully expurgated story that Berenice told, and noted its effect on the assembly. The chill with which they had regarded her had thawed perceptibly during her recital. Bruce and Jack and Dick were noticeably sympathetic; Janet's general hostility had relaxed, and Campbell's voice had lost its sternness. Young McCloud's eyes were soft with pity. There was even friendliness in the glances that Bob had cast at Berenice, though he had flinched sensitively at the revelations about his wife. Of them all, only Ismael seemed impervious to her pathos.

"Thank you, Mrs. Gordon. Now I want to ask you just one more question. Have you any idea what it was that your husband remembered just before he was killed?"

"No, I'm sorry," Berenice answered. "I was afraid to talk to Harry. As I said, I thought he had killed Ailsa, and I dreaded his telling me anything that might confirm my suspicions."

The officer consulted some notes which he had been holding in his hand, and then turned to Janet.

"Mrs. Durham, just before dinner last evening you were quarreling in your room with another woman. Was it Mrs. Brownley?"

Janet stiffened defensively. "No, it was not."

"Who was it?"

"If you really must know, it was Mrs. Gordon." Again there was a murmur of surprise as everybody once more looked at Berenice, who nodded without speaking.

"What were you quarreling about?"

Janet bit her thin lips. "It was hardly a quarrel," she said, "merely a difference of opinion. It had nothing to do with the murder."

"That is for me to judge," Campbell said sternly, "I have a reliable witness who overheard you, and I want to know what it was all about."

Her eyes flashed, but with an effort she controlled an angry retort, and answered with unaccustomed civility, "I wanted Mrs. Gordon to do a favor for me, and she refused."

"You weren't trying to persuade her to do away with Mrs. Brownley, were you?"

"Do you take me for a fool?" Janet scoffed. "Well, I suppose if I don't tell you, she will, and after all, there was nothing wrong. I wanted her to persuade Mrs. Brownley to stay in Singapore,—not to come to Manchester. I knew my husband was making a fool of himself, and from little things that he'd let slip, I suspected he was going to offer Mr. Brownley a position in the Manchester factory. Well, I didn't want the Brownleys in Manchester. I knew that Mrs. Gordon had lost heavily at bridge, and from what I could see of Harry's annoyance, I thought she might be afraid to ask him for the money to pay her debts. So, I told her that if she would persuade Ailsa to stay here, I'd give her the money for her bridge debts and she wouldn't have to go to her husband for it."

"And she refused?"

Janet laughed unpleasantly. "Yes, the little fool acted as if I'd insulted her. She simply wouldn't see reason at all. Apparently I'd been wrong in supposing she couldn't get the money from her husband." Janet dismissed the subject with a shrug of her thin shoulders.

"You must have been very anxious that Mrs. Brownley shouldn't go to Manchester to resort to such a scheme, Mrs. Durham. Just why were you afraid to have her go?"

Janet glared at him, and Durham shifted uneasily in his chair. "I didn't want her there. I didn't like having her make a fool of my husband. It was bad enough out here where no one mattered to me, but I wasn't going to have my family and friends back home know of his infatuation."

"But at dinner last night, you heard Mrs. Brownley refuse to go to England. Didn't that convince you?"

"No, I thought she was simply stalling for better terms. She knew that Dick was so keen about her that if she played her cards right, he would divorce me and marry her. He can't bear opposition, and he will pay any price to get what he wants. Usually after he gets it, it loses its value to him, but that would have been too late to help me."

"Did you approach Mrs. Gordon again on the subject?"

"Yes, I was desperate, and I still believed she could help me if she would. I made up my mind to tell her what Dick was planning, and so I asked her to come into my room with me when we went upstairs after the bridge game. She didn't want to, but I was so urgent that she couldn't very well refuse gracefully."

"What happened then?"

"We got along better that time. I apologized for offering her money and explained that I was desperate. She seemed to understand. I talked for a long time, telling her how Dick and I had worked together, and been happy until he began to make a lot of money. That made him discontented, with his home, and his friends, and me. He wanted to improve on all

of us, get something better. I showed her how vital
it was to me that Ailsa shouldn't come to England.
Berenice said that she was sure Ailsa had meant what
she said when she refused the Manchester job for
Bob,—that Ailsa didn't care a snap about Dick and
that she loved the East too much to leave it. She said
that Bob had had a lovely old place there in the country and that he had been crazy for years to go back to
England, but that Ailsa wouldn't hear of it. First she
persuaded him to rent it, and then when they were
hard up, she convinced him that he ought to sell it,
which he finally did."

A shudder passed over Bob's strained figure at
the mention of his old home, but he said nothing,
and Janet continued, "I felt a lot better to hear
that, and I began to think Berenice might be right
after all. I made up my mind that I'd have a showdown with Dick today and insist upon our sailing as
soon as we got back to Singapore."

"Mrs. Gordon," the officer looked at Berenice.
"Do you confirm what Mrs. Durham has said about
her conversations with you?"

"Yes, it was just as she said," Berenice replied.

"Do you think you succeeded in convincing her
that Mrs. Brownley wouldn't go to England?"

"I think so. She made me quite angry before dinner, but later that night she apologized, and when I
saw how upset she was, I tried to reassure her. I knew
Ailsa would never dream of marrying Dick, she used

to joke with me about him." A dark flush dyed Dick's face, but unconscious of the effect of her words, Berenice went on. "Of course, I didn't tell her that, but I said I was sure Ailsa would never dream of leaving the East. Mrs. Durham had calmed down a lot before I left, so I guess she believed me."

Once more Campbell consulted his notes. "Mr. Ames!" Jack started nervously. "Last night you said that someone had upset Mrs. Brownley just before you met her. When I asked you who it was, you refused to tell me. I hope, in view of all that has occurred since then, that you will think better of your decision, and will now give me the name of that person."

Jack hesitated. "I'm not absolutely sure of course, but as I stood there on the veranda, and Ailsa came up to me, I thought I recognized Durham walking down the road. I couldn't see his face, but he has a distinctive walk, a sort of bouncing strut, if you get my meaning. Anyway, I knew he was crazy about her, and he'd been pretty rough once or twice at dinner. I'd got his goat pretty badly on several occasions, and he resented her friendship for me. I noticed he kept the bar boy busy all the time he was playing bridge, so I just put two and two together. Last night I was a bit off my head, and I said a lot of things that must have sounded wild."

"You don't think it could have been Mr. Gordon you saw on the road?"

"No, it wasn't Harry. Harry was a lot taller, and he moved differently, more deliberately."

"I see," the officer looked down at his notes.

"Look here, Campbell," Dick broke in, "I told you that I'd been talking to Ailsa. What are you trying to do?"

The officer replied quietly, "Mr. Ames made certain ill-considered threats last night against the man he thought had been annoying Mrs. Brownley. This afternoon, Mr. Gordon was murdered. I wished to ascertain whether Mr. Ames had suspected Mr. Gordon of the murder."

"Good Lord!" the boy said sharply, "you don't think I killed Harry do you? Why I liked Harry. Last night I didn't mean I was going to kill the murderer, I was just going to beat him within an inch of his life, for my own satisfaction, before I turned him over to you."

Campbell smiled. "Well, I guess you've had your lesson now. Next time, just leave everything to the police."

"Whew! and how!" Jack heaved a sigh of relief.

Again the officer ran over his notes. "Well, I guess that covers most of the ground," he said at last, "I have already had frank statements from Mr. MacAlistair, Mr. Brownley and Mr. Durham, so unless one of you has something further to add, I won't worry you any more tonight."

Chairs were hastily scraped back as the guests rose hurriedly to their feet. The interview was over, and so far as any of them could see, the solution was as far distant as ever. "By the way," Campbell's voice halted them, "I want you all to be sure that your doors are locked tonight when you retire, and I want you all to stay in your rooms. That is an order, but it is for your own protection. The murderer is still among you, and none of you are safe while the killer is at large."

Berenice shivered, and her frightened eyes were raised appealingly to Campbell's face. "Haven't you any clues? Are these murders going on and on, until we are all killed?" In spite of their personal fears, everyone suddenly remembered the empty bed that was in Berenice's room, and felt an impulse of pity. For a perceptible moment Susan hesitated, then she said quietly, "Would you like to sleep in my room tonight, Berenice? We'll both feel better not to be alone."

"O Susan, thank you," Berenice said gratefully, "you don't know how I dreaded going upstairs by myself."

"I think what you all need is a sedative of some sort," Campbell said drily. "Have you any codeine left, Brownley?"

Bob looked at him quickly, shaking his head as he said ruefully, "No, I'm sorry. I took the last pill early this morning, and threw the box away. I was wondering how I'd manage to get to sleep myself."

"That's too bad," Campbell's voice was regretful, "I should have asked Dr. Bailey to leave some bromides. Do you want me to send out for some? None of you have slept much, and you will be under a hard strain until the murderer is caught."

Everyone refused his offer and moved restlessly toward the door.

"Well, if any of you want anything, I will be bunking down here in the hall. You can call me, but I don't want any of you rambling around alone. Just by way of giving you a ray of comfort, I want to say that this interview has been very helpful, and I think I can promise you an arrest very soon. Goodnight!"

As if glad to escape from the official atmosphere of the room, the guests hurried into the hall, closely followed by Ismael.

To Campbell and McCloud in the hot, shuttered little room, the next two hours crept by with intolerable slowness. The air was blue with the smoke from nervously lighted, half-consumed cigarettes, and in the haze, hundreds of insects and moths fluttered and died against the blazing, white shaded lights. In spite of the officer's repeated suggestion, young McCloud refused point-blank to go home and get some sleep until Ismael's return, though his head nodded and jerked above his scattered notes.

Gradually the sound of voices and movement in the big hall outside ceased and a few minutes later, Ismael's welcome figure slipped into the Recreation

Room. "All is ready, Tuan. The houseguests have retired, the local people who dropped in for a look-see
and gossip over a drink have reluctantly returned to
their homes, the bar is closed, and the servants have
gone to their quarters."

"Good, did you pick up anything new?" Campbell
asked.

"No, nothing," Ismael's eyes twinkled. "Tuan
MacAlistair spent a long time saying goodnight to
Mem Ames, and Tuan Wetherby held the hand of
Mem Gordon longer than seemed necessary—but
that was all I saw. Tuan Durham seemed very thirsty,
and increased his bar bill by many ringgits, before
his Mem could persuade him to go upstairs. Tuan
Brownley went direct to his room when he left here,
and Tuan Ames took a turn on the veranda with the
little American Mem until her father summoned her
to retire. I then had Own Ling close the bar, and
there was nothing more to detain the curious from
town."

"Are you sure you don't want me to stick around,
Ismael?" the magistrate asked hopefully, as he picked
up his papers from the table.

"No, Tuan, it will be better for all of us, if you
leave temporarily. Your presence might interfere with
our plans. Doubtless the murderer is already listening impatiently for the receding noise of your motorcycle."

"Well, far be it from me to interfere with the long arm of the law," McCloud said, turning his lagging feet toward the door, "but I'll be back the first thing in the morning."

"If we're lucky, McCloud, the next statement you take down will be at the jail," Campbell promised. "So long, and thank you!" With a nod, and a "goodnight," the young magistrate closed the door behind him.

As the snorts of his motorcycle faded away in the distance, Campbell turned to Ismael. "I guess I'll go out now and settle myself for the night."

The Malay padded behind him into the outer room saying quietly, "I have arranged your chair for you, Tuan, here near the foot of the stairs, just beyond the door to the servants' quarters, but under the balcony where the shadows are deepest." He lowered his voice still further as he added, "The pillar that supports the balcony at this end intervenes, as you see. It will be impossible for anyone on the balcony opposite you to get a good aim. In order to shoot, the slayer must come down the stairs. The shutters are all closed and fastened, and I will now lock the front door. The only approach to you will be these rear stairs, and I will be just inside the door of the servants' quarters, so that to reach you, the murderer must pass me. I have tried it out. In order to shoot you, the slayer must come down the stairs and stand within two feet of this door where I shall be stationed."

In spite of the warmth of the night, Campbell felt a shiver crawl up his back as he heard Ismael so calmly discussing his possible murder. A careful survey of the scene assured him that Ismael had placed his chair in the safest spot in the room. Cautiously the Malay turned the big key in the front door. "All right, here go the lights, Ismael!" Campbell pushed the switch, and in the sudden darkness groped his way back to the long chair. Slowly he stretched himself out in the shadows. It wasn't really dark in the middle of the room, just a dim, murky twilight, thanks to the lights in the ceiling two stories above. For a time he lay tense, his ears straining to catch every sound, his nerves twitching, but nothing happened, and gradually he became calmer. It seemed a fantastic idea of Ismael's, that anyone should want to kill him. He smiled to himself at the extravagance of the notion, and the way he would pull his assistant's leg in the morning. His eyes were tired of staring into the shadows and he closed them to shut out the familiar objects that his imagination had been distorting into menacing shapes and figures. The clock above the bar ticked steadily, monotonously. Time was passing.

He must have dozed off for a few minutes, but suddenly he was wide awake, roused by a sense of danger that seemed to be without foundation. The room was just the same. There wasn't a sound except the ticking of the clock. Hold on there was someone on the balcony. A vague white blur. Whoever it was must have been staring down toward him. He hoped he hadn't moved and given the show away when he woke up, but it was devilishly hard to lie still and wait for that shape to creep down the stairs. How long would it take, pausing between each step, stopping to listen and look behind? Did Ismael know the murderer was coming, or had he too dozed off. Campbell's hands were suddenly cold and damp. He remembered a young goat that he had tethered once as bait for a tiger—the poor thing had probably felt just as he did now, except that the goat could plunge and bleat. Ah! a board had creaked—that loose step halfway down the stairs. It couldn't be long now. Campbell held himself rigid, exerting all his self-control to make his breathing sound natural. A second for each step, he figured, forcing himself to reason calmly, and then five paces to the door where Ismael was standing. Would Ismael grab the slayer as he passed the door, or would he wait until the murderer had come close to his chair. It might spoil everything if he sprang his trap too soon. They were dealing with a perverted genius who would have some perfectly plausible explanation to offer—that he was walking in his sleep, perhaps. There, he could hear someone breathing. It couldn't be Ismael. It must be the murderer. Close now,—in a second more he would round the corner and be in the shadows that sheltered Campbell. No sound of Ismael yet. God! could he have gone to sleep? Silently the officer braced himself for a spring. This was al-together too much of a good thing. Flesh and blood could only stand so much. His eyes stared painful-ly at the entrance to the stairs. Ah, there he was, the black revolver outlined faintly in a white hand. Campbell threw himself sideways in his chair just as a second figure hurled itself forward striking down the assailant's arm as it grabbed him with an armlock. The revolver exploded with a flash and a roar that echoed and re-echoed through the closed building. There was a gasp of pain and dismay, and then a dull thud on the stone floor.

"All right, Tuan, I've got him. Switch on the lights!"

CHAPTER XX

As the lights flooded the room, doors upstairs were flung open, excited voices demanded to know what had happened, and pale faces peered anxiously over the balcony railing.

"It's all right!" Campbell called reassuringly, "you can come down if you want to." With bathrobes and negligées hastily clutched around them, the agitated guests, fearful of another murder, piled down the stairs.

"We have the murderer." The officer's quiet tone disguised his satisfaction.

"Where? Who?" demanded Bruce gazing around him with a stupefied expression.

Silently Campbell nodded toward the chair where, under the watchful eyes of Ismael, the figure of Bob Brownley was slumped.

"Not Bob!" Bruce exclaimed, hurrying to the side of his friend, "why, man, you're crazy!"

"No, he's damn smart!" gasped Bob, still convulsed from the effect of Ismael's knee in his stomach. At his words, the guests who had crowded forward, shrank back, staring with amazement and horror.

"You don't know what you are saying, Bob," protested Bruce, "Campbell is accusing you of these murders!"

"Yes, I know." Bob raised his head and looked defiantly at his friend. "He's got me at last."

"My God!" The color drained out of Bruce's face as he read the truth in Bob's eyes. "Don't say anything more. Not another word until I can get a lawyer for you," Bruce said, rallying his faculties with an effort.

Bob shook his head. "I don't want a lawyer. I've nothing to live for now, and I'd far rather die than spend the rest of my life in a tropical jail. All I want to do, is to get it over quickly, can't you understand?"

Still stunned by the revelation, Bruce stared at the man who was so calmly addressing him. Bob's familiar smile flashed up at him. "just give me a cigarette, old man,—lighted please,—and we'll get on with this." With a hand that trembled despite itself, Bruce produced a cigarette case from his bathrobe pocket. Bob reached for the cigarette with his manacled hands, and turned to Campbell, "Now, Sir, I'm ready."

"Anything you say now will be used as evidence against you," warned the officer.

Bob waved aside the formal words. "I know. I've given you a run for your money, and I'm ready to pay up. I killed Ailsa, and I'm glad of it. If ever a murder was justified, hers was. I've no regret there at all. The others,—well, I'm sorry about them. They were just the outcome of Ailsa's. Mrs. DeKok and Harry both thrust themselves into the picture, and it seemed to me then, that I had no alternative but to get them out of the way. I had nothing against either of them until they interfered, and it was their life against mine. It's strange," Bob glanced about him with a bewildered air. "My life seemed so important then, and now it doesn't matter a hoot to me. I was all keyed up to kill Ailsa, and that impulse carried me along until now. Now, well, nothing seems to mean anything." He brooded for a second before he went on. "Ailsa ruined me. She took everything I had, everything I cared for:—my friend," he nodded toward Bruce's bent head, "my home, my money, my country, and at the last, my self-respect. There's nothing left. She fooled me, lied to me, laughed at me, and finally, she made a puppet of me,—a mechanical toy that simply carried out her wishes. Even so, I would probably never have had the courage to kill her, if she hadn't deliberately snatched away my one chance of manhood. If I could have gone back again to England on the job Durham offered me, I knew I could make good. His offer seemed like an answer to my prayers, just as I'd resigned myself to rotting away here in the East. You see I knew all the time what the drink, and the idleness and the loose living were doing to me—I could feel myself slipping lower and lower all the time, without the guts to pull myself together. And Durham's job was a rope thrown to me to pull myself out of the mud." He puffed somberly on his cigarette, and then, with a shrug, continued. "Well, Ailsa turned her thumbs down on all that, though she knew it was a question literally of life and death to me. The doctor had told her that another year in the tropics would finish me. After the bridge game, I was feeling pretty rocky with fever, so I went up to my room to lie down. I still thought that I could convince Ailsa that we must go back to England—it was so clear to me that it was our one hope of ever leading a decent life. It didn't occur to me, even then, that Ailsa simply didn't want to be decent, that she was contented with things as they were.

"Pretty soon, the door opened and she came in, but she was in a hurry, in no mood to be reasonable. I tried to tell her what I felt, but she just laughed. I reached out and caught her skirt. Until then, I had believed, in spite of everything, that she still cared for me a little. She struck my hand away and told me not to be a fool; that if we went to England, the arrangement was for her to be Durham's mistress. She accused me of wanting to live off of her. She was so furious by then that she gave other things away too— the fact that she had been unfaithful almost from the start. She thought I had known all along, and kept silent for my own reasons. It seems strange now that I never guessed, that she had fooled me all those years, but you see," his voice was apologetic, "I had always trusted her in that way. If I'd known, I might have left her years ago, and gone my own way. None of this would have happened, if I hadn't been such a blind, trusting fool. O well, there's no use speculating about that, what you want are the facts.

"Let's see, where was I?" he resumed, "O yes, I remember now. I jumped out of bed and started for her, but she just gave a mocking laugh and went out of the door before I could reach her. I followed her. I'd grabbed the kris I'd taken earlier from Durham's room—"

"Just a minute, Brownley," interrupted the officer, "when did you get the kris, and how, and where was it?"

Bob glanced at him impatiently. "I saw it lying on the table just inside the door of Durham's room when I went upstairs after the bridge game. I suppose even then I had planned to use it on Ailsa, or perhaps on myself—I don't know. I just noticed it through the open door as I passed. No one was around, so I reached in and took it. I hid it under my pillow."

Campbell nodded. "All right. Go on."

"Well, I picked up the kris and followed Ailsa into the hall. She was a few feet ahead of me, but she didn't look back. The hall was empty except for us, and for Gordon's native boy who was curled up asleep on the mat outside his door. In a flash I remembered two things about him; first, that he was latah; and second, that he was an Achenese from Northern Sumatra, a tribe famous for its fighters and hunters. It came over me then, that I could put Ailsa out of the way without actually touching her. Mahat could drive a knife home better than I. I took hold of his shoulder and shook him awake. Then I motioned for him to follow me down the stairs. As we crossed the lower veranda, Ailsa was going down the steps toward the shrubbery. We followed her a little way, keeping in the shadow as much as possible. I knew I had to be quite close to her before I made the gesture, because a latah acts so quickly. If he doesn't, the impulse is lost. As she reached the shrubbery, I put the kris in Mahat's hand and said sharply, 'Pukol sumah dia kras!' (*'Strike her hard!'*) making a motion to strike. I turned to hurry back into the house, and then I saw the Dutch woman leaning over the veranda rail upstairs. I didn't know whether she recognized me or not, but she had certainly seen too much for my peace of mind.

"As I slipped into the house I was wondering what I could do about her. Absent-mindedly I put my hand into the pocket of my dressing gown. My fingers touched a wad of cotton I had had there that morning when I cut myself shaving. By that time I knew I'd have to get rid of the Dutch woman before she told what she had seen, but there was no time then, for as I reached the top of the stairs, Ailsa screamed. God! I'll never forget that sound. I hurried along in the shadow on the balcony to Mrs. DeKok's room. If anyone saw me, I could say I'd come out of my room to see what the scream was. No one appeared though, for at least two minutes. I crammed the cotton into the eye of the bolt on her door jamb, so that it would prevent the bolt slipping home and I could get in her room later. It only took a second, and I was safe in my own room before people began to run out onto the balcony." There was a breathless silence as he paused.

"You know the rest. Later, when everything was quiet, I went to her room and fixed her so that she would never be able to tell what she had seen that night." Bob's voice was appallingly matter-of-fact.

"Where did you get the second knife?" Campbell asked, glancing up from the notes he was taking.

"It was on a tray outside the door of the Americans' room," Bob said promptly. "Someone must have had something to eat, and the roomboy, or the waiter hadn't taken the tray downstairs. I noticed it as I went along the balcony on the way to Mrs. DeKok's room. Until I happened to see the knife, I was afraid I'd have to strangle her. A revolver shot would have brought the whole house about my head, just as it did tonight," Bob explained. "By tonight though, I'd become rattled. I couldn't seem to think and plan the way I did at first." He smiled faintly at Campbell. "Didn't that bloodstained handkerchief under my mattress fool you?"

"For a little while," the officer admitted. "At first I jumped to the conclusions you expected,— that it had been planted."

"I don't know just when things did begin to go wrong," Bob said frowning, "I didn't want to kill anyone but Ailsa, and then I found I had to go on and on. I killed her so that I'd have a chance to be decent, paradoxical as it may seem, and from then on, that was really what I was fighting for. Of course I was on the lookout for any hint of suspicion against me, and when Harry spoke to you after lunch, I knew that he suspected me. Several months ago, when I was visiting him in Sumatra, just after he'd hired Mahat, I had foolishly told him I thought it was a risk; that Mahat would be an ideal tool for any crime that a clever man wanted to commit. I hoped he'd forgotten my remark, but at lunch today, when Mahat brought his cigarette case, I saw that he had remembered. His eyes suddenly opened very wide, and he gave me an incredulous sort of look. I knew then that I'd have to kill him." He seemed almost embarrassed.

"You used Mahat for that murder too, didn't you?" Campbell asked.

"Yes. I saw him outside the Gordon room again. He was awake this time. I made him come downstairs with me. The hall here was empty, and Harry was lying in the chair just outside the door. It was easy. A word, a gesture, and Mahat had stabbed him. Unfortunately the boy was terrified this time when he saw what he had done, and instead of coming back into the house, he ran away."

"Where did you hide the knife between the time you killed Mrs. DeKok, and the murder of Mr. Gordon?" queried the officer.

"That was another time I fooled you. I knew the place would be turned upside down to find the knife, and I was at my wits' end to find a safe place for it. Finally, I took some adhesive tape and strapped it to my leg. It didn't show under my trousers. Before I gave it to Mahat, I wiped off the handle on my handkerchief so that my fingerprints wouldn't be found on it." He paused to reflect before he added, "No, I don't think you'd have had a thing on me if that damn native hadn't run away. I knew he was my greatest danger, and I had planned to kill him when he came back into the hall. Everyone would have thought then that Mahat had committed all the murders, and that I had killed him in self-defense after he knifed Harry. He upset all my plans when he ran off the veranda instead of back into the house." Bob broke off with a shrug of his broad shoulders.

For a few minutes Campbell questioned him closely on several points, all of which, with an air completely detached, the prisoner explained. "Now, I think it is my turn," he announced, "I've satisfied your morbid curiosity." He glanced sardonically at the faces around him. "And I think you might do as much for me. When did you first suspect me, Campbell?"

The officer smiled. "I didn't. It was Ismael who is responsible for this denouement. You might ask him anything you want to know."

A ripple of surprise spread through the spectators, and Bob's eyes widened as he turned to the stocky, little Malay, hovering modestly in the background. "Well, I'll be damned," he muttered to himself. "What made you think I did it, Ismael?"

"I tried to place myself in the position of the murderer," Ismael said simply. "I took you each in turn, and so far as I could, for a time I lived your lives. I studied over the motives of all of you. Then I narrowed the possibilities down to those who were capable of strong passion, love or hatred. That group included Mem Durham, Tuan MacAlistair, Tuan Gordon, and yourself. Tuan MacAlistair however, no longer loved Mem Brownley, nor did he have sufficient cause to hate her. His feeling had cooled with the passing years. Mem Durham hated her and might have killed her, but that meant that Tuan Durham must at least have known of the murder of Mrs. De-Kok. He has not the courage. Tuan Gordon was a possibility, but always, he might have separated his wife from Mem Brownley without resorting to murder. Then I came to you, Tuan, and it seemed to me that you alone had a real motive. I thought to myself, if Mem Brownley had been my wife and had dishonored my name, what would I do, and I knew that I would kill her."

Bob's eyes glistened. Of all his auditors only the insignificant little Malay had shown any real understanding of his suffering, and of his character.

"Against that," Ismael continued calmly, "was the fact that you were supposedly drugged with a sleeping medicine at the time of the crime. I telephoned the management of your hotel in Singapore. They told me that you and Mem Brownley quarreled bitterly, and from them I obtained the name of your physician. When I spoke to him, he denied that he had ever given you codeine, or recommended it to you. He said you had never complained to him of insomnia, that he had treated you only for malaria and that unless you left the tropics you would be a dead man in a year. If you didn't have insomnia, I asked myself, why then did you tell everyone at the bridge table that you were going to take medicine that night to make you sleep? Again, when I found the handkerchief under your mattress, I questioned myself, if I killed Mem DeKok, what would I do with the cloth on which I wiped the blade if I wished to divert suspicion from myself. The answer was ready to my hand. I would place the cloth under my own mattress where everybody would think it had been planted, for so clever a murderer would never make so foolish a slip. So far I had gone, when Tuan MacAlistair mentioned that Mahat was latah, and that told me how it was possible for the murderer to be at the same time in the shrubbery with Mem Brownley, and putting cotton wool in Mem DeKok's door bolt. While Mahat was killing Mem Brownley, you were already preparing another murder. It was all clear to me then. You alone had motive, opportunity and the knowledge of Malay essential to use Mahat as your tool. Those blunders of yours were just,—what do you say, fortunes of war? But when you tried to be yet more clever and told us your revolver was stolen, then you were just being stupid." Ismael's voice was severe. "You thought to throw suspicion again on someone else after you committed your next murder, but when your coat had lost its stiffness after your warm tea, I saw the outline of the revolver stuck in your trousers belt."

"That was bad," Bob admitted, "I got very careless toward the end, but how did you know that it was Campbell I was planning to kill?"

"There was no one else who menaced your safety, except Tuan MacAlistair, and him I knew you would never harm. It is rare, Tuan, to find a friendship so strong, but your feeling for Tuan MacAlistair is more than friendship,—I think it is love."

Bruce stared in amazement at Bob as the latter said softly, "You are right about that, as you are about

everything else. Bruce and Ailsa were the only people I ever cared for deeply, and long after I lost my
feeling for Ailsa, I cherished the memory of Bruce's
friendship." He glanced apologetically at Bruce. "It
was all mixed up with my feeling for England, my
memory of school days, and all that sort of thing.
When I saw you again, I seemed to realize how low
I'd sunk. I didn't want you to know about the way I'd
had to live, the shifting, the scheming, the cheating
at cards—O yes, Ailsa and I worked the same stunt
that she and Berenice did. It made me desperate for
another chance to become decent. O well, let's get
on with this thing." He motioned to Campbell and
struggled to his feet. "At least I can promise you that
I will make a better job of dying than I did of living."

As Bob rose from his chair, Bruce stepped quickly
forward and clasped the manacled hands in a hard,
wordless grip. Bob's sagging shoulders straightened,
and with Ismael and Campbell on either side, he
turned toward the door. Hastily, with shrinking aver-
sion, the other guests made way for him, all except
Susan. Slipping her hand understandingly through
Bruce's arm, she turned on her companions. "Who
are we to judge him?" she demanded with flashing
eyes. "Think what the tropics have done to all of us;
the way our judgment has been warped, our perspective twisted. Can't you see that none of this could
have happened except here in the Far East?"

DEATH OVER HER SHOULDER

To William M. Rockwell
In grateful appreciation

CHAPTER I

The girl who had been sitting so rigidly in the back seat of the taxi as it nosed its way like a half-drowned beetle through the tropical storm gave a sigh of relief when the battered Ford jerked to a final halt. Eagerly she tried to peer through the curtain of rain, but she could distinguish only the dark bulk of the house raised on piles above the driveway. The dim lights of the taxi stared blindly through the rainy night across a mass of wet, fragrant shrubbery, and even the vivid flashes of green and blue lightning showed nothing of the house save steep narrow steps leading up into a vague blackness.

Above the roar of the thunder and the crackle of lightning, Nancy heard the Chinese driver shout, "Hey, Boy! Hey Boy! Ada Mem!" There was no answer, no welcome sound of running feet, no glimmer of light through an opened door, and with a disgusted snort, "Boys pergi wayong!" the Chinaman scrambled reluctantly from his seat. The word "way-ong" reminded Nancy of the scene they had passed

337

a few minutes before: there had been a lull in the storm, as though, after its first furious onslaught, it had run out of ammunition. Through the breathless silence, she had heard the heavy beating of a metallic drum, the penetrating whine of native violins, and leaning forward on the seat, Nancy had seen that the tunnel of rubber trees through which the car had been crawling had opened into a clearing, and that on either side of the rutted, rain-washed road, squares and oblongs of smoky light glowed in the massed shadows of squat buildings. The Chinese taxi driver had slowed down and, partially turning a sleek black head and flat cheek, had said over his shoulder, "Wayong," with a splatter of explanation she hadn't understood. However, Nancy had read about wayongs, and although she hadn't seen any native dances or plays in her four months in the Far East, she had forgotten her anxiety long enough to stare wistfully toward the sound of Malayan revelry. Then the thunder and lightning resumed their attack with renewed vigor, drowning out the eerie wails of the violins, and dropping a grey veil of rain over the cluster of bamboo huts. Once more the car had lurched forward, slithering and groping for purchase in the flooded ruts, and once more Nancy had been submerged in the morass of her personal fears.

The taxi driver's temper as he now slammed open the door of the car was due, she realized, to the fact that servants should have rushed out to take her suitcase instead of going off to the wayong and leaving a respectable Chinaman to get wet and to perform the menial job of depositing her light baggage on the veranda. A smile flickered across her lips as Nancy stepped out into the rain. Her smart blue linen suit and hat were already shapeless, her bright bronze hair was plastered in dark loops on her pale cheeks, but she didn't care. Her nightmare journey was ended, and in just a few seconds now Lydia would be welcoming her, fussing about her wet clothes, calming her fears, laughing away her worry.

Lydia of course must have had some good reason for not meeting the train, otherwise she would never have permitted Nancy to wander forlornly along the strange cinder platform at Kluang, pushing her way through groups of Malays, Chinese and Indians as she searched for a taxi driver who could understand her halting scraps of Malay; nor would she have permitted a guest, even an uninvited one, to spend her last silver dollars for the long, fifteen-mile drive from Kluang to the isolated Semang Rubber Estate. Probably Lydia hadn't received the telegram which Nancy had sent from Tapah Roads announcing her arrival on the 9.05 train. That made it awkward of course, but it was more comforting than her alternative fear—that Lydia simply didn't want Nancy to come; that she hadn't expected her invitations to be taken seriously by the lonely American girl whom she had befriended on the long

journey from Southampton to Penang. Much as she
had liked Lydia, Nancy had never expected to take advantage of their shipboard friendship; never expected
to see Lydia again, nor visit the isolated rubber
plantation which Lydia had described so glowingly,
or to share in the intimate, circumscribed life that
existed among the manager and assistant managers
on that 2000-acre estate. Certainly Nancy had never
dreamed that she would one day make a headlong,
panic-stricken flight half way across the Malayan
Peninsula to throw herself on Lydia's mercy, trusting
that Lydia, the one friend she had in the Far East,
would shelter and help her.

Nancy, stumbling up the steep, slippery steps behind the Chinaman, was so busy trying to decide how
best to inform Lydia of her plight, that it was not
until she was on the veranda itself, had dropped her
last remaining dollars in the greedy outstretched
palm, and had seen the Chinaman plunge through
the rain into the waiting car, that she realized the
house was in complete darkness.

A wild unreasoning panic seized her, and she
rushed to the veranda door, shrieking for the Chinaman to wait, to take her with him; but the wind,
rushing through the tossing boughs of the lime trees
on the terrace, blew her cry away, and the car, having
manipulated the circular driveway, dipped down the
hill.

Nancy, getting a grip on her emotions, felt a glimmer of gratitude that the Chinaman hadn't heard her. If she had climbed back into the taxi, where could she have gone, how could she have faced the driver's indignation when she admitted that she had no money? She stood still, just inside the dusty screen door, staring around her with wide, frightened eyes, as the weird flashes of lightning revealed the rainswept veranda—and then, for a second she relaxed. One of her fears was allayed; dangling on the arm of a wicker chair was a familiar cretonne knitting bag, the one that used to hang uselessly on the back of Lydia's steamer chair. At least she was in the right house; the Chinaman hadn't misunderstood her badly enunciated directions and abandoned her at some strange bungalow. With more confidence now, Nancy awaited the next flash which would tell her more about the house and its occupants. It came, a wincing blue dagger, illuminating briefly the rain-clogged screens, the soaked grass rugs, the sodden pillows and magazines.

The house wasn't deserted then. People had been here recently. But where was Lydia now? A longer green flash cut across the sky, illuminating the rows of shining rubber trees whose ranks seemed to halt half up the hill to the house, while thunder grumbled and gargled through the tree-choked valley, echoing and re-echoing as the encircling hills tossed back its roar.

As the sound died away, Nancy was aware of the rain rustling on the atap roof, of a shutter inside the house banging drearily to and fro, and once again she felt a rising tide of fear. The dark, lonely house filled her with a strange dread. Still, she must go inside, she couldn't stand indefinitely on the wet veranda. Reluctantly she moved forward, and groped for the doorknob. The door, swollen from dampness, stuck at first, and then groaned open on creaking hinges. Despite the wind that rushed in with her, the air inside was pungent with mildew, and the fainter more subtle odor of decay. The noise of the rain on the roof was louder, and so was the monotonous banging of the loose shutter; and yet, somehow, both sounds served only to intensify the ominous silence of the house.

"The first thing to do is to find a light," Nancy said, matter-of-factly, hoping that the brave sound of her words would drown out the heavy thud of her heart. "Probably there is a note from Lydia explaining why she isn't here, telling me what to do." With trembling fingers she groped in her sodden handbag for her cigarette lighter, and then forced herself to close the front door. It took her several minutes to coax a flame from the little wick—her fingers were so wet, so clumsy with nervousness. Shielded by her hand, at first the tiny flickering light made no impression on the black, immense gulf of the hall that stretched before her, but as her narrowed eyes become

accustomed to the feeble spurt of flame, she saw close
at hand a hall table with two ornate Chinese candlesticks holding tall yellow tapers. Her spirits rose as
their stiff, virgin wicks flared into guttering points of
flame and threw grotesque shadows across the whitewashed walls and ceiling.

Half way down the hall two wide dark doorways
gaped at each other across the bare wooden floor, and
beside each of them gleamed the familiar dull brass
fixtures of electric lights. Her spirits rose as she hurried toward them, and then sank to a corresponding
depth of despair when no amount of button pushing,
or even of bulb twisting, elicited any response. She
had to have lights to counteract the waves of fear that
swept over her; she must find candles or lamps somewhere that would chase the shadows away so that she
could be sure the house, empty as it obviously was of
human occupants, hadn't proved a refuge for some
slinking tiger or panther, or worse yet, a snake.

Returning to the hall table for a candle, she
noticed for the first time that one of the heavy
candlesticks anchored a telegram to the dark polished
surface. Then Lydia had received her telegram after
all, she thought with relief as she picked up the white
envelope. Her eyes widened as she read the message,
and a bewildered frown wrinkled her forehead; this
wasn't her telegram at all; this was from someone
who signed herself Helene Chambers, saying she had
been lucky enough to get the lead in a stock company

leaving Singapore immediately for Australia, thank-
ing Lydia for a loan, and regretting that her visit must
be postponed until the next time she was stranded.
It was a gay message, full of hope and courage, and
Nancy's broad, sensitive mouth curved into a spontaneous smile as she read it. Lydia had been an actress too, before she had married Clive Bosworth and
come out East; she'd laughed with Nancy about it on
shipboard, saying that it had taken her three years to
overcome the prejudice of Clive's father. This Helene
Chambers was doubtless a friend from Lydia's stage
days.

Suddenly, Nancy's mouth quivered at the thought
of the contrast between her own position and that of
the other girl. Not only was Nancy out of a job, but
it was impossible, after what had happened, for her
ever to get one in the Far East; she was 10,000 miles
from home, and she had literally spent her last penny to come to Lydia. Her hazel eyes darkened with
dismay. What if Lydia refused to believe her story;
refused to help her?

Her own telegram, she saw, was underneath Hel-
en's—a brief message, "Arriving Kluang 9.05 tonight, Nancy Reynolds." She hadn't dared say more
than that, hadn't dared send the telegram at all until
she was just a few hours from her destination. She
had been afraid to send it from Penang, lest she be
traced—afraid to send it earlier lest Lydia wire her
not to come.

What, she wondered, had Lydia thought when she received that message? How would she act now when she returned to find a derelict on her doorstep? Nancy was distressed to find that she couldn't remember Lydia's face at all, nothing except her light, windblown hair, the grace of her movements, the joyous gaiety of her laughter. She felt that she could count on Lydia, but what if Lydia's husband objected to Nancy's unceremonious arrival? She knew so little about Clive Bosworth, nothing, really, except that he loved to hunt, and Nancy had suspected that he neglected not only his work as manager of the rubber estate, but his wife, too. Lydia cared deeply about him, that was evident from the very way she mentioned his name, even though she admitted laughingly that he was nothing but a charming, irresponsible infant, and she'd only had four letters from him in as many months.

Well, no matter whether he approved of Nancy's arrival or not, he could hardly put her out into the storm. The storm! Lydia must have left before the storm broke, or she would have closed the shutters. It was all very queer and disturbing. There was a hateful atmosphere about the house, a creeping horror that grew worse instead of less as the minutes dragged past. It wasn't the storm, nor the isolated estate hewn out of the Malayan jungle, it was something about the house itself which was frightening her so that her knees trembled and her breath came in short shallow jerks.

She couldn't control her thoughts or her fears, but at least she could stop the banging of the loose shutter that formed so dreary an accompaniment to them. Slowly she moved down the hall in the direction of the sound which came from the rear of the room on the right-hand side of the hall. It was the living room, Nancy saw, holding her candle high; a long, narrow, shadow-filled room whose furniture was distorted into vague shapes by the dimness of her light. The storm had played havoc there, too, for in addition to two unshuttered windows, the front of the room had no wall, being separated from the veranda only by a big, half-closed Japanese screen. The room was deserted, but, despite Lydia's efforts to make it attractive, the rain-streaked curtains fluttering at the windows, the broad couch opposite the door, heaped with gay cushions, and partially concealed by the long, low teakwood table on which a broken vase spilled flowers and water among the piles of magazines and books, Nancy found herself shrinking from it—it was worse even than the hall and the veranda.

It was the rear shutter that was swinging so maddeningly, and slowly Nancy moved toward it, fighting against the horror that was overwhelming her. She had almost reached the window when the circling of her candle flickered across the couch and she saw that someone was lying there, half buried in the pillows. Nancy's candle dropped from her nerveless fingers. Her scream was lost in a dap of thunder as her light went out.

The next thing she knew, she was wrenching at the front door, her breath sobbing in her throat. There was no sound of pursuit, no sound at all except the beating of rain on the roof, and the mocking slams of the shutter. Even the thunder with grunts and growls of rage seemed to have rumbled into the distance.

Nancy was ashamed of her panic. It must have been Lydia lying there on the couch; she thought she remembered the glimpse of a green dress against the darkness of the couch cover. But if it was Lydia, why hadn't she awakened at Nancy's scream—why was she lying there with the rain beating in through the open shutters? unless she were sick, unconscious from some sudden attack of fever. That was it, of course. Lydia in the other room sick, and Nancy indulging in "the vapors," scaring herself to death about nothing. Filled with self-disgust, Nancy snatched the lighted candle from the hall table, and hurried back to the couch.

The figure was still lying there motionless on its side, a white arm dangling helplessly over the edge of the blue velours cover, the head and one shoulder buried in a pile of bright-hued pillows.

"Lydia!" Nancy's voice was thin and strained as she bent over the head of the couch. Slowly, reluctantly, she forced herself to pull aside an orange pillow. The candle light wavered across a white profile, caught the gold in the halo of fair hair spread on the dark couch cover. With shrinking fingers, Nancy touched the green linen shoulder—it was soft and repugnantly chill, and it fell back suddenly exposing an ominous dark stain that had oozed across the front of the crumpled green dress.

CHAPTER II

How long Nancy stood there stupidly staring down at the body of her friend, she never knew. Her throat was too stiff and dry to emit the scream that was choking her. It was the hot grease dripping from her precariously tilted candle across her clenched hand that finally aroused her from her numb horror. "So that's why I was so afraid of this house," she thought dully. "It was because Lydia was dead here all the time."

Suddenly the full significance of the scene dawned on her. Lydia was dead, and yet, the shaking candle which she forced herself to shift back and forth along the couch, along the narrow aisle between the couch and the table, revealed nothing which resembled a weapon. If Lydia had killed herself and fallen back among the pillows, the pistol or whatever she had used would be somewhere close to her body. Anyway, Lydia was too full of the joy of living ever to kill herself—and even if that had flagged for some reason, there were too many people who needed her help.

Lydia would have believed that the world couldn't get on without her assistance. Who could have been brutal enough to have silenced forever Lydia's sweet, husky voice, her delightful laughter?

Just when the realization of her own predicament percolated through her shocked sorrow, Nancy didn't know. One moment she was brooding over Lydia's untimely death and feeling a slow cumulative rage at her murderer—she didn't even know when she became convinced that it was murder—and the next, she was shaking with terror at her own anomalous position. She had been alone in the house with Lydia for many minutes, how could she prove that they hadn't quarreled, that she hadn't grabbed a knife or a gun in a moment of rage and killed her? It would be a simple matter for Lydia's husband, or the police, to telephone Penang, to learn what had happened there—and then, no one in the world would believe in her innocence. At worst, she would be accused of Lydia's murder—at best, she would be turned away penniless and friendless from the house, which, much as she loathed it, was her only refuge. Wildly she stared around her. There was no place she could hide in that room, and outside there were just miles of rain-tossing rubber trees, and then black, impenetrable jungle. She couldn't even cable home for money and help; it would kill her mother to get such a message, and what could her mother do anyway? It was Nancy who had been the breadwinner of the family since her father had died.

She drew a long, shuddering breath. Somehow she would have to save herself, use every bit of ingenuity she could summon, use every atom of guile, if she were to fight her way clear. She couldn't afford to have any scruples, any consideration for anyone but herself. Her tortured mind twisted among the stark facts that confronted it, and despairingly she realized that all she could do was to await developments. It was impossible to plan ahead; she was trapped for the moment.

Suddenly she caught the sound of voices, the low babel of Malay, too swift and idiomatic for her limited understanding, the rustle of sarongs, and the shuffle of bare feet on the gravel walk. For the first time she was aware that the thunder had stopped and the rain had dwindled to a half-hearted dripping. The servants must be coming back from the way-ong. Could it have been one of them who had killed Lydia? would he come slinking quietly through the door to take a final look at the woman he had killed, and then, finding Nancy there, kill her too? Before her wild fear had completed itself, she had blown out the candle and was crouching in the shadows at the head of the couch.

The voices passed the side windows and died away around the corner of the house. A few minutes later, she heard the distant clatter of pans, the tinkle of dishes, and then the acrid smell of burning wood drifted through the windows. The servants had evidently started a fire, probably carrying out orders of their dead mistress. Suppose one of them had come into the living room and found her crouching like a criminal. Her face was flushed with shame as she scrambled to her feet, and picked up her candlestick. Slowly she lit the wick again with a steady hand; she must go out to the kitchen, explain what had happened and send them for help. If they didn't understand her limited Malay vocabulary, at least she could make one of them follow her into the living room and let them see what had happened.

Quickly she smoothed down her damp skirt, and ran her fingers through her disheveled hair, trying to pat it into its usual waves, so that she would look more normal. At the door into the hall, she paused. There were more footsteps grinding along the driveway, heavy-shod feet this time, and the welcome sound of English. "Quite a show, wasn't it? Didn't think those coolies had it in them," someone was saying, and then, "They certainly have pantomime down to a fine art. Even if you couldn't understand a word of Malay, you'd have known it was 'Aladdin and the Lamp'." "Especially the lamp!" another voice said laughing, "I nearly fell off my bench when I recognized the lamp off my bicycle, ingenious devils."

"Hello! the house is all dark. The storm must have put the plant out of commission again. That means

Hamilton is drunk or he'd have had it working by that time."

The steps were mounting now to the veranda, and a fresh voice with a worried note exclaimed, "Where's Lydia? There ought to be candles lighted or something."

"Probably has her head buried under the bed-clothes. These storms we have out here always put her wind up. What ho, Lydia! Come out of it, old girl. We're all feeling peckish—thought you said supper at eleven!"

It was ghastly, Nancy thought, their unconsciousness of what was waiting for them. Slowly she advanced into the hall.

There was a crash and an oath from the veranda outside, "What the bloody hell did I fall over? A suitcase!" Electric flashlights played around the porch.

"Shhh," someone warned—probably Clive. "They must belong to that friend of Lydia's, Helene something or other. Lydia was expecting her to show up one day soon. Haven't seen each other since Lydia left the stage and are probably so busy pitching tales they forgot to light up." His voice sounded relieved, as though he had been more worried by the dark house than he had admitted.

The door groaned open, and Nancy, with an unconscious sense of the dramatic, held the candle picturesquely high as she breathlessly awaited their entrance.

A tall, broad-shouldered man in a white suit was the first to enter, the others, she didn't know how many, crowding close on his heels. His eyes opened very wide at the sight of the slim, blue-clad girl, with the candle light flickering down on her bronze hair, and white, frightened face.

"Oh, I'm so glad you've come," she gasped. "Something ghastly has happened."

They were all staring at her blankly, a circle of brown faces above white coats, faces that wavered and blurred and then merged before her tortured eyes. "Lydia's dead," her voice seemed to come from a long way off. "She's dead. I think someone killed her." Her slender body swayed, and a pair of strong arms caught her before she hit the floor.

When she recovered consciousness, she was huddled uncomfortably on a long wicker chair, with a wet washcloth dripping icy water down her neck, while someone was trying to force a fiery liquid through her clenched teeth. Where was she? Who was the strange man stooping over her? In sudden terror, as her memory returned, she shrank as far away as the limits of the chair permitted.

"You're all right, Miss Chambers. Take a quick swallow of this and you'll be yourself in no time." The brandy burned her throat, and, spluttering, she jerked herself upright. Her quick glance into the man's worried face reassured her. No one with such anxious blue eyes, with freckles blotting a round face, pale beneath its tan, and upstanding sandy hair, she decided illogically, could be a murderer.

"I'm sorry to be so stupid," she apologized. "It's the first time in my life that I ever fainted. It was this house, first, so dark and dreadful—and then finding Lydia."

"It was a rotten experience. I'd have been knocked for a loop myself," he sympathized, and then, as he stretched himself erect, Nancy saw the rest of the room. Shades had been lifted from the electric lamps, all of them blazing at last, and a harsh glare exposed each corner of the room—smaller than it had seemed beneath the uncertain flicker of her candle. Her fearful eyes slanted toward the couch, and she felt a tremor of relief to see that Lydia's body had been decently covered with a sheet or something white. A man was slumped in a chair near the end of the couch, as though he had sagged there, and someone had shoved a support beneath his knees. His blond head was partially hidden in a crook of his elbow, and his shoulders bobbed with racking sobs which he was trying, unsuccessfully, to muffle. A tall, good-looking youngster was pacing nervously back and forth from the living room to the dining room, his feet automatically avoiding tables and chairs, while ashes dropped unheeded from a cigarette he had forgotten to smoke.

Seated at the desk in the front of the room, a man with a profile like a Greek god was speaking in a soft southern voice over the telephone.

While she was still endeavoring to orient herself, and gather strength for the ordeal which she knew lay ahead of her, a fifth man, with the unmistakable characteristics of an Irishman, came briskly into the room. "The servants say they know nothing about this," he declared, waving a slim, facile hand toward the couch. "They left early for the wayong—in fact, ten or fifteen minutes before Clive and me. They all sat in a row, and they declare by all that is good and holy, none of them left the group even for a drink of water. It will be easy for the police to check that, but I am inclined to believe them, they all 'wah-wahed' enough at the bad news to convince me, at any rate." He whirled toward the man at the desk. "Did you get the police station, Bill?"

The man at the telephone turned, and Nancy noticed with distaste that his full face was even more handsome than his profile, like an idealized portrait of himself, and he was probably as unbearably conceited as most attractive men.

"Yes," he replied, "I got McCleary himself. He'll be right over. It's only about fifteen miles to Kluang, and at the rate he drives, even on a night like this, he should be here in half an hour. He'll bring Doc Sparkes."

The Irishman nodded, and then crossed the room to put a hand on Clive's hunched shoulder and murmur something. Clive shook his head, but ignoring the gesture, the Irishman spoke to the youngster who was still fidgeting back and forth. "Get a shot of brandy for Clive," he ordered, "and make him swallow it, and then, for the love of Pete, sit down somewhere and give the floors a rest. You're making us all giddy." The younger man blushed to the roots of his fair hair, and bolted from the room.

"Now, then," the Irishman moved toward Nancy's chair, and automatically she braced herself to resist the personality that was directing the activities of everyone else in the room. "Are you feeling better, Miss Chambers?"

Why did everyone call her "Miss Chambers," she wondered, irritated—still dazed by the events which had taken place so rapidly. Then she remembered the telegram. Everyone knew that Lydia expected Helene, and apparently none of them knew anything about Nancy's coming. Surreptitiously her fingers touched the crumpled telegrams, which in her agitation she had thoughtlessly shoved into her pocket. Helene Chambers with her established friendship with Lydia, her claim on Mr. Bosworth's hospitality. Nancy's lips settled into a straight line. After all, she had to look out for herself—let them go on thinking she was Helene.

The Irishman was staring down at her with a puzzled expression on his lean, tanned face, the pupils of his cat-green eyes contracted, and she realized that she hadn't even heard his last question.

"I'm sorry," she faltered, raising dark-fringed hazel eyes to his green ones, "I'm afraid I'm still a bit wonky. What was it you said?"

He smiled then, a flash of white teeth in his dark face—she was so absurdly young and frightened, so obviously trying to seem composed. "Suppose I tell you who we are first—I'd forgotten you didn't know." He glanced at the sandy-haired man whom Nancy had first seen as he had poured a drink down her reluctant throat, and who stood a few feet away, scowling at the Irishman. "He is Jim Mason, a fellow countryman of yours, second assistant on the estate."

Nancy's smile flickered toward her first friend, and then a puzzled look crossed her face—Jim Mason's eyes were as hard and cold as blue marbles, and his fists were clenched as he glowered at the Irishman. He nodded an acknowledgment of the introduction, and then, turning his back, he strolled away to talk in low tones to the good-looking man who still sat by the desk.

The Irishman's eyes twinkled. "I ought to warn you that I am not overly popular here on the estate. Perhaps I should have introduced myself first—I'm Mike Sullivan, just a no-account fifty-fifty stengah, if you know the vernacular—American Mother, the loveliest creature God ever made, and an Irish father, with half my early life divided between the two countries, and the rest of it scattered here and there in the less-populated sections of the world. 'Tis my friendship for Clive Bosworth that brings me into the scene." Nancy looked puzzled, and he added patiently, "I mean I am not connected with the estate—everyone else is. You and I are the only outsiders."

Perhaps, Nancy thought, that was the reason for Jim Mason's antagonism—the estate and those who worked it might be sort of a closed corporation.

"To get on with it," Mike continued, "the youngster just coming in with the glass of brandy and soda is Dave Farnsworth, fourth assistant, and newest addition to the estate. He likewise is an American from the Middle West some place. From the way that glass is slopping over, and the stare in his eyes, I'd say he'd been fortifying himself a bit on the side." His smile quirked at her, but without waiting for any comment, he went on, "The Adonis at the desk is Bill Pearson, third assistant, so damn good-looking that it's a handicap, and he doesn't know what to do about the whole thing. And, of course, the poor devil there beside the couch is Clive."

Was she supposed to know Clive, Nancy wondered wildly if she was, she was sunk as soon as he snapped to, he would recognize her and then— Mercifully, Mike relieved her anxiety, "No, I guess you don't at that—I mean know Clive—he and Lydia were married in London, and your friendship with her dated from her stage days. Ah, now you are looking better. Do you feel equal to telling us what happened here tonight?"

360 DOROTHY COLE MEADE

At his words, the other men edged forward until they formed a little group around her, all except Clive Bosworth, who still slumped in his chair, too stunned, or too indifferent to move.

"I don't really know anything—at least nothing that will help you," she began in a low, hesitant voice, "I'm not even sure what time I got to the station at Kluang, because I'd forgotten to wind my watch last night." She realized with sudden dismay that Helene would have come from Singapore, not Penang, and she had no idea when the Singapore train would have arrived. She looked helplessly at Jim Mason, the only man in whom she felt confidence. He spoke up promptly, "Her train must have gotten in at 8.47—at least it is due then." The train on which she had actually come arrived at 9.05; not much discrepancy of time to fill in, she thought with relief, but she would have to watch her step, be as vague as possible.

"Well, it was dark anyway, and the storm was coming up. I got hold of a taxi man who knew where the Semang Estate was, and he drove me out. The storm broke before we got here, and the trip seemed endless, so I don't know how long it actually took. The house was dark, and no one came when the driver shouted for a boy—he said something about their all being at a wayong. He put my bags on the porch, and drove off. I called Lydia, but no one answered me. She had told me to come whenever I could." It was difficult to stick to the literal truth, but the men were too anxious for her to complete her story to notice her hesitations. "I thought perhaps Lydia had gone to the wayong too, so when no one came to the door, I came inside. I used my cigarette lighter and lit the candles in the hall, then I came in here and found Lydia. I didn't do it as quickly as that, of course—I was awfully frightened," she concluded simply.

"What frightened you? Was it something you heard, Miss Chambers?" the Irishman asked. He was the only one, she thought resentfully, who didn't seem satisfied with her story.

Nancy shook her head, "I didn't hear anything except the storm, and a shutter that banged."

"There's a candle and candlestick on the floor by the couch. Did you drop it, or was it already there?"

She raised candid hazel eyes toward him. "I didn't know you wanted all the details. I brought that candle in the first time—when I came in to close the shutter that was banging, it had got on my nerves. I happened to see someone lying on the couch just before I reached the window—I'd been so sure that I was alone in the house that I was startled. I dropped the candlestick and ran out into the hall before I had time to realize that it must have been Lydia. I knew that if she had just been asleep, my scream would have wakened her, even if the storm and the rain beating in hadn't, so I thought she must be unconscious—sick with a sudden attack of fever. As soon as I had a chance to reason that far, I took the other candle and went back." The Irishman nodded, but it seemed to Nancy that his gaze was skeptical. He started to speak, but the dark, handsome man, Bill Pearson, interrupted.

"Pardon me, Mike—but I wonder whether Miss Chambers saw anything of the weapon—a knife or a dagger?"

Nancy shook her head again, "No, when I realized she was dead, I looked around, as much as I could without touching anything—there was nothing."

"What I can't understand," Mike continued as though Bill hadn't spoken at all, "is why you were so frightened that you ran out of the room when you saw Lydia lying there. What was there about the scene to upset you, when you didn't know at that time that she was dead?"

"I don't know, exactly," Nancy said, "I was frightened about the house—frightened even when I was on the veranda—by its darkness, and its silence. Then I made up my mind that there was no one here. When I went in to close the window—shutter, I mean— my candle just gave me a glimpse of someone on the couch—I only saw the outline of a figure, there were so many cushions there, and her face was buried in them. I didn't think at all. I was so startled, my fingers just let go of the candle, it fell and went out. Then I ran back to the hall." She hesitated, "Perhaps I ought to tell you that I lifted aside an orange pillow that hid Lydia's face, and when I touched her shoulder, it fell back. It had been hunched over so she was lying on her side."

Mike Sullivan leaned forward eagerly. "You didn't say that before—about touching her. Will you tell us just how she was lying when you first saw her, and how you changed her position? That is very important."

Nancy shuddered and turned appealing eyes toward Jim Mason. Once more he came to her defense. "Go easy there, Sullivan. Miss Chambers has been through a pretty rough time. Sounds as though you suspected her of the murder."

Mike flushed, and for the first time seemed less sure of himself. "I didn't mean anything of the sort," he protested, "I only wanted to get the story straight while it was fresh in her mind. She'll have to go over it with the police, and if she thinks clearly about it now, it will make things easier for her later." He flashed a smile at the girl, one compounded of apology and camaraderie, but Nancy refused to respond,

"I've told you everything I could," she murmured, biting her lip. "When I went back the second time, she was lying just as I left her, and I must have noticed subconsciously that there was no sound of breathing, for suddenly I was dreadfully afraid, even more than I had been. I managed to pull one pillow aside, and I saw her face—her profile, rather, and her outspread hair. I must have known then that she was dead, but I touched her shoulder. It was hunched up, as I told you. I didn't press it, or anything, but at my touch it moved back, as though settling into place, and then I saw the stain on the front of her dress." Nancy's chin quivered—it was too dreadful, having to relive that moment so many times.

The Irishman's voice was gentle; they had all been affected by her story, and the very evident effort it had caused her. "Just one thing more. Miss Chambers—when you saw Lydia the second time, did you get the impression that she had collapsed into that position, or that she had been flung there?"

A horrified murmur came from some man in the group; Clive Bosworth groaned, and Jim Mason said in quick protest, "You're going too far, Sullivan. It's ghastly enough without putting on the screws."

Mike Sullivan's green eyes were staring down into Nancy's white, strained face, dragging the words from her pale lips. "Yes, that was it," she whispered, "I didn't realize it before. That was what was so dreadful—why I knew she had been murdered. She couldn't have fallen like that by herself—someone killed her and then flung her down."

Nancy had forgotten herself, the role she had assumed, and the effort she must make to play it out. She knew only that the Irishman's brutality had clarified her impressions. "It must have been someone she knew," Nancy continued, unaware that she had stumbled to her feet. "Don't you see? Lydia was strong, wiry, yet she didn't put up any fight." Her accusing gaze swept the group of men in front of her. "She was stabbed while she was facing her murderer—he was standing close to her, or she would have seen her danger. It must have been someone she knew—knew well, and trusted!"

CHAPTER III

Nancy's accusation had a startling effect on the group of men she was facing. There were exclamations of surprise, of protest, of dismay—and yet somehow none of them rang true—it was as though she had merely put into words what each of them had been secretly thinking. Glances met, clashed and shifted as each man tried surreptitiously to study the others.

Mike Sullivan was the first to break through the clammy cloud of suspicion that had settled on the room. "You're probably right, Miss Chambers, though it is hard to believe that anyone who knew Lydia could have harmed her. You mustn't forget, though, that in addition to a handful of white men, there are hundreds of coolies on the estate, to say nothing of a couple of dozen servants—any one of whom could have approached Lydia with a cooked-up story that would gain her sympathy. It is too early to jump to conclusions."

Nancy felt deflated. She had been a fool to be carried away like that—to make enemies when she so desperately needed friends—and yet, somehow she was sure that Lydia had been killed by a white man. She felt a fresh blaze of dislike for the Irishman who had rebuked her.

"I can't see that this discussion is getting anywhere," Jim Mason declared. "Let's skip it."

"Maybe not, but at least we have some idea now of when the murder took place," Mike said.

"I don't see it," young Farnsworth put in. "Lord, isn't it bad enough to have Lydia killed without talking, talking, talking about it!" His voice had a hysterical note as he glared at the imperturbable Irishman.

"What do you want to do, sit and drink yourself blotto?" Mike asked contemptuously. Dave flushed, and his hands clenched, but he said nothing in reply to the taunt. "If we can get certain facts established," Mike went on, "it will save time. What the police will want is a clear statement of what happened here so far as anyone of us know it."

"Well, no one knows what happened, so you might as well save your breath." Jim Mason was deliberately rude. He resented Mike's jibe at Dave, the poor kid drank very little as a rule—he was just upset tonight, who the hell did that Irish stiff think he was, anyway?

Instead of being angry, Mike Sullivan's voice was suddenly suave. "Oh, yes, we have collected several facts that are going to help: we know that it was murder and not suicide, for we couldn't find any weapon.

We know that Lydia was alive at ten minutes of nine when Clive and I left for the wayong—she didn't go herself because she said, after the first dozen she'd seen, they bored her with their sameness. She let the servants off for the evening, but they were to come back at ten-thirty so they could prepare supper for the crowd. Lydia said she would fix the flowers and set the table so that the servants could get an early start. Well, she had started to do that—I looked in the dining room a while ago, and saw there were fresh roses and candles on the table, and that she had counted out the flat silver, but it was still in a pile on the sideboard, so it seems fair to assume that the murderer interrupted her at that point."

He whirled abruptly toward Nancy. "How long would it take to put on a lace cloth, put fresh flowers in a bowl, change the candles in the candelabra and count out the knives and forks and so on?"

Nancy shook her head. "There's no way of knowing that. How quickly a person works, and how efficiently—she might have stopped to wash her hands after she'd fixed the flowers, and been distracted by other chores; powdered her nose, darned a pair of stockings—gone to the kitchen "

Mike nodded. "Yes, of course—I didn't think of that." He looked dejected for a second, and then his face brightened. "Anyway, she called good-bye to us from the dining room as we started—that was at 8.50, do you remember, Clive?"

Clive Bosworth was still sunk in a lethargy of grief and shock. "I don't know," he muttered, "I can't remember. God! if only I hadn't gone to that damn wayong—that's all I can think."

"Don't torture yourself, old man," the Irishman's long stride carried him to his friend's side. "I don't believe it would have made any difference. Whoever was dastardly enough to kill a defenseless woman would simply have bided his time until the first moment he found her alone." Clive shuddered, and after a warm, sympathetic grip on the huddled shoulders, Mike returned to his place beside Nancy's chair. "You see what I am driving at, don't you? After we left Lydia spent a few minutes in the dining room, we don't know what else she did, but when Miss Chambers got here around nine-thirty, Lydia was dead and the murderer had gone. Her body was cool, but rigor mortis hadn't set in, so she had been dead for some few minutes, but not overly long."

Nancy felt guilty. Mike Sullivan was assuming that she had arrived at 9.30, whereas actually it must have been nearer ten o'clock.

Jim Mason voiced a protest, "We don't know that Miss Chambers got here at 9.30," Nancy started, and then relaxed as he went on. "It would all depend upon how long it took the taxi to get here—the storm would have slowed it up."

Would the police question the taxi driver and discover that she had come on the Penang train? Perhaps she could shift the trend of the detestable Irishman's thoughts. "I didn't come right in, you know. I stayed on the veranda a long time trying to get up my courage, and then it took quite a while to find the candles and light them."

Mike waved away her explanation, "It would seem a long time to you, but it was probably only a few minutes, ten at the most." He paused as though struck with a new idea, and his eyes regarded her speculatively, Nancy's gaze leaped fearfully to meet the question she dreaded—if she had discovered Lydia's body even as late as 9.45, what had she been doing in the intervening forty-five minutes that elapsed before the men arrived at 10.30.

Before he could voice the question, if he were actually planning to do so, there was the sound of a car on the driveway outside, and automatically everyone stiffened to attention.

"It's not the police," Bill Pearson exclaimed. "It's the Harvys. I forgot all about them, but there's no mistaking Betty's voice." Light footsteps, followed by heavier ones, crossed the veranda, and a blonde, fluffy woman wrapped in a fur-collared evening coat appeared in the hall. "So sorry to be late, Lydia dear," she trilled. "But the car wouldn't start—water in its something or other, and I simply refused to spoil my new silver sandals by slopping through the mud." She looked remarkably pretty poised in the doorway, shaking raindrops from her curly golden head and glancing from under long darkened lashes and pruned eyebrows at the group of men who had moved forward to meet her.

Towering behind her, almost unnoticed, stood her husband, John Harvy, a middle-aged man with shoulders slightly stooped, a brown, close-clipped moustache, and friendly eyes set deep in a lined brown face. "Where's Lydia and Clive?" he asked matter-of-factly, his words booming through his wife's chatter.

For a second no one spoke, and then Mike said gently, "I'm afraid you are in for a bad shock, Harvy. Lydia has been killed." The group around the door shifted, and the Harvys had a clear view of the brightly lighted living room, and the shrouded figure on the couch. Betty smothered a little scream against her husband's white coat sleeve as he pushed past her.

"What happened?" Harvy asked bluntly.

"She was murdered," David Farnsworth exclaimed quickly, as though fearful that someone else would break the news first. "Stabbed!"

"My God!" Harvy ejaculated. His wife broke into hysterical weeping and mechanically he patted her shoulder, "Take me home, John, take me away. I don't want to see her," she moaned.

"You don't have to, Betty." Dave moved to her side. "Come in the dining room with me, and I'll get you a bracer."

"No, no," she pushed him away, "I must speak to Clive." Hurriedly she dabbed her eyes with a flimsy chiffon handkerchief, and with her gaze carefully averted from the motionless figure on the couch, made a circle which brought her to the far side of the man who was still sitting motionless in his chair. "Clive, Clive— It's terrible, but you must not give way like this," she took hold of his limp hand and pressed it between both of hers. "You must brace up, not sit here brooding—"

"Who did it?" John Harvy was asking in a shocked voice. "Not one of the servants?" He ignored Mike Sullivan, and addressed his question to Bill Pearson.

"I don't know, sir," Bill replied. "The servants all seem to have alibis. Sullivan talked to them." Bill Pearson was the only man in the room, Nancy thought, who didn't seem to be antagonistic to the Irishman. Was it because he was the only person who didn't have something to hide, or was he trying to curry favor? The room seemed full of undercurrents of distrust and animosity, and instead of Lydia's murder drawing them together in a common bond of sorrow and indignation, her death had apparently unleashed all kinds of ugly emotions. She didn't like any of them, except perhaps Jim Mason who had tried to be kind. Mike Sullivan was an officious bully; that young Farnsworth was a fool— look at the way he was hanging around Mrs. Harvy, like a dog drooling for a bone. Clive Bosworth's grief was too theatrical, too abject; if he was anything of a man, he would keep his feelings to himself and take charge of the situation instead of weakly sitting back and letting the Irishman do his job for him. Bill Pearson was so extraordinarily good looking that there must be something wrong with him. No, she decided, there was no one in that room that she'd trust around the corner of a glass house; and yet they were the people she would have to be associated with if she stayed here—and now she would have no alternative about that. Even if she had another place to go, the police would insist upon her staying around for a time; anyway, she'd like to see Lydia's murderer caught and punished.

Her reverie was interrupted by Jim Mason's appearance at her side, "Our manners have all gone to the dogs, I'm afraid, Miss Chambers. No one thought to introduce the assistant manager, Mr. Harvy, and his wife to you."

John Harvy came forward, and acknowledged Jim's introduction with a warm, friendly handshake that somehow matched the expression in his deep-set grey eyes. "Betty, my dear," he said in a loud voice, "you must come and meet Lydia's friend, Miss Chambers. She has had a tragic time of it."

Reluctantly his wife turned and crossed the room with a cold, appraising feminine look that raked Nancy from the top of her ruffled head to the toes of her muddy white brogues. "How do you do?" she asked in a remote little voice. "I didn't know that Lydia was expecting you today."

Nancy forced a polite smile. "My plans were uncertain. Lydia told me to come whenever I could, so I just descended upon her at the first opportunity."

"Oh, yes," Betty murmured vaguely. "You're an actress, aren't you?" And then as though she had disposed finally of Nancy and her erratic behavior, she returned once more to Clive. He was sitting up straighter now, as though Betty's low, urgent conversation had given him strength.

John Harvy's face seemed to furrow into deeper lines at his wife's rudeness, and ponderously he tried to excuse her. "Betty is very much upset—she and Lydia saw a lot of each other—the only white women on the estate, of course. It will mean a lot to her, when she gets over the shock, to have you here."

Yes, Nancy thought derisively, just about as much as Lydia meant to her. If that little cat isn't out to get Clive Bosworth, I miss my guess—and Lydia not dead three hours. Almost as though he had read her thoughts, John Harvy went on, "We saw a great deal more of Clive, of course, than we did of Lydia. He practically lived at our house while Lydia was home." Nancy nodded as though she accepted his awkward explanations—she was sorry for him.

To their mutual relief, the necessity for further conversation was eliminated by the arrival of the police car and the heavy tramp of feet entering the house. There was a feeling of strained expectancy in the room, a nervous shifting of position and a sudden

silence as a stocky, square-jawed, red-faced man in a
khaki uniform appeared in the hall, his usually jovial
expression constrained into one of gravity. He spoke
quietly, in a deep voice to the men who had gone forward to meet him; John Harvy, Bill Pearson and Jim
Mason, and then moved into the living room. For a
moment he stood by the doorway, his small, intelligent
dark eyes surveying the scene, the shrouded figure on
the couch, the grief-stricken husband sitting close by,
Betty Harvy standing beside him and David Farnsworth restlessly shifting his feet as he edged away;
Nancy sitting forlornly on the long Singapore chair,
her blue suit rumpled and stained; Mike Sullivan
turning to nod a greeting to the officer.

Betty Harvy stooped to murmur something into
Clive's ear as the policeman came slowly toward
them, and with a visible effort Bosworth stumbled to
his feet. It was the first time Nancy had had a clear
view of him, and much as she hated to admit it, there
was something very appealing about his hollow eyes,
his high-bred features, and the boyish mop of light
disheveled hair.

"I'm sorry, Clive. This is a damnable thing!" the
officer's big hand closed warmly over the Englishman's.

"Thanks, Joe," he said, and then added helplessly,
"I can't understand it! Who would want to harm Lyd-
ia? she was such a good sort, too good to everybody!"
His voice choked, and then with an effort he said,

"It's pretty well done me in. Mike will tell you what happened—he'll give you any help you need."

McCleary nodded. "I brought Doc Sparkes along with me. He'll want to get on with his examination, and I'd like to go over this room. Could you people adjourn somewhere the dining room, perhaps?"

"No, not there." Betty Harry's voice was shrill. "It's the way Lydia left it, partly fixed for the supper party she was having—it would be too ghastly to sit there watching those flowers and candles. We'd all rather sit out on the veranda, wet as it is."

The officer shrugged. "Just as you like, so long as this room is cleared." There was a concerted movement toward the hall, and a tall, elderly man with a grey moustache, gold-rimmed spectacles and tired shoulders, broke off his conversation with Bill Pearson and picking up the little black satchel beside him, moved with professional deliberation toward the couch. His matter-of-fact action hastened the exodus, as though each person present dreaded to see the sheet drawn back from that quiet form.

As soon as the room was empty, Doctor Sparkes pulled the covering away from the still figure, and he and McCleary stared down at the helpless form of the murdered woman. The living room was very quiet, but from the veranda came the sound of scraping chairs, creaking rattan, and the subdued murmur of voices. "God!" muttered the officer, wiping his forehead with the back of his hand. "What a shame!

She was a fine woman. Who would have thought a thing like this would happen."

The doctor grunted. His gentle fingers were already busy. McCleary turned away. "With eight or nine people milling around all over the place, I don't suppose I will find much, but I'd better get on with the job."

"Any sign of the weapon, Doc, now that you've moved her?" he asked hopefully a few minutes later. "If she had stabbed herself, it would simplify things for everybody."

"No," Doctor Sparkes replied. "And you'd better get the idea of suicide out of your mind. Start looking for a dagger, or a stiletto—something with a six-inch blade, sharp as a razor on both edges. She couldn't have killed herself."

Quickly and efficiently Joe McCleary began his systematic search, dividing the room into sections and painstakingly examining each article of furniture, shaking out cushions and chair seats, fingering the intricacies of wicker and rattan, lifting down etchings and hunting prints from the white walls, and then, dropping down on all fours to search the yellow wood floor and rugs. Not until he completed a painful circle of the room, and once more reached the couch, did he emit a grunt of satisfaction. His blunt fingers moved over some dark drops on the deep blue Chinese rug. The spots were still damp, and his fingers, as he held them up to the light, had a reddish-brown smear.

"She must have been standing here when she was stabbed," he announced. "Does that jibe with what you've found?" He glanced up at the doctor who was once more drawing a sheet across the body.

"Yes, I should say so. She must have been standing near the couch. The weapon entered the body in the center of the cardiac region, avoided the sternum bone, pierced the pericardial septum—that's the membrane separating the pericardium from the main body cavity, penetrated the fibrous layer of the pericardium, then the inner layer, and finally the anterior tip of the heart where the great blood vessels are. Quite a bit of the yellow pericardial fluid was spilled and there was a large quantity of blood which soaked through her clothes and into the couch. She's been dead between two and four hours—can't tell closer until after the autopsy."

"Don't expect me to remember all your dictionary words, Doc. You can put them in your report. It's enough for me that she was stabbed in the lower part of the heart," McCleary said, standing up and brushing off the dust he had acquired in his progress around the room. "She was killed instantly?"

"Oh, yes. I should say the murderer caught her after the blow and slung her onto the couch—otherwise there would be a lot of blood on the floor, instead of just a few drops." The doctor paused, and then added, "From the downward direction of the wound, she was probably killed by someone several inches taller than she. It might have been done by a big, strong woman, or even a tall one who was angry enough to make the wound."

"That doesn't help me much," McCleary grumbled, "Mrs. Bosworth was surprisingly small—always gave the impression that she was a lot taller than five feet two. Almost everybody is taller than that, even the Malays."

The doctor was staring at McCleary with a somber expression in his eyes, "Mrs. Bosworth was small, but she was very lithe and wiry, and her muscles are strong. Strange she didn't put up more of a scrap, don't you think? Strange that she'd let the murderer get so close to her; that she didn't try to run away apparently, or defend herself."

"Good God, Doc—" McCleary gulped, and his red face faded to a pale pink. "That means that the poor thing was killed by someone she trusted. She wouldn't let a native get that close to her, not even her own servants, unless it was her personal maid, and Saidi simply worshipped the ground she walked on."

Doctor Sparkes nodded. "Not a nice thought, Joe—but there it is. You'd better face it now; she was killed by someone she knew well, and that means someone we know too."

"But—Oh, Lord, it's incredible. Why, I know all these chaps. You couldn't find a finer, more upstanding lot of men on any estate. Why, I've hunted with them, drunk with them, played poker with them— and you get to know a chap pretty damned well under those conditions."

The old doctor shrugged. "Well, counting the men out, there are still the women, Mrs. Harvy and the American girl." His expression was solicitous as he watched the dismay on his friend's face. "It's a rotten mess, Joe. The first white murder you've ever had in your district, and it had to be one of your friends. If I were you, I'd call up Johore Bahru and ask for help. You're too close to all these people—you'll break your heart over this case if you try to crack it alone."

McCleary shook his head. "If one of them killed her, the rest of them will all be with me. They'll be as anxious as I am to uncover the swine."

From the disillusion of seventy years, Doctor Sparkes smiled sadly. "I hope you're right. Tonight should tell the story. Only, remember, Joe, it's human nature to resent a policeman, and practically everyone has something or other in his life that he doesn't want dragged out for public exposure." His tone became matter-of-fact. "I suppose you'll be here for some time. Mind if I drive your car back to Kluang? I'll send my sais back with it."

McCleary was once more the official. "Tomorrow will be time enough for that. I'll spend the night

here—I've got the servants to question after I've finished with the crowd outside. You'll send for the body,
and arrange for an autopsy, won't you?" He glanced
again toward the couch, and then said slowly, "We
can't leave her there tonight—we'll have to use this
room—and besides, in this climate?"

"I was thinking about that," the doctor said. "Is
there a room here that is cooler than this?"

McCleary nodded, "Clive's office, downstairs under his bedroom there," he nodded toward the rear
wall. "There's an inside stairway from his room, and
the office is concrete. Can you give me a hand, or
shall I call one of the other men?"

"I'm not a cripple yet," the doctor snorted. "Wrap
her up in the couch cover—and later you can throw a
rug over the stains here so as not to upset any of your
squeamish friends. Come on—I want to get home."

The veranda, lighted now by orange-shaded lamps,
still had a desolate air, despite its occupants. Wisps
of mist, aftermath of the storm, drifted past the rusty
screens, cicadas shrilled their rasping notes, and a
myriad of strange humming, chirping, twittering
sounds brought the mysterious menace of the jungle
closer. There was a sudden creaking of rattan, an uneasy shifting of position as the doctor and the officer
appeared at last in the doorway.

"Now then," McCleary said in a friendly voice,
as Doctor Sparkes, with a gruff "Good night," went
quickly down the steps. "If someone will just remove

the fancy shades from those lamps so that we can have a little light—"

Several of the men, as though eager for action of some sort, jumped to lift off the offending shades. At the resultant glare, the taut, white faces of the little group leaped into haggard relief, all of them nervous, shrinking.

"Bring your chairs a little closer, won't you? So that I can talk to you all at the same time," Mc-Cleary asked, pulling out a straight wicker chair and lowering himself into it. He waited until a reluctant semi-circle had been formed in front of him. It seemed to him that all of their faces looked hard, the eyes wary; hands were clenched on chair arms, or moved restlessly, picking at sharp ends of wicker, feet scraped, long white-trowsered legs crossed and recrossed themselves.

"There's nothing to be nervous about," McCleary began in a calm voice. "This is just a little informal talk among friends who are anxious to discover the person who killed Mrs. Bosworth. I know I can count on all of you to co-operate with me, and that you are just as eager as I am to bring her murderer to justice."

There was a murmur of agreement, but not a face relaxed its guard. "First, I want to ask whether any of you know anything that will throw any light on tonight's tragedy. Did you know of anyone who had reason to wish Mrs. Bosworth out of the way?"

Heads shook, glances shifted warily, but no one answered in words. "Well, then, we'll have to approach the problem from another angle," McCleary said, patiently, after an awkward silence. "We'll try to eliminate all those who could not have committed the murder, and in order to do that, we'll have to find out just when Mrs. Bosworth was killed, and just where everyone was at that time. I understand that Miss Chambers was the first to discover the crime. Is that right?"

Nancy caught her breath. It was coming now. If only she could keep the secret of her identity. She forced her hazel eyes to meet the officer's direct gaze as she nodded her bright curly head. "Yes, it was I who found her," she admitted, moistening her dry lips.

The policeman was pulling a shabby notebook from his baggy pocket and opening it on the table in front of him— "Will you tell me, please, in your own words just what happened."

It wasn't until after the second murder that Nancy realized how wrong she had been in every decision she had made that night, that if she had told the whole truth to the officer, Lydia's murderer would have been exposed and two lives would have been saved.

CHAPTER IV

Nancy's low, soft voice was the only sound on the veranda, as she once more told the story of her arrival, her fear of the dark, silent house, her eventual discovery of her friend's body. It was less of an ordeal than she had expected; the officer seemed to be taking down her statement without question, and mercifully in this informal examination, he was concerned primarily, not with Nancy herself, but with the scene of the crime.

"So the house was in complete darkness?" he asked as she finished her tale and leaned back against the damp pillow in her chair. "When did the lights come on?"

"I don't know. I tried them when I went into the house, and found they were out of order. I fainted when the men returned from the wayong, and when I came to, the lights were all ablaze."

"Who turned on the lights?" McCleary's eyes swept the group of men.

"I turned on the hall ones," Jim Mason said, promptly. "Sullivan got ahead of me and caught Miss Chambers as she pitched forward." Nancy turned a startled gaze on Mike's lean profile—she had thought it was Jim who had carried her into the living room.

Mason continued, "Sullivan yelled to me to turn on the light, and they flooded the hall as soon as I touched the button. No one really believed what she said about Lydia's being dead, you see, we were more concerned about Miss Chambers and the state she was in. It wasn't until Sullivan carried her into the living room, and someone switched on the lights there, that we found Lydia."

"I turned on those lights," David Farnsworth volunteered.

The officer glanced at him and nodded. "All right, you can tell me about that later— Where's Hamilton? He'll know about the lights. They're his job, aren't they?"

David Farnsworth, angry at what he regarded as another snub, turned to Betty Harvy, as though seeking sympathy, but she snapped something at him in an irritated whisper, and he slouched moodily back in his chair.

There was an embarrassed silence in response to the policeman's inquiry, and then Bill Pearson said reluctantly, "I'm afraid you won't get much out of him tonight, Joe. I sent one of the Malay boys to fetch him, and the boy found him down at the factory with a couple of empty bottles on the table in front of him. You know what that means—he was dead to the world."

The inspector nodded. "Wasn't he invited to the supper party tonight, Clive?"

Bosworth started at the question, and it was a moment before he seemed to grasp its meaning. "Yes, yes, of course. Lydia asked everybody. I remember she said it was her first real triumph with him, and that she'd make him like her yet."

The officer seemed to pounce. "Didn't Hamilton like Mrs. Bosworth, then?"

Clive looked bewildered. "No, not much. He hasn't much use for anybody, you know, except Bill Pearson."

"Did he have any special reason for disliking Mrs. Bosworth?" McCleary persisted.

"He thought she pampered the coolies—and that she shouldn't interfere." Clive looked uncomfortable. Bill Pearson was frowning, but it was John Harvy who spoke up. "There was really nothing to it, Joe. Ronald Hamilton wouldn't hurt a fly. You're wasting your time, if you suspect him."

"That may be, but just the same I want to know what the trouble was. If you know about it, suppose you tell me."

John Harvy frowned and shifted his long legs into a more comfortable position. "Hamilton prides himself on his efficiency, and he's been here so long that he knows his labor force inside out. Mrs. Bosworth was a very warmhearted, impulsive person, always helping somebody, and the natives used to take advantage. Her maid, Saidi, complained that her husband, a Malay named Sidin, who worked in the factory, was very sick, and that Hamilton made him work just the same. Sidin is the sort who always malingers, but instead of explaining that to Lydia when she spoke to him about the man, Hamilton went off the deep end and told her to mind her own business, and let him mind his. Lydia was quick-tempered too, you know, and she flew back at him. Later, when she told me about the affair, I explained that Sidin was always whining and that Hamilton had had him thoroughly examined by a doctor, so he knew there was nothing wrong. She apologized to Hamilton, but for all his dourness, he's sensitive, and the fact that Lydia had believed him capable of injustice to one of his men rankled. That all happened a year ago, before Lydia took the trip home, so you see it could have had nothing to do with this affair. Ever since she came back, Hamilton has been willing to forget the incident; the fact that he accepted her invitation for tonight showed that. He keeps very much to himself, you know, never goes anywhere."

The policeman looked at Bill Pearson as though for confirmation. "Is that right, Bill? Do you think Hamilton had got over his ill feeling for Mrs. Bosworth? You ought to know, since you live with him."

Bill nodded, and his firm, well-molded lips relaxed into the suspicion of a smile. "Yes indeed. He hasn't a great opinion of women, but he admitted to me last night that Mrs. Bosworth was 'nane th' worrse, as women gae.' High praise for him."

"He was definitely planning to come here tonight?"

"Yes. He was pleased at Lydia's insistence—and flattered because she was having kedgeree especially for him. He spent an hour telling her just what she mustn't do, in order to have it right."

"Humph!" The officer was clearly skeptical—it looked to him as though Hamilton was the guilty man. "Strange then that he didn't show up, wasn't it?"

"Not if you know Hamilton. He wouldn't leave the factory if there was any danger of the lights going off in the storm. He probably worked like a dog when he found something had gone wrong with them, and then, when they were fixed, took a drink. Once he tastes the stuff, you know, he can't stop."

Betty Harvy, piqued at being so long ignored, and at the interest with which Clive was following the inquiry, leaned forward. "I don't understand all this fuss about the lights being off, Mr. McCleary," she complained in a childish tone. "I was home all evening, and my lights didn't go out."

"What's that?" the officer turned to her sharply.

"I was home all evening, and the lights were on the whole time," she repeated. "I never knew them to go off in one of the houses here without having the whole place plunged in darkness."

"Anybody there with you?" he asked.

"No, I was alone. John went to the wayong with the rest of the men, and the servants all went too, of course."

McCleary grunted. "Any of you other men have trouble with your lights?" He glanced questioningly at Pearson, Mason, and Farnsworth.

They shook their heads, each of them replying that they had been away from their bungalows during the storm and had no way of knowing whether or not their lights had been affected; and of course, the native kampongs weren't wired for electricity.

"Ever know of the lights in just one house going off in a storm, and the others remaining intact?"

There was a silence as though they were reluctant to commit themselves to a statement which would impugn the veracity of either Nancy or Betty. It was Mike who broke the silence. "Perhaps the lights weren't damaged by the storm, but just a fuse blew here. That would explain why this house was dark and the Harvy house had lights."

"If that was the case, then someone must have put in a new fuse, after Miss Chambers got here, and before you arrived; and Miss Chambers is certain that she heard no one."

Nancy looked worried. The lights really had been out—so either Mrs. Harvy was deliberately lying in order to discredit her or— "Where is the fuse box, please?" she asked.

"In the rear of the hall, near the back door," Mike said.

"Then, I am sure no one could have touched it while I was here alone," Nancy said positively. "My ears were strained for any sound, and I spent most of my time in the hall. No one could have opened a door, and put in a fuse without my hearing him. Whoever it was, should have had to have a light, and I would have seen the reflection on the ceiling. It's impossible." Her gaze shifted from the officer to Mrs. Harvy, whose eyes refused to meet the challenge.

"We'll check all that later, when Hamilton is available," McCleary said. "That can wait, but I don't want to keep you people up longer than I have to, so we'll get on with your stories. I'll finish with the ladies first. Mrs. Harvy," Betty jumped as she realized he was addressing her, and her blue eyes opened wide, "where were you this evening, and what were you doing?"

"I was home reading," she said virtuously. "The English mail had come in and I had lots of papers and magazines to keep me busy. Time went so fast that I didn't know how late it was until John came back. Then we had trouble starting the car and didn't get here until last."

"You were alone all evening?"

"Yes, I told you that," her tone was bored. "I let the servants off early. I think it's a mistake to spoil them, but Lydia let hers go, and she persuaded everyone else. She had awfully radical ideas—I think she would have approved of a forty-hour week for the whole plantation."

"You didn't go out? Didn't run down here to help Mrs. Bosworth in her preparations for supper?"

Betty shook her head. "No, I didn't move from the house. I knew if I had come, I'd just have been in the way. Lydia was so appallingly efficient, and such a scrumptious cook that she wouldn't have wanted me around. I did wish that I was up there though when the storm broke—I'm terrified of lightning—and I never saw such a storm, why—"

McCleary, who had been making a few notes in his looseleaf notebook, looked up impatiently. "Yes, yes—it was too bad—that will be all for the present, Mrs. Harvy." There was a faint smile on Betty's red rosebudded mouth as she settled back, which vanished as the officer spoke to the man beside her.

"Clive, when did you last see Mrs. Bosworth alive?"

The young Englishman jerked up in his chair. "I don't know, exactly. What time did you say it was, Mike, when we started for the wayong?"

"I asked you, Clive," the officer cut in. "I'll talk to Mike later. Where was Mrs. Bosworth when you left?"

"In the hall. I stopped to ask her if she was sure she didn't mind our going. She laughed and said she was glad to get us out from under foot because she had a lot of things to do."

"What did she mean by that?"

"Oh, the usual things, I guess—fix up the table, empty ashtrays, and get dressed—the usual rigmarole a woman goes through before a party. She was in the dining room bustling around as we went down the steps, for she called 'Good-by' to us out of the window." Clive's face was very pale, and his hands fidgeted on the arm of the chair, but he spoke composedly.

"I see. What did you do for the rest of the evening?"

"I was at the wayong," Clive sounded surprised. "We all were, you know."

"Yes, yes, I know that," the officer's tone was patient. "But I want to know who you were with, who you saw, what you did. Did you leave the wayong at all? Did you come back to the house?"

Clive seemed bewildered by the cascade of questions, at any rate his expression changed suddenly, Nancy thought, and his answers came slowly.

"I walked down to the show with Mike. The natives had benches reserved for us right up in front, and we sat there. It was pretty dark inside—just those stinkin' little oil lamps. I saw all the rest of the chaps at one time or another. Let's see, Bill sat near us, and

Dave did too. John came in late and had a seat at the
back. I don't know where Jim sat, but he was there,
for I ran into him once during the evening when I
went outside to get a whiff of air."

"You didn't go back to the house at all?"

"No, not until later. We passed the word around
when we'd stuck it as long as we could, and we all
decamped together, a few minutes after the servants left. Those wayongs go on into the night, and
Lydia was having supper at eleven."

McCleary stared at him as though about to ask
more questions, and then stifling a sigh, said, "Well,
that's all for now." With an air of relief, Clive relaxed
into his chair as the officer addressed Bill Pearson.
"Give me a résumé of your evening. Bill. You know
the sort of thing I want."

Bill leaned forward. "I was busy finishing some
letters that I wanted to go out in tomorrow's mail,
and I didn't get down to the wayong until a little
after nine. My boy had a chair for me, and as I sat
down I noticed Bosworth and Sullivan were there.
During one of the intermissions I went over and
talked to them, and wandered about a bit. It was
frightfully stuffy inside, and my seat was too near
the orchestra for comfort. I was glad when Sullivan
gave me the high sign to leave."

"You didn't go up to the house for anything?"

"No, sir."

"When did you last see Mrs. Bosworth alive?"

"This afternoon, about four-thirty. She was apparently taking a walk, for she was a mile from the house and cutting across the corner of my division. I thought she might have a message for me, and I shouted, but she shook her head and just waved her hand."

"You didn't speak to her then?"

"No, she was too far away. I just happened to notice her, that was all."

McCleary frowned. "Did you ever see her there before? Was it usual for her to wander around the estate alone?"

"I never saw her so far from the house, or in that particular place alone, but she was a very active person and interested in everything about the estate."

McCleary turned to Clive. "Was there any significance in Mrs. Bosworth's being out there this afternoon? Did she say anything to you about it before or afterwards?"

Clive shook his head. "Not that I know of. She took a walk almost every day, but usually she'd stick to the tracks. I don't know why she'd be going in that direction except that she might have been looking for new specimens for her wild garden—flowers and ferns."

"She'd hardly find anything suitable in the cleared ground, would she?"

"No, but between Pearson's division and Mason's, there was a neck of jungle, and I told her at tiffin that Harvy thought we ought to clear that out; that our production had been falling off and we ought to plant more rubber. That might have reminded her of the place and decided her to look around before it was burnt over."

The officer frowned—it sounded screwy to him for a white woman to go for a stroll in the jungle. She must have known she was apt to meet snakes or a tiger, or God knows what—and yet her husband and her friends didn't seem to think it strange. If she'd been the flirtatious type like Mrs. Harvy, he would have suspected a rendezvous. No doubt it was a trifling matter, but it worried him.

"And Mrs. Bosworth didn't mention her walk to you at teatime, Clive?" he persisted.

Clive flushed. "I didn't come home for tea. I cut work early so that Mike and I could drive over to Batu Pahat. He'd heard there was a man-eating tiger in the district, and that they were organizing a hunt. When we got there, though, we found it was just a yarn, there was no tiger at all, so we had a few beers and came back. Didn't get here until around eight, and Lydia ticked me off because we missed the early dinner she had planned. It was just a snack because of the supper party later. She never mentioned her walk. I'd have told her I was going to Batu Pahat, of course, but I just didn't think—Mike said 'Can you give the jolly old job a miss this afternoon? I'd like to get in on that tiger hunt up around Batu Pahat—

it's coming off in a day or so, I heard!' That was all I needed to know. We were in the car and away."

The other rubber men glowered at Mike Sullivan, and even the officer looked disapproving, but, though Mike's smile was mocking, he said nothing.

Clive looked distressed belatedly at his thoughtlessness. "I ought to have told Lydia—I was always a rotten husband."

McCleary turned to Mason.

"It's your turn now, Jim."

Jim straightened in his chair beside Nancy and leaned forward. "I went to Kluang this afternoon to see a shipment of rubber off, and was held up there at the Rest House talking to a gang of roughnecks." He grinned at the officer, who smiled faintly in return. "Yes, I remember that session, but you left after I did, so carry on from that point."

"Well, my drinking today was very conservative. I had only three beers, so I was perfectly compos mentis when I left the Rest House, as everyone there will tell you; it elicited surprise rather than admiration. I collected the supplies I had ordered earlier, and started home, but my radiator began to boil soon after I left town, and I had to stop at every stream I came to, to put in fresh water. I couldn't figure out what was wrong with the blasted thing, spent a lot of time fussing over it, and then it occurred to me that my fan belt might be greasy and not letting in the cool air. It was pitch dark by then, of course, so I had to use my flashlight to get it off, and then I didn't make much headway cleaning it, so I rubbed some dust on it, and just hoped it would carry me home. As I passed the kampong, I saw the wayong had started, but I had to clean up so I went along to my place. Farnsworth had already left, so I hurried into a fresh suit and set out again. I saw the storm was apt to break any minute, and as a matter of fact I only beat it by about thirty seconds. I met Bosworth outside the door, and I told him my adventures."

"That's right, by Jove, you did!" Clive exclaimed. "I'd forgotten. He told me about his fan belt, and I said he'd better have his kabun rub it with kerosene." His thin, pale face brightened at the memory of his advice, "Best thing in the world—"

"When did you last see Mrs. Bosworth?" the officer interrupted, looking up from his notebook.

"Last night," Jim said. "I walked down to the house with Clive, and she suggested that I come in and have a whisky soda with him. I mentioned that I was going into town today, and she asked me whether I'd mind getting her some stuff. She made out a list." His voice held a queer, regretful note as he added, "the things are still in my car."

Nancy shivered—poor Lydia making out a list of things she would never have occasion now to use.

"Harvy!" McCleary's voice sounded loud and abrupt in the silence which had been filled with the thought of Lydia's last hours of life. "How did you spend the evening, and when did you last see Mrs. Bosworth alive?"

John Harvy's face looked old and sad. "I saw her at nine o'clock, or a bit after."

There was a sudden, surprised shifting and creaking of chairs as everyone turned to look at him, and the air was tense with excitement. Even McCleary's stubby pencil ceased to scratch. "Go on," the officer exclaimed tersely.

"I stopped by to see whether Clive had left. I had some things to talk over with him; a sudden idea as to why our production had dropped off; but that isn't what you want to hear, is it?" He passed a hand across his brow as though to smooth out the deep lines of his frown. "I didn't go inside. I just called from the driveway, and Lydia answered me. She was in the dining room and came to that window—" He pointed toward the window facing them, and automatically everyone glanced up as though expecting to see Lydia there. "She said that Clive and Mike had left ten or fifteen minutes before, so I went on. I sat in the back at the wayong, which upset the natives— they had saved a place of honor for me down beside Clive and Sullivan. I was very tired, and I knew I couldn't stand being so near the gamelons. I'm afraid I didn't pay much attention to the wayong, I was too absorbed in my own thoughts; and I had lost all track of time when Dave tapped me on the shoulder and said it was time to go."

"You didn't go into this house at all, Harvy?"

"No, just hallooed for Clive from the driveway."

"Did Mrs. Bosworth seem worried? Did she seem to be alone?"

"So far as I know. I had heard her singing as I approached—singing the way one does when one is alone. And she seemed cheerful enough when she spoke. Her back was to the lighted room, and there was the screened porch between us, so I couldn't see her face, but there was nothing different in my impression of her."

"You didn't have any reason to dislike Mrs. Bosworth, or to fear her, did you, Harvy?" The officer's gimlet eyes bored into the lanky planter.

"God, no!" Harvy nearly leaped from his chair in his surprise.

McCleary leaned back, twisting the pencil in his blunt, hairy fingers. He was discouraged at the progress he was making. Every lead seemed to peter out. That was the worst of dealing with white men—friends. Give him a nice straightforward native killing, or a gang robbery, and he'd know where he was at. Wearily he turned to David Farnsworth. "Make your story as brief as you can, Dave, will you? It's getting late, and there's a lot to be done yet."

Young Farnsworth, who had been anticipating his questioning with a morbid eagerness, looked sulky at the request. He was always being pushed aside as though nothing he could do or say was of any importance. Betty Harvy was the only one on the estate who treated him like a man, and now Betty had dished him. The nips he had taken from the brandy bottle gave him courage—he'd show them how they'd underestimated him; that he wasn't the dumb cluck they thought him—

From across the sluggish, alligator-infested Sungei Sengbrong River that formed the western boundary of the estate, came a snarling, blood-chilling AAUM! Terrified, Nancy grabbed Jim Mason's arm. "What's that?" she gasped.

"Just a tiger," he said matter-of-factly, without turning his head. His eyes, bright with excitement, were watching David Farnsworth stumble to his feet.

"I'm not going to keep quiet any longer," he squealed in a shrill, defiant voice. "You're all scared to tell what you know, but I'm not. To hell with all of you! I know who killed Lydia, and I'm going to tell."

CHAPTER V

There was a stunned silence on the veranda as young Farnsworth paused to get the full flavor of the sensation he had caused. Every eye was fixed on him, everyone was tense, either with interest or fear, even the officer edged forward expectantly on his chair.

"I don't care if it does cost me my job," Dave blustered, clenching his trembling hands. "It was Bosworth who killed Lydia, the Tuan Besar himself!"

"Shut up, you drunken fool!" Mike Sullivan jumped to his feet. "You don't know what you're saying."

"Oh, yes, I do," Dave sneered. "I know why you want to shut me up too. Because you helped him. You hated Lydia because she didn't want you sponging on Clive, dragging him away from his work."

"Go back and sit down, Sullivan," the officer snapped as the Irishman, eyes blazing, plunged toward his accuser. Arrested by the tone of authority, Mike stopped. "You don't expect me to take that sort of talk and not do anything about it, do you?" he demanded, glaring from the policeman to Dave.

"I expect you to sit down, Sullivan. You'll have a chance to answer the accusations. This is an inquiry into murder, not a private feud. SIT DOWN!" Mc-Cleary's voice rose to a roar. Reluctantly, the Irish-man dropped back into his seat.

"Now, Farnsworth," the officer said sternly, "you have made accusations against two people. What foundation have you?"

"I know Clive was fed up with Lydia and the way she tried to keep his nose to the grindstone. I know he was away from the wayong for half an hour, be-cause I saw him sneak out and go up the road. I timed him because—well, I had my own reasons." Dave hes-itated, his facts didn't sound very convincing as he put them into words. "He lied about that, didn't he? Look at him! Let him tell you where he was if he hasn't anything to hide!" Clive had shrunk back in his chair and was staring helplessly at his accuser.

Betty nudged him. "Speak up, Clive. Tell the little worm where you were. You just went out to watch the storm, didn't you?"

"There, you see! She's telling him what to say!" David shrieked. "She's the real motive for Lydia's murder. He killed his wife so that he could marry Betty."

"That's enough, Farnsworth!" John Harvy was on his feet. "You leave my wife out of this."

"Your wife," David sneered. "Why don't you look after her then, not let her make a fool of herself over every man on the place? It would suit you down to the ground to be rid of her. If she and Clive cleared out, you'd be manager—that's what you're hoping for. You've always hated Clive, and you knew he wouldn't have lasted here two months if it hadn't been for Lydia."

John Harvy's face was white with rage, and his voice choked as he turned fiercely on the officer. "Either you will make this drunken fool shut up, McCleary, or I will."

The officer nodded. "That will do, Farnsworth. I want facts, not mudslinging."

"Mudslinging! Oh, my God! I've told you who committed the murder and you call it mudslinging!" David yelled. "It's a conspiracy, that's what it is. You all want to cover up the scandal, but you won't get away with it!" Beside himself with rage, Farnsworth whirled around to face his muttering associates. "I know plenty about all of you. Where's that fancy little Malay kris, Mason? The one Lydia admired at your cocktail party. Just the thing to stick into a defenseless woman!" Jim Mason's face whitened beneath his freckles and he checked an exclamation.

David was glaring at Bill Pearson now. "You, Pearson, with your pretty face—I saw Lydia weeping on your shoulder and you trying to shake her off, shut her up when you saw me coming. Why don't you tell about that?"

McCleary jumped to his feet with a shout, but he was too late. Bill Pearson's left arm shot out as he leaped forward, and his fist caught the point of David's chin. There was a wild scramble and shouts of approval as Farnsworth slumped to the floor. Mc-Cleary, white with rage, pushed Bill aside and stooped over the inert form— "Get away, Pearson I'll settle with you later," he roared as Bill, ashamed of his outburst of temper, tried to lift Dave's body. "Mason, take hold of the boy's feet and help me carry him inside. The rest of you stay right where you are."

Jim Mason returned in a few minutes, a grin on his homely, round face. "You certainly landed a pippin," he said to Bill. "He's just come out of it."

"What's he saying now?" Betty Harvy asked anxiously.

"Nothing much. As soon as he came to, McCleary chased me out. Clive's kabun is on guard outside the bedroom door."

"I shouldn't have lost my temper," Bill said. "He was drunk and wasn't responsible for what he said, but it made me see red when he implied that Lydia, that I—" Pearson turned to Clive. "There wasn't anything to his insinuations, you know—" Clive was too preoccupied with his own thoughts to do more than nod indifferently.

"He certainly said plenty," Jim agreed. "I hope to God I can find that damned kris of mine, or I'll be talking to you from behind bars." Despite his levity Mason was obviously worried. "Can't for the life of me remember seeing that kris lately either."

"What's Mr. McCleary doing?" Betty asked in a strained voice.

"He's telephoning to Johore. He's in a frightful temper. Didn't know good old Joe could get so mad. The less we see of him in his present state of mind, the better off we'll be."

As though in answer to the words, the officer appeared in the doorway, his face a grim red mask, and his voice, devoid of all friendliness, was harsh as he said, "In view of what has happened, I will have to keep you all here for the present,"

"Why? What for?—" questions crackled in the sultry air.

"Because you've all lied to me; because I'm not getting co-operation from anyone; because Farnsworth was attacked when he tried to give me information. I've tried to play cricket with you, but it's impossible. A man is coming up from Johore to take over the investigation, and he wants everyone kept here until he arrives."

"Who's coming? Anyone we know?" Mike Sullivan asked, an undertone of anxiety in the voice he tried to keep casual.

McCleary, who had started to turn away, stared at him with hard eyes. "Sergeant Ismael will take charge. He is leaving at once."

"Ismael!" Betty Harvy sniffed. "Sounds like a native."

Without deigning to reply, McCleary vanished indoors, but Mike Sullivan, with a worried expression in his cat-green eyes, said slowly, "He *is* a native— and one of the smartest detectives in the East. God damn Farnsworth!"

"Well, I don't care about any native." Betty's voice was petulant. "I'm going home. Come on, John!" She rose imperiously, gathering her coat about her.

"Sit down, Betty!" her husband commanded. "There's no use drawing any more attention to yourself than you already have. I don't know whether McCleary has any right to keep us here, but I think we'd be fools to antagonize him any more than we have done."

Bill Pearson, who had moved quietly toward the steps, halted. "I suppose McCleary wants a chance to search our bungalows!" He sounded disturbed, and his hand reached for the doorknob, as though in defiance of the officer's command, he was about to hurry away. Then, changing his mind, he turned slowly and went back to his chair.

Nancy, who had been watching and listening with the detached interest of a person who knew she was living in a nightmare, and with the dim assurance that she would eventually wake up safe in her own bed, became suddenly aware of her own danger. McCleary had been gentle with her, interested only in what had happened in the house since her arrival, but she couldn't hope for such an attitude on the part of

another detective. He would want to know all kinds
of personal things about her, would tangle her with
questions to which she knew no answer. Where had
Helene Chambers come from? what was she doing in
the East? what were the names of the plays in which
she had appeared? Lydia probably had letters from
Helene with which the police could check Nancy's
random replies. Was there a chance that Nancy could
get hold of the letters first so that she would know
more about the girl she was impersonating? She almost wished she had told the truth in the beginning
and yet, how could she expect anyone to believe in
her after they knew what had happened in Penang?

With an effort she controlled her rising panic. She
was Helene Chambers, a hard-boiled actress from
New York—not a frightened little librarian from a
small New England village. She ought to act her part
better, look it too. Thus far, fortunately everyone had
been too overwrought, too concerned with their own
affairs to pay much attention to her but at any moment one of them might notice incongruities, and
certainly the strange detective would take nothing
for granted.

It was lucky she hadn't had her baggage marked
with her initials, and that she had had the presence of
mind to scrape off all the labels before she fled from
Penang. At that point, her complacence received a
shock. Had she put her letters in the trunk which
she had checked at the steamship office in Penang, or

were they in her suitcase? She couldn't remember. If
they were in her suitcase, she'd have to destroy them
before the police began to search, and above all, she
must get rid of those telegrams. She glanced around
the group on the veranda with a calculating eye; who
could help her?

Impulsively, Nancy rose and made her way across
the semi-circle, until she stood in front of Clive.
"Mr. Bosworth," her tone was apologetic, "I'm sorry
to be a nuisance, but I wonder whether there is some
place where I could change these damp clothes?" Her
eyes were wide and appealing. "I'm chilled through,
and it looks as though we'd have to be out here indefinitely?"

Clive looked up dazed, and for a second he blinked
as though trying to remember who she was and why
she was there. Then he was on his feet, the well-bred
English host. "Of course, Miss Chambers. *A'fully* sorry to have been so remiss. Forgotten all my manners.
I fancy Lydia has a room fixed for you— Boy!" He
raised his voice to a shout. Nancy drew a sharp breath
of relief. Betty Harvy shifted her head to stare at
the washed-out, insignificant girl who had suddenly
asserted herself, and Mike Sullivan's face lighted into
a grin. It had taken the Chambers wench to arouse
Clive to his responsibilities—the old die-hard English hospitality would pull the poor chap out of his
depression yet, with luck.

A scared Malay boy in a white coat and brilliant hued sarong hurried onto the veranda. "Take these bags along to the Mem's room," Clive said in sing-song Malay, and then to McCleary, who had appeared in the doorway, "Miss Chambers must change her wet clothes—been sittin' around in them for hours."

The officer's glance was skeptical as he met Clive's steady blue gaze, but the picture Nancy made, forlorn and drooping, capped by a well-timed shiver, made him capitulate. "All right, she can go in."

"I'll show her to her room—want to be sure it's all right," Clive said calmly, motioning Nancy to follow the Malay boy whose bare feet were padding along the hall as he balanced the suitcase and hatbox on his head.

McCleary was taken aback by Clive's sudden assertiveness. "Keep out of the other rooms. Farnsworth is in your bedroom and I don't want him disturbed, nor anything in the place. And see that you come right back."

"That's quite all right," Clive nodded. "I'll take Miss Chambers along to her room, but I want to speak to the cookie too. Time we all had something to eat and drink if we have to make a night of it. I ought to have spoken to the servants before this, the poor beggars are probably quite demoralized."

The officer frowned. "I don't want you talking to the servants. Tell the boy there to order supper, if you want to, but it'll have to be served on the porch. I expect to use the dining room."

Clive shrugged, and his expression was sardonic. "I'll take Miss Chambers to her room, and then you can come along and hear what I tell the boy, if that would make you feel better. My only desire is to see that my guests are provided for."

McCleary grunted, "Good!" but he watched Clive's tall figure moving easily down the hall behind the girl, with a puzzled expression. What the deuce had come over the bugger?

Unconscious, apparently, of McCleary's straining ears and suspicious gaze, the Englishman was saying to Nancy in a pleasant voice, "You know where the living room and dining room are." He motioned his head backward without glancing at either door. "This one next to the living room is ours, er, mine. Farnsworth is in there recuperating." He gave a friendly, reassuring nod to a young Malay boy who had risen from the floor outside the door. "McCleary has pressed my kabun—gardener—into service as guard, I see. The room opposite is Mike's—he's here so much that he leaves a lot of his barang, er, baggage, guns and whatnot, you know, so he doesn't have to pack them with him when he comes. The room next to his, second door below the dining room, is the guest room. I fancy Lydia has it ready for you." He peered rather helplessly into the rose-lit room where the young Malay was painstakingly unstrapping Nancy's hatbox and suitcase. "Looks all right, but I don't know much about that sort of thing. I'll send Saidi, Lydia's maid, along to help you."

"Oh, no, please don't," Nancy said quickly. "I'm sure everything is all right. See? there are even fresh flowers on the dressing table and on the bedside table. I'd rather do things for myself. I'm not used to a maid, and I don't know enough Malay to direct her."

"Well—" he turned away. "The guest bath is next to yours—you and Mike can share that—or better yet, you can have that to yourself and he can use mine." He rubbed a hand across his forehead impatiently. "I can't adjust myself to Lydia's—" With an effort he controlled his feelings and went on. "The door at the end of the hall opens out on the rear veranda. Steps go down to a covered passage leading out to the kitchen and servants' quarters. I'll have the boy tell Saidi to put hot water and towels in the bathroom for you, and if you need anything else, just shout." He smiled vaguely down at her, and calling to the boy, strode back along the hall.

Poor Lydia had done her best to make the room attractive, Nancy thought, as she locked the door behind her, but the chintz curtains at the window hung limp and faded, and the heavy fragrance of the jasmine and passion flowers didn't quite drown the smell of mildew. The big bed, shrouded with mosquito netting, and the huge dark wood wardrobe, constant reminders of the tropics, dominated the whole place and somehow made the cushioned wicker chairs and well-equipped, taffeta-petticoated dressing table seem like frivolous intruders. Moths fluttered across the whitewashed ceilings and hurled themselves suicidally against the rose-shaded lights until their singed bodies dropped on the table. Mosquitoes buzzed voraciously around her head, and the dank air sifting through the partially closed slats of the shutters seemed a direct message of warning from the fever-infested jungle.

Half an hour later Nancy nodded approval of the transformed figure reflected from her mirror. Her bronze hair had been piled high in a mass of careful curls, bright rouge enhanced the depth and color of her eyes, lipstick brought out the tender humorous lines of her mouth, and the long, soft drapery of a yellow chiffon frock gave her slender figure added height and dignity.

There was no trace left of Nancy Reynolds, not a scrap of paper in her baggage nor a familiar look or smell about her person, for she had used the powders and perfumes which were part of the furnishings of the dressing table. For better or worse, now, Nancy thought, she was Helene Chambers—mercifully unaware at the moment that the real Helene was a

petite brunette with the amusing vocabulary of a
street gamin.

Nancy turned from the mirror, and with the dramatic gesture decided upon to initiate herself in her
new role, threw open her bedroom door. Resentfully
it hurled itself back against the flimsy wall with a reverberating bang, and almost simultaneously a shriek
of mortal terror echoed through the house.

For a second Nancy cowered back too horrified to
move, but something in the sheer terror of the cry
still echoing in her ears impelled her across the hall
to the door which a dazed Malay boy was still guarding. The scream had come from there, but her limited
knowledge of the language was a barrier between her
and the suspicious kabun.

McCleary was suddenly beside her. "What's the
matter? Did you cry out?"

Nancy shook her head. "Not I. I am sure it was
Mr. Farnsworth. I was just coming out of my room,
and the sound came from here."

McCleary threw open the door, and cursed under his breath as he floundered for a light. Behind
him the kabun was importantly denying entrance to
the excited white people who had crowded into the
hall. Nancy, however, with heavy beating heart had
crept into the room behind McCleary, and stood just
inside the door, shivering in the damp breeze that
blew in from the windows. As the light flashed on,

it was Nancy who first saw that the bed was empty, the sheets impatiently entwined with the open
mosquito netting; and it was Nancy, emboldened by
the light and the obviously deserted room, who discovered the blood marks on the white window sill
below the desolately swinging shutters.

CHAPTER VI

Two hours later a squat, brown-faced Malay, smartly clad in a khaki uniform, alighted from a mud-spattered car and mounted the steps of the vine-festooned bungalow. McCleary, who for the last half hour had been pacing the hall with long, nervous strides, hurried out onto the veranda. "Glad to meet you, Ismael. I'm McCleary of the Kluang office," he said, extending a blunt, hairy hand.

"Sorry to keep you waiting so long a time," the sub-inspector's smile revealed teeth surprisingly white. "A prou would have been swifter on some of the roads than that petrol eater." His calm brown eyes surveyed the other occupants of the veranda, five white-suited men, and two women, one in blue and the other in yellow, all trying to look at ease, all obviously worried or frightened.

McCleary hesitated, and then said in an undertone, "I'll just introduce you to these people, and then we'll go inside and I'll outline the situation." Ismael nodded. "As you will, Tuan."

With a jerk the white officer turned toward Clive. "Mr. Bosworth," he announced, "owner of the bungalow, and manager of the estate, and his guests, Miss Chambers, and Mr. Sullivan." Clive stepped forward to shake hands, and Mike followed him, while Nancy merely stretched her stiff face into the semblance of a smile at Ismael's bobbing bow. McCleary, obviously anxious to get down to business, went on in an abrupt voice, "Mr. Harvy, first assistant, and Mrs. Harvy. Mr. Mason, second assistant, and Mr. Pearson, the third assistant." Betty's nod was curt, expressing her disapproval of a native official, but the men greeted Ismael with a semblance of cordiality.

Impatiently, McCleary waited for Ismael to make his stiff little bows, his formal acknowledgment and polite excuses, and then led the way into the house.

"This is the room where Mrs. Bosworth was found. She was lying on the couch, partly hidden by sofa pillows—Doctor Sparkes and I carried her down into the office under the house, where it is cooler. Do you want to see the body, and look things over here first, or shall I tell you what I have discovered?"

It was obvious that McCleary was anxious to talk about the case, and although Ismael would much prefer to make his own discoveries, glean his own impressions of the people involved, it seemed diplomatic, for the present, to follow McCleary's wishes. "Tell me, if you will, Tuan, what happened. Inspector Campbell told me only that Mrs. Bosworth had been stabbed while the servants and the officials on the estate were at a wayong, and that you wished assistance from his office. He would have come himself had he not been working on another case which he couldn't leave."

McCleary nodded. "That's all right. I know something of your work, and if anyone can get to the bottom of this blasted affair, I think you can. Sit down now, and we'll get on with it." He settled himself in a wicker chair beside the Malay in the farthest corner of the living room where they could talk without being overheard from either the veranda or the hall.

"About quarter of eleven tonight, Bill Pearson, the third assistant on the estate, called me up to report that Mrs. Bosworth had been stabbed. He was naturally upset, and from his statement I got the impression that she had killed herself. I knew all the outfit here, knew them well, and so I got hold of Doctor Sparkes and drove out as fast as I could. Didn't think it necessary to bring any of my men with me. It was obvious, even before the doctor made his examination, that she had been murdered, and murdered by someone she knew well—you see, she must have been facing the murderer and permitted him to come very close, close enough to stab her. There was no sign of a struggle, and no trace of the weapon, a dagger, or a sharp, two-edged knife of some sort."

McCleary drew a long breath, and his face contracted with an expression that seemed almost to be pain. "Well, as I said, I thought I knew these chaps, regarded them as friends, with the exception of Sullivan, perhaps; and I expected that I'd get co-operation from them. Mrs. Bosworth was a charming woman; you'd naturally think her husband and her friends would do everything possible to discover the murderer, wouldn't you? But not at all. I hadn't talked to them five minutes before I knew they'd raised a wall against me. I wasn't a friend any more, I was a policeman, someone to distrust, to deceive."

Ismael's smile was sympathetic. "It was a difficult position for you. In trouble of this sort a policeman, like an undertaker, is a necessary evil—his unpleasant work overshadows all else."

"This is the first white murder I've ever had in my district," McCleary declared in an aggrieved tone. "I'd have sworn these chaps here were as fine and upstanding a group as you'd find on any estate in Malaya—and yet— Well, I'll get on with it, I got no change at all from any of the people I questioned; just the impression that they were each hiding something, and everyone was afraid of what I might unearth; until I came to young Farnsworth. He had been lifting the brandy bottle at frequent intervals to steady his nerves—he isn't much of a drinker ordinarily, and apparently he had a grievance against everyone on the estate. He definitely accused Bosworth of killing his wife, and Sullivan of being an accessory; and then slashed out at everybody, except Miss Chambers whom he didn't know. I'll read you my notes in a minute. There was a lot of confusion; everybody trying to shut him up, and then, before I could stop him, Bill Pearson knocked him out."

McCleary paused to pull forth a stubby pipe and a worn tobacco pouch. His fingers shook slightly as he packed the bowl and applied a match. "Are you a pipe smoker? No? Don't know what you miss. Cigarettes?" He made a motion toward a can on the table nearby. Ismael shook his head, "None of the lesser vices are mine, Tuan."

McCleary seemed to relax some of his stiffness under the soothing influence of tobacco. "Where was I? Oh, yes—with the help of Jim Mason, I carried Farnsworth into Bosworth's bedroom, next door to this room, and brought him around. He was in no shape to talk so I left a kabun on guard at the hall door to see that no one bothered him, and then I called up Johore. Campbell thought I'd better keep everyone involved here at the bungalow until you arrived. I decided that was as good a time as any to question the servants, so I had them come in one at a time—I sat in the dining room where I could see the hall, and at the same time, through the front windows, keep an eye on the people on the veranda. The only white person besides myself in the house was Miss Chambers who had asked to be allowed to change

her clothes—she'd gotten wet in the storm. Bosworth
showed her to the room, and then, in my presence,
told his boy to have the servants serve supper out on
the veranda. It was while they were waiting for supper that I started to interview the servants. Suddenly
there was the most ungodly scream I ever heard. It
echoed through the whole house, and I couldn't tell
where it had come from. I thought Miss Chambers
might have been frightened by something, but she
was all right. The kabun was still in front of the door
guarding Farnsworth, and he said he didn't know
where it had come from either, that no one had been
in the hall. He was scared and dazed, and I suspected
he'd been asleep, so I hurried into Bosworth's room.
Farnsworth was gone. The room was empty, but there
was a bloodstain on one of the window sills, and the
shutters of that window were swinging loose."

Ismael had leaned forward, his eyes bright with
interest. "Pardon, Tuan, but were there no other
openings in the room?"

"Besides the entrance to the hall, there is another
door at the head of a stairs leading down to Bosworth's office; he has it down there so the coolies
and laborers can come and go without entering the
house, but that door was locked, and the key was
on the bedroom side of the door. I locked it myself
after we'd carried Mrs. Bosworth down. No, Farnsworth must have gone through the window, either
voluntarily or involuntarily. Everyone had come

running into the house to find out what had happened, and I herded them all back onto the veranda. Then I sent the servants out to look for Farnsworth. Didn't dare leave the house myself; had an idea the whole thing might have been staged to get me away. I called up the office and had four of my constables come out—all I dared take away from headquarters, and when they arrived, I put them to work looking for the missing man. So far no one has found hide nor hair of him. There are footprints under the window, but whether they are Farnsworth's or someone's else, I don't know. I looked over the shoes worn by the people on the veranda, but none of them showed recent signs of mud and wet; hard to tell, of course, for the men had all been walking earlier in the storm. Anyway, I had had them all under my eye the whole time, except Miss Chambers, and she had clean, new gold sandals on, so that lets her out."

"And the servants, Tuan?"

"I can only vouch personally for Saidi, Mrs. Bosworth's maid. I was questioning her in the dining room at the time the scream came. The rest of the servants claim that they were all busy preparing supper. Their stories check and unless they are all lying, none of them could have gotten in to Farnsworth."

"The servants also had an alibi for the time of Mrs. Bosworth's death?"

"Yes, they all went to a wayong. The servants sat together, and left in a body about 10.00; they were to be back in the house by 10.20 to serve an 11-o'clock supper. The white men were there, too, for part of the wayong, but some of them came late, and all of them moved around. I'll read you their statements." McCleary pulled out his battered notebook, and leaned forward so that the light fell on the scrawled pages.

Ismael produced a similar black loose-leaf book, and with small, distinct handwriting began to jot down the points that interested him in the officer's singsong recital.

"Anything more I can tell you?" McCleary asked as he finished the last page of notes. His gaze, fixed on the precise characters which Ismael had been making, was unmistakably curious.

"You are sure, Tuan, that Mr. Hamilton was not the person who attacked Mr. Farnsworth, or helped to get him out of the room?"

"No, I don't think that's possible. I sent Bosworth's boy down to the factory immediately to check up on Hamilton. He said the Scotchman was sound asleep with his head on the table, just as Pearson reported earlier. The boy couldn't rouse him, but he said there was no trace of Farnsworth's having been there. What else is on your mind? I see you've a number of things written down. If you can see any glimmer of light in this affair, I'd like to know what it is."

For a brief second Ismael hesitated. This was the first time he had ever worked on a case with anyone except Campbell, and he realized that he couldn't

hope for the latitude which his own superior officer always permitted. He was accustomed to working
things out by himself, and only reporting to Campbell when he had something of definite value. The little Malay stifled a sigh at the difficulties he foresaw.
McCleary looked like a good man, an honest officer,
but all the people who were suspect were McCleary's
friends. How much could Ismael afford to tell him as
the investigation progressed—and yet it was essential
that the two policemen work together harmoniously.

"These poor notes of mine are just suggestions,"
Ismael said with seeming candor. "My thought was
this: that we cannot keep those people outside indefinitely. It is not seemly that all of them should suffer
for the evil of one, or perhaps two. I would like to
ask each of them a question or two before we permit
them to retire."

McCleary looked dubious. "I thought we ought to
keep them here until we had a chance to search their
belongings—no telling what they may destroy if we
let them go to their own bungalows. We ought to
search their persons, too, in case they are concealing
the weapon."

"Of course, Tuan, that might be done, but I think
the murderer will have already covered his tracks,
and we would find no evidence of the crime in his
house. As for the others it would take hours to search
their houses, and it would arouse much ill feeling.
The same is true of searching their persons—it could

be done; but we must remember the murderer had an hour or more in which to hide the weapon, and surely he would be too cunning to carry it around with him."

McCleary looked relieved. "I'm glad you see it that way, Ismael. I hated snooping around their personal things, but I didn't want to let my own feelings interfere in anything you thought ought to be done."

Ismael's smile was understanding. "It shall be done only if it becomes necessary. I think, too, Tuan, that if your men have not found any trace of Farnsworth after all this time, it would be well to wait until daylight to continue the search. If he does not appear then, we will get beaters to go through the jungle, and drag the river, but I have an idea, Tuan, that he will be found without so much trouble."

"You don't think he was killed, then?"

The Malay shrugged his plump shoulders. "You found no sign of a crime save some blood on the window sill. It seems unlikely that anyone could have crawled into his room, attacked him—at which point he would have emitted the scream—and then, before you opened the door into the room, drag his body through the window, and make off with it. It seems to me rather, considering the state he was in, that he was frightened by something, and, fearing the vengeance of the men he had denounced, ran away."

"There was a loud bang," McCleary said thoughtfully; "Miss Chambers' door crashed against the hall wall. That may have startled him—the scream came almost at the same instant."

"At any rate, we can do nothing more for him to-night," Ismael announced. "But, these other people, we must watch and protect. You have four men, you said. Why not then send one to guard each bungalow; one for the Harvys, one for that occupied by Pearson and Hamilton, one to the bungalow of Mason and Farnsworth, and the other to the factory? That will prevent any foolish move to run away, or to commit an indiscretion, and will also serve as a protection from harm for the innocent."

"Good, good!" McCleary exclaimed. "The men can keep us informed about what goes on. You and I will stay here, of course—that will give you an opportunity to look over this house. Now, about those questions you want to ask, do you mind telling me what they are? You don't have to, of course," he said hastily. "But I'd like to see how you work, and what I have overlooked. This is my first white murder case, and I admit I'm out of my element; you've made your mark in a lot of them, so I'd like to pick up something of your technique." He swallowed a gulp, and then said stumblingly: "I never thought I'd have a murder like this on my hands, but if it could happen once in an ideal place like the Semang Estate—it can happen again— I'd like to be more prepared next time."

McCleary was pathetic in his disillusion, his self-abasement, Ismael thought, and furthermore, what he had said was true, he should be prepared to cope with crime among the white men of the district who were his own friends. Next time, it would not hurt him so much—he could better balance himself on that hazy line between friendship and official-dom. "The questions, Tuan, are all suggested by your notes," Ismael said. "I am no Pawang to work magic on people I do not yet know." Ismael's voice was deprecating. "I will tell you the questions which I would ask; and this, Tuan, is no reflection, you will understand, on the work you have already done. Without that, I could not even see so far as the blank jungle wall that has been raised by all these unfortunate people."

The little Malay glanced down at his notes. "First, I would like to know more about Miss Chambers who came here from out beyond to discover her murdered friend. That seems like more than one question, but I can sum it up so, 'Why did you come here now?' Of Mrs. Harvy I would ask, 'How did it come that a gentle lady like you, timid I am sure of storms, stayed alone in the house without even telephoning for companionship to your friend Lydia?'

"Of Mr. Pearson, I would ask more details about the walk that Mrs. Bosworth took alone this afternoon, when most white women are sleeping—where she seemed to be going, from which exact direction she had come.

"And there, Tuan, I include questions to her maid, whether the poor lady was upset upon her return, and from the gardener, whether she brought back flowers and ferns. From Mr. Mason, I would request the kris mentioned by Tuan Farnsworth. From Tuan Farnsworth, I would like to know whether it was the brandy that spoke tonight, or whether he deliberately bared his fangs? Of Mr. Bosworth, and this is very delicate, of course, I would ascertain his real feelings for his wife. I would like to know what Mr. Harvy wished to say to Mr. Bosworth that was important enough, at that time, to make him walk a mile out of his way, when he could easily have found other opportunities, more convenient, in which to speak to him. I would like to know exactly what is the motive for Mr. Sullivan's interest in Mr. Bosworth. Hamilton, of course, I would like to ask about the lights." He paused, and though his face was as impassive as Buddha's own, he added, "Of course, Tuan, one question may lead to others, or, as I hope, to voluntary statements."

McCleary's red face broadened into a grin. "More power to you, Inspector. You certainly picked out the kernel in each instance; but if you get a straightforward answer to those questions, I'd say you were qualified to hang out your shingle any day as a full-fledged Pawang."

Ismael's brown, oriental face was serious. "I must learn those answers, Tuan. I must have them, for their own sakes more than ours, they must tell me!"

McCleary, disconcerted by the Malay's gravity, started. "What do you mean?"

"Only the truth, in all its starkness, can combat the evil that stalks this plantation. Can't you feel it, Tuan? It is in the very air of this house!"

Involuntarily the officer gave a deep sniff. "Can't say I do. The house seems all right to me—a bit damp, and there's the smell of mildew of course, and decay always get that in damp weather. A bit gruesome too—the poor little lady downstairs, but tomorrow early, she'll be gone, and things will be normal."

Ismael shook his head. "They can't be normal until we have caught the murderer. At least one of those people sitting so quietly on the veranda is the murderer, unless it is Tuan Hamilton, of course—and another, knowingly or unknowingly, holds the murderer's or murderess' fate in his hands—and so long as he does so, he, or she, is in mortal danger."

"Good God, you think there'll be another murder?" McCleary jumped to his feet, his chin outthrust aggressively at the idea.

"I hope not, Tuan, but I feel strongly that these people must be persuaded to tell the truth at whatever cost to their own feelings. They are all hiding some little personal matters which might cause them to lose face with their friends—about which the police would care nothing—but in that morass of secrets is hidden the face of the murderer and that is what concerns us. Let us peel away the lies and the fears, and we shall see him. But, the murderer too knows that danger—he is counting on the personal vanity, the ambitions perhaps, the dread of scandal, of his or her associates. He is watching, waiting, listening for the first hint that he is known; he is even now trying to influence them, to misdirect suspicion, and if his efforts fail—? Well, he has killed once. What has he to lose now by killing again to protect his secret?"

McCleary gave a strong pull on his pipe which had gone out, and strangled on a mouthful of nicotine—unpleasant as it was, it was more palatable than the things his colleague had been saying. "I see what you mean. Yes—it's quite in order, damn it all," he spluttered, and then added meekly: "What can we do? Who do you think is in the most danger? Tell me that and I'll watch over him like a wet nurse. I can't fight ideas or fears, but give me something tangible, and I'll stick till hell freezes over!"

Ismael looked troubled. "If only we could know that, how simple it would be! I can't be sure." He glanced down at his notebook, flicked its pages, and then shook his head. "I can't tell—it is too soon," he muttered, half to himself. "I must talk to them all, get to know them—and then, it may be too late." He closed the notebook, and for a moment was absolutely still, every muscle in his plump body relaxed as though he were making it vulnerable to unseen forces and emotions.

It all seemed a bit theatric to McCleary who was drawing placidly now on a cleared pipe, and yet— there was something about the funny little beggar that got under your skin. "I don't know, Tuan," Ismael said frankly, "but my feeling is that we should watch over the little American girl with exceeding care. It was she who found the body, who spent such a long, unexplained time in the house, and who has told us so little of herself. Who knows what she may have discovered here; what trace of the murderer she may have found? Without even realizing it, she may be holding his life in her small hand. He left—she came later, so he had no chance to cover up any loose ends or clues he may have left. Oh, yes, Tuan, it is clear that it must be she the murderer is watching more than the others. Allah protect her!"

CHAPTER VII

Nancy, quite unaware of the fact that her safety was a subject of concern to the officers in the next room, was feeling a growing sense of confidence. She was no longer a little nonentity in a crumpled suit, crouching unnoticed on the outskirts of a group of strangers. Her radically changed appearance, her assumed poise, had had its own reward in the homage that was being paid her by the men. She could read the measure of her success in Betty Harvy's hard eyes, and ill-disguised hostility. The men who had rushed into the house at the sound of Farnsworth's terrified shriek had regarded her with varying degrees of admiration and solicitude, and despite their reaction to the new mystery, and to McCleary's abrupt orders, had accorded Nancy a new position. She was not only an honored guest now, but the hostess.

The houseboy, carrying the coffee tray on to the veranda, had deposited it matter-of-factly on the table in front of her, and Clive, noticing her involuntary glance at Betty Harvy, had said quietly, "Don't mind serving the coffee, do you, Miss Chambers?"

Betty, who had expected to act as hostess, exclaimed, "Perhaps I had better pour, Clive; it is an art, you know, to get just the right proportions of syrup and hot milk, and Miss Chambers is still a stranger out here."

Clive, oblivious of her intent, had remarked easily, "She'll have to get used to it—I'll show her," He moved to Nancy's side. "The coffee essence is in that small jug, and the hot milk in the tall one. Mike and I like our coffee strong, so you can make it half and half for us. The others can tell you how much they like of each—you'll soon get the hang of it."

Betty bit her lip. "You seem to be assuming, Clive, that Miss Chambers is going to stay on here indefinitely, but you know, of course, that that is out of the question. She will want to go back to Singapore as soon as possible. No girl could afford to stay on in the house with two men."

John Harvy spoke up promptly, "Of course, Betty, Miss Chambers will come to us. I thought you would have arranged that." His wife glared at him, but before she could reply, Mike Sullivan interposed, "I don't think we will have much to say about any arrangement so long as the police are in charge. I'm sure Miss Chambers appreciates your concern, Betty, but really, with six policemen in the house, I don't believe anyone is going to worry about her reputation." Mike smiled at Nancy, whose hands were hovering uncertainly over the coffee cups.

Was he really being friendly, Nancy wondered, or was he just using her to annoy Betty Harvy?

Conversation during the picnic supper had been desultory, and no one had been able to eat very much from the heaped plates passed by the white-coated Malay boy. However, as soon as he had removed the traces of solid food, Nancy was kept busy filling and refilling coffee cups. Everyone was distrait, and the knowledge that McCleary, moving restlessly back and forth, scorning both supper and coffee, could hear everything that was said, acted upon them all like a damper. Each time one of the native policemen who had been sent out to search for Farnsworth returned to report his failure, the officer's voice grew sharper with fresh directions, and the tension on the veranda tightened.

It was Mike who, seated on Nancy's right, broke the oppressive silence by starting a discussion about hunting—the only subject sufficiently impersonal to be safe. Although it was to Nancy he was ostensibly speaking, it seemed to her that the topic had been chosen primarily to interest Clive, and to release him from Betty's proprietary whispers. If that had been the Irishman's purpose, he succeeded, for with more animation than he had displayed all evening, Clive leaned across Jim Mason and Nancy to join Mike in reminiscences of various hunting experiences with boar, seladang, tiger.

Jim Mason had lapsed into a somber reverie, his efforts to establish a bond between himself and Nancy having been lost in the excited argument about the relative danger from tigers and from boars. Nancy turned to him suddenly. "Tell me, Mr. Mason, do tigers and panthers and things ever get inside a house like this?"

A smile brightened his homely face. "So, you've been reading some of those damned travel books, have you? And scaring yourself to death. I'll bet you looked under your bed for hamadryads, and shook out your shoes in case a coral snake had cached himself there!"

Nancy flushed. "Well, I was afraid—especially when I first went into the house and couldn't find a light," she admitted confidentially. "That's what took me so long. I was scared to death that something would pounce on me, or worse yet twine itself around me."

His voice was sympathetic, and appreciating that her fear was still haunting her, his words were comfortably matter of fact. "The house is on piles, you see, in order, among other things, to keep snakes out. Of course there are pythons and various other kinds of snakes in the jungle, but you can walk there for miles without ever seeing one. Tigers and panthers are cowardly beasts, and as a rule they shun habitations—there is plenty of easier game for them in the jungle. I think there is only one case on official record of a tiger going into a house; that was years ago, and it was a native hut on the outskirts of a kampong. Once in a blue moon you hear of a panther getting into some isolated dwelling, but I've been out here two years, and I've never known anyone who had an actual experience. You are really a whole lot safer here, so far as wild animals and snakes are concerned, than you'd be in New York traffic."

Nancy sighed her relief. "I remember now that it is India where the snakes crawl into bed with you, and drop from the ceiling. Thank you for telling me about this place though. I'm sure I'll sleep better tonight than I expected to—that is, if we are ever permitted to go to bed."

Jim Mason smiled. "It's bound to seem strange to you at first, but it's surprising how quickly you'll get used to the life here, and what a hold it will get on you. But then, of course, you are used to adapting yourself to strange environments."

Nancy looked surprised, and he explained, "Being an actress, I mean, travelling about, putting up in all sorts of places. Lydia told me about some of her amusing experiences, and some that were darn near tragic. And you were in her company, weren't you? How did you happen to get so far from the States?"

Instantly Nancy was on guard. "Oh, I have always wanted to come to the Far East, so I jumped at the first chance that presented itself."

Jim shook his head disapprovingly. "The East is no place for a girl on her own. Particularly a girl like you—somehow you are quite different from what I expected, but that just makes it worse."

"What do you mean?" Nancy asked sharply.

"Oh, I don't know. I thought somehow you would be older—Lydia's age—thirtyish—and more hard-boiled. You look so young and, well, sort of vulnerable, as if you hadn't been around much."

At that moment, before Nancy had had to reply, everyone caught the sound of a car crawling up the hill, and McCleary had hurried forward to meet the detective from Johore.

Nancy's first sight of Ismael had been disillusioning. He looked like an ordinary Malay servant dressed up in a khaki uniform. His round, brown face was bland and inscrutable, and during the introductions that had followed, his expression had never changed. "Oh, dear," Nancy had thought; "he'll never find the murderer," and then, with an elation purely selfish, "At least I needn't fear him. He'll never know who I really am." She thought with complacence of the telegrams and letters she had concealed almost under McCleary's nose, of the way she had elicited Clive's support, and of the noticeable effect she had achieved with her changed appearance.

She was surprised to notice, after the policemen had gone indoors, that no one else was sharing her feeling of relief. The men had drawn closer together, and were talking in low tones. "You'd never think to look at him that he is the smartest detective in the East," Mike Sullivan warned. "Don't let that Buddha-like expression fool you." "Yes," chimed in John Harvy. "Look at the way he solved the murders in the Johore Rest House, and at the Crag Hotel in Penang," "And don't forget that affair of the English Mess in the old Malay Palace," Jim Mason said; "I think that was his best job." Even the rather silent Bill Pearson had a word to contribute. "He gets his dope because white people underestimate him. He's so damn polite, with his brown face, that people come to regard him as casually as they do the native servants."

"Well, I don't care what you say about him," Betty said with a toss of her blonde curls; "I'm not going to give him any change, and I'm not going to have his brown hands pawing through all my personal belongings, either. I don't know what the Government is coming to, when natives start bossing white people around. No wonder we are losing face out here."

The next half hour seemed endless to the people on the veranda. The men moved restlessly back and forth half consuming cigarettes and leaving them to smolder on ash trays; while the two women constantly shifted their positions in the creaking rattan chairs whose ridges bit through their scanty clothing.

The air seemed more breathless than ever, and the atmosphere on the veranda grew momentarily more strained and ominous, as though the fears emanating from the seven people there were on the point of assuming definite and horrible shapes.

It was a relief when McCleary and Ismael once more appeared, and the white officer announced, "Sub-Inspector Ismael would like to ask a few questions, and then those of you who wish to may go home." He turned to the stolid little Malay. "I'll leave you now for a while. I want to look around a bit outside, and check up on my men. I'll have them back here by the time you are through."

Ismael bent his head politely. "Very good, Tuan," and then as McCleary clumped down the steps, he addressed the expectant group on the veranda. "As Tuan McCleary explained, I will keep you just a little longer now, and then you may be free to go to your rest. Tomorrow is yet another day, and this night is already overfull of sorrow and trouble." His narrow Mongolian eyes surveyed each strained white face, and then he continued, "Those who have farthest to go, I think should be first released from this unpleasant vigil. Mrs. Harvy, if you will be so good?—" He motioned toward the hall door.

For a moment Betty hesitated, her full lips a stubborn red line, but John Harvy's pressure on her arm was urgent, and she said ungraciously, "Well, what do you want to know?"

"That I will tell you, Madame, when we are alone, I think it is better to talk to each of you apart. If you will go inside?"

"I'm not going into that living room," she declared even as she found herself rising to her feet.

"Have no fear of unpleasantness," Ismael assured her patiently; "Mrs. Bosworth's body is no longer there to disturb your feelings."

Leaving a trail of heavy perfume in her wake, Betty, followed by the little Malay, walked slowly into the house. Having ensconced her solicitously in the chair recently vacated by McCleary, Ismael settled himself at a respectful distance and pulled out his notebook.

"Why do you think it was that the lights in this house went out during the storm, and the lights in your house remained on?" he asked.

It was obviously not the question she had expected, and her stiff body relaxed as she said with a shrug, "I don't know. I'm not a mechanic. Perhaps a fuse blew out or something."

"No, that can hardly be," Ismael said gravely. "There is no sign in the fuse box of a new fuse— they are all in the same condition, tarnished, and the cover of the box is coated with dust."

"Then, all I can say is that Miss Chambers was—" she hesitated, and her voice was spiteful as she said, "Shall we say, 'mistaken.'"

"That is a possibility," Ismael conceded, "though I think under the circumstances, a stranger coming into a dark house would have made every effort to find a light. No one with an electric fixture before his eyes would choose the romantic glimmer of a candle. There is another possibility, Mrs. Harvy—" his voice hardened as he leaned forward to stare into her startled, shrinking face, "and that is that your lights were off too."

Betty started. "If you are implying that I lied—" she shrilled.

"Not at all," Ismael disclaimed. "I merely believe that you do not know whether your lights were on or off."

"You mean, I fell asleep. Well, I didn't."

"No, I mean that you cannot know, because you weren't there."

Fear stared for a second from her eyes before her lashes curled over them, and her hands clenched in her lap. "No," she declared. "No. I was in the house all the time. The lights never went off."

Ismael shrugged. "That is all then. I have no more to ask you now. Only, I warn you, I am going to find out the truth." For a second time she stared at him, and then shaking out the folds of her blue georgette dress, rose and swept out of the room.

"Will you be so kind as to ask your husband to come in, Mrs. Harvy?" Ismael asked mildly as she reached the door.

Betty didn't deign to reply, but a moment later, John Harvy was seated in the chair opposite Ismael.

"What can I do for you, Inspector?" he asked in a pleasant voice. "I've been thinking all evening about this dreadful thing, but for the life of me, I can't recall anything that would throw any light on it. It is inconceivable that anyone would have wished Lydia harm."

"We will reach the truth in time, Tuan," Ismael said, and then asked, almost casually, "What was the business you wished to consult Tuan Bosworth about this evening?"

John Harvy blinked, obviously disconcerted so that it took him a second to adjust his thoughts. "There has been a steady decline in our rubber production," he said reluctantly. "Nothing really serious as yet, but it has worried me since I got the last figures from Hamilton. The trees are all healthy, the coolies have been working well, and yet, for the last three months the output has fallen off steadily. I had been thinking about it all day, and wanted to go into the matter with Clive. As you may have gathered, he doesn't take much interest in the estate, and it is difficult to pin him down to a serious discussion. I had hoped to talk to him this afternoon, but I saw him drive off with Sullivan, so I made up my mind that I'd get hold of him this evening, and insist that he set a definite time tomorrow to go into the matter. I thought he'd be in a good humor tonight, and that if I approached him properly, he'd be reasonable." John drew a long breath. "Clive is a good enough chap, but he is what the Americans call a 'playboy.'"

"How does it happen then that he is Manager of this estate?"

"That's easy." There was a bitter note in the older man's voice. "His father is Chairman of the Board of Directors of the Semang Rubber Estate, and the principal stockholder. Clive is the second son, and was a bit difficult; too much of a good fellow. The father lost patience and as a last resort sent him out East to work on one of the estates in Sumatra with the understanding that when he learned the business, he would have a responsible position. Clive has brains enough when he wants to apply himself, and he really did very well, so well that when the manager of this estate retired, Clive was put in charge."

"I see," Ismael nodded. "And since he has come here, he has not been, what you English say, 'pulling his weight'?"

"No, I don't consider that he has." John's eyes looked frankly into Ismael's. "I realize that it isn't diplomatic for me to say so under the circumstances, but everyone knows it—even Bosworth senior, who is nobody's fool, began to suspect it. He put the matter squarely up to Lydia when she was home a while back—told her she would have to keep Clive's nose to the grindstone or he'd be out of a job. The old gentleman had a great deal of confidence in Lydia, after his first prejudice had worn off, and they understood each other. For a little while after she came back from

England, Clive took hold, but lately he has been slipping again—"

The little Malay tapped his pencil thoughtfully.
"So you didn't have an opportunity as yet to speak to
Tuan Bosworth about the rubber yield?"

"No, as I said, he and Sullivan had left for the
wayong when I got here, and on the way up to the
house later, the other men were around, and I didn't
like to say anything in front of them. I'll have to wait
now, I suppose, until he gets over this shock."

"Thank you for your frankness, Mr. Harvy." Ismael
rose and accompanied the Englishman to the veranda.
"May I speak with you, Mr. Mason?" his soft voice
interrupted Jim's conversation with Nancy.

As he led the way back into the house, the detective paused at the living-room door. "I am interested, Tuan, in the Malay kris which Mr. Farnsworth
said Mrs. Bosworth admired. Will you tell one of the
'boys' where it can be found and let him get it?"

Jim frowned, "Sure, I'd be glad to," he said slowly.
"The trouble is, I can't for the life of me remember
seeing it since the day Lydia commented upon it. It's
been worrying me ever since Farnsworth brought up
the subject. You see, it is just the sort of weapon that
might have been used tonight—and anyone could
have picked it up. Mahat, my boy, might know where
it is, but he's at the wayong."

"That can be easily remedied. We will send
Semut—that I believe is the name of Tuan Bosworth's

boy, down to the wayong, and he can tell your Mahat to find the kris and bring it here."

"Fine," Jim looked relieved. "Of course there's probably nothing in it; but I'll feel a lot better when I see it. I'll look up Semut now and send him off with the message."

At Ismael's nod of approval, he hurried down the hall and through the door leading to the servants' quarters. The detective turned back to the veranda, and beckoned to Bill Pearson who jumped up nervously as though he'd been awaiting the summons.

"Tuan," Ismael said when they were seated in the living room, "I would like to know more about Mrs. Bosworth's stroll this afternoon."

Bill stared at him in surprise. "I told all I knew to McCleary, and I presume he passed the word along. I just happened to notice her cutting across the corner of my division, about a mile from the house."

"From which direction was she coming, and where did she seem to be going?"

Bill's smooth forehead wrinkled into a frown as he tried to recall his glimpse of Lydia. "I'd say she had come from the house, and was headed toward the neck of jungle between my division and Mason's."

"Was there anything else you can recall about her appearance?" Ismael asked, stifling his disappointment. He had hoped she was on her way back to the house, and that there might have been something in her attitude that would indicate her state of mind.

"No, she was some distance from me. I couldn't see her plainly because of the trees, she had on a light green dress, and a big straw hat that shaded her face. She didn't seem to be hurrying, but neither did she seem to by strolling aimlessly if you know what I mean. I shouted to her, and she waved her hand."

"Did she have anything in it, in her hand?"

"Yes, by George, she did!" Bill exclaimed. "Funny, but I didn't think of it until now—she had some sort of basket."

"Thank you, Tuan, that will be all for the present."

Bill looked startled at his dismissal, but instead of welcoming his release, he sat still for a moment. "Look here, Inspector, I was a damn fool to lose my temper over Farnsworth this evening—but I don't want you to get a wrong impression about it, or about my relations with Mrs. Bosworth. I hated to hear Dave making such a blithering idiot of himself, of course, and when he implied things about Lydia and me, I hit without thinking. Which, of course, only made things look worse. I'd just like to tell you about the episode he referred to, if you don't mind?"

Ismael stared at the handsome troubled face opposite him and then nodded permission.

"It really didn't amount to a row of beans," Bill said eagerly. "I'd come in looking for Clive. He wanted a pig shoot and had asked me to get hold of the beaters. Lydia was sitting in the chair over there—the

long one." He pointed to the Singapore chair opposite them, where Nancy had lain earlier in the evening. "And when she got up, I saw she had been crying. It was a jolt to see her in tears—she was always
so gay, and efficient—never let things get her down,
the way most of us do. I asked her what the trouble
was and whether I could help her, and, of course,
that was just the wrong thing to do, for she began to
sob. She was all broken up over something, no doubt
about it. I put my arm around her shoulder, and patted her. She said she was at her wits' end, and had
to tell somebody; but before she could control herself enough to talk, young Farnsworth came bursting
in. I heard him coming, and gave her a little shove
by way of warning; and hoped that he wouldn't notice anything was wrong. He's something of a snoop,
as you may have noticed; his way of making himself important. That's all there was to it. I went out
with him; he'd come in to borrow some magazines for
Betty Harvy, and I didn't want him to get the idea that
I was hanging around for a *tête-à-tête* with Lydia."

"She never told you what had been troubling her?"

"No," Bill said. "The next time I saw her, she told
me to please forget what a bally fool she'd been, and
she showed plainly that she didn't want to say anything more about it."

"Your impression was that it was something serious?"

"It must have been. I've known her for two years, and I never saw her out of control before, or since—not even when Clive was shot."

Ismael blinked. "When was that?"

"A couple of weeks ago. We were pig shooting. Cripes! it must have been the one I'd gotten the beaters for. Yes, it was the day after she'd been crying, because that was the first chance I'd had to speak to her again. And it was on our way over to the other side of the river that she told me to forget it."

"What happened to Mr. Bosworth?" Ismael leaned forward.

"No one quite knows. He and Lydia were stationed at a point in the bluker when the pigs broke. There was a lot of shooting, and one of the bullets struck Clive in the thigh. There had been lots of running around and excitement, and we couldn't find the bullet, so there was no telling whose shot had gone wild, or whether he had somehow managed to hit himself. Everyone was awfully concerned, of course, but there was no real harm done—just a scratch. Clive didn't think anything about it, laughed it off as an accident, and said he'd really rather not know which of his friends was such a rotten shot."

"You were all there? Mrs. Harvy, too?"

"Yes, everybody. Betty put on a show; she wouldn't miss a chance like that. Screamed and fainted. Lydia was the one to keep her head."

Ismael hesitated, uncertain whether to question Bill further on the subject. There were many details he wanted to know about the episode, but it might be wiser not to emphasize the matter at this time lest Pearson, suspecting his interest, might put the other men on their guard.

Bill, apparently engrossed in his own line of thought, continued, "No, Lydia wasn't easily upset. She was more like a man in her attitude toward life. I don't mean that she wasn't feminine, but that she had the humor and tolerance and efficiency that you'd expect from a man. That was why I liked her. As a rule I manage to steer clear of women—one reason I took a job off in the wilds like this. The only women that could stick this life would be those that were married to it, and the visiting girls that cropped up occasionally—well, I could dodge them."

Strange that a young man so virile, so handsome, should speak with such bitterness, Ismael thought. Doubtless he had been disillusioned by women who had run after him. If that was true, was it possible that Mrs. Bosworth, of whom he spoke so warmly, had attracted him more than he was willing to admit? Had he misjudged her feeling for her husband, made overtures which she had repulsed, and then in anger or shame, killed her? After all, it was only when Farnsworth insinuated things about Mrs. Bosworth and himself that Pearson had struck him—and it was interesting to note that it had been Pearson who resented the aspersions, not Clive.

"Thank you, Tuan." Ismael was suddenly conscious that Bill had stopped speaking and was gazing at him with a puzzled expression. "I am very glad to have had this talk with you. Will you please ask Mr. Sullivan to come in?"

Was it possible that the shooting of Clive Bosworth had not been an accident, but a deliberate attempt upon his life? All of the people on the Estate were experienced hunters—it was strange that one of them should have been so criminally careless. Had the shot which grazed the husband perhaps been intended for the wife? Had that been a first attempt to murder Lydia Bosworth? Ismael had thought that the murder had been done on the spur of the moment, but the absence of the weapon indicated that the murderer had come armed, and, if there had been a previous attempt to shoot her, then it meant that they were not dealing with a hot-headed man or woman who had struck in a moment of fear or rage, but with a cold-blooded, ruthless killer.

CHAPTER VIII

Ismael's unpleasant brooding was interrupted by the appearance of Mike Sullivan, his jaunty manner not quite concealing the wary expression in his green eyes. A few moments' conversation convinced the detective that he had small hope at present of penetrating the Irishman's guard.

"What do I do for a living?" Mike laughed. "I have a small patrimony, and I eke out a lean existence here and there. In spite of my American mother I have the Irish luck at horses and cards, and none at all with women. Not that I want any I've seen yet, thank God. Give me a good dog and a good gun, and I ask nothing more."

Only when Clive Bosworth's name was mentioned did the Irishman show any feeling. "I knew him since he was a little lad. He's five years younger than I— just the age my brother would have been. They were inseparable pals. I got the habit of looking after the both of them."

"What happened to your brother?"

It seemed to Ismael that Mike's face whitened under its tan, and that there was a throb of pain in the deep voice. "He was killed in an accident. I don't talk about it."

"Do you think your influence has been good for Mr. Bosworth?" Ismael asked.

Mike showed no resentment of the question, and his answer was prompt. "I know it. I know him better than anyone does. He's got to have a certain amount of diversion, or he wouldn't stick it; he'd go off the deep end. And hunting is safer than women."

"You liked Mrs. Bosworth?"

"She was fine," Mike said simply. "I wish now that I had told her some of the things I knew about Clive; my reason for acting as I did. She mistrusted me, you know, and that made me stubborn—I couldn't tell her—" He stopped.

"You mean that you were afraid he was too much interested in Mrs. Harvy?"

Mike nodded. "That was part of it. I thought I could break that affair up, keep Clive away from her without his knowing what I was about. I couldn't tell Lydia—you see, when he first got interested in Lydia I did everything I could to discourage it, and he told her so. I'd only met her once casually before I came out East, and when Clive wrote that they were engaged, I raised merry hell about it. I thought she was just another American gold digger, and that when she found Clive didn't have any money of his own, she'd dish him. I didn't want him to get in deep enough to be hurt. She never forgave me for that. I don't blame her—she didn't know I'd completely changed my mind about her; and that all I ever wanted was Clive's happiness and security." He shrugged his shoulders.

"Hunting is not always so safe a sport, Tuan, even among experts, as you imply," Ismael remarked. "I understand that Mr. Bosworth had an accident not long ago."

"Yes," Mike said frowning. "Damned careless on someone's part. Clive might have been killed. Someone shot directly into the thicket where he and Lydia were standing, the bloody fool. If I'd known who it was I'd have broken his gun over his thick head."

"How is the situation now with regard to Mrs. Harvy?" The detective casually changed the subject, satisfied that it hadn't occurred to Mike that the shot at Clive might have been deliberate, or that it might have been meant for Lydia.

"I don't know. I haven't given him much time lately to be with her. She asked him for tea this afternoon; that's why I whisked him away to Batu Pahat on the trail of a mythical tiger." His grin at the success of that ruse faded, however, as he went on. "I don't like the present look of things—Betty acts as though Clive had been signed, sealed and delivered to her."

"You think she is in love with him?"

"I think she'd like to marry him," Mike said bluntly. "She wants to get away from the East, and Clive is the only person she's found recently that hates it out here as much as she does, so she's been playing up to him."

"And what are his feelings?"

"I think he is flattered by the fuss she makes over him, and she made him think that Lydia was a tyrant, but I don't believe for a minute that he is in love with her, or ever thought of marrying her. She got in her fine work, of course, when Lydia was away—he practically lived at the Harvy bungalow—as I discovered when I came back from Africa."

"What does Mr. Harvy think about it?"

"It's hard to tell. Betty is the sort of woman who always has to have another man hanging around, so I imagine he's gotten used to it. I don't think he'd stand for any real monkey business—but on the other hand, he might be glad to get rid of her. I know I would be."

Jim Mason appeared in the doorway. "I don't want to interrupt, Sergeant, but Mahat just brought the kris, and I thought you'd want to see it right away."

"Good." Ismael rose. "Mr. Sullivan and I were completed."

Mike sauntered toward the door, he was rather pleased with his share in the interview; he had told,

with seeming frankness, everything that the detective
would have been bound to discover.

Jim, his face shining with relief, handed the little
weapon to the detective. "Mahat found it in the back
of my desk, in its usual place; and it doesn't look to
me as though it had been touched for weeks. See?
The blade is clean, and the gold handle is tarnished,
even the little tuft of hair is dusty." Ismael examined
the dagger carefully. It was a clever bit of workman-
ship, a tiny replica of an old Malay kris, a slender
steel blade about six inches long, topped by an intricately carved handle of gold and silver, with a waving
tuft of black hair. There was no indication that the
weapon had ever been used; the edges of the blade
were razor sharp, but the steel, though clouded, was
unstained. Particles of dust had lodged in the carving
of the handle, and there was a greyish tinge in the
dark plume of hair.

Jim Mason had been watching the detective anxiously. "You see, don't you, that it hasn't been used?"

"No, that is obvious," Ismael agreed. "It is a clever
bit of work, Tuan. Where did you find it?"

"It was pushed back in my desk," Mason repeated, and then laughed. "Oh, you mean where did I
buy it? I picked it up in the Dutch East Indies—I've
forgotten whether it was in a Pasar at Batavia, or in
Belawan Dewi. I bought a lot of stuff on that trip to
send home, but I liked this baby and kept it." His

eyes narrowed as he saw Ismael place the dagger on the table instead of returning it to him. The Malay smiled. "I will cherish it, Tuan, have no fear, but I would like to keep it a little longer."

McCleary appeared in the doorway. "I have the men all in now, Ismael. They didn't find a trace of Farnsworth. The servants had tramped all over the tracks under the window, and the road, though I particularly warned them." His tone was disgusted. "That's the worst of not being able to superintend the job yourself." He glowered at Mason as though blaming him for the fact that he hadn't been able to leave the house.

"We may be able to see more in the morning, Tuan," Ismael consoled. "Allah's light is better than man's. The sun may show us things that the flash-lights overlooked." He moved to McCleary's side and lowered his voice. "You have explained to your men what their duties are?"

"Yes, they understand they are to guard the various buildings and report everything that happens." The officer looked grim. "Did you get any change out of the people you've talked to?"

Ismael's smile was inscrutable. "Yes, Tuan—a number of interesting facts raised their heads, but what they mean, I cannot tell at present. We will have a talk together later if you will." He glanced sideways at Jim Mason, and McCleary nodded his understanding. "I think I will not question Tuan Bosworth tonight, so there remains only Miss Chambers. Perhaps you will be so good as to ask her to come inside when you return to the veranda to dismiss your unwilling guests."

"The sooner they are out of the way now, the better I'll be pleased," McCleary grunted. "I wish I never had to set eyes on any of them again."

Ismael smiled. "That feeling will pass, like everything else, Tuan. When we know the truth, your friendship will be even closer with all save the murderer. Do not judge hastily."

Nancy came slowly into the room, as though the slowness of her feet would disguise the rapid beating of her heart. The other people who had been interviewed had all seemed worried and depressed as they straggled back to the veranda, and with the departure of the Harvys, Pearson, and Jim Mason, she felt strangely defenseless. Clive Bosworth and Mike had been so engrossed in their low-voiced conference that they didn't even look up to give her an encouraging nod.

"Sit down, Miss Chambers." The squat little Malay motioned to the chair opposite his own. "I will not keep you long from your bed." Nancy sank down on the seat he indicated, and waited nervously for her ordeal to begin.

"When did you last hear from Mrs. Bosworth?"

"A week or so ago," Nancy improvised, and then added, as though to forestall further questions, "She wanted me to visit her, but at that time I had a position which I couldn't leave. Then, suddenly I lost my job, and so I was able to come after all."

"Her last letter to you—it was cheerful?"

"Oh, yes," Nancy replied, smiling at the memory of the gay little note she had had six weeks earlier.

Ismael's almond-shaped eyes stared at her thoughtfully. The girl was concealing something. Her hazel eyes, raised so candidly to his, didn't match the slim fingers that were twitching the edges of her chiffon handkerchief.

"Did you write Mrs. Bosworth of your change in plans?"

Nancy caught her breath. "I told her the last time I wrote, that I would come when I could, but I didn't say when that would be. I wanted to see something of the country on my way." The handkerchief was a ball now, crumpled in a small damp fist.

"And did you enjoy your trip, from—where did you say you were?"

"Rangoon." Nancy desperately named the first place she could think of. "But I didn't see much of the country—I had an attack of malaria."

Ismael noted the white translucence of her skin which showed no trace of the yellowish aftermath of malaria. What had the girl been up to during this past week? She was a pathetically obvious liar.

"Tell me what occurred when you reached the house tonight," he requested, dropping the subject of her travels.

Nancy's tautness immediately relaxed, she was on familiar ground now, and her voice, for the first time during the interview, had an unmistakable ring of truth as she once more described her arrival, her fear of the dark house and its ominous stillness—the shock of finding Lydia's body.

"You heard nothing—not the sound of a closing door, of footsteps?"

"No, nothing," Nancy replied earnestly. "The house felt deserted, if you know what I mean. I was afraid, yes—but it was of the darkness, of the strangeness of everything—I even thought there might be a snake, or a tiger or something. But I had no feeling, at any time, that there was a human being around, and I was so keyed up, I think I would have known instinctively if there had been anyone here."

It sounded unconvincing to herself as she spoke, but the little Malay seemed to understand. He knew what she meant, and he liked her sensitiveness of perception—few white people had it.

"You didn't touch anything in the house? You left all as you found it?"

"I used both candlesticks, as I told you," Nancy said, trying to remember again every-thing she had done, "and I pressed the electric-light button, turned the key close to them, and I even fiddled with the bulbs themselves to be sure they weren't loose. In the living room, I pulled aside the orange pillow, I touched Lydia's shoulder—" she shivered at the recollection, "but I am sure I didn't touch anything else—not even the furniture. I held my candle up high while I looked around the room, and down low when I tried to find whether Lydia had killed herself—if she had the pistol or knife it must have fallen to the floor. There was nothing. And anyway, I think I knew from the beginning that someone had killed her."

"You didn't destroy anything? Take anything away with you? Even something that seemed unimportant?"

Nancy, remembering the telegrams, felt herself flushing. "I took nothing from the room," she affirmed—after all, the telegrams had been in the hall, and they had nothing to do with Lydia's murder.

Ismael sighed; the girl was lying again. What in Allah's name was she concealing!

"You had never met any of these people before, except Mr. Bosworth?" he asked.

"No," Nancy said. "And I had never met Mr. Bosworth either."

If that was true, and he felt that it was, whatever she was hiding was something which concerned only herself. She was playing a lone game, and one that was even more dangerous than he had thought.

"What do you think of these people? How have they treated you?" he asked abruptly.

Nancy looked surprised at his question, and he explained. "It is more important than you think, than you can understand. You will help me if you will tell me what you feel about them, and how they have acted toward you. You wish me to find the person who murdered your friend, do you not?"

"Yes. Oh, yes!" The girl's voice was eager, genuine. "I'll do anything to help punish him—only," she threw her hands apart in a helpless little gesture, "what can I do?"

Ismael smiled as he would at a child. "You are a stranger here—you are not involved in the politics or scandal of the estate. Your coming was unexpected to the murderer, for you are an unknown quantity. You understand what I mean? He must have been able to predict to some extent how the others would react, but he knows nothing about what you will do, or say or think!"

Nancy nodded. "I see what you mean." She was quiet for a moment or two, and then shook her head. "There was nothing significant about the behavior of anyone of them, so far as I can judge. Of course they are strangers to me, and I don't know how they would act at all under normal circumstances. After their first concern for me, when I fainted, you know, their chief desire, quite naturally, was to hear what I had seen and done. After that was over with, they rather forgot me—it wasn't until I asked Mr. Bosworth whether I might change my clothes that he seemed to realize that I was there at all. I looked like something the cat dragged in anyway—and I was an outsider—everyone had plenty on his mind." Her lips curved into a smile. "After I had fixed myself up a bit, and repaired the damages, I seemed for the first time to register as a person."

Ismael's eyes twinkled. "At first you were a little wet mouse, and then, behold, you were a peacock!"

Nancy laughed. "Something like that. Clothes made the woman!" Suddenly her face was quiet, sad. "The dreadful thing to me is the fact that none of them seem to want Lydia's murderer discovered, and," her voice quavered a bit, "I don't think any of them feel any deep sorrow—not her husband, not one of those people who she must have thought were her friends. Even I—" she broke off with a frightened glance at the detective— "Oh don't misunderstand me— Lydia was my friend, I want to see her murderer captured—I loathe myself when personal consider-ations crop up!" With sudden fear she realized that she had said too much, implied, God knew what. Leaning forward so that the light shone on her bronze hair, her eager young face, she added, "It is hateful being mixed up in a murder case, you know—it is going to damn me from here to yon—and I do have to think of that, hateful as it seems."

The little Malay looked grave. "I realize, Miss Chambers, that there are many things I do not know. I have two duties: one to find the murderer; and two, to protect the innocent. I do not wish to alarm you, but I want you to be very careful with these people until the murderer is discovered. Do not go anywhere alone with anyone, under any circumstance. Keep your shutters fastened at night, and lock your door when you are in your room."

The girl stared at him with wide, incredulous eyes. "Why, what do you mean? Who would want to hurt me? I don't even know them!"

Ismael sighed. "You were the first person to discover the body. You alone had the opportunity to see anything that the murderer had overlooked; your presence may have upset his plans in a dozen ways, just because it was outside his expectations. Do you not see that? The person who killed Mrs. Bosworth will be watching you to find out what you may have discovered in the time you were here—" he waved a brown hand— "Perhaps nothing of which you are conscious now; but later you may remember some little thing that was strange, was out of its accustomed place, which you cannot judge until the room is in its usual order." She looked skeptical, and Ismael added, "If you are hiding anything, I beg you, for your own sake to tell me now. Your life may depend upon it."

For a second his earnestness moved her almost to the point of telling him about the telegrams, about her horrible experience in Penang, but her faith in human nature had received too deadly a blow. She was no longer the trusting, friendly girl she had been when she left America—besides, her own Yankee shrewdness told her that the telegrams she had

suppressed were of no moment except to herself,
and to the fortunate Helene Chambers who was safely beyond reach of this tragic affair.

"I know nothing that the murderer need fear,"
Nancy declared. "If I did, at whatever cost to myself,
I would tell you." She meant every word, and Ismael
recognized the fact.

"Come, then, I will escort you to your room," he
said, rising. Sobered by his solicitude, Nancy led the
way into the deserted hall and along the corridor to
the guest room where the rose-colored lights cast a
pink glow across the white ceilings.

"Well, here I am," she said, turning at the door.

"One moment, please." Ismael entered the room
ahead of her. Matter-of-factly he peered under the
bed, opened the wardrobe and explored its damp
depths, and then, going to the window, glanced out
before he firmly closed and fastened the shutters.
"Now," he gravely motioned to her to enter, "you may
rest easy. Be sure to lock your door, and do not open
it again unless you hear the voice of Tuan McCleary
or myself. If you want anything, you have only to
call. I will hear you."

With his polite little bow, Ismael stepped outside
and waited until he heard the bolt creak into place.

Nancy lowered her trembling figure into a wicker
chair and stared around her. It had been an ordeal,
talking to the detective, and her thoughts were still
confused—one moment he seemed more sympathetic,

more understanding than anyone she had ever met; the next, he was an enemy against whom, despairingly, she was pitting all her puny wiles. Of one thing only did she feel convinced; that he was deeply concerned about her personal safety, and that was too incredible to grasp. Why would anyone want to harm her? She knew nothing—all she had done was to keep the telegrams which she had absent-mindedly stuffed into her pocket; and certainly they could mean nothing to anyone here except herself.

Suddenly, she started from her chair, realizing vaguely that something was missing from the room. Her shoes were gone. The muddy-white brogues she had worn earlier in the evening; they weren't beside the bed where she had left them, nor were they in the wardrobe either, she discovered after groping along its wooden floors and feeling the length of its dusty high shelf. It wasn't the loss of the shoes themselves that worried her, inconvenient as that was apt to prove in her present state of bankruptcy, but the fact that wadded in the tissue paper with which she had stuffed the soggy toes were the torn bits of the telegrams and the three personal letters she had destroyed. Had the police taken them? Had one of the servants removed them for cleaning? Or, she shivered, had the murderer been there and carried them off? Why would he want them, except perhaps as a hold over her; to force her to help him! She knew now why all her instincts had revolted against this dark, lonely house. It wasn't because of its isolation; its somber silence; not because of the wild animals and snakes that lived close by, but because the most horrible thing in the world lurked within its damp, flimsy walls—murder.

CHAPTER IX

In the chill blackness of the hour preceding dawn, Ismael sat hunched over his notebook. The data he had collected during the past hours had been carefully inscribed in his precise handwriting, but they were cold facts—black and white—and until they had been dyed with the emotions behind this crime, they were meaningless to the little Malay, He had seen fear in the faces of those he had interviewed, had heard lies and evasions from everyone, but he hadn't yet felt the forces of love or hatred. In other words, he thought, sucking the end of his stubby pencil, he had not yet been able to connect the atmosphere of this damp, isolated bungalow to any one person. His smile was involuntary, as he glanced across the room to the long Singapore chair where McCleary was sprawled, his mouth open, his red face peacefully upturned toward the blazing lights—how impossible to explain to this earnest white officer his own methods of crime deduction! How disgusted that conscientious, square-faced man would be if Ismael were to say, "Tuan, I smell murder on this estate, but I do not yet get the scent of the murderer." It was the sort of thing he never even risked saying to his own chief, although he sometimes thought that Campbell would come closer to understanding it than any other white man he had ever known. The little American girl he had talked to this evening had surprised him with her sensitiveness to impressions—she too had felt the horror of this house; she had differentiated between her fear of the darkness and of wild animals, and that of human beings; but she hadn't gone far enough.

McCleary stirred, as though conscious of Ismael's stare, and sheepishly opened his eye. "Ugh! must have dropped off," he muttered apologetically as he struggled into an upright position. "Discovered anything new in the bedroom, or in here?"

The Malay shook his head. "Nothing, Tuan. Too many people have been in here—and in the bedroom I found nothing to indicate a crime. I think Tuan Farnsworth was frightened and scrambled through the window, scratching himself as he went, and so making the blood marks. Apparently he had told all he knew, when he was brave with brandy—of what use to kill him under such difficult circumstances?"

"Well, I hope you're right, but I'd like to get my hands on the bloody young fool." McCleary swung his feet to the floor and stood up yawning. "Must be almost dawn—you can hear the birds. And there goes the tong-tong!" The notes of a deep bronze gong rose and fell on the damp, chilly air, echoing and re-echoing through the rubber trees.—Business as usual!

Ismael frowned. "I wish today was a holiday, Tuan. I do not like the thought of these people being scattered over countless hundreds of acres."

"You mean Bosworth and the assistants?" McCleary asked in a surprised tone, and then shrugged his broad, muscular shoulders. "They'll be all right. Remember, there are four hundred coolies on the estate. Anyway," he added briskly, "there's nothing we can do about it. I couldn't possibly get a constable to guard each of them, and if we stopped work here until we caught the murderer, we'd both be out of a job. The best we can do is to post a man at each bungalow, as we have done, and at the factory at night—which we have also done."

Ismael's smile was sardonic. "You white men with your teachings of the sacredness of human life!"

McCleary grinned. "Human life is only sacred in the home, Ismael, not in business. A few more crimes in the rubber industry would hardly be noticed."

Through the open window drifted the chatter of Malay servants, the clink of dishes, the sharp tang of wood smoke, blending with the fragrance of fresh coffee. From across the hall, they heard Sullivan's Irish voice, "Up ye get, ye spalpeen. The tong-tong's gone." There was an incoherent mutter of annoyance, and then Mike spoke again. "Sure you're goin'

to work. It's meself that's tellin' you. You're through
with loafin'."

McCleary grinned. "The pot calling the kettle
black."

"A strange man, Tuan Sullivan," Ismael said, rising
and stretching his cramped rotund body.

"What's next on the program?" McCleary asked,
looking enviously at the Malay, who, despite his
hard, sleepless night, looked as fresh and immaculate
as ever. "I've got to have a bathe and a shave before
I'll be good for anything."

"By the time breakfast is finished, it will be light,"
Ismael said. "Then I will try to find the elusive Farnsworth, and talk to the servants."

Half an hour later, Ismael, fortified by several cups
of coffee, stepped out into the dampness of the new
day. It was drizzling half-heartedly, and a blanket of
mist shrouded the valley like a fog, obscuring all but
the nearest rubber trees. Moving like a squat, bulky
ghost, Ismael trotted down the muddy roadway, his
sharp eyes picking out the tracks he had followed
from beneath the bedroom window. The footsteps
had been blurred and half obliterated by the marks of
the barefooted servants, the boots of the constables,
and the light, spasmodic drizzle, but the marks he
was following, deep toe prints of a running man, appeared frequently enough to assure him that he had
been correct in his surmise. As Ismael came out of

the aisle of rubber trees into the clearing where the low rambling factory stood, the sleepy-eyed constable on duty saluted him.

"Is Tuan Hamilton awake?" the detective asked, pausing half way up the deep rutted drive.

"Sahaya, Tuan. He is bathing. A remarkable man, Tuan Hamilton—one moment drugged with whisky, then came the tong-tong, and I heard the engines start up. I went in and told him he must come with me, but he said he must bathe first, his head hurt, and I could wait outside for him."

"Did you tell him why he was wanted?" Ismael's tone was sharp.

"No, Tuan, he didn't ask me." The man's simple face beamed at his display of intelligence.

"Well, keep your eye on him, and tell him nothing. Just take him to your Tuan McCleary."

The constable saluted again, and with ill-concealed curiosity watched the detective disappear around the corner of the building, like a plump beagle hound on the trail of a rabbit. Ismael, oblivious of everything save those staggering toeprints, followed them to the back of the factory where they stopped abruptly beside the narrow mark of tires. The little Malay emitted a sigh of satisfaction; a bicycle had rested there against the dull, unpainted wall of the covered passage leading to the electric shed. Again he took up the trail. The tire marks swerved around the far side of the factory and returned to the road.

As he neared the coolie lines below the factory, Ismael met the first signs of activity; gangs of Malays, Chinese, Indians, clad in dirty, white shorts, or grimy g-strings, straggled past him, marshalled by sharp-voice mandurs. Wide brown eyes in yellow and brown faces stared at him with childlike curiosity, and stood aside respectfully for him to pass—a Malay mata-mata (policeman) whose reputation was a matter of pride to natives throughout the length and breadth of Malaya. He would find the evil one who had killed the Mem, they whispered, for the news of Lydia's murder had spread through the usual underground route that made even the stupidest coolie aware of all that happened on the estate. The mandurs, as befitted the importance of their position, were the first to recover themselves, and with loud authority urged along the gangs of weeders and tappers.

The air around the native kampongs was heavy with the odorous weight of newly built fires, spices, dried fish and coconut oil, and in the doorways of the little woven bamboo huts, under the broad pale leaves of banana trees, or behind the blazing crimson of poinsettia hedges, Malay, Indian, and Chinese women paused in their household tasks to gaze round-eyed and solemn as he passed. "Why was the mata-mata walking so fast, with head downbent as though in prayer?"

Suddenly Ismael stopped, staring in perplexity at the tire marks. "This is wrong," he muttered to himself. "One track leading down toward the highway, as I expected, and then crossing it in places, another track leading off through the rubber. He must have come back then—but what happened to put him off the road?" With a new burst of speed, Ismael hurried along beside the narrow marks that bit deep in the reddish earth between the tall trunks of serried rubber trees on the eastern side of the road. And then, through the thinning mist, he saw a crumpled white figure sprawled against a tree trunk.

It was Farnsworth, lanky, boyish legs twisted beside a wrecked bicycle, his suit a mass of mud and blood stains, his face cut and scratched beneath the swells of mosquito and insect bites. As Ismael stooped down to ascertain his injuries, Farnsworth opened blank blue eyes. "Go way, Semut," he croaked. "I'm too sick to work. Tell Tuan Mason—"

"Come, Tuan Farnsworth," Ismael said, putting an arm beneath the soggy shoulders, "try to get up."

At his touch the boy emitted a shriek of terror. "Don't kill me, don't kill me! I won't tell. I won't tell!"

"I won't hurt you," Ismael soothed. "I will help you. You are sick. You must go to your bed."

"My bed—not that other," the boy begged. "He will kill me there. Oh, God, he's after me!" His eyes stared wildly around at the tree trunks, and then, as though reassured at finding himself out of doors, he spoke coherently. "Don't know how I got here. Must get back to my own bed."

Pushing, tugging and coaxing, Ismael got him to his feet, and half carrying the limp form, staggered back to the road. The timely arrival of a passing bullock cart, reporting for work at the factory, solved the problem of transporting the injured man to the house. The surprised Malay driver helped to lift Farnsworth into the rough wooden cart, and then, with Ismael walking behind, he whipped the bullock into a fast lumbering pace.

As the cart jolted back up the road, the constable who had been on guard at the factory came stumbling to meet it "Tuan, Tuan," he gasped, his usually brown face a sickly yellow. "Tuan Hamilton is gone."

"What do you mean?" the detective asked. "How could that happen with you on guard?"

"He was bathing, Tuan, as I told you. I could hear the water splashing and splashing all the time, but he took so long that I went inside to tell him to hurry. The door was locked, and he didn't answer. Then I went outside and looked in the window—the shutters were open and no one was in the bathing room, just the water running from the pipe. I didn't know the water came so, I thought he must dip it from a jar."

"Fool! Imbecile!" Ismael exclaimed. "What sort of a policeman are you? Even a crocodile should have known better! Here, walk beside this cart and take this sick man to your Tuan. Tell him what happened. Allah help you, for no one else can, if you let this man get away from you!"

"Yes, please, Tuan," the constable said humbly. "I will guard him like my own poor soul."

"What a case!" Ismael groaned to himself as the driver swung his whip and the rough-hewn wheels of the cart lurched forward. "It is like a game of hide-and-go-seek. Always someone I must find before I can get down to any real work."

Turning, he hurried into the low, rambling building. In the grey twilight of its interior, he saw the skeleton frame of the weighing machine at the right of the door, and beyond the long row of empty vats waiting for the arrival of the latex. Great bottles of acid gleamed palely on the shelf above the vats, and on the opposite side of the long, low ceiling room, bulked the dark shapes of the massive rollers. From the room beyond, connected by a covered passage, the throb of gas engines generating electricity shook the building with regular pulsations.

On the left of the front door was a small, dusty office, containing a roll-top desk, a filing cabinet, a table and two chairs. Above the throbbing of the engines, Ismael could hear distinctly the splashing of water in the locked bathroom that opened off the little office.

Swiftly he whirled around and hurried through the factory, his dark eyes searching each nook and corner as he proceeded into the building containing the electric plant, then along a covered passage into the smoke room, through another passage into the packing shed. All were deserted. Glad to escape from the nauseating smell of rubber and lysol that permeated the factory, Ismael stepped through a rear door into the fresh air. The mist was disappearing, and although the air was still heavy, the drizzle had stopped, and the sun was struggling to break through its prison of clouds.

Underneath the bathroom window were the large, heavy footprints where the Scotch engineer had made his escape. The man had walked fast—his strides were long, but they moved evenly, and in a direct purposeful line through the rubber trees. There was no attempt at concealment, no dodging or doubling. The aisles between the white-flecked trees were alive with moving brown and yellow figures, the weeders bent over their scraping hoes, the tappers with bright knives moving from tree to tree, and behind them other coolies emptying the white cups into big zinc pails.

Hamilton's footprints led in a diagonal line through the rubber to the rough, muddy ruts of the track that bisected the estate, leading from Harvy's bungalow on the east side of the main roadway, to the bungalow occupied by Pearson and Hamilton near the steamy, mangrove-choked river that formed the western boundary. "This is a waste of time," Ismael grumbled, as the footprints turned westward along the track. "The man has only gone to his bungalow to change his clothes, and the constable on guard there, unless he is as big a dolt as the one at the factory, will take charge of him."

He was aroused from his irritating thoughts by a shout, and looking up saw the slender, broad-shouldered figure of Bill Pearson coming toward him under the canopy of overhanging branches. "Looking for Hamilton, Inspector? He came along to the house about half an hour ago, and the constable rushed him up to McCleary."

"Thank you, Tuan." Ismael smiled at the attractive picture which Pearson unconsciously made in his khaki shorts and shirt, his bronze face toning into the tan of his terai hat. "You saved me time and trouble. Now I can go with a free mind to the house of Tuan Bosworth. Are you coming my way?"

"Yes." Pearson adjusted his long stride to the Malay's short quick steps. "Harvy didn't show up at roll call, and I thought I'd go along and see how he was after I'd put my men to work. If he isn't feeling fit, I'll have to take over for him down at the factory. I hope McCleary won't hold Hamilton up long—the latex will be coming in now, and we're short-handed. Mason is taking over for Farnsworth."

"Tuan McCleary realizes the importance of rubber," Ismael said blandly. "He knows that nothing must stop the work on the estate, not even death."

Pearson glanced sharply at the expressionless face of the man beside him, and an unwilling smile twisted his lips. "It does sound heartless—but the estate really can't afford to slack off even for a day." He raised his head to stare up through the rising mist to the low, heavy grey sky. "I hope it clears up so that the coolies can work, but it doesn't look too good. We're way behind in our production for some reason or other, and the Board of Directors will tear their hair when they get this month's figures. If we don't speed up somehow, we'll all be on the dole." He changed the subject abruptly. "Mason tells me you've found Farnsworth."

For the thousandth time Ismael pondered the speed and accuracy with which news traveled among the natives until it reached even the white bosses.

"Yes," he said noncommittally.

"Out of his head, so Mason heard, babbling about the murderer being after him. What do you suppose he was doing on the bicycle out in the midst of the rubber?"

"I don't know. Perhaps he was the murderer trying to escape. Perhaps he was trying to escape from the murderer," Ismael said absent-mindedly. He was too worried to pay much attention now to the man beside him. And he didn't know exactly why he was worried either—a depressed feeling that something was wrong, and that there was something he ought to do immediately.

They had reached the main road running north toward the Bosworth bungalow, and south past the factory and the kampongs, to the highway. The little Malay stood hesitating, his smooth brown forehead wrinkled into a furrow.

"You just follow the road up the hill," Pearson volunteered. Ismael paid no attention to him, he was staring with dark, troubled eyes along the continuation of the rough track winding between rubber and jungle. Something was urging him to follow that track, but with the knowledge of all the work awaiting him at the bungalow, he struggled against it. He knew now what was troubling him: the fact that Harvy had not appeared at roll call. There might be a dozen reasons for his delinquency, but none of them tallied with the impression Ismael had of the sober, conscientious Englishman he had talked to—the man who was the real backbone of the estate, who cherished it even above his wife.

Automatically, Ismael crossed the road and hurried along the rutted track. The crude road, just wide enough to permit the passage of the Harvy automobile, was a feeble demonstration of the conflict between man and nature. On the left marched row upon row of symmetrical rubber trees, with their white cups attached by wire to the trunks, their bark disfigured with markings; circles, dot—arrows. On the right, a patch of uncleared jungle lapped its dark sinister tongue, in the form of thickets and lianas, along the very edge of the road.

"We're going to clear this patch out next week," Bill Pearson volunteered, looking resentfully at the tangled mass of rattan and bamboo, which, knotted together with lianas, rose in a defiant wall. "This patch, and one like it up between my division and Mason's are the last on the estate. The State Forestry Reserves just about circle us, though, so it won't spoil the hunting—" He broke off abruptly. "What's up?"

Without replying, Ismael broke into a run. Through the overhanging trees Bill Pearson too caught a glimpse of something white on the ground beneath a dark mass of thicket. His face paled under its tan as he sped after the Malay. It was just a gleam of something white he had seen, but it was out of place; whatever it was it had no business to be there at the edge of the jungle. He refused to acknowledge the fear that hammered at him; he only knew that the estate and the jungle were places of browns and greens and greys; green trees, brown trunks, brown earth, brown natives; grey g-strings and shorts. White was the color of civilization—white was worn by white men, by white women.

Ismael's squat figure was crouched beside the white patch now, blocking Pearson's view. Not that

Bill wanted to see; and yet he had to know. Anything was better than this horrible, gnawing suspense.

"What is it?" Pearson's words came in gulps "Oh, God—not—?"

Ismael turned a grey, haunted face toward him. "Get McCleary," he ordered in a harsh, unnatural voice. "Tell him that Mr. Harvy has been killed—stabbed in the back."

CHAPTER X

It was the sound of running feet, of deep vibrant voices that aroused Nancy from the drugged sleep into which she had finally fallen. She had been dreaming of home—of bright autumn foliage, of white houses facing elm-shaded streets, of the classic red-brick college buildings on the hill, and she lay bewildered for several minutes after she opened her eyes, trying to remember where she was.

Daylight creeping through the shutters fell in even, greyish bars on the mattinged floor, and in the dim light she distinguished, through the veil of mosquito netting, the unfamiliar furnishings of Lydia's guest room. Nancy shivered and pulled the sheet higher around her shoulders as though to shield herself from the tide of hateful memories that swept over her. She mustn't think about Penang—if she once started to relive that ghastly experience, she wouldn't have the courage to carry on. It was even better to think about Lydia's murder, and the fact that she herself might actually be in danger, as the funny little Malay detective had hinted. Here at least she had nothing with which to reproach herself; she couldn't help anything that had happened in this horrible house, except, of course, that she had taken advantage of their mistake in her identity. And that didn't harm anyone. Later, after Ismael had caught the murderer, she could explain—strange how sure she was that the absurd little man would succeed where McCleary had failed. Had it been he who had taken her shoes and found the papers, or had it been one of the servants? Last night, in her upset state she had thought it might even have been the murderer, but now, in the cold light of morning, that theory seemed fantastic. She was a stranger; why should he worry about her? She knew nothing; if she had, she would have turned him over to Ismael with a smile on her face. Poor Lydia. Her gaze brooded somberly on the bowl of flowers beside her bed. It must have been almost the last thing Lydia had done—to add that welcoming touch. She hadn't thought of it before, but now it seemed a message. Lydia had known she was coming, had wanted her. Nancy's heart felt lighter, almost as though Lydia had spoken to her—as perhaps she had.

Half an hour later, bathed and carefully dressed in white linen whose crispness had been wilted by the damp, she wandered through the hall toward the front veranda. The door of the Bosworth bedroom was closed, and a constable was on guard there—a

determined-looking little Malay who stared at her
suspiciously as she passed. From inside the room
came muffled babblings, sometimes shrill, insistent,
sometimes low, but always incoherent.

"Tuan Farnsworth?" she asked.

"Sahaya, Mem," the constable answered, straightening himself as though he feared she would try to
enter the room.

With a nod, she passed on. Where had Farnsworth
gone last night, she wondered, and how did Ismael
find him when no one else had been able to?

The living room was deserted, but a white-coated Malay boy was lazily swishing a cloth and mop
around, raising clouds of dust which glimmered in
the grey light for a second before settling in a new
location. "I'd show him what for, if this was my
house," Nancy grumbled, all her New England ances-
try outraged by his methods; and then her indignation faded under his broad smile of welcome, "Tabeh
Mem, ada copee?" He dropped his mop and duster,
and padded eagerly past her toward the kitchen.

The dining room was still dressed up in its lace and
silver—a sad reminder of the supper party which had
never taken place. Hurriedly Nancy stepped out onto
the veranda, and stood drinking in the beauty of the
scene before her. Beyond the wet, blackened gravel
of the driveway was a strip of carefully tended
lawn, as soft and green as plush, and then a series
of three terraces riotous with flowers, sending

up wave after wave of perfume, dazzling the eyes with their color. Below the flower beds stretched the dark, shining green of hundreds of rubber trees receding into the mist that still hung over the valley.

So absorbed was she in her surroundings that she was quite unconscious of the long, grim-faced man who was watching her from the depths of a wicker chair, or of the Malay constable squatting on the steps below her. "Hrrumph! and who might you be?" a Scottish voice broke in upon her pleasure.

Startled, she whirled around and stared down at the indolent figure in the crumpled white suit. His red-rimmed eyes looked hollow in the long, dusty brown face, and there were freckles on the tanned bald spot above the close-cut grey hair. Was he another policeman?

"Th' name's Hamilton, if that means anything to you," he said sardonically, "and after you tell me who you are and what you're doing here, I'd be pleased to hear what all this fuss is about that's keepin' me frae m' wurrk,"

Nancy smiled at the indignation in his voice. "I'm a friend of Lydia's. I got here last night. My name is—" she caught her breath a little— "Helene Chambers."

"Yus, she was speakin' about you yestere'en," Hamilton nodded, and brought his heavy grey eyebrows together in a frown. "But 'twas not like you are she described you."

Nancy's hazel eyes darkened in alarm. What had Lydia told this disagreeable old man about Helene that made him challenge her identity? "What did she say about me?" she asked, forcing a friendly smile to her unwilling lips.

"That's neither here nor there," he grunted, hitching his chair around so that he might stare at her more comfortably from beneath his shaggy eyebrows.

"Well, it doesn't matter." Nancy shrugged her slim shoulders in assumed indifference. "She was probably just spoofing you. Anyway, I understood that you didn't like each other."

He was taken aback by her frankness, she noticed with satisfaction. "Not at furst, we didna," he admitted. "I let nae one mind my business for me—but after she'd learnt her lesson, she was none sae bad for a woman."

Nancy bit her lip at his masculine complacence, but before she could reply, the houseboy pattered out on the veranda bearing a large tray.

"Put it over there, awa' frae me," Hamilton barked. "I don't want to see nor smell the stuff." He turned his aching head away as the boy hurried to place a table at a careful distance from him.

"Won't you have some coffee?" Nancy asked maliciously. "I've always heard that coffee was a good antidote for too much whisky. My, those eggs and bacon smell delicious!"

Hamilton choked back his nausea at the thought of them, but he said nothing until Nancy had seated herself.

"Noo, then. Tell me what deil's wurrk went on here last night," he commanded. "Nary a wurrd of sense can I mak oot o' it. McCleary was juist aboot to tell me when up runs Pearson, eyes goggling oot o' his face, and whisks McCleary awa wi'oot sae much as a by your please."

"Somebody killed Lydia," Nancy said, suddenly ashamed that she could eat and drink with such zest.

"Sae mooch I gathered—" the Scotchman's tone was dry. "'Tis the who and how and why I'm wantin' to ken."

"She was stabbed. That's all I really know. The police think that someone on the estate must have done it—a white man, not a native," she added, watching him closely over the rim of her coffee cup.

His brown sandstone face didn't change its expression, but his shrewd grey eyes narrowed. "Noo, who wad be like to do such a thing?" he mused aloud.

"Who do you think?" Nancy asked. "You know all these people here better than I do."

Caution veiled the brightness of his eyes, and his voice was cold. "I dinna ken mooch aboot them. I mind my ane business, and if everyone else did the same, the wurrld wad be the better for it."

Nancy flushed angrily at his words, but before she could find a sufficiently crushing retort, a white topee appeared below the vine-draped railing of the veranda, and Jim Mason ran breathlessly up the steps. "What's this about Harvy being killed?" he demanded.

"Mr. Harvy killed!" Nancy exclaimed, her cup slipping from her nerveless fingers to smash in a brown puddle on the white cloth.

"Ye're daft, mon," Hamilton growled. "'Twas Mrs. Bosworth was killed, not John."

"John too—they found him just a little while ago, my mandur told me. Stabbed in the back. He was lying on the edge of the jungle—must have happened when he was on his way to roll call."

"Sae that's why Pearson came after McCleary," Hamilton muttered. "Sma' wonder he looked as if he'd seen a ghost."

"I suppose they took him up to his own bungalow," Mason said. "I thought they might have brought him here. Good Lord! It's unbelievable. Who'd want to kill poor old John?" Jim dropped limply into a chair beside Nancy. The girl looked white and shaken, and he felt a pang of compunction at his tactlessness. "I'm sorry, Helene," he said softly, reaching out to pat her cold fingers. "I thought of course you knew about it, or I wouldn't have come bursting up here the way I did."

"No, I didn't know—I just got up." She pushed her chair back from the table with a gesture of repugnance.

"Wait, I'll get rid of that debris for you. Hey, boy!" he called, and an alert young Malay appeared. "Makanan habis bawa pergi pinggan semua."

"How about a drink, old man?" he asked Hamilton as the boy began to stack the dishes on his tray. "I could do with one, and I'll bet you could."

"I'm needin' it bad," the Scotchman admitted. He'd liked John Harvy, and in spite of his reluctance he'd come to like Lydia too. He kept seeing her as she had stood in the doorway of the factory yesterday, the sun making a halo of her fair hair. Perhaps if he hadn't been drunk last night, he might have saved her. His big-knuckled hands clenched.

"Kasseh dua whisky soda, besar," Jim murmured to the boy.

A light rain began to rustle on the atap roof and drip from the overhanging eaves. Jim frowned. "More rain. Damn this climate—there go the coolies." He stared morosely at the group of natives hurrying for shelter.

"It's the awful uncertainty," Nancy burst out; "not knowing who did it, or who will be next." She shivered.

"You don't have to worry anyway," Jim assured her. "I imagine Harvy was killed because he knew who had killed Lydia, and the murderer was afraid he'd tell the police. You haven't any idea who killed her, have you? Not hiding his identity under those brown curls of yours, are you?" He was smiling, but his eyes were anxious.

"No, I have no idea," Nancy said frankly. "If I had I'd have told Ismael last night. I'd like to see the brute, whoever he is, boiled in oil. Poor Lydia—she never hurt anyone in her life, and I don't believe Mr. Harvy did either. It's a horrible world where such things can happen to people like them."

"What price virtue?" Jim sighed, and then turning to Hamilton asked, "Have you any ideas on the subject?"

"Nay—I know naething. I was drunk last nicht, and I'm wishing I was drunk noo."

Ignoring the rain which was streaming from the edges of his terai, and darkening his khaki shirt, Bill Pearson came slowly along the driveway, his shoulders bent like an old man's. Wearily, he climbed the steps, and without a word dropped into the nearest chair. His face was still good-looking in spite of its haggardness, Nancy thought resentfully.

The houseboy appeared with tall clinking glasses, and Jim motioned for him to give one to Bill. "Take a swig of that, old man—and then tell us what happened."

Absent-mindedly Bill drained his glass, and then raising his head for the first time, seemed aware of the other people on the veranda.

"Sorry, Miss Chambers," he said with an apologetic smile. "It's such a ghastly thing. Finding poor old John like that, and then breaking the news to Betty."

"How is she?" Nancy asked, forgetting her distrust of the other woman in a rush of sympathy. "Is there anything I can do?"

"Not just now. Perhaps later." He hesitated and then said bitterly, "She didn't want anyone but Clive. I sent for him, and he and Mike are with her now."

Hamilton turned his head, and the eyes of the two men met in silent understanding.

"Not wasting any time, is she?" Jim Mason said with a cynical smile, and then, as though dismissing Betty, asked quickly, "How did you happen to find him, Bill? What do Ismael and McCleary make of it?"

"I don't know what they think," Bill said. "I was walking along with Ismael when he noticed the body. Funny thing—it was just John's white sleeve that showed, and you could see it from only one point in the road—the rest of the body was hidden in the bushes. He sent me along for McCleary, and together we carried John up to the house." His lips tightened at the thought of that journey; John had been a heavy burden, a lifeless weight rolling from side to side on the crude litter they had fashioned. "They sent me in to tell Betty. She couldn't believe it, of course. Seems she'd gotten up early and walked part way with John. She blames herself for having left him."

Hamilton looked up sharply. "What for was she sae early up, and walkin' wi' John?"

"Don't ask me," Bill shrugged. "Couldn't sleep, perhaps."

"What I don't see is how anyone could have slipped up on John without his noticing it," Jim Mason said thoughtfully.

"Easy enough, along that track. It was very misty early this morning, remember, could hardly see your hand before your face. John is, or was, an absent-minded beggar—wouldn't expect to meet anyone. Here come Clive and Mike now!" His voice changed as the two friends hurried through the sheets of rain that were now bouncing on the gravel driveway.

"What's the latest news?" Jim asked while the new-comers were still on the steps.

Clive, with the old dazed expression on his white, strained face, walked into the house without replying, but Mike said shortly, "I don't know. Doc Sparkes is there. Ismael and McCleary aren't saying much— just asked Clive and me where we'd been this morning, and what we'd done. I suppose they are trying to eliminate as many suspects as they can, but as nearly as I've been able to figure, everyone's in for it—even Farnsworth, and Hamilton here."

"Eh, what's that ye're sayin'?" the Scotchman growled. "I had naething to do wi' all this."

Mike's grin was malicious. "It's up to you to prove it then, and unless you have a better alibi than I think you have, you're in the same boat as the rest of us." His cat-green eyes shifted away from Hamilton's indignant face, to rest on Nancy, and his expression softened. "All, that is, except Miss Chambers. She seems to be in the clear. That's the reward of an easy conscience. You sleep late and have no time to slip around in the mist sticking knives in people's backs."

"Oh, don't," Nancy said with a shiver. "How can you be so heartless!" Her eyes flashed their dislike of the man who could sit there so easily taunting them all.

Clive Bosworth, looking more than ever like a sleepwalker, came slowly out onto the veranda and, after glancing about uncertainly, dropped into the empty chair which Mike pushed toward him

"How about footprints?" Jim Mason asked. "Did they get a look at any before this last shower came up?"

"I don't know," Bill Pearson answered doubtfully. "The coolies had been along part of the road, and their bare feet were all over the place. I didn't think to look for marks near the body, but I suppose Ismael had a look-see while I went for McCleary. He's too clever to overlook a bet like that."

Mike Sullivan yawned, and swung his long legs up onto the Singapore chair which creaked dismally as he settled himself back in its embrace. "Personally, if I had been wanting to slip up on Harvy, I wouldn't have risked meeting him face to face. I'd have gone along the path through the jungle—there's a trail there that the natives use, you know—"

"You seem to know all about it," Jim Mason said sharply.

"Sure, and why wouldn't I?" Mike grinned. "I've got eyes, and I've got brains. Everyone here knows about that path, and unless I'm very much mistaken some one of us used it this morning."

There was a sudden silence. With a shock Nancy grasped the full intent of his words; one of the men sitting there on the veranda with her was the murderer. Her eyes, bright with suspicion, searched their faces for some sign of abnormality. Was it Mike Sullivan, lying there with a mocking smile still lingering around his lips? Was it Clive Bosworth, whose yellow head was resting so despairingly on his hand? Was it Bill Pearson, who was staring stonily over her head at some unseen horror? Was it the disagreeable Scotchman, whose inscrutable face betrayed absolutely nothing of his feelings? Or was it Jim Mason, whose quick blue eyes were scanning each of the other men, as she herself was doing?

It couldn't be any of them, she decided. They all looked so normal, in spite of the horror and the strain. It must be Dave Farnsworth, she thought, or perhaps even Betty Harvy. Then impatient at herself, she shrugged. She always decided that it was someone who wasn't present. Last night she had been sure it must be Hamilton, simply because he wasn't there to disarm her with his presence. And now, watching these people on the veranda she couldn't bring herself to believe such evil of any of them.

She was glad she wasn't a detective, she decided, her thoughts turning to the little Malay upon whose

shoulders rested the task of ferreting out the murderer. It was strange, Ismael had seemed to have a
presentiment last night of danger, only he had feared
for her safety, not for John Harvy's. What had he
said to her? "Do not go anywhere alone with anyone,
under any circumstances. Keep your shutters closed
and your door locked when you are in your room." If
he had given that advice to Mr. Harvy, the poor man
might still be alive. Why did Ismael think that Nancy was in danger? Something about the possibility
that she had the clue to the murderer's identity, just
because she had been the first on the scene. Well, he
was wrong—she'd gone over and over all that she had
done and seen, and there was nothing—all she had
done was to hide the telegrams and let people think
she was Helene Chambers. Surely that was something
that could concern only herself. It had been sheer
luck that she had found the telegrams lying on the
table where Lydia had left them, and that no one except Lydia had known of their arrival.

Suddenly all the color drained from her face, and
she swallowed hastily to choke back the exclamation
that trembled on her pale lips. O God! why hadn't
she thought of that before? She felt overwhelmed at
the ugliness of the fact that had so suddenly confronted her. Here she had been acting blindly on the
assumption that only Lydia had seen the telegrams,
and she had been wrong. The murderer knew who
she was. Even if Lydia hadn't told him of the change

in Helene's plans, and of Nancy's arrival, he would never have overlooked the telegrams lying openly on the table. Whoever knew that she was Nancy Reynolds, and not Helene Chambers, was the murderer.

Once more she scanned the faces of the men around her. What had they said to her? How had they acted? Frantically she tried to remember. Mike Sullivan had been skeptical about the time of her arrival and what she had done in the house. Jim Mason had asked her just a few moments ago whether she knew anything about the murderer. Mr. Hamilton had openly questioned her identity. Bill Pearson had spoken to her only once or twice, but he watched her a lot— as he was watching her now. Hurriedly she lowered her long lashes. Betty Harvy had implied that Nancy was unwelcome. Clive Bosworth, and Farnsworth— well, she didn't know what their attitude had been. Certainly at first Clive had ignored her, as he might any intruder—it wasn't until she had appealed to him directly that he had acknowledged her as a guest.

It was all very confusing, but one thing was certain, sooner or later the murderer would betray his knowledge of her identity. If she could lead each of the men on to talk to her, if she played her part cleverly enough, she would be able to point him out to the detectives. The realization that she alone had a clue to the murderer was so intoxicating that a confident smile curved her lips. All she had to do, she thought, was to be sweet and sympathetic to these

lonely men, listen to them, watch them, and then
when the murderer had been lured into betraying
himself—her hands clenched themselves fiercely at
the thought of her triumph.

It wasn't until much later that Nancy was to remember Ismael's warning, and to realize, when it was
too late, that she had been playing directly into the
murderer's hands.

CHAPTER XI

Ismael, plodding slowly along the muddy road, was too engrossed in the gloom of his thoughts to notice the rain beating on his shoulders, streaming from his sun helmet in warm trickles down the neck of his khaki tunic. "Surely, Allah," he protested, "these tears of yours are unnecessary. For a week now you have wept each day until the rice paddies are flooded, and your children sit in idleness watching their crops wash away. If you were again moved to tears today, why could you not have waited but a brief hour before you gave way—time to you is nothing; but to your humble servant here it is everything. One short hour, and I might have discovered the son of Shaitan who is working this evil among us!" The little Malay sighed, and then continued his childish arraignment of his deity. "And why, O Allah, with your infinite wisdom, did you trouble to create so witless a creature as the Constable Karimun?" Words failed him as he thought of the policeman he had sent to guard the spot where John Harvy's body had been found—the stupid Malay, who, at the first warm drops of rain, had taken shelter in the underbrush, and had been so busy protecting his empty head from the downpour that he had made no effort to preserve the precious footprints he had been set to watch.

"Why did you not then cover them, son of a pig?" Ismael had thundered when he had been at last free to hurry to the jungle's edge. The constable had peered up at him through the screen of wet foliage with stupid oxlike eyes and murmured piously, "It was the will of Allah, Tuan, to wash them away. He sent the aya panas (literally, hot rain; figuratively, blood of warriors). It would have been bad luck to interfere."

With an exclamation of disgust, Ismael turned away from the cowering native, squatting under his crude shelter at the edge of the jungle. The marks had all been smoothed into an even surface of mud—the footprints behind the tree where the murderer had lain in wait for John Harvy, the marks where his body had been dragged from the road into the underbrush, the footprints around the body, and the tracks which the murderer had made coming and going along the jungle path.

The rain had started while Ismael was busy questioning Mrs. Harvy and the servants, as he waited for Doctor Sparkes to make his examination, and he had had no time to examine the footprints at the scene of the crime. Having put a constable in charge, he had made the mistake of assuming that the man would do

his job—he had been used to the trained co-operation
of a corps of conscientious helpers in Johore, and the
stupidity of the local police here handicapped him at
every turn. There was so much to do, and he was fast
realizing that none of the duties could be relegated
to anyone else.

It was strange about that kris of Tuan Mason's.
Doctor Sparkes had said it fitted the wound in Mrs.
Bosworth's as well as that in Mr. Harvy's body, like
a sheath, and yet, it hadn't been used even in the
first murder. And in the second, there could be no
question, for it was still in the desk in the Bosworth
living room, where Ismael himself had locked it. But
that was only one of the many queer angles to this
case.

There was little use, he admitted, in going now to
the place where he had found Tuan Farnsworth; the
imprint of the bicycle tires would have been beaten
out by the rain, but there was a dim chance that some
friendly tree or bush might have preserved some of
the marks, and it might still be possible to discover
from them what had happened to the unstable young
American.

The factory was crowded with peering natives as
he passed it, but there was no sign of life in the kampong, where the women and children cowered indoors
away from the "evil" warm rain. The rubber tree under
which he had found Farnsworth still bore the scars of
the impact, and the twisted, useless frame lay in its

same resting place, but the marks of the tires had been washed away. Slowly, methodically, Ismael searched the sodden ground between the rubber trees, but it was not until he reached the narrow opening in the almost impenetrable barrier of jungle that he found a fresh scratch on the tall, smooth trunk of a tree where a pedal might have scraped it. Search as he might, he found nothing else to enlighten him about Farnsworth's movements. Had he alighted and gone along the jungle path to come out on the other side of that primitive path, or had he been riding around aimlessly during the hours he had been missing? How had he wrecked the bicycle? Had he run into a tree as Ismael at first supposed, or had he been struck from behind by the man who had murdered Harvy? Or, was Farnsworth the killer, and his own disaster just an accident caused by the mist?

Someone had certainly been along that path, Ismael decided as he pushed his way carefully through the creepers and trailing vines, shouldering aside the wet leaves and clutching brambles while his feet sank deep in black, sucking mud. A twig was broken here, a fresh leaf was pressed into the black soil there, but the rain had obliterated any footprints that might have been retained in the swampy ground. Monkeys scolded overhead, a dainty mouse deer peered curiously at him from behind a clump of rattan, a snake slithered across the path; the underbrush was alive with twitterings and murmurs of bright-hued birds, the squeaks and squeals of small startled animals, but there was nothing to identify the merciless killer who had passed that way.

"Go and report to Tuan McCleary," Ismael ordered the constable, who with an exclamation of fright had jumped to his feet, clutching his baton, as the detective silently emerged from the jungle behind him. "You are a fool and a coward. You are no use to me."

McCleary was restlessly pacing the veranda of the Harvy bungalow, his red face scowled with worry; his dark hair upended showed the passage of blunt, nervous fingers. "Where did you disappear to?" he asked in an irritable tone as Ismael clumped up the steps. Without waiting for a reply, he continued in a husky whisper, "I think we've got a case against Bosworth and Mrs. Harvy. I found an insurance policy making her the beneficiary to the tune of ten thousand pounds. I put the screws on her maid and some of the servants, and they admitted that Bosworth was her lover, had been ever since Mrs. Bosworth took that trip home. Today, for the first time since the servants have been here, she got up in time for breakfast with Harvy, and walked down the road with him. At first she said it was because she was frightened and upset, and then she admitted that she hoped to see Bosworth, said she was worried about him. Pretty thin, eh?" His broad mouth stretched into a grim smile. "Let's go along and question Bosworth. Strike while the iron is hot—"

"One moment, Tuan," Ismael said. "I think first it would be well to send some cables."

"Cables?" McCleary looked blank. "Where to? What for?"

"To London, and to New York. We should know more about these people, and, since they will not tell us about themselves, I want to know what they are hiding."

"I don't see that that will help us much," McCleary protested; "Bosworth and Mrs. Harvy are the only ones who had a motive. Bosworth was tired of his wife, and she was anxious to get rid of her husband. By removing them both, the road is clear, and they have ten thousand pounds to boot."

"Nevertheless, Tuan, I think the cables should go," Ismael insisted, and then, noticing the stubborn set of McCleary's heavy jaw, he added tactfully, "If Scotland Yard tells us that the Semang Rubber Estate is in good shape, that Hamilton, Harvy, Mrs. Harvy, Bosworth, and Sullivan have nothing in their past lives to conceal; and if the New York police can find nothing against Mason, Pearson, Farnsworth, and Miss Chambers, then we will know that the crime had its roots here on the estate, that it did not creep from out of the past."

McCleary's nod was reluctant. "I don't suppose it can do any harm—may clear away some of the lies and evasions; but I don't think you'll find out anything of real value. This is a clear case of lust and

greed." The detective's face was eloquent of his opinion of the motives.

Ismael, taking advantage of McCleary's reluctant
agreement, hurried into the deserted Harvy living
room, and with an exclamation of annoyance removed
the silken doll that prissily concealed the telephone.
The room, with its dark-shaded lamps, its incense, its
low, black satin divans heaped with ornate pillows,
was as frivolously out of place on the rubber estate as
the futile, scatter-brained woman who had staged it.

Half an hour later, Ismael and McCleary were
seated in the damp, mildewed room beneath the
Bosworth bungalow—Clive's office—and Clive himself, white and shaken, was facing them from across
his flat-topped desk. "I tell you, I don't know anything about Harvy's murder, any more than I know
who killed Lydia. I don't know how the estate will
manage without him—my God! he was the estate.
He ought to have been the manager. He knew more
about rubber in ten minutes than I'll ever know."
Clive buried his tousled head in his hands.

"What did you do this morning?" McCleary asked
in a businesslike tone.

"Nothing. I haven't done a damned thing. Been
too upset."

"That isn't what I mean. I want to know where you
went, whom you saw, what you did; everything, from
the time you got up, until now."

Clive lifted his head. "I got up at four thirty when
Mike routed me out for roll call. We had breakfast
on the porch. When the second tong-tong sounded,
we started down toward the coolie lines. Then I remembered that Harvy had given me some papers yesterday that he wanted me to go over. I was supposed
to read them, and return them to him this morning. I thought I'd better get them and glance over
his notes; he'd been pretty insistent, and he'd kick
up a fuss if he found I hadn't had time to go over
them. I told Mike to go on, and I ran back here. I'd
left the papers on this desk, but when I got here, I
couldn't find them. Then I suddenly saw Lydia lying
on the settee over there, and it gave me such a turn,
I nearly collapsed. I got outside, and was sick. When
I got to the factory, roll call was over, and I saw the
coolies going to work. Pearson and Mason came up
and said that Harvy hadn't put in an appearance. I
didn't think much about it then, though it was very
unusual—still everything was topsy-turvy—we were
busy planning the work, short-handed, you know, on
account of Farnsworth. Mason offered to take over
Farnsworth's division this morning, and Pearson was
to take it this afternoon. I went into the factory to see
how things were going there. Josephs, the half-caste
clerk, said he could handle the place until Hamilton
got there, so I started out to make the inspection
rounds. I was over in Mason's sector when Harvy's
boy caught up to me and told me that Harvy was

dead, and that Betty—er, Mrs. Harvy—wanted to see me. Mike went along with me, and, well, you were there, so you know the rest. When Doctor Sparkes gave her something to quiet her down, we came back here. It had started to rain, and the coolies always quit then, so there was no point in trying to work—I was too upset to be any good, anyway."

McCleary's glance at Ismael was exultant. Clive hadn't an alibi for the vital moments when Harvy had been killed.

"Did you see anyone, Tuan, when you came back to look for the papers?" the Malay asked.

"No, I came right in here through the outside door. No one ever comes here except in my office hours; then, of course, there is a string of coolies—but that is later in the morning. One of the house boys is supposed to clean, but he hadn't gotten around to it—it's just the way it was yesterday, now that they've taken Lydia's body away." He glanced distastefully around the dirt-tracked floor and dust-filmed furniture.

"You didn't go upstairs to look for the papers?" Ismael persisted.

"No, I just looked here, where I'd left them, and when I suddenly saw Lydia lying there on that settee, everything else went out of my head. Anyway, Harvy probably took them."

"What were the papers like, Tuan?" Ismael asked.

"Oh, just papers," Clive said vaguely. "Notes, you know—some writing and a lot of figures. They were on two pieces of blue paper, clipped together. He had some crazy system—blue pad for one thing; yellow pad for another, and so on—I never paid much attention."

The Malay leaned forward eagerly. "What did he use blue paper for, Tuan, can you remember?"

"Blue was for anything dealing with production, I believe. Yellow I know was for labor."

"There was nothing like that among Harvy's stuff," McCleary stated. "I went through everything he owned."

"Maybe he destroyed it, changed his mind or something," Clive volunteered. "All I know is that he gave it to me, and I put it right here." He thumped the desk. "And it was gone when I looked for it." Restlessly he began pulling out desk drawers, shifting books and papers, feeling into crevices, while McCleary watched him impatiently. "Here, that's no way to look for anything," he exclaimed. "Let me get there." Even the Inspector's systematic search, however, failed to produce the missing papers. "I don't suppose they matter, anyway," McCleary announced. "We're just wasting our time." He turned abruptly to Clive,

"Did you know that Mrs. Harvy walked part way with her husband this morning?"

The Englishman nodded indifferently. "Yes, she said that if she had only gone on with him instead of

turning back to the house, he'd be alive now. That's
what's worrying her, I told her it was no use reproach-
ing herself; I'd felt the same way about having left
Lydia, and Mike had said it wouldn't have made any
difference—the murderer would have killed her the
first time he'd caught her alone."

"Oh, so Mike Sullivan told you that, did he? And
how did he know so much about the murderer?"

"Mike doesn't know—he just figured that if it was
important to kill Lydia, the murderer would do it the
first chance he got."

"Why do you think they were killed—Mrs. Bosworth and Mr. Harvy?" Ismael asked before McCleary
could say anything more.

"That's what I'd like to know," Clive said thoughtfully. "I can't see for the life of me why anyone
would want to kill either of them. Whoever did it
must be crazy—just wanted to kill for the sake of
killing—like an amok, you know, only an amok keeps
on in one single tear until he's killed himself." Clive
looked rather pleased with his theory, until Ismael
said quietly, "A mania such as that would show itself,
I think, Tuan. Have you noticed anything strange in
the behavior of your friends?"

Clive's face fell. "No, and I've been watching for
some sign. Damn awful feeling, if you know what
I mean—thinking someone you know might stick a
knife into any one at any minute. But everyone seems

so normal. Puts my wind up a bit. I mean anyone who is crazy enough to go around killing people ought to show it—and nobody does."

McCleary shook his head impatiently. "That's all nonsense. The person who committed these murders did it in cold blood, and had a reason for both of them. Once we get hold of that, we'll have the murderer." His small dark eyes narrowed into slits, and his voice was harsh as he said meaningly, "So far, you and Mrs. Harvy are the only ones who have gained by the murders."

Clive's body jerked in surprise. "Why, what do you mean? What have I gained? You don't think I had anything to do with it, do you? Or Betty? Why— Good Lord—" words seemed to fail him.

Ismael frowned, but ignoring him McCleary continued, "You are lovers, you and Mrs. Harvy. You want to get married. The two people who stood in your way were both killed, and—Mrs. Harvy will get ten thousand pounds, perhaps twenty thousand, if there was double indemnity!"

Clive gasped, his face flushed a deep scarlet, and then grew ghastly while a cold perspiration stood out in visible drops on his forehead. "No! No! you're wrong. You can't believe that. I wouldn't have touched Lydia or John—I was a'fully fond of them both. I did make an ass of myself over Betty but that's the worst that can be said of me—I never once thought of marrying her— Oh, you must believe me!" His blue eyes held a hurt expression, like a child who had been unjustly accused and realized his helplessness.

Ismael intervened before McCleary could say anything more. "I think, Tuan, we should talk to some of the other people—Tuan Hamilton is impatient to go to the factory—and we have much to do."

McCleary frowned at the interruption, but something in the expression of the little Malay checked the recitation of the evidence against the estate manager. McCleary, strangely enough, felt no pity for the man who had been his friend; in his opinion Clive had outraged every code of decency, forfeited every right for consideration. "All right," the officer said gruffly. "You can go now, Bosworth. Tell Hamilton to step down here."

As Clive stumbled from the room, McCleary glowered at Ismael. "Why did you stop me? The bastard's as guilty as hell. I'd have gotten a confession out of him in another half hour. And to think I used to regard him as a friend!"

"I don't think you would have had a confession, Tuan," Ismael said calmly. "If he was the guilty one, if he planned and carried out these murders, he is too cold and calculating to be frightened into an admission. You really have no case against him, you know, nothing but a motive. Unless you can place him at the scene of the crimes, it is worse than useless to arrest him." His voice softened. "You are taking this case too hard, Tuan—it comes too close to you, and

in your anxiety to do your duty, you lose your perspective."

The long, lanky figure of the Scotch engineer,
entering the doorway, prevented further discussion,
"It's aboot time ye got ower ye're business wi' me,"
Hamilton growled. "Keepin' me frae my wurrk wi'
yer dilly-dallying." He seated himself gingerly on the
edge of a chair, his dour face expressionless. "Weel,
get on wi' it."

"Tell us what you did last evening, Tuan," Ismael
said, after waiting vainly for the white officer to
speak. McCleary obviously had taken his implied
criticism of harshness to heart.

"I did naething. I was drunk," the Scotchman said
bluntly.

"Why were you drunk?"

"And why not?" Hamilton asked. "A sturrm outside, twa guid bottles of whisky at ma elbow. Wha
wad ye hae me do?"

Ismael stared at him without speaking, and after
a moment's uncomfortable silence, the engineer said
cautiously, "I'm not sayin' I meant to get drunk, ye
ken. No, I was coming up here later for some kedgeree.
It was juist a drink or twa I was meanin' to tak—to
pass the time. And the next thing I knew the tong-
tong was beating as loud as if it was in ma head."

"When did you see Mrs. Bosworth last?"

"Yesterday forenoon," Hamilton said promptly.
"She stopped by the factory to mind me o' supper."

"How did she seem—was she cheerful?"

"She was as she always was," Hamilton said glumly. He didn't want to think about the way she had looked, or her joking kindness—the ripple of her laughter still echoed dimly in his ears. He'd been a fool to soften to her as he had. Life had taught him that if you liked a person, sooner or later he hurt you. "If ye're lookin' for saething to do, ye might find oot who was busyin' theirsels wi' my engines last nicht."

"What do you mean?" McCleary was startled out of his sulkiness.

"Juist that. Someone was in the factory, monkeyin aboot ma engines. 'Tis a miracle all the lichts dinna gae oot."

McCleary's small eyes sparkled. "They did. So Miss Chambers said. Mrs. Harvy, though, claimed that the ones in her place were on all the time. Can you account for that?"

"If th' switch was pulled, the lichts a' over went out. The only way the lichts wad go oot in one house and not in a' is if a wire gaes doon, or a house fuse is blown."

"How do you know that someone was in the factory?"

Hamilton snorted, "I ken those engines like a mither does her chield. There was mud twa, on th' floor, and marks on the machinery."

Ismael nodded. "I saw them, Tuan. I was going to ask you whether you had made them."

"Not I. 'Twas some clumsy lout blundering aboot, touching this and that till he found the switch."

"Ought to get some finger prints then, eh, Ismael? The first we've been able to isolate!"

"Nae ye doon't," Hamilton said. "I wiped them off—d'ye think I'd leave ma engine room messed aboot?"

"When did you wipe them off? Why did you touch them?" McCleary raised his voice in disappointment.

"When I started ma engines this morning," the Scotchman replied, "I picked up a rag and gave a bit of a polish—ma engines are as clean, I'll hae ye know, as a hound's tooth."

"You'd no business to touch anything," McCleary exclaimed. "That was the one chance we had of getting finger prints, and you, you old busybody, spoil it!"

"And why not? It's ma business to mind my engines. I'll not be leaving them dirty for anyone—not, mind ye, that I mightn't hae done for an hour or twa if it wad hae helped you catch the mon ye're luikin' for—but I dinna ken thot then, ye'll understand."

The Scotchman was more upset than he was willing to admit, Ismael thought—his Scotch was intermixed with perfectly good English, but which came the more naturally it was difficult to decide.

"Well," grunted McCleary, "it looks to me as though you'd done your damnedest to help the murderer. How do we know you were really drunk last night? You might have poured the contents of those two bottles down the drain pipe!"

Hamilton chuckled. "Y' dinna ken the Scots, ma lad. And if you think I wad hae lifted my hand tae touch a hair o' Mrs. Bosworth's heid, or John Harvy's either, ye're a bigger fool than I thocht—and that's sayin' o'er mooch."

McCleary's red face turned an apoplectic purple, and Ismael said hastily, "Tell us what you did this morning, Tuan Hamilton."

"I woke when the tong-tong sounded like I told you. I went to my engines and saw someone had been there, so I wiped off the marks and started them up. Then I came back to get a bathe; my head was twa big for its skull. A policeman came in and spoke to me, and I told him to wait outside. With my head achin' like it did, I couldna be troubled wi' him juist then. I thought there'd been a fight at the wayong last e'en, and a head or twa bashed, so I ganged along to the hoose to get some aspirin and a change o' clothes. Pearson saw me and told me what had happened afore the policeman there could stop him. A guid laddie is Pearson. Then I came along here under police escort, and here I've been ever since. Now ye ken as much as I do, and I'll be gangin' back to ma wurrk afore the latex is a' ruined." He rose with deliberation and stood waiting for McCleary to speak.

"One moment, Tuan, if you please," Ismael said. "Do you know anything about a memorandum that

Tuan Harvy gave Tuan Bosworth yesterday. It was on blue paper, and I understand that blue is used only for notes about rubber production."

Hamilton rubbed his grey stubbled chin. "Likely 'twould be saething aboot ma report. I gae John my figures for the month's production the nicht before, and he was sore worrit. I dinna ken for sure, but likely 'twas aboot that, for I mind his sayin' he must hae a serious talk wi' Bosworth."

"Have you a copy of the report you gave him?" Ismael asked.

"O' course, mon. I keep one copy for ma files, and the original and a second copy I always gie to John. Richtly it should gae to Bosworth, but John's the one who does a' the wurrk. He'd send ma figures, along wi' his ane report to London, and he'd file away the second carbon for himsel'."

Ismael looked thoughtful, "Did you see carbons of production figures when you went through Tuan Harvy's papers?" he asked McCleary. "According to Tuan Hamilton, there should be a whole file of them, perhaps many files."

"I didn't notice anything of the sort, but I wasn't looking for that kind of thing," the officer, who was bored with the apparent irrelevance of the conversation replied indifferently. "What did he keep them in?"

"In a blue folder in the bottom drawer of his desk—in the office back of the living room," Hamilton declared. "He took out the folder whilst I was there, and looked up last month's record."

McCleary shook his head. "I saw a lot of colored folders in that drawer—all business stuff, but there wasn't a blue one among them. What's the use of wasting time over that, anyway? Let's get on with our questioning. All we have to do is to find someone who saw Bosworth or Mrs. Harvy near the place where Harvy was killed, and we'll pin the murder right on them. Someone must have seen them; the servants or the coolies. As for Bosworth's talk about a blue memorandum, I think it's all hokum he made up to account for his time while he was murdering Harvy. Who'd bother stealing a couple of sheets of paper!"

"That, Tuan, is what I wish to know," Ismael said rising. "I think while you are questioning the rest of the people, I will go with Tuan Hamilton and see what there was of interest in his report."

"All right, go on if you want to, but there's nothing to it," McCleary growled. "Perhaps by the time you get through chasing mare's nests, Farnsworth's fever will have dropped and we can find out what he was up to last night. He may be able to identify the murderer."

Ismael was silent on the swift walk down to the factory, but Hamilton marveled at the speed with which the Malay's short muscular legs traveled along the muddy road. The rain had stopped temporarily,

and a line of coolies with zinc pails of latex was waiting outside the factory, while just inside the door,
the half-caste clerk, Josephs, cursed and muttered as
he weighed the contents of each pail and jotted down
the figures. The air was acrid with the smell of rubber
and acid in the great vats along the side of the room,
and the damp, perspiring bodies of the natives.

Josephs gave a sigh of relief as Hamilton pushed
past the coolies and entered the building. "You'll have
to carry on for a bit longer, Josephs," the Scotchman said, and then in an irritable voice he addressed
Ismael. "See how ye're holdin' up the wurrk wi' ye'r
foolishness. Pearson or Mason should be down here
doin't the weighin'. 'Twas Farnsworth's day for it. I'll
gie you the folder o' reports, and you can tak it along
wi' ye, and tell McCleary he's got to let one o' the
assistants free—even Bosworth wad be better than
nae one."

Matter-of-factly the engineer went to the filing
cabinet and yanked open a drawer. His big, gnarled
hand paused in midair, and his expression was suddenly blank as he stared at the neat array of folders.
Quickly he began to toss them out onto the table until the drawer was empty. "It's not here," he muttered,
and jerked open the other two drawers. "This year's
file is gone—naething sen December o' last year."
He turned to his desk and began to search frantically among the papers under its rolled top, and then

angrily dumped the contents of the desk drawers onto the floor.

"It's not here. Not any place." He raised a flushed face from the litter he had been pawing through, and scratched his grey, prickly chin. "Feckless, that's what it is. Feckless! Who wad want my reports?"

"Perhaps someone is afraid of losing his job when the Tuan Besars in London should see the report," Ismael suggested.

"Nae, that is nonsense. The report went to London yesterday."

"Are you sure it went, Tuan?"

"Josephs!" bawled Hamilton, "did you mail the report for Mr. Harvy yesterday or did you not?"

The dapper, half-caste clerk came to the door. "Yes, Tuan. I took it in to Kluang as always and registered it at the post office."

"Tell me just what you did," Ismael said. "When did Tuan Harvy give it to you? Was it sealed? Did anyone touch it besides yourself?"

"Mr. Harvy sent for me to come to his office," the clerk said precisely. "He was sealing the envelope with red wax. He gave it into my hands and told me to go right in to Kluang and register it. I did, and when I returned, I gave him the receipt. No one touched the letter save myself and Mr. Harvy."

"All richt, gae back to ye'r weighin'," Hamilton ordered, ignoring the curiosity in the half-caste's yellowish face.

"You see, Sergeant, it doesna mak sense. The report went to London all richt, and for why wad anyone steal the carbons and let the original gang?" the engineer asked belligerently.

"Perhaps the person who stole the carbons was anxious only to suppress the facts here on the estate, and didn't care what your Tuan Besars thought."

The Scotchman looked thoughtful. "Onless, it wad be a question o' time, that sething wad happen, or wad not happen, afore the mail reached London."

"That might be so," Ismael frowned. "The question is whether that could have anything to do with the murders."

Hamilton was dubious. "Mayhap it micht account o' John's death, but Mrs. Bosworth could hae ken't naething aboot it."

"She never asked you about the amount of rubber produced, or showed any interest in that side of the business?"

"Nay, never. I wad nae hae told her—such things were not her business. Nae more wad John. But she dinna care aboot that part. She was interested in the coolies and their families, and learned what the markings meant on the trees—the good producers and the bad ones, and the diseases. She liked live things—a great one she was for bein't out o' doors."

"Could she have understood the reports if she had seen them?" Ismael persisted.

"Nae, I doot it. They're quite technical, and abbreviated, and she had nae ower mooch schoolin', so she told me one time. Always pesterin' her mither to let her be an actress, and when her feyther died, her mither said she micht as well get it oot o' her system, for she'd be guid for naethin' else till she tried the stage."

No, it didn't make sense, Ismael silently agreed with the Scotchman: stolen carbons of the monthly reports, a delirious young assistant, a drunken engineer, a missing weapon—a dead woman in a dark house, a dead man on the edge of the black steamy jungle, and the unrecognized figure of the murderer striking through the darkness and the mist.

CHAPTER XII

The house, perched above the wet tossing sea of rubber trees, seemed to be cut off from the rest of the world by the grey monotony of the rain; drizzle that changed to spasmodic, angry shakes of rain, clogged the wire screens, sprayed the sticky rattan furniture, rustled the atap roof, and dripped drearily from the eaves. Yet, despite the damp discomfort of the veranda, none of the people gathered at the main bungalow had any desire to remain indoors. They had hurried through a listless luncheon in a dining room which, although stripped of its festive candles and drooping flowers, was still pregnant with memories of Lydia. At least the air outside was fresh, heavy with the perfume of rain-drenched flowers, the familiar smell of wet leaves, moist earth. Behind its closed doors, its shuttered windows, the house seemed to brood darkly over the tragedy that had taken place within its walls. No amount of electric light could banish the shadows that lived there; they merely slipped to the outskirts of the bright pools made by the shaded lamps, and clustered in corners as though biding their time. Floors creaked suddenly, walls groaned, window curtains and draperies stirred, and the air was weighted with the bitter taste of mildew and decay.

Nancy shivered. "Was it always like this?" she murmured, shifting her gaze from the blank shuttered face of the house.

"Like what?" Jim Mason asked, roused from his reverie by the sound of Nancy's voice. No one had spoken for several minutes.

"The house," she said, flushing at the realization that she had spoken aloud. "It seems to be watching us from behind the shutters; waiting, listening—I can't explain, only it's horrible. I was just wondering whether it missed Lydia, and hated us all because we are alive, and she is gone; or whether it had hated her, too, and was glad she'd been killed."

Mike Sullivan looked at her with interest, but Jim Mason merely blinked. "I don't know what you're driving at. I guess it's just the damnable rain that's making you imagine things. Enough to get on anyone's nerves, the eternal drip, drop."

Mike's smile was sarcastic. "Trouble is, Helene, you haven't been in the tropics long enough to blame the weather for everything that happens."

"It's not the rain, though," Nancy insisted. "Why, home I used to love a rainy day. It gave me a chance to get caught up on my mending, or to read— It's cozy indoors in front of a log fire, and it's nice out too, sloshing through puddles with the rain on your face, and the wet sidewalks reflecting the street lamps." Her voice had a homesick note.

Clive Bosworth nodded. "I know what you mean; roaring fires and a tea tray heaped with crumpets and cakes after a day's shooting. Jolly people milling around trying to dry themselves—laughin' and talkin'." He sighed. "Lydia always loved the rain. Wanted to get right out in it. Used to put on old clothes and work in the garden. She'd look a sight when she came in. I got a snapshot of her that way once—sun came out just in time." He smiled wistfully at Nancy. "Would you like to see our albums; some of the pictures date back to Lydia's baby days—might be some of you in it."

Nancy caught her breath at the suddenness of the danger, but her voice was steady as she replied, "Some time, but not now. I don't think I could bear to look at them today." She turned quickly to Jim Mason. "But why were you expelled from college?" she asked with assumed interest. "You had just started to tell me when lunch was announced."

Jim Mason smiled retrospectively. "Oh, a gang of us got in a scrape, and I just happened to be the goat. I decided college was a waste of time for me anyway. I wanted to get out and do things."

Mike Sullivan rose and stretched his long arms. "I wish to God I knew what McCleary and Ismael are up to," he said. "How long are they going to keep us penned up here? They've spent hours questioning us, going over every move we've made since yesterday morning, and still they keep us hanging around." The stolid little Malay policeman stationed by the veranda door watched his restless movements with round wary eyes.

Bill Pearson rubbed a nervous hand across his forehead. "Ismael is questioning the servants, I believe, and McCleary is down in the coolie lines. I suppose they are trying to find out whether any of us were seen over there—" he stared with haunted eyes in the direction of the spot where John Harvy's body had been found. His handsome face was haggard, and he seemed to have aged ten years since the previous night. He had scarcely spoken all morning, just stared into space with a tortured expression, and at lunch had barely touched his food.

Clive Bosworth, on the other hand, seemed more normal and self-possessed than he had at any time, in spite of the fact that McCleary obviously suspected him of the murders. Mike Sullivan was far more upset about the situation than Clive was—the big Irishman's muscles had tensed each time McCleary had gone near his friend.

"There goes Ismael now," Jim Mason said, peering through the rain-silvered screen. "The kabun is with him, and they're going down toward the garden." Everyone leaned forward to watch the two figures moving quickly across the glistening lawn to pause at one of the flower beds. The kabun was pointing, and Ismael was down on his knees in the mud examining some plants. Presently the kabun hurried away, to return in a few minutes with a green wicker basket in one hand, and some gardening tools in the other. "That's the basket Lydia had yesterday!" Bill Pearson exclaimed with a show of interest. "He must be trying to check up on whether she got any plants."

"What's that got to do with the murders?" Jim Mason asked impatiently. "Fine detectives they are—fussing about plants and blue papers and missing folders! Why don't they do something to catch the murderer! I'm fed up with their puttering around, and their eternal questions about this and that, till you don't know what you're saying. Why don't they get on with something useful?"

A car crunched along the gravel driveway and stopped at the steps. Betty Harvy, frail and pathetic, looked up at the veranda. Clive sprang from his chair beside the door, and went down the steps to meet her. "I couldn't bear to stay over there all by myself," she murmured, tears dazzling her lovely eyes, "so I made the policeman bring me here. You don't mind, do you?"

"Of course not," Clive said, helping her up the slippery steps. "I didn't think you'd feel up to coming out, or seeing people, or we'd have suggested your coming over."

Betty smiled wanly at the men who had risen, and then sank gracefully into a chair. "You've no idea how ghastly it is over there—all the servants slinking around and peeking at me from corners, and the policeman watching every move I make. You don't suppose Mr. McCleary will mind my coming over, do you?" She looked up anxiously into Clive's face as he bent to light her cigarette.

"He'll probably be glad," Bosworth said grimly, and then over his shoulder, "get her a shot of brandy, will you, Mike—she's shivering."

With a muffled sound that was almost a snort, the Irishman slammed into the house, and the door groaned shut behind him.

Nancy jumped to her feet—now was the time to find out what had happened to her shoes. Somehow, she hadn't had the courage to go into the house alone, even though she knew there were servants inside, and a policeman on duty outside the room where Farnsworth lay. She'd ask Mike Sullivan to inquire whether the servants had taken her shoes, or where they were—she could say the sandals she had on were uncomfortable.

Nancy paused for a moment beside Betty's chair—she ought to say something to her—after all, the woman had lost her husband under horrible circumstances. "I'm so terribly sorry, Mrs. Harvy," she murmured. "Is there anything I can do for you? Anything

I can get you? A sweater, or a wrap perhaps?—it's damp out here."

Betty held out a fragile, carefully manicured hand. "Thank you, dear." Her voice was dulcet, but it seemed to Nancy that the blue eyes were hard, suspicious, in the brief second before her long lashes drooped over them, "There's nothing I want now—later I may impose on you, if Clive is willing. I don't think I can face a night alone over there—" She hesitated and glanced appealingly at Clive.

"Why, er—of course, Betty," the Englishman said, "we can fix up some place for you. Perhaps Miss Chambers won't mind your bunkin' in with her?" He looked rather helplessly at Nancy. So, that was her game was it, Nancy thought grimly, but there was nothing for her to do but to acquiesce as graciously as she could, repulsive as the prospect was.

Nancy opened the door, and at the sound of the groaning hinges, Mike Sullivan came out of the dining room. He looked startled at the sight of her standing there in the greyish light of the hall, and in some indefinable way she had the impression that he was glad to see her. "I wonder whether you will ask the servants what happened to my shoes," she said. "The ones I wore yesterday disappeared, and these are too new yet to be comfortable."

He nodded. "Boy!" His voice echoed hollowly under the high ceilings, and the sturdy little Malay

policeman, who had been eyeing them suspiciously
from his post beside Clive's bedroom door, started
at the sound. Semut opened the door at the rear of
the hall, hastily buttoning a fresh white coat, "Apa,
Tuan?"

Mike addressed him in rapid Malay, glancing
down at Nancy's slim white sandals. Semut popped
back through the door like a wooden jack-in-the-
box, to appear smiling a moment later with Nancy's
brogues—a damp grey—in his hands. Behind him
came another houseboy holding a can of bianco and
a sponge. His brown face was worried, his splutter of
words and his gestures apologetic.

"He is just cleaning them now," Mike explained.
"All the work had been held up by the police and he
hasn't had time to finish yet. Anyway, it is too damp
for the shoes to dry today, so there was no hurry."

"Give them to me, please." Nancy stretched out
her hand toward Semut, who moved unwillingly to
hand her the shoes. Swiftly her slim fingers explored
the toes. The stuffing was gone! What had happened
to the letters and telegrams? Her worried eyes met
Mike's curious gaze, and she flushed. "I had some
tissue paper stuffed inside to keep them in shape. It's
gone now. Will you ask what they did with it? Who
took the shoes out of my room, anyway?" she asked
irritably. "I always clean my own white shoes. No one
ought to have touched them."

"I'll tell the boy to find some shoe trees. Nothing to get the wind up about, is there?" he asked lazily.

Nancy bit her lip. "No, of course not. Only I don't like people touching my things, and I don't want shoe trees; they leave ridges in the suede when it's damp."

Once more Mike addressed the boys and listened to their singsong replies. "The houseboy said he found the shoes on the back veranda this morning, with Clive's and mine. There was nothing inside them, but if you want them stuffed with paper, he will find some. He's probably lying—threw your tissue paper away—it must have been wet. But, that's as near the truth as you'll get. Better give the shoes back to him. You can't wear them until they've dried." He seemed suddenly bored with the discussion, annoyed at the stubborn set of her chin. Why did women fuss over such trifles? He had thought she was different. Two murders committed on the estate—the killer still prowling around, the place overrun with policemen; and this girl thinking of nothing except a foolish little pair of wet shoes. He shrugged his broad shoulders and turned toward the dining room. "I have to get some brandy for Mrs. Harvy, or Clive will be on my neck."

Reluctantly Nancy handed the shoes to Semut. It was as much a mystery as ever; she still didn't know who had taken them out of her room, or what had happened to the papers. All she could do was to hope that the houseboy actually had destroyed them. And, far from making any headway in finding out which man knew that she wasn't Helene Chambers, she had annoyed Jim Mason by leaving him so abruptly, and had disgusted Mike Sullivan by her fussiness over her shoes. The outlook wasn't very encouraging, but she felt she ought to try at least to penetrate his guard, and she knew that she could do that only by antagonizing him; he would have no patience with attempted coquetry.

"You are worse than a mother hen with a duckling," she accused, following him into the dim greyness of the shuttered dining room.

Mike turned to glare at her. "What do you mean by that?"

"Just that you are always worrying about Mr. Bosworth. Anyone would think he was three years old, instead of thirty, and with a subnormal I.Q. at that. It's ridiculous, you know—makes you both look so absurd."

His green eyes flashed at her insolence, but his angry rejoinder faltered at the realization that there was some truth in her accusation. Good Lord! what were people thinking? Did that snip of girl believe—? Suddenly, he pushed the electric light button, and a cold, harsh light flooded the room, rushing the shadows back into the hall. Mike stared down at Nancy. No, her small, upturned face was impudent, but there was no insinuation in her wide hazel eyes. Still, he felt sensitively, there was no knowing how other people might be regarding his friendship for Clive.

Why was he looking so queer? Nancy wondered. Why did he take out his handkerchief and mop his forehead as though the room was hot instead of chilly? And above all, why didn't he snap back at her, instead of holding the echo of her last words in this strange, uncomfortable silence?

When at last he did speak, his voice sounded queer and choked. "I can't explain—but long ago I swore that I'd look out for Clive. It was a penance. I can't turn back on it."

"Well," said Nancy matter-of-factly, "you may have promised long ago to look out for him, but that doesn't mean that you have to draw every breath for him. You are being false to the spirit of your promise, in my opinion, if you don't make him stand on his own feet. You kill his initiative. Whoever asked you to take care of him must have meant that you were to help him be a man, not keep him a perpetual child."

"'Twas a child asked it," Mike said softly his voice a breath from the past. An old familiar horror dilated his pupils, whitened his face.

"Don't! Don't look like that!" Nancy, con-science-stricken at the effect of her careless words, was shaking his arm. "Whatever it is, it's over—done with." Oh, she thought wildly, she'd never try to pry beneath surfaces again.

He brushed a hand over his face as though he were wiping away his memories. "Sure, I didn't mean to frighten the wits out of you like that. Some ghosts stirred, that is all, but maybe 'twas their last walk, so we'll not begrudge them." His hand shook a little as he lifted a decanter from the side table and poured out a stiff drink. "Have one?" he asked and, as Nancy shook her head, swallowed the brandy in one gulp.

The front door creaked open and shut, a damp current of air swept through the house; and then Jim Mason stood in the wide doorway, a tight, strained expression on his freckled face. "What's taking you two so long?" he demanded in a harsh voice. "I thought something must have happened to Helene."

Nancy flushed at his proprietary tone, and to her annoyance found herself feebly maundering excuses about her wet shoes. Jim's look was so frankly skeptical that her voice changed. "I don't have to account for everything I do. You have no right to question me."

"No, of course not. I didn't mean anything—only I was worried because you'd been gone so long," he said humbly, but his narrowed eyes traveled past her to Mike, who was loading a small tray with decanters and glasses. Not until everything was arranged to his satisfaction did the Irishman turn and glance at Jim with a mocking smile. Mason stiffened, but neither man spoke as Mike, with a leisurely smile, moved past them.

Jim glowered at the broad back receding into the shadowy light of the hall. "I can't stand that guy. There's something phony about him."

"What do you mean?" Nancy asked sharply.

"Well, look at the way he acted last night, for instance—all over the place, questioning everybody, reconstructing the crime and what not, and then, when the police came, he had nothing helpful to say at all. If he is so anxious to find the murderer, why doesn't he spout all his smart ideas to McCleary or Ismael? But, no siree, he's afraid now that they'll pin the murder on his friend Clive, and he's in for it too, if Bosworth is guilty, for Clive hasn't the initiative to do anything on his own."

There was some truth in Jim's criticism, Nancy had to admit. Mike's attitude had definitely changed since the previous evening, but it was Mr. Bosworth he was protecting, she felt sure, not himself. Somehow, since she had had that strange, intimate insight into Mike's suffering, she felt as though, in spite of all the mystery about him, she knew him better than she did the man beside her. After all, she assured herself patriotically, Mike was half American, and Jim was a bit boring—the way he was continually waving the star-spangled banner about—real Americans didn't have to do that. It wasn't so much in what he said, it was his implication that because they were both born in the United States, everyone else was naturally suspect. With a start, she realized that Bill Pearson, the reserved, and Bob Farnsworth, the loquacious, were Americans too, as Lydia had been. Jim was staring at her with troubled eyes. "What's the matter with you, anyway? You haven't fallen for him, have you?" he asked in dismay.

"Good heavens, no!" Nancy exclaimed with transparent sincerity. "I never even thought of such a thing. And as for him, I'm sure he must loathe me. But, I do think, we ought to forget the fact that we are Americans, or Englishmen or Irishmen, or Scotchmen—after all, what we all want is to find the murderer, whatever nationality he is."

Relieved at her spontaneous denial, and ingenuous outburst of internationalism, Jim grinned. "Well, you had me worried. First I was scared pink that something had happened to you when you were gone so long, and then when I dashed in and saw you standing safe and sound beside Sullivan, I had the crazy idea that you trusted him; had fallen for him. After all, he's the sort of guy women do fall for, Helene, and he's so damn coldblooded, he doesn't give a hoot in hell for them. I know his sort. I know it's none of my business, but you're a nice kid, and you come from back home, and I just don't want to see you hurt." His hand was warm and comforting on her chilly arm. "Oh," he exclaimed solicitously, "you're cold—wait, I'll get you something to put on over that silly white dress. The weather here is very deceptive, especially when it rains."

She realized then that she really was chilled through, but while she was still protesting that she would get a wrap of some sort herself, he hurried out into the gloom of the hall, and she heard the quick beat of his heavy footsteps along the bare wooden boards. In a few minutes he was back, carrying a yellow-woolly sweater in a dangling arm. "Here you are, put it on, and let's get out of here."

A haunting fragrance, reminiscent of Lydia, bringing her back poignantly, with all her charm and vivacity, emanated from the soft, golden folds.

Nancy shrank, back shivering. "Take it away I can't wear that. It's Lydia's!"

Jim stared from Nancy's horrified face to the limp yellow sweater in his hand. "What's the matter with it? She kept things like this in the wardrobe down the hall; they were for anyone to wear."

"I don't care," Nancy's chin was set stubbornly. "I'd rather freeze to death than have it touch me. Can't you understand that things are different now? Lydia's dead!" She was impatient of his masculine denseness; the bewildered way in which he was turning the sweater in his hand as though seeking an explanation of her repudiation. Probably he had gone dozens of times to fetch that same garment, or similar ones from the wardrobe, at Lydia's behest, and he simply couldn't grasp, with his male indifference to feminine reactions, that at this particular time, the sweater was abhorrent. Men were just plain dumb, but you couldn't explain anything so fundamental. Either they got it, or they didn't. Jim definitely didn't.

"Never mind," Nancy said with a wavering smile. "I'll get something of my own."

The sweater slipped through his fingers, a golden heap on the dark wood seat of the chair beside the dining room door. "Well, of all the silly nonsense!" he ejaculated! but without waiting for him to complete his indictment, Nancy hurried along the hall. The rain, in one of its sudden tempers, beat for admission on the resistant roof; the hall seemed longer and colder than ever, and over her shoulder she saw Jim, with hunched disgruntled shoulders, at the veranda door. So, he wasn't going to wait for her! Nancy shivered again, and then, seeing the policeman beside the opposite door, felt reassured, even though his almond-brown eyes gleamed with suspicion as she passed him.

The idea of expecting me to wear Lydia's sweater! She flagged her indignation to distract herself from the chill hostility of her room. Rain was drumming on the window sills, falling in thin grey strings beyond the half closed slats of the shutters; a damp breeze fluttered the soggy curtains. Hurriedly, she rushed to the wardrobe and flung open the door. Her garments drooped dejectedly from the hangers; dresses above, shoes and slippers on the wardrobe floor beneath them, like headless, legless ghosts swaying from their scaffolds. They stirred in protest as a wet breeze sighed through the room, and the wardrobe door creaked on its rusty hinges.

"Where did I put my sweater!" Nancy murmured, hoping that the sound of her own voice would steady her nerves. Her hands shook as she groped through the clinging, swaying folds of silk and linen, feeling for something soft and woolly. She should have turned on the light—it was as dark as pitch in the wardrobe, and the musty odor of mildew was almost overpowering. "Darn the sweater!" she exclaimed. "I'll take my white flannel coat." It was the last garment in the closet, and as she touched the familiar sleeve, she stiffened. What was that sound! A board creaked as though someone was creeping up behind her. There was someone behind her. Her dresses were suddenly enemies seizing her, catching in her hair as she tried to escape, and one of them slid from the hanger, a maddening, silken noose over her shoulders, until she shook it off.

She heard the wardrobe door creak again, a rusty warning, and she felt a hot breath on her bare neck, as a sinewy hand seized her throat, choking back her scream. Something suffocating was thrown over her head, twisted tight across her mouth. It was soft and woolly and held Lydia's faint fragrance—her sweater that Nancy had repudiated. Frantically she tried to struggle, expecting every second to feel a dagger plunge into her helpless body. A rough hand shoved her face forward into the wardrobe, and she fell into a heap of dresses that had slipped from their hangers. The wardrobe door groaned shut. Paralyzed with fear, she lay motionless where she had fallen, expecting every moment that the door would be flung open again and that the murderer would seize her.

"This is just a warning, Nancy Reynolds," a hoarse voice, elusively familiar, whispered, "in case you are tempted to tell anyone what you know—"

CHAPTER XIII

Ismael watched the last saronged, white-coated servant slip through the open door of the underground
office, and disappear into the rainy gloom of the
late afternoon. For hours he had been sitting there
behind Clive's flat-topped desk patiently, tactfully,
questioning the servants of the various households
on the estate; house boys, gardeners, chauffeurs,
cooks, babus—coaxing replies from blank brown
faces, pouncing swiftly on each glimmer of fear in
the wary, almond-shaped eyes; cajoling them, reassuring them.

He had received some information for his pains,
though he had nothing tangible to offer to McCleary.
The white officer dealt only with facts, and would be
satisfied with nothing less than the complete identi-
fication of the murderer, or, perhaps direct evidence
that one or both of his pet suspects had been wit-
nessed on the scene of the crime.

Ismael's broad brown face relaxed into a smile as
he glanced down at his notes, and visualized his white
superior's disgust.

Saidi, Lydia's maid, had been the first to contribute to the pictures Ismael was slowly forming of the chief actors in the tragedies. She had never seen her mistress weep, though when she first came back from her journey she had looked worried and a little sad. Saidi didn't know whether her mistress had known of the Tuan's intrigue with Mem Harvy or not—certainly she had never spoken of it in Saidi's hearing. No, her Mem she was sure didn't like Tuan Sullivan, but that was because he took the Tuan Besar away so much. The servants all liked him; he was kind to them, and generous. Better, wasn't it, that he took the Tuan away hunting than leave him to the wiles of Mem Harvy? Mem Bosworth was too good to think evil of anyone. Saidi knew of nothing unusual that happened the day before, except, of course, the wayong. Her mistress had been cheerful. It was not strange for her to go to the jungle for flowers or ferns for her garden. She had found some new plants on her walk yesterday, and had planted them with her own hands—she had growing hands, things lived for her that would die with even the kabun. No, she was just as usual when she returned from her walk, only when the Tuan Besar and Tuan Sullivan didn't come home for dinner she was annoyed a little, but even then she laughed—the Mem was always laughing. No, never, never, never, was Mem Bosworth interested in any man except the Tuan. She was not like Mem Harvy, unfaithful by nature. Saidi knew of no one

who would wish to harm her mistress, unless perhaps
it was Mem Harvy, that was truly a snake in the grass,
but Saidi admitted reluctantly, that she was too mouse-
spirited to kill anyone. As for the Tuan Besar doing
so terrible a thing—Saidi threw up her arms in repudiation of the idea—the Tuan was a child really, but
he loved Mem, he needed her.

The Harvy servants, under pressure, confirmed the
story of the affair between their mistress and Clive
Bosworth, adding dates and details, and wondering
mildly that Tuan Harvy and Mem Bosworth should
have been so blind. Their Tuan was too trusting,
their Mem too sly. But their Tuan worked too hard;
he thought always of the estate, and he left the Mem
alone too much. No, Tuan Bosworth was not the first
lover she had taken, but she seemed to like him best;
at least, she had stopped seeing Tuan Farnsworth, and
Tuan Farnsworth was handsome and fresh and young,
and crazy with love for her. He hadn't been her lover,
but he wanted to be. Everyone liked Tuan Harvy; he
was kind and just. No, he had never quarreled with
any of the white men—the assistants he treated like
his younger brothers, helping them always, so long as
they did their work. Yes, they all worked well, except,
of course, Tuan Bosworth; but he was the Tuan Besar,
so even their master could do nothing about that

Hamilton's boy was as stubbornly loyal as his master, but eventually he admitted, with caution, that
sometimes, not often, his Tuan drank too much.

Then he might get into a rage, swear and throw things about, but in the morning he had forgotten all about it. He was a good man when he didn't drink, and even when he did have too much, he was still far and away the best man on the estate.

From Bill Pearson's boy, Ismael elicited the fact that the engineer was difficult to handle when he was drunk. Once when Tuan Pearson tried to stop him, he had thrown a chair at him, and broken a mirror. The next day he remembered nothing, but he was very sorry, for he liked Tuan Pearson, and he had bought a new mirror for him. Tuan Pearson was a good man to work for—always even tempered and considerate. Even when he was in trouble, he didn't get angry at the servants. No, he didn't know what the trouble was, only that it had come in the mail about a month ago. Tuan Pearson had shut himself in his room for a long time, and when he came out, he seemed sad. He tried to hide it when he was with other people, but since that letter had come, he had slept badly, sometimes his light had burned all through the night, and his bed would not show a wrinkle. On those nights he would smoke two cans of cigarettes, a hundred, but even so, he was never short tempered. He had been like that when he first came to the estate—walk, walk, walk—all night, and smoke, smoke, smoke. Then he was better; for a long time, he was like other men; but after the letter came he had heard his Tuan saying a name over and over, "Sheilah!" and he had been surprised to hear a woman's name, because his Tuan didn't seem to like women. Strange, was it not? when Tuan Pearson was so virile, so handsome!

There was something about Mahat, Jim Mason's boy, that Ismael disliked. He was too smooth, too self-possessed, too voluble. It was often true of boys who worked for Americans; they didn't seem to know how to handle natives—either they were too hard on them, or too easy. Mahat was full of glib praise for Jim, but when he mentioned Tuan Farnsworth, his tone was disrespectful: Tuan Farnsworth was a child who didn't know his way around the world. He wanted to be a man, but when he played cards, he always lost; when he tried to drink, a little whisky made him foolish. Mahat's broad mouth stretched into a leer—why, he couldn't even get a woman when he wanted one! Mem Harvy had made a monkey out of him, when everyone knew how easy she was. Then there was the Malay girl who used to do the washing for Tuan Mason and Tuan Farnsworth—a bold piece who had made up to Tuan Farnsworth, and he, like a fool, had fallen for her blandishments. Almost, she had talked him into taking her to be his mistress; and then someone had told Mem Bosworth, and she had called him to the house and scolded him until he came back cringing like a dog, with his tail between his legs. Tuan Farnsworth had no faith in himself; he wanted everyone to like him, and if people paid him attention he would be happy, saying

they were "swell," and if they snubbed him, he'd call
them all louses and sonsofbitches, and say they'd be
sorry someday.

Farnsworth's boy was more reticent than Mason's,
but it was obvious that he had no respect or affection
for the man he served, and rather resented the fact
that his master had caused him to lose face.

Ismael was so busy fitting together the bits
of information he had garnered that he started
when McCleary paused on the threshold. Water
dripped from the officer's rain-soaked sun helmet,
making rivulets on the dusty floor, and his khaki
uniform was black with rain. "How about a little
light?" he asked, switching on a high white
glare. "I hope you had better luck than I did. I
saw more Chinese than a Jap's nightmare, and
enough Malays and Indians to overthrow the British Government—and not a damn one of them
apparently was within a quarter of a mile of the place
where Harvy was killed—at the approximate time he
was killed, that is. Model coolies, according to their
stories; they heard no evil, saw no evil, and certainly,
they spoke no evil."

He threw his wet topee down on the desk, and
rubbed the dark red crease it had pressed into his
forehead. "How did you make out?"

"I have some notes here, Tuan, that may interest you," Ismael said, pushing his close, meticulously
written pages across the desk, "but I got no direct

evidence against anyone. I am sure the servants are concealing nothing of importance."

McCleary blinked down at the delicate handwriting. "I'm too tired to wade through all that now. Just give me any highlights, will you?"

"Do not expect too much, Tuan," Ismael said disparagingly. "The things I learned are but parts of an unknown whole." Briefly he summarized the information he had obtained from the various servants. As he finished, McCleary sighed and shifted his position. "And what does that add up to?" he asked in a discouraged tone. "Nothing! I tell you, Ismael, Bosworth's our man, with the Harvy woman accessory before and after the fact." The officer perched himself on the edge of the desk, swinging a soggy, rain-soaked shoe. "I've gone over this affair until I'm giddy, and every time I run up against the only solid facts we have: Bosworth and Mrs. Harvy are the only ones who had a motive to kill Mrs. Bosworth and John. And, in addition to the two strong motives—lust and greed," his lips curled with distaste, "they had the opportunity. Neither of them has alibis for the time of either murder."

Ismael's smooth brown face looked unconvinced. "No one had an alibi for the time of Mrs. Bosworth's murder, and only the American girl has one for this morning when Tuan Harvy was killed. You know how carefully we have questioned everyone today, and checked their statements not only with each other, but with the servants and the police who were on guard. The answer is the same in the case of Pearson, Mason, Sullivan and Bosworth. The men arose at their usual time, had breakfast, and went out into a morning thick with mist and drizzle. More than that we cannot discover, for only the murderer knows whether he ran swiftly through the fog to ambush Tuan Harvy, or walked slowly and directly to the coolie lines."

"But they were all on time except Bosworth, don't forget that!" McCleary said triumphantly. "And don't forget either that for the first time in the memory of man, Mrs. Harvy got up early this morning and walked part way with her husband. If she wasn't doing that to distract his attention from danger, I'll eat my hat."

"You also forget two things, Tuan," Ismael grinned. "Tuan Hamilton admittedly was wandering around this morning—he who flies into a rage when he is drunk, and then remembers nothing about it; and Tuan Farnsworth who evidence shows was at the edge of the jungle path—Tuan Farnsworth whose behavior has been so strange throughout."

McCleary frowned. "I'm not overlooking either of those birds," he protested. "It's been clear to me all along that either these murders are the wanton killings of a crazy man, or they are component parts of a cold-blooded plot. I don't really believe though that Hamilton, drunk or sober, committed the murders; as for Farnsworth, I'll admit he's a bit 'gila,' but that's a long way from being a homicidal maniac. Anyway, we'll know more as soon as we're able to question him. If he did commit the murders, in his weakened state we ought to be able to get it out of him, and if he didn't—well, I'm just hoping he saw the murderer come out of the jungle. Doc said his fever ought to go down this afternoon. He didn't think there was a question of concussion—just shock and exposure, and a bad bumping. You haven't heard anything from the nurse, I take it? She was to let us know as soon as he was fit to talk."

Even as Ismael shook his smooth black head, a polite knock sounded hollowly on the open door, and they saw the trim figure of a Malay policeman outlined against the darkening grey oblong of light.

"Apa?" McCleary inquired, motioning the constable to enter. "Why did you leave your post?"

"The nurse sent me to tell you that Tuan Farnsworth's head is clear now, and that you may speak to him for a short time."

McCleary slid from his perch on the desk. "Good! Now we'll get somewhere. No need to go out into the rain again, we can go up these stairs."

Ismael leaned across the desk and addressed the constable. "Who is on duty upstairs? Did you leave someone at your post?"

The little policeman shifted his feet uneasily. "No, Tuan. There was no one to leave. The nurse said I must go directly to Tuan McCleary." His heavy face brightened. "There is my brother on the veranda outside, and my cousin is having kopee in the kitchen. Surely no harm can come of my leaving."

"Come on, Ismael." McCleary moved impatiently. "You're as fussy as an old maid schoolteacher." He yanked open the door and disappeared up the narrow enclosed stairway leading into the bedroom overhead.

Ismael sighed. "All right, go back quickly to your post," he said and, still frowning, followed McCleary's heavy footsteps.

As the door from the stairway opened, the long figure on the bed twitched uneasily, and Farnsworth's blue eyes, dilated with sudden fear, stared at them from beneath a white bandage. A half-caste nurse moved with a rustle of starched uniform to the bedside, and placed a yellow, efficient hand on his wrist. "It is all right—only the police who are guarding you. You have nothing to fear." She turned apologetically to the officers who were blinking in the glare of lights. "There shouldn't be so much light here, but he fears the dark. There must be no shadows anywhere in the room."

McCleary nodded. "That's all right." His glance banished the nurse to the other side of the room, and he took her place beside the sick man. "Feeling better, Farnsworth?"

"My head aches like the very devil," Dave complained, "and my mouth feels like the inside of a last year's bird's nest."

"That's too bad, but the nurse will be able to fix you up in a little while. Suppose you tell us what happened to you last night, and how you got in such a fix."

Farnsworth's eyes shifted from McCleary's red face to Ismael's brown one. "Who's he?" he demanded. "I haven't seen him before."

"He is Inspector Ismael from Johore, who has come up to help me with this case. It was he who found you this morning. We both want to know why you left this room last night, and where you went." McCleary's voice was patient, coaxing.

"Why wouldn't I leave? Do you think I was going to stay here and be murdered in my bed? Someone tried to shoot me, but I got away from him, out of the window over there. Scratched my arm on the catch as I scrambled out, but I didn't know it until later. I ran and ran—but it was so dark and muddy I couldn't make any time. After awhile I remembered seeing a bicycle down by the factory, so I made for that—"

"Just a moment, Tuan, please," Ismael interrupted. "When did you see the bicycle?"

Farnsworth looked uncomfortable, and then with a forced laugh he said, "I suppose I'd better admit it. It was all just a joke, you know, my switching off the lights."

McCleary started, but before he could speak, Ismael interposed smoothly, "Whom was the joke against, Tuan?"

"Bosworth, of course—Bosworth and Betty. I thought I'd teach them a lesson. I knew he was going up to see her, and so, when he slipped away from the wayong, I followed him outside. She had it coming to her for treating me the way she did. I knew she was alone up there waiting for him, and I thought I'd throw a scare into her. Hamilton was dead to the world, and the watchman had slipped off to get a squint at the wayong, so it was easy enough. I only left the lights off for about ten minutes; I didn't want really to inconvenience anyone, you know. It was while I was waiting to put them on again that I wandered out the back door and stumbled against the bicycle."

So, Ismael thought, Mrs. Harvy was either lying about the lights, or had gone to meet Clive and really knew nothing of the sudden darkness. But, by the same token, since the lights didn't go on again at the Bosworth bungalow, it meant that someone there, Mrs. Bosworth, the American girl, or the murderer, had turned them off. Those facts must somehow fit into the pattern of the crime, but he didn't yet see just how.

"And after you found the bicycle? McCleary prompted him, "where did you go then?'

Farnsworth seemed relieved that the officers had accepted his confession about the lights so matter-of-factly. "I decided I'd go to Kluang and put up at the Rest House there, and in the morning, I'd come back and pack. I knew I'd queered myself here on the estate by shooting off my face about everyone, and besides, I wasn't going to stick around and be killed."

"Did you go to Kluang?"

"No, it was too far; it was pitch black too, and raining, and the roads were flooded in places. My head still ached from where Pearson had socked me, and I was dizzy. I knew there was an old abandoned hut that had belonged to a Chinese kabun, a couple of miles down the road, and I decided to go there and spend the night. Things looked different in the dark though, and I had quite a time locating the place. It's a bit off the highway, but I finally found it. It was pretty lousy though; the roof leaked like a sieve, but it was better than being outdoors. As soon as it began to get light, I started back to the estate to get dry clothes on, and to pack up, but the mist down there was so thick you couldn't see your hands before your face, and after I turned off the highway, I must have wandered off the estate road, for the first thing I knew, I was bang up against a wall of jungle as black as your hat. I knew I was wrong then, and started back. The next thing I remember, I woke up here in this bed." In contrast to the first part of his story, the finish which should have been the climax was very much curtailed, and Farnsworth's attitude too had subtly changed. His eyes no longer looked into Mc-Cleary's, and his thin, nervous fingers automatically creased and smoothed the edge of the bedspread.

"Did you see anyone, or hear anything when you were near the jungle?" the inspector asked eagerly.

"No, not a soul," Farnsworth said. "How could I see anyone in that fog?" His voice was higher, more penetrating, and held a faint note of hysteria. Ismael knew he was lying.

McCleary had apparently accepted the statement at its face value, for he sounded discouraged as he asked, "What about those accusations you made last night?"

Farnsworth winced as he shook his head emphatically. "Lies," he declared. "All lies. I had quite a lot to drink, and it made me ugly—I was sore at everybody and in a mood to make trouble. Rotten of me. I didn't mean a word I said—you tell the other fellows for me, will you? Tell them that I realized what a damned fool I made of myself, and that I'm resigning; that I'm going back to America on the first boat I can get. You fix it all up for me, will you, like a good chap?" His hot hand clutched McCleary's hairy paw. Funk, pure, unadulterated funk; the officer had difficulty in concealing his repulsion.

"That won't wash, you know, Farnsworth. You may have had a drop too much, but you knew what you were saying, and you must have had some grounds for your accusations."

"No, no, I didn't!" in the eagerness of his denial, Farnsworth sat upright. "I don't even remember what

I said. That shows you, doesn't it? It was all hooey—all of it—and you be sure to tell everybody."

The nurse moved forward with a severe rustle. "You've upset my patient, Mr. McCleary. He's talked enough. Now he is going to have a bromide and go sleepy bye—" her hand rested soothingly on Farnsworth's forehead, pressing him back onto his pillow and with the fatuous confidence of a child from whom responsibility had been lifted, he smiled up at her.

For a moment McCleary looked baffled, and then he said, "Just a minute, nurse. I think I can relieve your patient's mind; he has a kind of persecution complex or something." She hesitated, a bit out of her depth, and McCleary addressed Farnsworth again. "You think someone tried to kill you last night, don't you? And you're afraid they may try again if you say anything more. What you thought was a shot, though, wasn't a shot at all, it was just Miss Chambers' door banging against the wall when she flung it open. A man was on guard outside your room the whole time, and no one came near it. The door at the head of those stairs was locked, and the shutters closed until you opened one yourself. What's more, everyone was on the veranda except Miss Chambers, and you certainly can't believe that she knocked out your guard, crashed into your room and fired a shot at you. She had no reason to dislike you, and furthermore the guard hadn't been touched."

Farnsworth's eyes opened wide. "You're just trying to make me feel good. I tell you I heard him, I
know—" He bit back whatever it was that he started
to say. "I don't want to be killed—" his voice rose
into a wail.

"Wait, Tuan, calm yourself," Ismael said. "What
Tuan McCleary says is quite true, and I will prove it
to you. You will believe it, will you not, if you hear
the same sound again? And you will not be frightened, because the nurse will hold your hand, and
Tuan McCleary will be here and also, outside your
door there is a policeman on guard."

Farnsworth slowly digested Ismael's statement.
With all the lights on with two people he trusted in
the room, and with a man outside. Slowly he nodded
his head.

"Good," Ismael encouraged him. "Now I will open
this door, cross the hall, and throw back Miss Chambers' door, as she did last night. You will hear it crash
against the wall, and you will tell us whether it is the
same sound."

Swiftly Ismael left the room. The little constable,
leaning against the wall outside, drew himself to attention. The hall was almost dark as Ismael crossed
it diagonally and paused in front of Nancy's room.
"Turn on the lights in the hall," he called suddenly to
the policeman. Strange how this house affected him,
he thought. He couldn't remember ever before craving physical light as he did here, and more and more,

as though the evil that lurked in the house was always just a few steps ahead, in the shadows, and could be banished by the click of a switch.

The shadows leaped away as the electric lights came on, illuminating the harsh whitewashed walls and ceiling, the rough boards of the floor. The hall, as he expected, was empty, save for the table by the front door, and the heavy wardrobe by the back door; the constable moving sedately back to his post, and he himself standing afraid beside the girl's bedroom. Impatient of his own imaginings, Ismael jerked open the door, and it swung back, as he had expected, with a sharp, reverberating bang. The light from the hall rushed a short way into the bedroom, and settled into a long yellow wedge between the phalanxes of shadows.

Something was lying there huddled on the floor, at the edge of the shadows. With an exclamation of fear, Ismael dropped on his knees beside Nancy's body.

CHAPTER XIV

Leaving a constable on guard outside Nancy's room while she, recovered from her frightening experience, repaired the damage to her appearance, Ismael hurried downstairs to rejoin McCleary. The white officer looked up eagerly as the Malay appeared in the doorway. "What did she say after she recovered consciousness?" he asked. "Did she recognize him? Why did he attack her?"

Ismael smiled noncommittally. "To the first question, she said much, after some persuasion. To the second question, she didn't recognize her attacker, for he grabbed her from behind and pushed her face foremost into the closet; and to the third question, the murderer warned her to keep quiet about her identity, but why he did that, she doesn't know, nor can I understand."

McCleary blinked. "Identity? What about her identity? What's it all about anyway?" His voice was fretful.

Ismael settled himself in a straight-backed chair opposite the inspector. "She is not Miss Chambers; she is another American girl, Nancy Reynolds, who met Mrs. Bosworth four months ago when they were shipmates." He motioned for McCleary to wait, as the officer began to splutter. "I will explain her motive in a few minutes. Miss Reynolds came to Penang to act as secretary for Doctor Gordon, the great historian on the Far East. He came from the same town in New England, and knew her family. Apparently, for all his wisdom, the famous scholar was as much a child, in worldly ways, as the American girl, for he expected his young English wife to receive her as a friend. The situation, Tuan, was like the motive of a wayong, for in addition to the idealistic professor and the two antagonistic women, there was a young Englishman who, apparently courting Miss Reynolds, was actually the lover of Mrs. Gordon. And Mrs. Gordon, to protect her own interests, let it be known that the new secretary was her husband's mistress. Not a nice situation for the ingenue."

McCleary nodded, and then frowned. "But, didn't Doctor Gordon kill himself recently? I got a report— suicide while temporarily insane from overwork."

"Yes," Ismael said. "He shot himself, but that was after he found his wife in her room with her lover. Miss Reynolds, too, had discovered the intrigue that day, and was packing to go home, when Doctor Gordon returned unexpectedly from Angkor Vat and the dénouement followed. Miss Reynolds was just entering the library when he shot himself. Mrs. Gordon, fearful of what the girl might tell, accused her of murdering her employer, and threatened to tell the police unless she left Penang immediately. Miss Reynolds, frightened and bewildered, believed that she might be arrested, and so she allowed herself to be driven away, without her salary, or her return passage, or even a letter of recommendation. The only person she knew in the East was Mrs. Bosworth and so she came here. And, we know what she found upon her arrival."

"But how did she happen to take the name of Helene Chambers? And what has that got to do with the murders and with the attack on her? Did she know any of these people here?" McCleary asked, still hopeful of tangible evidence against someone.

"No, she knew no one. But she found her own telegram to Mrs. Bosworth, and one from Helene Chambers, and so later, when people assumed she was Miss Chambers, she hid the telegrams, and said nothing. It was wrong, of course, Tuan, but it is understandable in view of her experience in Penang. She thought no one would accept her word against that of Mrs. Gordon, that perhaps the police were already looking for her—and now she found herself in a strange house with her murdered hostess."

Ismael waited while the white officer struggled with his conscience, and then smiled as the inspector said slowly, "Well, she shouldn't have lied to us, but I can see why she'd have the wind up. What did she do with the telegrams?"

Ismael explained their disappearance, and added hastily as McCleary once more began to look choleric, "Actually, Tuan, the only part of Miss Reynolds' experience that concerns us is the fact that she suppressed the telegrams, and that when the murderer attacked her it was to warn her not to tell us of her real identity."

McCleary's mouth gaped open. "He knew who she was? But what difference did that make to him?"

"That is what puzzles me. Miss Reynolds too can offer no reason. I find the American young women truly remarkable, so strange a mixture of wisdom and innocence, of courage and nerves. Even when I left she was exalted into the belief that she must bait herself to capture the murderer—like a young bull buffalo staked in a pit to lure a man-eating tiger."

McCleary rolled his eyes, and once more his worried fingers upended his dark hair. "I hope you put the fear of God into her, and told her not to mess things up any more."

Ismael sighed. "I told her, yes, but I have no faith in my persuasions. Look at all the American missionaries! Her final words to me were, 'But I must, don't you see I must try to make him betray himself to me? I am the only one that he fears, and if he so much as hints that I am not Helene Chambers, I will know who he is, and you can arrest him!'" The little Malay drew a deep, deploring breath. "The worst of it is, Tuan, that she is right. And that is one thing that no man, no matter what his race, can ever forgive a female."

For the first time in forty-eight hours, McCleary laughed; he was warmed by a sudden kinship to the little Malay; after all, no matter what the difference in color, in creed, in politics or in methods of crime deduction, they were both bachelors.

Ismael's face relaxed into a smile, but his mind relaxed even more. McCleary had accepted Nancy's story, and he would appreciate the importance of guarding her. "I have talked over much, Tuan," he said. "What did you glean from your questioning of the guests and of the servants?"

McCleary rose restlessly to his feet and began to pace the damp stone floor of the basement office, while Ismael, still sitting stiffly upright, tried to segregate the facts from the flow of curses and invective that exploded from the inspector's lips.

"There you have it all," McCleary said more calmly. "Bosworth went indoors, so he says, to get a wrap for Mrs. Harvy. He didn't see the yellow sweater on the chair, but went to the wardrobe at the end of the hall. Hamilton had come up onto the veranda soaked to the skin, and Sullivan went into the dining room to get another glass for him. That makes two of them indoors, mind you—two of them so far. As if that

wasn't enough, Hamilton decides that instead of a
cold drink, he'd rather have a hot toddy, so he went
in to look for one of the servants, and then, having
been gone for several minutes, he says he changed his
mind and went back to the veranda without calling
anyone.

"Mason says he didn't go out on the veranda after
he dropped the sweater but wandered into the living room to wait for Miss Chambers." He paused. "I
think we'd better keep on calling her that, don't you,
so that we won't slip up perhaps in front of other
people?"

"Most assuredly, Tuan," Ismael approved. "I must
remember to watch my own lips carefully."

McCleary nodded, and went on. "Where was I?
Oh, yes, even Farnsworth isn't in the clear so far as
alibis go, because the nurse decided he ought to have
a sedative before we talked to him. The ice-water jug
was empty, so she went out to the rear veranda, leaving his door open, and called a boy to bring her some
water. She says she was gone for only two or three
minutes, but who knows? She might have been gone
the whole time the constable was down fetching us.
I made the constable go through his motions while I
timed him. It seems he stopped to speak to the constable on the front veranda who was grousing about
a relief. If they talked say for two minutes, and it
took him two to go through the house, out onto the
veranda, down the steps and around to this door, two

more to give us the message, and two to get back to his post, that means that the murderer had at least eight minutes in which to attack Miss Chambers and get away. He could have done the job in three at the outside."

"How did their stories check, Tuan?" Ismael asked, calmly.

"Oh, Sullivan, of course, says he saw Clive go through the hall and come right back with a coat over his arm. Clive said he saw Sullivan in the dining room, but he didn't see the nurse, and that Farnsworth's door was closed. Mason says he didn't see anyone, though he heard footsteps going back and forth. He says he had picked up a magazine from the table at the back of the room and got interested in a story, so he didn't realize how long Miss Chambers had been gone. Bosworth says he saw Hamilton come into the house as he went out, and Hamilton checks that. Hamilton says, too, that he saw the nurse leave Farnsworth's room and go out on the rear veranda; that was what made him change his mind about the toddy; thought he'd better not bother the servants if they were getting things for the nurse. Semut brought the water, but there was no one in the hall when he went through, though he heard the front door close as he came through the back one. The lights weren't on in the hall, you know, until you ordered the constable to put them on, but the dining room was lighted, and Mason had switched on the table lamp in the living room. Incidentally the light was still on, and there was an open copy of a *New Yorker* on the table. Mason said he left it when he heard you bang open Miss Chambers' door. He was afraid something had happened, and ran out into the hall. By the time the constable had called me, of course, everyone was milling around out there, to say nothing of the servants and the constables; all of them pushing around, asking questions and trying to see into the girl's room. Well, you know what it was like, and how long it took to herd them out."

"And where was Tuan Pearson? You didn't mention him," Ismael commented.

"No, I didn't. And that's another funny one. He says he was sitting over in the shadows by those living room screens, and never moved until he heard all the commotion. Mrs. Harvy was on the veranda too, the whole time, but she was lying back in one of the long chairs near the dining room, and had her eyes closed, so she didn't notice him at all. He could easily have slipped around the screens, cut through the living room without attracting Mason's attention, and then gone down the hall. Of course Pearson denies that he moved from his chair until he heard the row inside and Betty and everyone rushed in, but he was as nervous as a witch, hands and feet twitching—"

Ismael shook his head. "It is certainly a difficult case. Shaitan seems to be protecting his own this time. There is no trace of the weapon in any of the houses, as I saw for myself after the constables failed to find it. There are no fingerprints, for the man who attacked Miss Reynolds was careful to wipe the handle on the wardrobe, and the knobs on the bedroom door. The bruises on her neck are not sufficiently discolored to show a fingerprint—it is obvious that he didn't intend to harm her and so pressed lightly. Even the weather has favored the murderer; the rain has washed away his tracks, and the mist has hidden him."

McCleary reached into a baggy pocket and took out a pipe which he slowly filled from a shabby suede pouch, "All we really have to go on is motive, and that brings us back to Bosworth and his paramour."

"They had a motive, Tuan, that I grant," Ismael said slowly, "but if they are guilty, we still have too many things unexplained; first, the shooting accident to Mr. Bosworth; then the disappearance of the reports that Mr. Harvy gave him; and lastly, the strange fear of Miss Reynolds, and the attack on her. Bosworth could have had no purpose in any of those things— he wouldn't shoot himself in the leg; he had no reason to steal the reports—all he had to do was to keep silent about them if he had wanted them suppressed; and above all, he had no reason to care whether it was Miss Chambers or Miss Reynolds who came to visit; both were friends of his wife, both unknown to him, and he to them."

McCleary puffed slowly on his pipe. "It's a nasty mess, however you look at it, and no sooner do we seem to be getting one bit clear, than something else happens. We'd just found out that Farnsworth was the one who turned off the lights, and I was getting ready to put Bosworth and Mrs. Harvy on the mat for lying about their meeting, when Miss Reynolds is attacked and we have to follow up that lead." His indignation was fanned by his memory. "Good Lord, it's been like that all through: I was trying to get a line on Mrs. Bosworth's murder, when Pearson knocks out the one person who was willing to talk; then Farnsworth gets the wind up and disappears; you find Farnsworth, and before he can tell us anything, Harvy is killed; and while we are trying to sift that down, Miss Reynolds is attacked."

"Tuan Farnsworth would say nothing more, even when he was satisfied that it was the door which banged and not a shot?" Ismael asked.

"Farnsworth is a white-livered young pup," McCleary declared. "He knows something all right, but I doubt if we'll ever be able to drag it out of him until the murderer is under lock and key. He got himself so worked up when the crowd from the veranda started trooping into the house, that the nurse gave him another bromide."

Ismael frowned. There was something nagging at the back of his mind, something that had occurred to

him just before he found the American girl unconscious, and now it was lost. He clucked his tongue
in annoyance; he shouldn't have forgotten, it was important. Ah, well, it would come back to him later,
when he relaxed his mind from all these other worries.

There was a knock on the outside door, and Semut's
soft voice said, "Telephone for Che Ismael."

"Probably some answers to your cables," McCleary
commented. "When you go up, would you mind asking Mrs. Harvy to come down here? I'll tackle her
first about Farnsworth's story."

"Now, Mrs. Harvy—" McCleary's red face was
grim a few minutes later when he addressed the
woman gracefully draped in the chair opposite him—
"I hope this time you will tell me the truth about
what you did last evening, though it is my duty to
warn you that you don't have to answer my questions."

"You mean," Betty gasped, looking at him with
wide, terrified blue eyes, "that you suspect me?"

McCleary nodded, impervious to her pathetic fra-
gility.

"But you can't! I had nothing to do with Lydia's
death—I know nothing about it! I was miles away
from here—or at least nearly a mile—nowhere near
the house. Oh, how can you think such a thing!"
There was a very real note of distress in her voice.

"We know that you lied to us about the lights being on in your house all evening. We know that you met Bosworth."

The woman's face paled beneath her rouge. "How do you know?" she whispered.

McCleary concealed his satisfaction. "It's enough that we do know. You weren't home, you met Bosworth, your lover, and you were up here with him while he killed his wife."

"No, no!" she moaned, wringing her small jeweled fingers. "It isn't so. We never came here, we never even crossed the road. I didn't mean to lie to you about the lights; I didn't know they'd been off. They were burning when I left, and they were on when I got back. We only talked for a few minutes—we didn't have time to come so far."

"Why did you meet him?" the officer asked, and repeated perfunctorily, "You don't have to answer that question if you don't want to."

"I'd rather tell you. I've nothing to hide," Betty said. "Anything is better than having you think that I killed Lydia, or that I knew about it. I wanted to see Clive. He was to have come to tea, but instead, that awful Sullivan person took him to Batu Pahat. I had to see him. He'd been keeping away from me ever since Sullivan came back. I ran up here after tea—" her head drooped a little; "I pretended that I wanted to help Lydia with her supper party, but I knew she wouldn't let me, of course. I left a note here on

Clive's desk for him, saying I would wait for him at the turn in our road at nine fifteen, and he'd have to slip away from the wayong. I knew he'd come—he wouldn't let me stay there alone in the dark waiting."

"Why did you have to see him so urgently? You would have had an opportunity to see him later at supper, wouldn't you?"

"That wouldn't have been any good," she said. "Lydia would have been here then, and Sullivan. I could have managed Lydia, but not the combination of Lydia and Sullivan. Don't you see?" She sounded slightly hysterical. "I had to know that Clive still cared for me—I was afraid he might have had another attack of conscience."

"What happened when you met?"

"Oh, everything was all right. I can always manage him when people don't interfere. Lydia was never his type—she was too strong for him. He needs someone dependent upon him, not someone he can lean on. That's been his whole trouble; he's always had Mike Sullivan, and then Lydia, to tell him what he ought to do, or to do it for him; when what he has really needed was someone weaker than himself that he'd have to protect." She leaned toward the officer, and for the first time her face was soft and appealing. "I know what you think about me, but you are quite wrong. I really love Clive; he's the only man I have ever really loved. Lydia was too good for him, just as John was too good for me; neither of us could measure up to their standards. John and Lydia were both crazy about the Far East, and both Clive and I loathed it."

"So you thought that if you could persuade Clive to run off with you, Mr. Harvy and Mrs. Bosworth might make a go of it too, just shift partners—was that your idea?"

Betty nodded. "It was the only sensible solution."

"But it didn't come off," McCleary announced. "You realized that Clive didn't really care for you; so you decided to get rid of Lydia and your husband, and so force his hand."

"No, Clive does care about me. He was just afraid to make the break, he didn't want to hurt Lydia. But in time she would have driven him to it."

"And now, you are independent. No matter what Bosworth decides to do, you have twenty thousand pounds and can go back to England and the life you crave!"

"Yes," Betty flared, "I can and I will. I'm sick of the East and everything in it, and for the first time in my life my happiness isn't dependent on the whims of any man. I've told you the truth. You can take it or leave it, but I warn you, you can't make a case against either Clive or me, for we're innocent. However, I am going to advise Clive to get a lawyer, and to cable his father immediately."

McCleary scratched his chin. If she got old man Bosworth steamed up, there would certainly be hell to pay, unless McCleary could present an airtight case. Ismael's return saved him the embarrassment of answering the woman's threat, and with as much confidence as he could summon, he dismissed her, saying, "I'll talk to you again later." Of course she'd tell Bosworth about the interview, but that didn't matter much; if their story was faked, they already had it down pat. Bosworth might get his wind up waiting for his interview, and prove more malleable than Mrs. Harvy had.

"Did you get a line on anyone?" he asked, turning to Ismael as Mrs. Harvy slammed shut the door. "Whew, that woman is a hellcat—she ran the gauntlet from near hysterics to threats; one minute declaring that Bosworth was the only man she ever loved, and in the next breath exulting because she'd have her husband's insurance money and would be independent of all men."

"Shallow water is easily stirred, Tuan," Ismael said. "I have several interesting lines of information, all spreading in a different direction. Tuan Campbell read me the replies from Scotland Yard and from the New York police. I thought it better to act through him so that no one in Kluang, or on this estate, would know of my inquiries or their results."

For a second McCleary looked annoyed, and then his face cleared. "Of course my office would have been discreet, but the operators might have let the cat out of the bag. Get on with the story."

"Scotland Yard reports first that there have been persistent rumors lately about the instability of this estate. Mr. Bosworth senior has vainly tried to run them to earth; he says there is no truth in the assertions, that although the production has fallen off to a considerable extent, he had every confidence in Mr. Harvy's ability to discover the trouble and rectify it. He has been very abrupt with offers on the part of various large rubber interests who showed a desire to purchase the estate. The gossip has had a bad effect on the stockholders of his company, and before he could convince them that there was nothing wrong, many shares had been unloaded on the market. He and other members of the Board of Directors offered to purchase any shares, and that stopped their panic.

"These murders won't help the estate any," Mc-Cleary said grimly. "It's nothing short of a miracle that the newspapers haven't got wind of it already."

Ismael glanced again at his notes. "There is nothing against John Harvy; he was well liked, and the directors of the company had great confidence in him. They had not the same confidence, however, in Clive Bosworth. It was only the fact that his father had the controlling interest that gave him this position. Their distrust was not based on fear of his dishonesty, but because of his former reputation as a 'playboy,' and the fact that he doesn't take his work seriously.

"Nothing is known about Mrs. Harvy, or Mrs. Bosworth. Hamilton, however, had some difficulty with the authorities five years ago when he was chief engineer on the *Osiris*. There was a drunken brawl in a pub in Liverpool, and Hamilton badly injured the first mate. For a time they thought the man was going to die and Hamilton was held by the police. The officer recovered, and at the insistence of the Steamship Company, who had already discharged Hamilton, refused to prosecute. Hamilton insisted he remembered nothing about the affair, that his mind was a blank. He couldn't get another berth, and drifted out East, where Harvy got him his present job.

"Mike Sullivan had a good war record, enlisting when he was sixteen. He was twice mentioned in despatches before he was invalided. He is the only living member of his family. His father was killed in action, and his younger brother and his mother died within a week of the father. He has a very good income, derived from his mother's estate. Her father was a pioneer in the rubber industry and had large holdings in several big American rubber companies. Of late Mike has displayed an unusual interest in the activities of those companies, and has made inquiries in London through a private detective agency about the status of the Semang Rubber Estate, Mr. Bosworth senior speaks very highly of him and his devotion to Clive, but regrets his lack of ambition."

Ismael laid down the page he had finished. "So much for Scotland Yard. Here is what the New York police reported: a list of plays in which Mrs. Bosworth, formerly Lydia Handly, had small parts, and notice of her marriage to Clive Bosworth. Also a shorter list of plays in which Helene Chambers appeared—we aren't interested in her now, of course. David Farnsworth's father is a vice-president in a large American rubber company. David is the only son; went to a number of expensive private schools in the States, and several colleges, but never stayed long. His father finally sent him out East to get him away from his mother's influence and try to make a man of him. Jim Mason's father is the manager of a rival rubber company in the Middle West, but his history differs from Farnsworth's, he was expelled from college, but went directly to work in his father's factory, and eventually came out to this estate in order to learn the business from every angle."

The Malay's face was suddenly sober, and he hesitated a second before continuing his recitation. "Bill Pearson's story, Tuan, is a sad one. His people come from old Atlanta families, where his father is in the export business. When Bill's sister Sheilah was born fourteen years ago, his mother went insane. She had been slightly deranged at her son's birth, but had recovered. However, from the second birth she did not recover and eventually had to be placed in a private institution. A short time ago, the girl Sheilah developed dementia praecox, and she, too, is now in the same institution."

"Good God!" McCleary exclaimed, his eyes opening very wide. "I told you he was acting queer. Look at the way he attacked Farnsworth; the way he sits and broods—like a Malay before he runs amok. You should have told me about him first, so that we could have gotten him away quietly. He may go haywire any minute and kill someone else!"

Ismael's voice was calm. "I am not a doctor, Tuan, but I know that it is not unusual for a woman to lose her reason at childbirth, and I also know that dementia praecox is not hereditary. If you were to assume that Tuan Pearson is insane because of his mother and sister, you might actually drive him over the abyss into which he is now staring."

McCleary frowned. "I can't understand you, Ismael. Standing there shaking your head, and refusing to do anything with a maniac loose upstairs!"

Ismael clapped his hand to his forehead. "That is it! Now I remember that little maggot that was gnawing at my mind. Tuan, when you went up the stairs to see Tuan Farnsworth, was the door at the head of these stairs locked?"

The inspector looked blank. "No, no; I don't think it was. I just turned the knob and went in." His expression changed to one of consternation. "Good Lord! it should have been locked, of course—what—"

A woman's scream, shrill with terror, echoed above their heads.

Ismael recognized the voice of the half-caste nurse, and even as he dashed across the room, his heavy heart told him that in spite of all the protection the police had provided, the murderer had struck again—the frightened young American Tuan would never be able to tell them what he knew.

CHAPTER XV

As Nancy slowly opened the front door and stepped out onto the veranda, it seemed to her, in her exalted state of self-sacrifice, that she would be able to look into the faces turned expectantly toward her, and point an unerring finger at the murderer. She wasn't sure whether she would recognize him by his blanched, cowering figure, or whether justice itself, by some mysterious method, would make her aware of the truth.

It was a bitter disappointment, therefore, to find that nothing in the way of miracles happened at all; that the familiar faces looked the same to her; that everyone acted in a normal way to her sudden appearance. Jim Mason sprang up with an eager welcome, and rushed to her; Mike Sullivan brought forward the most comfortable chair; Clive Bosworth appeared at her side with a whisky soda in one hand, a can of cigarettes in the other; Bill Pearson roused himself from his reveries long enough to produce a lighted match, and Ronald Hamilton untwined his length of limbs from his chair and came solemnly to shake her hand. "It's verra guid to hae ye wi' us safe an' sound." Betty Harvy's voice was cooing as she said languidly, "You should never have gone in there alone; apparently the murderer was simply waiting for a chance at you. I wonder why that could be, when you are a stranger here. Unless of course, you met someone before."

"No," Nancy said steadily; "I didn't know any of you until last night—was it really only last night?" She shook her head. "So much has happened that it might have been last week, or last month, or last year."

Questions were pelted at her from all sides: "What happened?" "Didn't you see something?" "What did he do?" "Did he say anything?" "Wasn't there any way you could recognize him?"

Ismael had warned her what to say. She mustn't admit that the murderer had spoken at all; he would be listening for that; trying to gauge from her first remarks just how much she had told the police. She must let him think that she had heeded his warnings; and she must remember that there were two policemen close at hand, one standing beside the front steps, one concealed behind the screens that separated the front of the living room from the veranda. Ismael had told her to sit there. Was there any significance in the fact that Mike Sullivan had placed her chair on the opposite side near the dining room windows; any special reason why he wanted her to sit there? Was there perhaps poison in the drink Clive Bosworth had given her? A knife concealed in Jim Mason's hand—she shivered as he touched her arm. Was Hamilton's deep-throated voice the one which had whispered through the closet door? That one hadn't had any Scotch accent, but she had noticed that Hamilton's accent rather waxed and waned— when he wanted to, he sounded just like anyone else. She glanced at Bill Pearson's slim brown fingers as he lighted another match for her cigarette which, in her abstraction, had gone out. Were they the hands that had choked off her scream, thrust her into the blackness of the wardrobe? She didn't know; it was as dark a mystery as ever; but, she had to get a grip on herself and not let her imagination run rampant. After all, only one person to whom she had to speak wished her ill; the others were sincere.

Smiling, she shook her head at them all, and then to Mike, "If you don't mind, I'd rather sit back there in the shadows—no, don't bother." She moved quickly across the damp grass rugs and seated herself in a vacant chair beside the living room screens, outside the orange halos of the lighted lamps. "But," Jim Mason protested, "you're so far away from us there. I don't think you ought to sit with your back to those screens."

"She's safe enough," Mike Sullivan growled. "We're all here, aren't we? No need for her to move until one of us goes indoors."

There was an oppressive silence as the significance of Mike's remark reached their consciousness, a silence broken only by the drip, drop of the rain, the soft swish of the night breeze through the lime trees. Clive Bosworth was the first to speak, "Oh, I say, old chap, why keep harpin' on that? Let's hear what Miss Chambers has to say."

Chairs were shifted forward, sideways, until, to her discomfort, Nancy was confronted by a semicircle of eager faces, white where the orange light touched them, sinisterly black where the shadows obscured their features.

"There's really nothing to tell," she said slowly, "I just went to the wardrobe in my room to get some sort of wrap a sweater, or coat; so I didn't bother switching on the lights, I was so sure I could find it at once. While I was fumbling inside the closet, I thought I heard a floor board creak, and then before I could turn around, I realized that there was someone behind me. A hand grabbed me backwards, and two hands went around my throat so that I couldn't scream. Something woolly was wrapped around my head a second later and I was shoved face foremost into the closet again. The door was closed, but luckily for me, there was no key in the lock, so when I managed to get to my feet, I opened the door quite easily. I had just backed out into my room, when Ismael banged open the bedroom door. I thought it was the murderer coming back to finish me, and over I keeled. So stupid to faint twice in twenty-four hours, wasn't it? When I came to, I was on the bed, and Ismael was there. That's all." No need to tell them of her abject panic in that horrible wardrobe, of the way she had held her breath, listening and straining every sense before she ventured to move—it might have been seconds, it might have been hours. But no one must know how terrified she had been; how terrified she was even now.

"Didn't the fellow say anything to you? Why did he attack you at all?" Mike Sullivan demanded.

"And," chimed in Jim Mason, "why, if he wanted to kill you, didn't he do it then and there? If he didn't want to hurt you, what did he want?"

"I don't know," Nancy said. "It all seems so pointless. It isn't as though I knew anything, had anything to conceal that would help him." She was suddenly tired of their questions, and annoyed by Betty's Mona Lisa smile. "The only thing that has occurred to me—" she hesitated. Everyone leaned forward eagerly, and she said slowly, "He might have mistaken me for Mrs. Harvy." In the shadows she could permit the laughter that came into her eyes as Betty Harvy emitted an exclamation, and to her annoyance found herself suddenly the center of the group.

"How can you say such a thing?" she squeaked, her voice so angry that it was beyond control. "What would I be in your room for?"

"Well, I didn't reason as far as that," Nancy said, carefully keeping her amusement out of her voice. "I just thought that since we were the only white women here, and I was a complete stranger, as you've emphasized yourself, he, the murderer I mean, would have more cause to frighten you than me. And you were cold, as I was, and we are the same size approximately."

After that theory was adequately discussed, and eventually rejected under Betty's vehement disclaimers, attention was once more focused on Nancy. "Was anything missing in your room?" Clive Bosworth asked. "Money or valuables?"

"I have neither. Nothing that anyone could possibly want," Nancy said with a twisted smile, remembering how pathetically bereft she was of anything she could commercialize.

"Perhaps," Bill Pearson said suddenly, "the murderer had left something there—the knife, or something he had to get before you found it."

"By Jove, old boy," Clive exclaimed, "that must have been it—that would explain everything. He was in the room looking for it when she came in, and he was afraid she'd spot him, so he shoves her in the closet!"

Nancy shook her head. "He couldn't have been in there first, because he wrapped Lydia's yellow sweater around my head, and that was in the dining room on a chair when I went down the hall. You remember, Jim?"

Jim Mason frowned, and then his face brightened. "Yes, I remember, if it's the sweater I brought you and you were so uppish about. I didn't know what color it was, but I dropped it on the chair when you refused to wear it—"

"Well then, instead of being in the room first," Clive said, "he followed you, afraid you'd find the knife or whatever it was before he could get it."

"Well, perhaps," Nancy admitted dubiously. "But I don't see why he'd have hidden anything in my room. If Lydia had been the only one killed with the knife, it might have been possible; but Mr. Harvy was killed with the same weapon this morning and whoever killed him had the whole estate, to say nothing of the jungle, to hide it in. I can't see how, or why, or when, he could hide the weapon in my room."

"Yes, of course," Clive said in a dejected tone, "that won't wash."

"Are you sure it was a man?" Mike Sullivan asked, and at his words, Betty Harvy stiffened.

"Yes. That is all I am sure of," Nancy replied. "I don't know, but I'm sure the hands that grabbed me were a man's hands. And I don't believe he was looking for anything. He didn't have time, and none of my belongings were disturbed. Besides Ismael searched the whole place and he couldn't even find a fingerprint, much less anything material—I mean, no fingerprints except Saidi's and mine. And it wasn't Saidi because she is shorter than I, and whoever grabbed me was a lot taller."

Surreptitiously the people on the porch began mentally to measure each other, but soon gave it up—every one there, except the two women, was six feet, or over.

The sharp tinkle of the telephone cut into their gloomy silence, and everyone strained his ears to catch Semut's low-voiced replies. A moment later he padded out onto the veranda, and in answer to Clive's sharp question, said, "For Ismael, Tuan—a call from Johore Bahru."

"Now what wud that be?" Hamilton speculated aloud as Semut hurried down the steps and disappeared into the darkness. They were still debating the possibilities when Ismael's bulky form appeared in one of the circles of light, "Tuan McCleary would like to talk to you, Mrs. Harvy, if you don't mind."

Clive Bosworth stumbled to his feet. "I'll go with you, Betty—"

Ismael shook his head. "Sorry, Tuan, she must go alone, but Semut will take her to the door, and wait outside."

Bosworth held open the door, and with a final murmur of warning, or assurance, waited until her slender figure, escorted by Semut, vanished around the corner of the house. "How about a spot of dinner?" he asked, turning to the others. "Rotten host, I am. Must all be feelin' peckish, eh what?"

"Good idea, old man, if there's anything in the house to eat," Jim Mason exclaimed.

"Ought to be," Clive grunted; "told the cookie to order plenty. Got to keep them busy, you know." He waved a vague hand toward the servants' quarters. "I'll see what progress they've made, and when things will be ready to serve."

"You see," Nancy said in soft triumph to Mike Sullivan, who had leaned forward to pass her a cigarette, "he's much better when he's on his own."

Mike scowled. "I'm afraid he's getting in deeper all the time with that Harvy cat. She's appealing to his chivalry, and he's so credulous he can't see through her." His sudden smile mocked her. "Now, if it was you, I wouldn't have a word to say."

Nancy was annoyed, although she wasn't sure why. "I am quite capable of managing my own affairs without any assistance," she snapped.

"I doubt it," he grinned. "You certainly haven't been very successful so far. On second thought, perhaps it's just as well that your type doesn't appeal to Clive. I'd have two babes in the woods on my hands then."

"You flatter yourself," she said coldly, and turned to smile up at Jim Mason.

"Have you forgiven me, Helene?" Jim stepped between Nancy and Mike.

"Forgiven you, for what?" she asked, refusing to meet the mockery in Mike's green eyes, or to watch the jaunty set of his shoulders as he strolled across to Ronald Hamilton.

"For letting you go to your room alone. I ought to have gone for your wrap myself, or at least tagged along to look after you. Every time I think of that murderous brute touching you, it drives me wild." His fingers caressed the bruise on her throat. Panic-stricken, she shrank away from his hand. "Don't! Don't!"

"Poor little girl. I'm sorry. I didn't mean to frighten you. I'm an awful dub where women are concerned, always putting my foot into things." He sat down humbly in the nearest chair.

"I'm just jittery," Nancy admitted, "and when you touched me—it brought it all back."

"Good God!" Jim exclaimed, staring at her with accusing eyes. "You don't mean you think I was the one! That I'd harm a hair of your head? Can't you see how I feel about you? I want to look out for you; I resent everyone who comes near you. I'm jealous of them, and at the same time, I'm afraid for you. How do I know which of them attacked you, what he may be planning? It's driving me nuts."

Nancy was startled by his vehemence, and at the deep note of emotion in his voice. "Why, you hardly know me," she protested. "Please don't say anything more. Don't look at me like that; everyone is watching."

He jerked himself erect in his chair, and glanced self-consciously around the veranda. "I don't care; I'm not ashamed of my feelings," he muttered, and then in a pleading whisper, "Helene, marry me. Marry me quickly so that I can look out for you!"

It was comforting, Nancy admitted to herself, to have someone she could depend upon, even though it was impossible to take him seriously. At least if he thought he was in love with her, she could eliminate him from the people who would have to be watched. He wasn't handsome, like Bill Pearson; or attractive as Mike Sullivan was; he didn't even have Clive Bosworth's charm and breeding, but he was thoroughly nice, and he had been consistently kind to her from the beginning. She leaned toward him. "Don't, Jim— not now—I'm too bewildered by all that has happened to be able to think."

Jim Mason turned and stared earnestly into her face, and then his rather infrequent smile crept across his broad, homely face, illuminating it into attractiveness. "All right, I won't say anything more now."

Ismael finished his low-voiced conversation on the telephone, and crossed the veranda, a sheaf of white notes in his brown hand, but he hurried down the steps without speaking. Clive Bosworth returned from his interview with the cook. "Dinner at 8.30," he announced, and moved deliberately to the veranda door to peer through its rain-silvered screen.

"Halloo, here you are," he exclaimed as Betty's slim figure emerged from the darkness. Semut, who had been following her at a respectful distance, dropped back and vanished into the rain.

"What's left of me," Betty sighed. "But I don't think I came off so badly at the end."

"He put you through it, did he?" Clive sounded anxious.

"Rather," she said, dropping into the chair she had vacated earlier, and motioning to Clive to sit down. "McCleary knew about our meeting last night; that I was away from the house; and, of course, he had jumped to the conclusion that we had been up here killing Lydia; and then that I led poor John this morning into an ambush to let you kill him." In spite of the fact that she knew everybody on the veranda was listening, Betty made no effort to lower her voice.

"So that's where you were last night!" Mike stared accusingly at Clive, "Why the devil didn't you say so?"

"Oh," Clive exclaimed blankly. "Did you see me go out of the wayong? I didn't know—thought I was pretty nippy about it." His smile was conciliatory. "Nothing to it, really. I just slipped off to see Betty. Didn't want anyone to get the wrong idea about it, don't you know, when I found what had happened to

Lydia. Bowled me over so that I've only been about half functioning ever since—things have happened so damn fast."

"Anyway," Betty said, "I think you ought to cable your father, Clive, and then get a good lawyer. You've nothing to hide now, you can't whitewash me, and as things look to the police, you and I had the best motives."

"Motive?" Clive exclaimed. "I didn't have any motive—I was a rotten husband to Lydia, but I was awf'ly fond of her, and she knew it."

"That isn't what the police think," Betty said drily. "They think you wanted to marry me; that you killed Lydia for that reason, and then killed John to get hold of the insurance money, so that we could go back to England to live."

Clive flushed to the roots of his fair hair. "Of all the bally rot! Why, it never occurred to either one of us, did it, Betty? We were bally fools enough to compromise ourselves, but as for anything serious! Good Lord!" He ran an agitated hand through his hair. "I haven't any intention of going back to England. I'm going to stick right here on this estate and make something of it—made up my mind today; and felt better right away. Something to do for Lydia and John."

Betty shrugged. "You can do as you like, of course; but personally the sooner I can get back to civilization the better."

Mike Sullivan said slowly, "It might be a good idea to cable your father, Clive; it's bound to be in all the papers as soon as the first reporter gets wind of it. He'd be prepared then. Didn't you realize after Mc-Cleary talked to you what a tough spot you were in?"

Clive blinked. "I'm afraid I didn't take it very seriously. I thought he was just taking a pot shot at each of us in turn, hoping to surprise a confession out of us. You see, I knew I didn't kill Lydia, and I couldn't believe anyone would really consider it," he said naively. "I can't yet. Anyway, I'm not going to bother my father with my troubles ahead of time, and I'm not going to have any bally lawyer hanging around."

Mike and Betty, for the first time in agreement, both started to protest, but Clive's face became momentarily more stubborn.

"Is this all the whusky ye've got, Bosworth?" Hamilton interrupted, "Because if it is, I'm hopin' no one else wants a drink this nicht." He tipped the contents of the bottle into a glass and drained it at a gulp.

"Better go easy, Hamilton," Bill Pearson warned, his voice rising above dive's shout, "Boy, kassi whisky!"

Hamilton smacked his lips. "Ye'd all be better for a drink instead o' mouthin' and gawpin' and wonderin' aboot everyone here. Naethin' like a bellyfu' o' liquor to dull the feel o' a knife in yer ribs."

"Oh, don't," Nancy begged. "It's bad enough thinking about it, without putting it into words."

Hamilton's somber glance shifted from the empty whisky bottle to Nancy's white face. "Aye, lass, you do well to be fearfu'. 'Twas o' you I was thinking. Go you to the police noo afore 'tis too late. Tell them a' ye ken. 'Tis for your ain guid that I'm speakin'—"

"I don't know what you are talking about," Nancy protested, moistening her dry lips.

"Aye, ye do," the Scotchman contradicted. "You think you are sae clever that you can catch out the murderer your ain self, but you are nought but a fool to think it. I dinna ken what it is you ken aboot him—'twas for something sure that he choked you a whilst back. There was more to it than ye've telt. Like enow he spoke to you, and ye're hopin' to recognize his voice, or saething aboot his hands. I've seen you watching hands ever since ye came oot, and turnin't yer hand this way an' that to catch the sound o' a voice." His long gangling arms gestured wildly, "Go you to the police now, afore it is too late!"

Every eye was focused on Nancy, and she could think of nothing light and casual that might counteract the effect of Hamilton's solemn warning; all she could do was to think dully, "That's torn it. The old fool has taken away my last chance. Nothing can save me now—no one."

CHAPTER XVI

The half-caste nurse was still screaming, as shrilly and automatically as a police siren, as Ismael and McCleary burst through the door at the head of the stairs. The bed was only a few feet from the door, and, ignoring the nurse, the two men hurried toward the sheet-covered figure that lay there, so ominously quiet, the head face downward between the two pillows. McCleary pulled a pillow impatiently aside, while Ismael stooped to lift the dark, suffused face. Slowly he laid it back—there was no need for words. They both had seen the cord twisted tightly around his neck.

"Shut up, you!" McCleary whirled on the screaming nurse, and when she still kept on with her nerve-wracking shrieks, he flung the contents of a glass of water into her face. The last scream ended in a spluttering gasp, and McCleary waited grimly until she had caught her breath and began automatically to wipe her streaming face.

"Now then, tell us what happened."

"I don't know, I don't know!" she wept. "I just found him like this, and then I screamed."

"We know about the screaming. Just tell us who was in here."

"No one, not a soul. And I didn't leave the room either," she stated.

McCleary looked incredulous. "Well, then, tell us what happened from the time I left."

"One moment, Tuan. Let her sit down and calm herself a little while I speak to those outside. We cannot hear her over those voices." The nurse sank gratefully into a chair on the far side of the room, while the Malay opened the door and spoke quietly to the worried, excited group of people in the hall, "Tuan Farnsworth is dead. That is all we know at present; the nurse just discovered that his spirit had fled, and so she screamed. When we learn more, I will tell you. You will help us best now, if you will all go back to the veranda, and keep as calm as you can."

He ignored the eager questions, the grumbles and appeals, and spoke in swift Malay to the constable on duty. Apparently he was satisfied with the reply, but nevertheless he raised his voice, and the guards on duty in the living room, and on the veranda poked their heads into the hall to assure him that they were "truly" at their posts. "Now go," he addressed the white people and the servants; "I mean this. You will be safe if you will stay together, but you mustn't delay me longer."

McCleary was impatiently tapping his foot, and glaring at the door, as Ismael returned to the room, but the nurse had recovered some of her professional veneer of calm, and seemed anxious to speak. "I gave Mr. Farnsworth his second bromide as soon as you left the room—I was already mixing it, Mr. McCleary, at your suggestion. For a minute or two, while the noise in the hall was at its worst, he clung to my hand, but he quieted almost immediately. Coming on top of the first draught so quickly, it acted with great speed. He was very susceptible to soporifics anyway, I had discovered, but in his excitable state, I thought it a good thing for him to get a good sleep. I fixed his pillows and his bedclothes, and by the time I had rinsed out the glass in the bathroom," she nodded toward the door at the rear of the room where a light disclosed part of a stone floor and a white enamel sink, "he was asleep. I felt his pulse, which was good, pulled the bedclothes over his shoulder—he was lying on his side, his head burrowed into the pillow—then I lowered the shade on the lamp so that it threw a shadow across the bed, I turned the key in the lock of the door opening into the hall, and then, having nothing more I could do for my patient, I decided that I would bathe myself and change into a fresh uniform. That, I thought, would help me keep awake, since I had been on duty all last night, on another case, and had only taken this one to oblige the good Doctor Sparkes. Here, too, I had had a strenuous day, and I realized that I must be alert for the time when the bromide wore off, and the poor young man would begin demanding attention." She paused, and her brown eyes, with their faintly yellowish whites, turned from one policeman to the other. McCleary cleared his throat, but he could find no fault with her behavior. "Go on," he muttered huskily.

"I left the bathroom door ajar, so that I could hear if my patient called me. I could have heard that even above the running of the water; but I heard nothing. I bathed and dressed, slowly, I don't know how long it took me. I had the whole night to use up, you will understand, save what part of it my patient needed. I felt refreshed when I came out of the bathroom; Mr. Farnsworth hadn't changed his position, and the bed was still in shadow. The rain started up again about that time, if you will remember?" She looked expectantly at McCleary, who shook his head: "I don't know, it's been going off and on in spurts all day; I don't even notice it now." Ismael blinked his almond eyes. "I remember that it grew ferocious about seven o'clock and that it kept on, as it still is." For the first time they seemed to realize the beating of the rain on the roof, no longer a rustling, for the atap was too sodden, but a steady drum-drum; and the trees outside loaned their sullen, reluctant swishing as the wind shook their rain-heavy branches.

The nurse continued in her rather flat voice: "That was what I heard, all I heard. If it had been a still night, I would have found myself breathing with my patient, one-two-three—a nurse cannot help that, and, in a heart case, it is very disturbing—the irregularity, and the way one must, somehow, accompany it with one's own breathing." McCleary shuffled his feet—this was getting nowhere. What he wanted was facts, and the sight of Ismael gravely following the nurse's intake and outgo of breath made him purple with anger.

"And then," Ismael said gently.

"Oh, I was manicuring my fingernails by this light over here," she pointed with a yellow hand to the light that was shining down on both Ismael and McCleary, and the white man drew back involuntarily from the litter of buffers, nail enamel, and other small bottles on the table at his elbow.

"Suddenly the rain let up. I hardly realized it at first. Everything so quiet all at once. I kept on for a minute or two doing my last finger, and then suddenly I knew there was something wrong. I didn't stop to think what it was; I just jumped for my patient, spilling everything in my lap on the floor." Both men glanced down at a scattering of emery boards and a pair of manicure scissors. "I had realized without knowing it that I didn't hear my patient's breathing. His face was still burrowed in his pillow, and apparently he

was lying just as I had left him, and yet I knew—"
Hastily she pressed a handkerchief against her lips
and gulped once or twice. "I knew that he was dead."
She drew a deep breath and finished calmly. "I lifted
his head, and saw his face. I thought for a moment
he had been suffocated by the pillows—drugged as he
was, you know. And then I noticed the cord around
his neck. It was the realization that he had been murdered, with no one in the room, that made me lose
control and scream as I did." She pushed a weary
amber hand through her blue-black hair. "I don't
understand it. But, awful as it is, I am glad that it
wasn't an accident, that his death was no reflection
on my nursing."

McCleary had a dozen questions to ask, but the
nurse was unshaken in her story. Ismael moved heavily toward the door that opened on to the basement
stairway. "Here is the key, Tuan." He bent over and
picked up a long rusty key from the rug between the
door and the bed. "Too late we know what happened."

The white officer blinked and sprang to his feet.
"What do you mean, 'we know what happened'?—
damned if I know!"

"Sometime this afternoon, or this evening, probably when the nurse left the room to get drinking
water, the murderer stepped inside the room. Nay,
he needn't have entered the room—just reached three
feet with his arm, turned the key which opened the
door, and moved away. Doubtless that was just as he

left Miss Reynolds' room. By so doing, he left the way open to silence Farnsworth when he had later an opportunity. That opportunity came quickly, the first time everyone rushed indoors, when I banged Miss Chambers' door, and found her lying on the floor. There was much confusion, you will recall, and the constable from the veranda followed the crowd indoors. I think, Tuan," Ismael looked thoughtful, "the murderer first slipped behind the living room screen, and then when everyone had gone inside, went swiftly from the veranda, around the house to the office, and up the stairs. By that time, the nurse had gone into the bathroom; or he may have waited outside the door until he heard water running—the rest was simple. He had only to step to the bed where his victim lay in a drugged sleep and slip the cord around his neck, pull it tight, and arrange the pillows."

McCleary nodded. "It must have happened about like that," he admitted, "but think of the risk he took! The downstairs office was empty only about half an hour, all told, and during fifteen minutes of that time, you and I were here in this room." The officer pushed a weary hand across his forehead. "If only I could remember which of them were in the hall, and which were in Miss Chambers' room, I could figure out who was missing; but with everyone milling around, and jabbering, servants and guests and constables—if that bloody fool had stayed on the veranda, this wouldn't have happened. He'll hear about that!"

There was a gleam of satisfaction in Ismael's eyes; the constables had been a thorn in the flesh throughout the case, good enough Malays, but untrained and stupid in comparison with the Johore police. Sensing Ismael's silent criticism, McCleary said defensively, "They are good men but they are not used to a case of this kind; give them a good clean case of gang robbery, or a straight native killing, and you couldn't ask for better men. They're out of their element in a white murder, just as I am."

Ismael changed the subject; in his opinion that didn't excuse the lack of discipline, the casual disregard of orders. "The doctor should be notified, Tuan, and the body removed; and then, we must question the people on the veranda, see whether any of them noticed anything amiss."

"I suppose you are right, but I am sick to death of asking questions, and I haven't any faith at all in the replies I get, when I get any. Well, come on, there's no use putting off the evil hour any longer. Though mark my words, it is going to be time wasted."

McCleary's gloomy prediction proved to be correct. None of the frightened, overwrought guests had been able to contribute anything of value; each could account only for his own actions at the time; the rush into the house and their anxiety to know what had happened, concern for Miss Chambers. Certainly by the time McCleary had herded them out onto the veranda, everyone was present, but who had been missing for part of the time, no one could, or would, tell. The same situation held with the servants; they had run into the house, those who hadn't been too frightened, to see what the noise had portended, and had hung around in order to satisfy their curiosity, until the Tuan Mata-Mata had hurried them off about their business. The constable on duty on the veranda announced quite simply that with all the white people in the house, he had naturally followed to see what had happened. He could be of more use indoors, he thought, than outside guarding an empty group of chairs. If, as he thought, the murderer was inside, then it was his duty to protect the people he was to guard, by going with them, and despite the blast of McCleary's rage, his stolid face maintained its approval of his own reasoning.

Doctor Sparke, looking very much harassed, had come and gone, and Farnsworth's body had been carried away to lie briefly beside those of the other victims of the murderer in the tiny morgue at Kluang. A dried, belated dinner had been served, in which no one had been interested, and at midnight the guests had been despatched to their beds.

Ismael lay back in a long wicker chair which he had dragged into the hall of the bungalow. The back of the chair rested against the rear door, and the long, brightly lit hall stretched in front of him, the blank, shut faces of the three bedrooms, the dark yawning maws of the living and dining rooms, and then the brown scabby paint of the front door. In spite of the fact that he had had no sleep for eighteen hours, he knew there was no danger of his relaxing his vigilance; his eyes were wide and staring; his ears strained to catch every sound in the sleeping house: the spasmodic beat of rain on the roof, the soft scurry of lizards and mice across the atap thatch, the twitching of the night breeze through the dripping lime trees. He heard the occasional snore emitted by the exhausted McCleary who had thrown himself down on the couch in the living room, the restless turning and tossing of Mike Sullivan or Clive Bosworth as they twisted about on the bed so recently occupied by young Farnsworth. Mike had given up his room to Betty Harvy, at the diffident suggestion of Clive who obviously dreaded sleeping alone in that desecrated bed. A constable had accompanied Jim Mason to his bachelor quarters, and another was guarding Pearson and Hamilton; and this time, Ismael thought with grim satisfaction, the policemen would perform their duties. The two remaining constables were patrolling the grounds outside the Bosworth house. Ismael could hear the scrunch of their shoes at periodic intervals on the gravel driveway, the rattle of the doorknobs as they assured themselves that no one had entered, the rattle of shutters as they in their turn were tested.

Despite all those precautions, however, Ismael had taken upon himself the guarding of the American

girl. The diabolic cleverness and speed with which
the murderer had killed the hapless Farnsworth had
shaken Ismael's confidence in everyone except himself, and he was determined that, for this night at
least, Nancy's safety should rest on his shoulders.

Why, he wondered, did the murderer fear the
American girl? Obviously, it was due to the telegrams, and to her adoption of Helene Chambers' identity; but why was it so important to
him that she persevere in the role of Miss Chambers? Could it be that the murderer knew, from
some indiscretion of Mrs. Bosworth's, that Helene
Chambers had information that would connect him
with the crime?—a bit of gossip, an anecdote that
Lydia Bosworth had written to her friend? If she had
imparted such information, it would explain why
the murderer was so anxious for Nancy to continue
the impersonation. Nancy herself knew nothing, but
might it not be that Helene Chambers, miles away at
sea, and ignorant of the murders, might hold the key
to the murderer's identity? At least that theory would
explain why it was so important to the killer that the
police should continue to believe that Nancy Reynolds was Helene Chambers.

It was too bad that the telegrams had been destroyed, for, under pressure, the frightened houseboy had admitted to Ismael that he had thrown away
the damp wads of paper, and that they had been
burned with the rubbish, and Saidi had admitted

matter-of-factly that she had been the one to put the Mem's shoes outside to be cleaned. So, that one small mystery had been cleared up. Tomorrow, Ismael would get copies of the telegrams; possibly there had been something significant in Miss Chambers' message which Nancy had overlooked.

There was so much that should already have been done; but as McCleary complained, no sooner did they make a little headway in one angle of the case, than a new tragedy occurred, and all the routine work and questioning had to be started over again. Ismael hadn't even had time to think about the case in an attitude of peace and receptiveness which was always essential for him. Now, in the quiet of these early hours, he was confident that he could make progress.

First, he decided, he must get a new report about the month's rubber production from Hamilton. The man who had rifled the files at the factory apparently hadn't realized that the engineer still had the rough notes from which the report had been made. Of course, it was possible that Hamilton himself had destroyed the blue sheets, but even so, the figures could be obtained from the Government offices; they had a record of all rubber shipped; they did their own weighing, too, so that their figures would be absolutely accurate. When he talked to them, Ismael decided he would get reports on the rubber production for the whole district. Not that he could see exactly what bearing they could have on this case, but he was meticulous about details, and painstaking both in the acquisition of information and in piecing it together. Only by knowing as much as possible about the life, the history and the character of everybody involved in a crime could he discover the guilty person.

Vaguely in Ismael's mind the personality of the murderer was taking shape; a man, cold and cunning and ruthless; whose every word and look and deed was calculated; a man who, during his life on the estate had assumed a role so successfully that no one had penetrated it. No one, that was, except Lydia Bosworth in the last second of her life—she alone had seen the cruelty and purpose behind the mask of friendship. John Harvy had been spared that knowledge; he hadn't seen which trusted hand had struck him from behind; nor could Farnsworth have known which of his comrades had cut off his life.

Ismael changed the direction of his thoughts. He remembered when he had first arrived at this house he had told McCleary impulsively that he wanted the answers to just one or two questions from each of the people involved, and, although he hadn't actually committed himself in words, he had thought at the time that if he had truthful replies to those key questions, he could solve Lydia Bosworth's murder. He wondered now whether those answers would solve the two additional murders. Some had already been answered: he knew now why

Nancy Reynolds had arrived when she did, and about
her relations with Lydia. He knew that Betty Harvy had been out with Clive Bosworth, and so had
been unaware of the lights being off; he knew too
how the lights had happened to go off. He knew
what John Harvy had been so anxious to discuss
with Clive that night; and he knew about Jim Mason's kris. He knew that Clive Bosworth had probably cared as much for his wife as he was capable of
caring for any woman; and that unless he was a more
successful liar than Ismael considered him, his feeling for Mrs. Harvy was a passing one. Nor, according to his statements on the veranda that evening,
which had been duly passed on to Ismael by the constable, did he hate the East as much as people had
assumed. There were still some questions to be answered: he didn't know what hold Mike Sullivan had
on Clive, or perhaps, what hold Clive had on Mike
Sullivan. Likewise, he was not yet satisfied about the
walk that Mrs. Bosworth had taken the afternoon of
her death, despite the flowers she had brought back
with her. Would the answer to those questions dis-
close the identity of the murderer? No one knew
better than Ismael himself how vital it was to solve
the murders as quickly as possible if the life of the
little American girl was to be saved. The murderer
was willing to take any desperate risk to preserve his
secret; and it seemed to Ismael, thinking over the
circumstances of each murder, that the killer was

becoming progressively bolder, more contemptuous of the forces pitted against him. When a man became so confident of his superiority over others, he grew careless, although, Ismael admitted with a sigh, in spite of the brief time he had had to commit Farnsworth's murder, the criminal had left no fingerprints even on the door key. So far, the killer, from his own viewpoint, had made only one mistake; he had spared Nancy's life; and that was a mistake, Ismael felt convinced, which would be rectified the first moment he found the American girl alone.

CHAPTER XVII

If only she knew what to expect, whom to fear, Nancy thought as she moved restlessly about in the big, mosquito-nettinged bed, she could meet whatever happened with some degree of fortitude. It was the uncertainty that made the situation so demoralizing. Never before had she gone to bed deliberately and left the lights all burning so that at intervals she could raise herself on her elbow and peer into every corner. She could hear the measured tramp of the constables' feet as they circled the house, hear their testing of her shutters every ten minutes. Outside in the hall, she caught the occasional creak of the rattan chair as Ismael shifted his position. The house too was awake; above the swishing of the breeze, the spatter of rain, and the sudden scurrying of lizards and mice, she could hear the floor boards groan as though invisible feet pressed them, and the white plaster walls seemed to creak and strain.

Nancy shivered. She didn't want to die; but if she had to, she wanted to meet death face to face, not have it clutch her from behind with strangling fingers or a stabbing stroke as it had John Harvy, not have it smother her in her sleep, as it had Dave Farnsworth. "My curiosity will be the death of me," she said with a thin humor that didn't at all divert her thoughts. The most horrible thing of all was the knowledge that one of the people with whom she had been so closely associated, some of whom she had come to like, was even now planning how he could eliminate her. In her last moment would she have an opportunity to know whether it was Mike or Clive, Bill Pearson or Jim, or Ronald Hamilton? Betty was out of the picture actively, at any rate, though what part she might have in the plot, Nancy couldn't tell. The very fact that she had spoken so frankly to Clive on the veranda, early in the evening, made Nancy skeptical; and his repudiation of her, his sudden determination to stick to his job, sounded just a bit too good to be true. On the other hand, Betty was obviously mercenary; she was very good-looking, and just the type to appeal to the majority of men—well, with a hundred thousand dollars, she would know that she could do a lot better than Clive Bosworth. She had probably been giving him notice that she was going to run out on him.

Not until a chill, drizzly dawn had changed the blackness of night into the light wet grey of morning, did Nancy finally fall into a deep, dreamless sleep. It was ten o' clock when she was startled into fearful wakefulness by a banging on her door. "Are you all right, Helene?" She shivered and shrank farther under the bedclothes as she recognized Mike Sullivan's voice. He had repeated the inquiry with growing alarm before she could steady her dry lips to reply, "Yes, I was asleep. You woke me."

"Sorry," he apologized. "I got the wind up a bit when you kept on not putting in an appearance—if you understand what I mean."

"Where's Ismael?" She tried to make her question sound casual by adding, "I'm under police orders not to open the door except to him or to Mr. McCleary."

"Good Lord! I don't want to come in," Mike exclaimed in alarm. "I just wanted to be sure you were all right. I don't know where Ismael has gone; he simply faded away a couple of hours ago, but there's a policeman outside here who is regarding me with the deepest suspicion, and fingering his baton as though he itched to place it in the back of my scalp. McCleary is taking poor Pearson over the hurdles at the moment—not that that will do him any good, or Pearson either—but I'll tell McCleary you are ready to have the embargo lifted."

An involuntary smile curved her lips, and her heart felt at least two tons lighter for listening to the Irishman's nonsense. Mechanically she started to dress, pleased, half way in the process, to find herself absorbed in the choice between her yellow linen with schoolgirlish white round collar, or the more sophisticated tan and brown pongee with its smart brown jacket. It was embarrassing, when McCleary's hearty voice sounded outside the door, to tell him he would have to wait until she had gone to the bathroom. Her face was very pink and young as she scuttled past him, clutching her peach-colored negligee around her, but he was so completely matter-of-fact when she gave him a sideward look from under her long lashes, that she found herself completely unembarrassed as she cleaned her teeth and made a thorough job of her ablutions.

He was still standing there when she emerged from the bathroom, talking in Malay to the constable, and she gave him the most fleeting of smiles. "Two minutes only now, Mr. McCleary—the worst is over. You'll be surprised."

He was not only surprised but pleased; that lady maid's job had irked him, but Ismael had been so insistent—and anyway, here she was, in exactly two minutes, as sweet and fresh as a man's heart could wish—which was not completely sterile as was his own. No coquetry either, just a nice young girl in a fresh yellow dress. In spite of himself, McCleary's heart warmed to her.

"It's damper than ever outside," he said. "Sullivan thought you'd be more comfortable having breakfast indoors. Funny," he added as he drew her chair back and pushed her with a mighty shove forward so that her kneecaps hit an undersupport, "everyone seems to shun the house. Here you are all comfortable with a breakfast tray in front of you, and yet, do you know, most of those bloody, beg-your-pardon, bally fools— er idiots, preferred to sit on that wet porch, and balance a plate on one shivering knee, and a shaking coffee cup in his hand? It's beyond me. Sullivan was the only sensible person; he and I had our breakfast here in peace and comfort."

Nancy felt guilty at accepting McCleary's approval, for she too would have preferred to do a juggling act with plates and cups than eat where she was, although she was vaguely pleased that Mike Sullivan and McCleary had assumed that she felt as they did.

"Where is Ismael?" Nancy asked cautiously, sipping the steaming coffee.

"I don't know; queer tight-mouthed little beggar. Makes it a bit hard to work with him because you never know what is going on behind that flat brown face of his. He routed me out to say that I was to keep my eye on you; and then, as calm as you please he said, 'I think, Tuan, when I return, I will be able to point out the murderer,' and off he buzzed!"

Nancy leaned forward, her face alight. "Oh, what a relief it will be!" and then she paused uncertainly and her anxiety was obvious as she added, "Whom do you think he suspects?"

McCleary, aware suddenly of his indiscretion, shrugged his shoulders. "I don't know. And please regard what I just said as a confidence—no use fore-warning the murderer. Not," he added hastily, "that I believe the case will be solved so quickly. Are you through there?" he asked, "because I've work to do."

"Oh, I'm sorry," Nancy said impudently, "I thought you just wanted to keep me company. I'd forgotten for all of five minutes that I was a sort of ward in chancery. However, I don't want anything more. What do we do now?"

"I don't care what you do, so long as you take care of yourself , and don't run into trouble," McCleary growled. "You'd better keep close to the crowd on the veranda. They're all out there—the laborers aren't working again on account of the rain, so no one has anything to do except cool his heels and criticize the police."

"Well, my heels are cool enough, goodness knows. This dampness has penetrated right through to my marrow—and I certainly don't intend to criticize the police. I don't see how either you or Ismael could possibly have done more than you are doing." Her smile was unexpectedly sweet as she pushed back her chair. "However, I'll take myself off your hands anyway by going out with the others."

"So here you are at last, lazybones," Jim Mason said, coming forward to take her arm with an affec-tionate grip. "I thought you were never going to come out. Been waiting hours. Come over here—I've a chair all ready. I spent most of the night thinking of the things I wanted to say to you—I'm afraid I bungled yesterday." His voice was low and anxious. "I didn't mean to crowd you. You can take all the time you want, of course. Only, if you could give me a little bit of hope, some right to take care of you—"

Nancy laughed a little breathlessly, but she allowed Jim to lead her to the chair he had reserved beside his. Mike Sullivan, engrossed in a three-cornered conversation with Pearson and Hamilton, had merely nodded to her. His green eyes weren't mocking as she expected; they were worse than that, they didn't notice her at all.

"What I really want to know is," Jim said, awkwardly tucking her coat around her—he had none of the easy grace, the skilled competence in small attentions which came so naturally to Clive Bosworth; but Nancy found herself liking him the better for his clumsiness, "is whether I am repulsive to you? If I'm not, then I am sure I can make you care for me. Believe it or not, you are the first girl I've ever asked to marry me. I just never had time to fall for anybody before, I guess; been too busy. But, I've got quite a bit of money saved up, and I'm ready now to go back to the States and take over the job that's waiting for me there."

"But I thought you liked the East so much!" Nancy exclaimed. "I thought you were planning to be out here for several years."

Jim shook his head. "No, I'm going back home. The things that have happened here have spoiled this place for me, and I can't see taking a job on another estate. I know about growing rubber now, and about its raw state. I'm going back to the manufacturing end. There's more money there; and I want to be near my old man—he's getting on, you know. I want to repay him a little for all he has done for me." His voice was so deeply stirred that Nancy gazed at him in surprise—she had never heard a man express, in a tone, the adoration of his father that Jim's did, nor seen a man's face so illuminated. As though aware of her surprise, Jim said hastily, "And anyway, the East is no place for a wife."

"You haven't one yet," Nancy reminded him, still thinking about Jim's devotion to his father, "and you can't be really sure that you'd want to marry me when you know me better. You might not like me at all." She'd have to make some plans soon, Nancy thought, remembering suddenly that she was penniless, and thousands of miles away from home. It seemed very coldblooded to be considering this proposal as a means of escape; but she must do something, and she honestly did like Jim; there was something reassuring about his very homeliness and sincerity. Of course he wasn't exactly the answer to a maiden's prayer, so far as looks and background were concerned, but her disillusioning experience in Penang, her knowledge of Clive Bosworth's disloyalty to Lydia, made her deeply distrustful of men with physical charm and easy manners.

"But what will happen here to the estate if you leave?" she asked to gain time. "Surely now that John Harvy is dead, Clive is going to need all the help he can get. Isn't it rather deserting the ship?"

"No, I don't think so," Jim said gravely. "It seems to me the best thing that could happen to the place would be for it to have a clean sweep; a new manager, and all new assistants. Bosworth will never be able to pull it up, even if he sticks to it. I doubt if even poor old John could have. The best thing that could happen for the Semang Rubber Company would be to sell it. Let somebody else have the headaches. Once an estate gets a bad name, everything seems to go haywire with it. I don't know why, but I've seen it happen even in my time; the managers and assistants seem to feel that the whole thing is hopeless, they expect things to go flooey, and they do. Psychology, I suppose—though I'm not up very much on that. Anyway, if you ask any of the old-time rubber men they'll tell you the same thing, some estates are lucky, and some are unlucky, like ships. And once a place gets a bad name, believe you me, it's sunk!"

Nancy was impressed with his vehemence, and his concern about the estate. She knew that what he really had in mind was the fact that Clive Bosworth had committed the murders, and that after his arrest, Jim didn't want to profit by the promotions which would follow— Why, Jim would be manager, and Bill first assistant! How dreadful for both of them; and how impossible for either to accept. How could they stay on with the memory of the tragedies haunting every nook and corner?

"Say something, Helene!" Jim's voice was close to her ear, his bright blue eyes searching her face. "You seem so far away! What are you thinking? Are you frightened—worried? Tell me and let me help you!"

His use of the name "Helene" brought her face to face with the unpleasant fact that Jim didn't even know who she really was; that in all fairness to him, she must tell him the truth before he committed himself any further. And yet, she had promised Ismael not to divulge her identity to anyone, so all she could do was to prevent Jim from saying anything which he might later regret when she was free to tell him about the affair at Penang, about her deception.

"Don't, Jim. Don't say anything more," she said, withdrawing the hand he had seized. "Wait until Ismael gets back. I must talk to him first."

For a moment he stared at her as though about to make another appeal, and then abruptly he rose from his chair. "It's up to you," he muttered grumpily, and stalked into the house.

Nancy's face was rueful as she heard the door slam behind him. She hadn't meant to hurt his feelings, but if she had done so inadvertently, he needn't have gone off the deep end like that. Everybody was looking at her now, as though she had done something outrageous; and Mike Sullivan was coming across the veranda with his usual jaunty swagger and his laughing eyes.

"How's the Lord High Executioner this bright and glorious day?" he asked, dropping into the chair that Jim had just vacated. "And what was the crime for which poor Mason has been exiled?"

"You aren't funny," Nancy said coldly.

"I know I'm not, but it was the best I could do on the spur of the moment. I've nothing against Mason except the efficiency with which he managed to corral you, and now I can forgive him even that."

"You are certainly an adept at concealing your emotions," Nancy replied tartly. "A casual observer would have thought you were completely immersed in your conversation with Mr. Pearson and Mr. Hamilton. You all looked as though the League of Nations depended on your verdict."

"So, you noticed that, did you! Poor Mason!" He grinned at her flushed and furious face.

"You're hateful," she flared. "I wish you'd go away. Why don't you go over and spoil Betty and Clive's *tête-à-tête*, since you enjoy being where you aren't wanted?" She glanced across the veranda at the two fair heads bent earnestly toward each other.

"No, you've reformed me in that direction. Once Clive is clear of this mess, I am through interfering in his life," Mike announced flatly.

Nancy's wide eyes were turned toward him expectantly, and Mike inwardly cursed the behavior which had aroused her interest, although at the same time he had an inexplicable desire to justify himself to her. "Clive," he explained carefully, "was a close friend of my young brother Denny—the places in Ireland where we spent our summers adjoined. Clive was a lonely chap, his mother died when he was born, and neither his father nor his older brother had any time for him, so he practically lived at our house. I was a bit older, of course, but I used to pal around with them. One day when we were out swimming on a bit of forbidden coast, the two little chaps got beyond their depths, were swept away in the current. I went for Denny, but he said he could hold out, that I should help Clive. I managed to fish Clive ashore, but—Denny was gone."

"Oh," Nancy's voice was distressed. "How dreadful! I understand now why you feel so responsible for Clive." Mike's smile was sardonic—if she was satisfied with that explanation so much the better. He wouldn't tell her about his mother's dropping dead at his feet when she realized that Denny was lost. It had seemed unbearable at the time, but later he had been glad that she had gone so swiftly, before news of his father's death had come; that she had died believing that her husband was a hero. At least she hadn't had the pain of disillusionment which had been Mike's when he had gone through his father's private papers and discovered that the man he had worshipped was also the father of poor little Clive. How much Mr. Bosworth senior knew, Mike never fathomed; but he must have suspected there was something out of the way, for he had never taken any interest in the poor little beggar, just performed his perfunctory duty. Mike had burned the incriminating letters, and then, oppressed by the guilt and responsibility which had never apparently worried his father, had determined to watch over the brother he could never acknowledge. The people who had known of Denny's death had accepted Mike's devotion to Clive quite matter-of-factly; and Clive himself had never questioned the sacrifices Mike had made at times to get him out of scrapes. And Mike himself had never doubted the wisdom of his own actions, until Nancy had challenged them. It was bitter to realize, as he did now, that he had been doing more harm than good to the one person in the world for whom he gave a damn— that Clive would be better off without him.

Nancy said nothing, she sat very still, her hands clasped in her lap, suffering vicariously the tragedy that had darkened Mike's boyhood. She sensed that there was more behind the story than he had told, but she didn't want to hear it; she couldn't bear to see the stricken expression in the Irishman's eyes.

Mike glanced at her, his voice once more mocking. "As soon as I see Clive safely settled, even if it means marrying him off to Betty, I'll be away—this time for good and all. I'll never again try to be a *deus ex machina*."

"Where will you go?" Nancy asked.

Mike shrugged. "I haven't thought about that. Perhaps to Borneo—I've never been in the interior there; and I've never shot a Kodiak Bear either, so I may decide on Alaska; or perhaps I may make a complete right-about-face and settle down in America, cut my own coupons for a change, and harry the Tycoons in the rubber business because my dividends aren't as large as they might be. On the other hand, I might throw in my lot with the C. I. O. and go on a permanent sit-down strike."

Nancy was annoyed she hated his flippancy, "And what will you do if they arrest Clive?" she asked. "McCleary told me—" She stopped short, remembering that the inspector had spoken to her in confidence.

"They won't touch Clive!" Mike's face darkened. "I'll confess myself before I'll let them arrest him." Without saying another word, or glancing down into Nancy's horrified face, he sprang from his chair and started across the veranda toward Clive and Betty.

"Tiffin is served, Tuan," Semut announced from the doorway; and slowly, reluctantly, the occupants of the veranda rose and made their way into the dining room.

Whether it was the usual depressing effect of the house, or the undercurrent of fear and suspicion engendered by the knowledge that one of their number was the murderer, Nancy didn't know, but none of the people gathered around the luncheon table could make much pretense of eating, nor any effort at conversation. Mike's words still rang in her ears, and she knew now that they had been merely a confirmation of her own suspicion. If his lawyers pleaded insanity, if they showed the dreadful lasting effects of his boyhood tragedy, proved that Clive had become an obsession with him, couldn't they prevent a death sentence? But then it would mean he would be shut away for the rest of his life in an insane asylum; and that would be even worse.

As though suddenly conscious of her gaze, Mike turned and addressed her quietly, "You won't repeat what I said, will you? If Clive is in the clear, it won't be necessary for me to take any action. I hadn't any right to burden your poor little New England conscience. Forget it all."

"Never," she declared fiercely. "I won't be made a party to anything so dreadful. Of course I'll tell, I'll stop you somehow."

"Shut up, you little fool." His voice was a hoarse whisper, hauntingly like that other whisper outside her wardrobe door, and his eyes seemed to flash their hatred. "I warn you to keep out of this."

She glanced swiftly around the table. Apparently nobody had heard him; people were pushing back their

628   Dorothy Cole Meade

chairs, moving toward the door. With a half-muffled cry she sprang up, terrified that she might be left alone with Mike.

"Halloo, there's the sun!" Clive exclaimed, pointing to the rather watery pale light that had seeped through the clouds. "Come on, fellows, that means work. The coolies will be going out now, and we'll all have to work to make up for this rainy spell. Will you take a hand, Mike? If you could manage to take over for Farnsworth for a bit, it would help us out no end." Everyone suddenly felt more normal at the prospect of something to do, and the men acted quite cheerful as they hurried off down the driveway.

"Oh, Mr. McCleary," Betty addressed the inspector who had strolled out onto the veranda, "will it be all right for me to go over to my bungalow and get some fresh clothes? I won't be gone long."

"Certainly," McCleary agreed, "I'll just speak to one of the constables." Betty laughed, "Let me take the little roly-poly one, won't you? He is the cutest of them all; I am thinking of buying a collar and leash for him and taking him back to England with me."

"You haven't gone back to England yet, my lady," McCleary growled, "'and if you go where I think you're going, to take a policeman along would be like bringing coals to Newcastle." He strode to the door and shouted "Katidjo!"

Betty looked disconcerted. "Still has me cast for the role of villainess, apparently! I suppose it is easier for him to go on thinking that, than it is to exert a little intelligence and find the real murderer." She shrugged her shoulder, and moved over to the screen door where she stood impatiently tapping her foot, until a small, jolly-looking little constable appeared around the corner of the house. "Escort the Mem to the house of Tuan Harvy, and wait there with her, then bring her back here, Katidjo. Watch her carefully, do you understand?"

Disdaining to speak, Betty stalked down the steps and began to pick her way among the muddied puddles on the drive. McCleary stared grimly at her stiff back. "Brazen piece she is," he muttered, and then turning abruptly to Nancy asked, "What are you going to do with yourself?"

"I hadn't thought," Nancy said. "It seems so good just to be lying here in the sun, and not having a crowd of people around, with all the under currents and tension."

McCleary nodded. "I know how you feel; they keep me stirred up too. Good idea for you to relax while you can. With everyone out of the house, you ought to be safe enough, but I'm not going to take any chances: there's a constable squatting down there beside the front steps, with orders to admit no one, and there's another on the back veranda, with the same instructions. The servants have cleared the dining room and are back in their quarters, so the house is empty. Of course, if you are nervous, I'll stay here with you, but if you think you'll be all right, there are some things outside on the estate that I'd like to check up on. I'd be back in about an hour."

Nancy smiled. "Run along, I'll be all right." She was glad to see his broad back retreating; it was impossible to forget the murders when he was there; and now that he was gone, there was nothing to remind her, for the Malays were out of sight, if not out of sound. For a few minutes Nancy lay quietly in the long chair, but instead of finding the peace she expected after the inspector had left her, she found her mind running in circles about the murders, selecting first this person and then that one as the guilty one; and rejecting each in turn, while all the time, try as she might to silence it, she heard Mike Sullivan's hoarse voice warning her, as the murderer had done. And Ismael would be back soon now, any minute, to name the killer. In an attempt to get her mind off that prospect, she began to think of her own discouraging future; a stranger masquerading as another person; twelve thousand miles from home, penniless and discredited for any job that required references. What to do about it!

She felt suddenly cool and realized that the sun was obscured once more by ominous clouds and a gusty small wind was again sprinkling drops of rain on the long-suffering porch. She decided that she would go inside and read; the men would all be

coming back, since work apparently stopped automatically on the estate when rain began to fall, and
she had no desire to be there when they arrived. She
had taken a book to her room last night, a current
best seller on which she had been unable to concentrate, but which, according to her favorite reviewers, merited attention. Perhaps now, in her different mood, with fear removed, she could concentrate
upon it, and forget her surroundings. Remembering
Ismael's grave warnings, she stepped to the veranda
door and spoke to the unseen constable, telling him
in groping, kindergarten Malay that she was going
to her room. Apparently he grasped her intent, for
his face was stretched into a broad grin as he sprang
into sight on the steps, and although she didn't understand his spurt of conversation, she gathered from
his actions, and an occasional familiar word, that he
would now guard over her safety from the veranda
where it was comfortably dry. He squatted contentedly beside the open hall door. Nancy hesitated for
a second. Ismael had said that a constable must be
outside her bedroom whenever she was in there, and
yet, with the house empty, McCleary had only ordered his men to watch the front and back entrances.
She didn't want to cause any more trouble than she
already had; she would just go to her room and get
her book, and then come back to the veranda until
Ismael or McCleary returned. They could settle the
matter to their own satisfaction.

The hall was once more gray and dreary, as Nancy hurried along to her room, and it had the same depressing effect on her spirits. Well, it wouldn't take long to dash in, grab the book from the table beside her bed, and be out again. Nancy opened her door and stepped into her dim shadowy bedroom. The shutters were still closed, but the slats had been opened to admit thin bars of drab light that merely accentuated the damp gloom of the rest of the room. She shivered a little as she stepped inside—Ismael, she remembered suddenly, had made her promise always to bolt her door, and though she knew there was no one in the house, she turned punctiliously to carry out his instructions. Even as her hand groped for the bolt, she was aware of something behind her, but before she could throw open the door, or a scream could reach her lips, long, merciless fingers gripped her throat, drawing her back into the room. Frantically she tried to free herself from the strangling hold, her body, twisting and wrenching, disputing every inch of the way. If she could only kick over a chair, do something to bring help, but she had been dragged now into the center of the room where there was no furniture within reach of her kicking feet, and her rubber-soled shoes made no sound on the grass matting. She was going to die. Nothing could save her this time. With a final, despairing twist of her exhausted body, she turned sideways, and her bulging eyes stared into the distorted, merciless face of the man who had killed Lydia, John Harvy, Dave Farnsworth—and now was going to kill her. Outrage, as she recognized the murderer, gave her a bit of strength—enough to fight backwards a few steps, and with a last, desperate effort hook her foot around the leg of the dressing table.

CHAPTER XVIII

At ten o'clock that Monday morning, Ismael was sitting in a small, dusty office in the Kluang police station, his ear glued to the telephone receiver, his right hand busily taking down notes. The white pages were covered with hastily scribbled figures, listed under separate headings, and at the moment were as meaningless as the inscriptions on the Rosetta Stone. The voice at the other end of the wire, in the Johore Government Record Office, stopped its monotonous recitations. "That's the whole lot. I've given you the rubber production now for the Semang Estate for the last six months, and also the rubber produced by the entire district. Anything more I can do for you, Inspector?"

Ismael studied the columns of figures and then asked thoughtfully, "Do you not think it strange, Tuan, that although the production of rubber from the Semang Estate has steadily decreased, the total production for the district remains approximately the same?"

There was an exclamation. "You're right. Something out of the way there. The Chief would have spotted it right away, but he's home on leave, and his number One is down with fever. The figures are handled by different clerks here; that's what took me so long to get them for you. We'll look into the matter immediately and send an inspector up."

"How would you account for the discrepancy, Tuan?" Ismael's body was tense as he asked the question. "I am only seeking unofficial information, you understand, but it is very important that I have something to work on until your inspector arrives."

The voice hesitated. "I don't like to commit myself without an investigation, but, if you are just looking for a lead, I'd suggest that you look into the coolies on the Semang Estate, check up and see whether the rubber is being pirated."

Ismael concealed his satisfaction. "Can you suggest how that can best be done? I am unfamiliar with the routine, and I must work swiftly and alone. I can't trust any of the people on the estate."

"Well, the usual way rubber is pirated is by an extra, possibly a night tapping of the trees. Then the latex is smuggled off the estate and sold to some of the small native kabuns whose yield is low, and those fellows ship it out in the regular way with their own stuff. It's quite a racket, and hard to check if the coolies are careful, and the stolen rubber widely distributed among the small growers. Better get the mandurs together and work on the coolies through them, or else put out guards and catch the thieves red handed."

So that was it, Ismael thought after he had expressed his gratitude and hung up the receiver. He knew that in good tapping, the bark was cut only one inch a month, but on the Semang Estate, instead of that, the trees were probably being tapped again at night, and the little white cups emptied not only in the morning, but in the afternoon or evening as well. Was that what Lydia Bosworth had seen the afternoon of her death; a coolie emptying the cups at an unusual hour, or had she perhaps stumbled on an unexplained supply of latex hidden in the jungle awaiting removal? It was probably a coolie she had noticed, something that seemed a bit out of the ordinary, but not of tremendous importance, for she had not spoken of it when she returned—or—if she had, no one had admitted it. If she had found a concealed supply of latex, Ismael felt sure she would have reported it immediately. He frowned. And yet, wasn't it possible that she had commented upon it to the man who had killed her; might not that have been the motive for her murder?

How much money was involved in the theft? Was it enough to warrant the risk, or was something even larger involved? He remembered the rumors current in London about the Semang Estate, the offers for purchase which had annoyed Mr. Bosworth senior;

the record sheets which had been stolen from the
estate, and the fact that no attempt had been made
to prevent the original reports from going to London. Could it all be part of a plot to get control of
the estate?

He mustn't waste time theorizing, Ismael reminded himself—already he had been away longer than he
had planned, and he still had two errands to do before his work in Kluang was finished. He had to go to
the telegraph office for copies of the telegrams which
Nancy had taken, and he must make a round of all
the kedais to learn whether any white man had made
suspicious purchases within the last week or two.

Two hours later, a mud-stained, rain-streaked car
was skidding crazily over sodden, rutted roads. Ismael
was hunched over the wheel, his eyes fixed on the
streaming windshield, his body braced to resist the
wild lurching of the speeding car. It was a race between him and death. In his pocket he had evidence to
convict the murderer; the copies of the telegrams. He
knew now not only who the murderer was, but why
it had been essential to him that Nancy conceal her
identity; she was all that stood between him and the
scaffold. It was so obvious, so simple. Ismael cursed
himself for his blindness, cursed Nancy for her deception, but most of all he cursed the storm-drenched
miles of road that still lay between him and the
estate where even now the murderer might be

carrying out his deadly work. Allah grant that he be in time.

"Where is she?" Ismael panted, flinging himself from the car and dashing up the steps.

The group of people on the veranda broke off their conversation to stare at him in amazement, "Who? I don't know, we just came back from the factory; what's wrong?" The constable outside the hall door said quickly, "The young Mem went to her room maybe three-four minutes ago. But do not worry, Tuan, the back door is guarded, and I myself have seen that no one entered this door except the Mem until Tuan McCleary returns. He comes now."

Ismael didn't wait to hear the sentry. His first apprehensive glance at the veranda showed him that both Nancy and the man he now knew to be the murderer were missing. As he raced into the house, he heard a heavy crash, the sound of shattering glass, and an instant later Ismael hurled himself against Nancy's door. The flimsy catch gave way, and the murderer, dropping the girl's limp body, sprang at the detective's throat. His viciousness was his undoing, for he stumbled over Nancy's motionless form and spread-eagled at Ismael's feet. Before he could struggle up, or Ismael could act, the sturdy but dumb little constable, who had been guarding the back door, dashed into the room and brought his truncheon down with terrific force on the murderer's head.

McCleary thrust his way through the group of people who were swarming into the house, and hurried into Nancy's room. "What's going on here?" he demanded, staring in bewilderment at Ismael who was lifting the girl onto the bed, and at the proud little constable who had mounted guard over the prostrate figure of a man sprawled face downward across the wreckage of the dressing table.

"Please, Tuan, tell the constable to guard the door and keep people out," Ismael requested over his shoulder, "and also handcuff that son of Shaitan on the floor before he again becomes his evil self."

McCleary barked an order at the constable who promptly took his place in the doorway, blocking the excited people who were clamoring for admittance. Lights flashed on; and white, incredulous faces peered into the room over the rigid shoulders of the constable; their horrified gaze shifting from Ismael who was rhythmically pumping air into the lungs of the half-strangled girl on the bed, to McCleary who was snapping handcuffs on the recumbent figure on the floor.

"But how did you know it was Jim Mason?" McCleary asked when the excitement had died down sufficiently so that his voice could be heard above the babel of exclamations and questions. Jim Mason, a constable on either side of him, slumped in a chair by the window, his face turned sullenly away. Betty Harvy was holding a bottle of aromatic ammonia under Nancy's nose, while Mike Sullivan, with hands surprisingly gentle, bathed her forehead and her bruised neck with ice water. The rest of the group, under a pledge not to molest the prisoner, were allowed to enter the room. It was unusual, McCleary knew, but he wished to make amends for his former suspicions, and it seemed to him that they were entitled to hear Ismael's explanations.

"It was the telegrams, Tuan." Ismael's soft voice sounded loud in the hushed expectancy of the room. "I should have known as soon as Miss Reynolds told me of the murderer's anxiety that she conceal her identity, but I was handicapped by my unfamiliarity with the routine of the estate. I looked for something that might have been in the telegrams, and thus, I missed what was so obvious. I had pieced together the greed behind the murders. I was sure that rubber was being pirated, but the money from that was secondary. The real object was to force the sale of the estate to a large American rubber company which coveted it.

"When I had learned so much from my telephoning this morning, I went to all the kedais in Kluang, seeking to learn if a white man had recently purchased a dagger similar to the one belonging to Tuan Mason which had fitted the wounds on the first two victims, but which had not been used to commit the crimes. I found at length a small Chinese shop on the outskirts of the town, and the owner told me that on

the day Mrs. Bosworth was killed, a white man had
purchased a small dagger from his assistant. Unfortunately the assistant had been discharged for dishonesty, and I had no time then to seek him. The owner, of course, could not describe the man who had
bought the dagger, but from his description of the
weapon, it seemed just such a one as Tuan Mason's.
I went next to the telegraph office to request copies
of the telegrams, and there, with the first words of
the operator, the case was finished. He asked, 'Didn't
Mr. Mason deliver the telegrams? I was just closing
up Friday night when I saw him come out of the Rest
House, so I asked him to take them out to Mrs. Bosworth—saved us a thirty-mile run.'"

Ismael paused. "So simple as that, Tuan."

"But why did he kill Lydia?" Clive cried indignantly. "She'd always been decent to him, and he seemed
to like her. Buying her a present, and then, by God!
killing her with it!"

"If you would like it, I will tell you what I think
happened," Ismael said. "But you will understand it
is only as I see the happenings in these sad days—we
have yet to prove many things."

There was an eager murmur of assent, and the
little Malay began his reconstruction of the crimes.
"I do not think Tuan Mason intended to kill Mrs.
Bosworth when he came to the house that night,
but after he had given her the telegrams, she made
the mistake which cost her her life. She remembered

something she had seen on her walk that afternoon, and in all innocence, she asked Mason what it meant. She had either seen coolies emptying the latex cups at an unusual time, or had come upon buckets of latex hidden in the jungle. That will be discovered when we question the coolies. Now that we know of the pirating, they will talk, and so will the kabuns to whom the latex was sold, for all natives have a fear of being mixed up in a white murder. Mason knew that Mrs. Bosworth had only to mention what she had seen to anyone connected with the estate, and his plot would have been exposed. So, he stabbed her. Frightened by his crime, he turned off the light and hurried away, forgetting about the telegrams. Before he had an opportunity to come back to the house, Miss Reynolds had arrived and found the body. She had also taken the telegrams, and for reasons of her own later decided to masquerade for a time as Miss Chambers. Mason felt that he was safe so long as she concealed her real identity, for then there was no occasion for anyone to know about the telegrams he had delivered."

"But why did he kill John?" Betty asked.

"Murder breeds murder," Ismael declared. "A man can die only once, and after he has taken one life, he has nothing to lose by killing again and again. Tuan Harvy was killed because he was determined to get to the root of the rubber shortage and I think, from his anxiety to talk to Tuan Bosworth, something had

aroused his suspicions. His mistake had been in trusting his assistants so completely that in his search for
the cause of the lower production, he didn't suspect
pirating of the rubber, for only with the connivance
of one of the assistants could the theft have been
carried on over so long a period, without discovery.
So Tuan Harvy had to die. And then, because Tuan
Farnsworth saw Mason come out of the jungle, he,
too, had to be killed. Then only Miss Reynolds remained to endanger him, but for her, he felt a soft-
ness. If he could have persuaded her to marry him,
to trust him as an accepted lover, or to frighten her
into keeping silence, he would never have harmed
her. But instead of turning toward him, he saw her
alienated, interested more and more in the Irishman
whom he feared and hated. And so, he made up his
mind that she too must die."

The look of abhorrence which his former friends
cast in the direction of Mason attested eloquently
to their feelings, but the blunt-featured profile by
the window showed no emotion. His half-closed eye-
lids veiled his hatred of the insignificant little Malay
who was responsible for his predicament, who was
so uncannily tracing his thoughts and his actions.
But they'd never have the satisfaction of hearing the
truth from him. "Least said, soonest mended!" His
father would get him a good lawyer—his father had
seen him through plenty of scrapes. He'd be pretty

sick about this one though—but he'd have to help, just to save his own face.

It was Pearson who broke the hostile silence, a Pearson rejuvenated since, at Ismael's suggestion, he had had a blunt talk with Doctor Sparkes and been convinced of his own mental health. "What happened to the dagger he used on Lydia and John? Why didn't he use that on poor Farnsworth, and Miss Chambers—er, Reynolds? It was quicker, and he wouldn't have been caught."

"For that, Tuan, we must all thank Allah!" Ismael said in heartfelt tones, glancing at the bed where Nancy was sitting, her bright head resting against Mike's broad shoulder. "Of course I do not know, but I think that after Tuan Mason committed the first murder, he hid the dagger somewhere on the estate, between this house and his own, or between his bungalow and the kampong. It doesn't matter, for in the morning when he hurried off to kill Tuan Harvy, he unearthed it once more. After his second evil deed was done, back he plunged the weapon into the earth, for he couldn't have concealed it on his person when he reported at the coolie line in shorts and an open shirt. A small reward offered to the coolies will, I am sure, produce it. Later, when he had the chance to kill Tuan Farnsworth, he had neither the time nor the opportunity to get the dagger, so he used a cord. The same holds true for this afternoon;

he had no weapon to use on Miss Reynolds save his own bare hands."

Jim Mason stirred restlessly. Was nothing hidden from that damn Malay? How did he manage to follow the thoughts of a white man?

"And how did the murderin' bastard get in here today, with both doors guarded?" Hamilton asked belligerently.

McCleary looked uncomfortable. "That was my fault," he admitted. "I had a man at both doors, and the house was empty. Miss Reynolds was on the veranda resting when I left. I forgot the door at the head of the basement stairs, or rather I forgot that it wasn't locked—I'd sent the key off to Kluang to be examined for fingerprints. I know you said there weren't any on it, Ismael, but I didn't want to take a chance. I knew the men were all off working, and as soon as the rain started, I hurried back. I was looking for the dagger." He glanced sheepishly at Pearson, whose bungalow he had so fruitlessly ransacked.

To relieve McCleary's embarrassment, Ismael said practically, "I think, Tuan, it will be well to send a cable to America, for obviously it was there that the plot was born."

Jim Mason started; his thoughts were confused, but between them, fear ran like a panic-stricken rabbit. With things buzzing in America, his father and the rest of them would leave him out on a limb—no one would dare raise a finger to help him. Under heavy lids he glanced furtively at the windows, at the door. If he made a dash, enough of a furor, they might shoot him, and that would be better than hanging.

"I think, Tuan McCleary, it would be well to remove the prisoner," Ismael said quietly. Thankful of an excuse for action, McCleary barked an order to the constables and picked up his topee as the important little mata-matas urged Mason toward the door.

There was a general movement, people rising to their feet, and pressing forward to express their gratitude to the man who had solved the case, who had vindicated, and at the same time avenged them. "Wonderful—simply marvelous," Betty Harvy exclaimed with a soulful roll of her eyes. "But I want to ask him—" Her words were lost in the jumble of deeper voices, Hamilton proposing a toast to Ismael, Pearson saying, "Are you going to stick it, Bosworth? Good, would you like me to stay on?" Mike Sullivan, with eyes on Nancy, said firmly, "I'm staying too—feel like a spot of work."

Ismael saw them all moving toward him, and perspiration broke out on his forehead. He dreaded the ordeal of congratulations, of praise. He didn't deserve credit; the little American girl had blocked him, fooled him almost to the last minute. He felt hot all over when he thought of the report he would have to make in Johore, and of Tuan Campbell's laughter. He must get away from here.

"One moment, Tuan McCleary," Ismael called as the officer started down the hall, "I will come with you."

McCleary looked back at him in surprise. Ismael was suddenly just a small plump Malay. "Tabeh, Mem Reynolds—tabeh, Mem Harvy, tabeh, Tuan-Tuan." His voice was the humble one of a native servant, his ducking bobs, as he backed through the doorway, those of a shopkeeper. The white people paused uncertainly, their words of appreciation lost, their outstretched hands falling lifelessly to their sides as Ismael slipped unobtrusively past them. "Why," Betty Harvy exclaimed in a disappointed voice, "he's nothing but a native after all. I'd forgotten."

Outside in the teeming rain, Ismael smiled happily.

COACHWHIP PUBLICATIONS

COACHWHIPBOOKS.COM

VIRGINIA RATH

DEATH AT
DAYTON'S FOLLY

COACHWHIP PUBLICATIONS
COACHWHIPBOOKS.COM

SAMUEL ROGERS

YOU'LL BE
SORRY!

YOU LEAVE
ME COLD!

COACHWHIP PUBLICATIONS

CoachwhipBooks.com

COACHWHIP PUBLICATIONS

CoachwhipBooks.com

TYLINE PERRY

THE OWNER
LIES DEAD

COACHWHIP PUBLICATIONS
CoachwhipBooks.com

THE STRAWSTACK
MURDER CASE
K I R K E
MECHEM

MURDER A LA MODE

ELEANORE KELLY SELLARS

CLASSIC RED BADGE PRIZE MYSTERY

COACHWHIP PUBLICATIONS
CoachwhipBooks.com

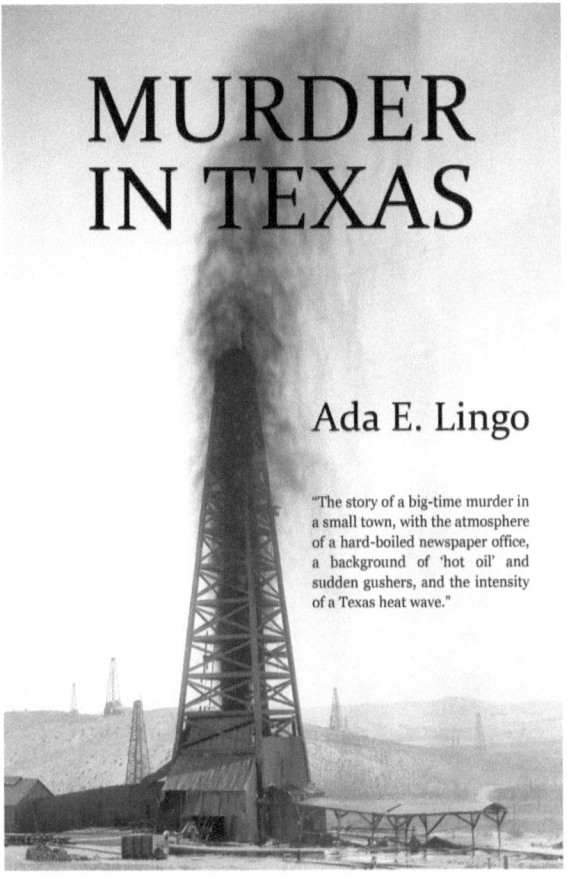

MURDER IN TEXAS

Ada E. Lingo

"The story of a big-time murder in a small town, with the atmosphere of a hard-boiled newspaper office, a background of 'hot oil' and sudden gushers, and the intensity of a Texas heat wave."